THE
PLAINS
OF
FORGET

THE PLAINS OF FORGET

STRANGER THAN FICTION

— BOOK 4 —

T. B. MARE

Podium

This is a work of fiction. Names, characters, places, and incidents are either products of the author's imagination or used fictitiously. Any resemblance to actual events, locales, or persons, living, dead, or undead, is entirely coincidental.

Cover design by Barbara Ciardo

ISBN: 978-1-0394-5481-1

Published in 2024 by Podium Publishing
www.podiumaudio.com

THE
PLAINS
OF
FORGET

PROLOGUE

Most people took the concept of direction for granted. Below was where your feet lay. Above soared over your head, while hands identified left and right. And not just hands, but eyes, ears, cheeks, legs—the entire symmetry of the human body, as well as the natural geometry of the world around you expressed itself beautifully in the language of directions. Part of the dizziness that came with being in the dark sprang from the inability to ascertain one's direction.

But that dizziness was nothing . . . *nothing* compared to being inside the Haze.

Haze. Ginnungagap. Inner reticulum of the now-fragmented Ikai Realm. Call it whatever you want. But, for Lukas Aguilar, the entire thing could be summed up in one single word.

Directionless.

Everywhere was mist and color, making it almost impossible to peer through it. Pump in lifeforce to expand his senses and the world to his left glowed a bright shade of neon pink. To the bottom right was now a particularly light shade of teal. The pink had fled to his feet and was moving away from him. Was he going forwards, backwards, spinning in circles? Horizontally, vertically? Did geometry even matter in this endless mist of color? A metallic blue line shot out of nowhere towards him. He stepped back and found his leg in water—

Water?

It was a dark shade of beige. Still . . . watery? No, his leg definitely didn't feel wet, yet the sensation was there.

Closing Nexus
Reverting Consciousness to Host

Lukas opened his eyes. The Haze had no concept of geometry, Euclidean or otherwise. It had connections, not directions. Even the Nexus he had was akin to the Rosetta Stone for the Haze. He knew A plus B equals C in the Haze, but the reason why it was so was not clear.

And with good reason.

Lukas suppressed the urge to yelp out in surprise, and scowled. "How many times have I asked you not to do that?"

Many? said his newest headache.

"Seriously, Empress," said Lukas drolly. "You're, quite frankly, a pain in my ass."

Joke is on you, said Meynte. *You had the bright idea to trap me in your inner-world.*

Funny thing about voices in your head. When you first get them, you absolutely hate them. Especially when that voice belongs to an ancient god-queen with a superiority complex the size of the freaking solar system. An entity that is so impossibly large in sheer personality, power, and history to make you feel like you're nothing but an ephemeral candle to them, and that's discounting their constant attempts to turn you into their personal hatchet man. But after you get to know them for a bit and then the voice "sacrifices" itself to resurrect you, you actually realize how much you had gotten used to them and how much you miss them.

But only until you get a replacement, and you realize that, even without the temptation of becoming their enforcer in exchange for impossible skill and power, it's really annoying to be renting out your headspace in the first place.

Regardless of how good the rent was.

Technically, he was still alone in the eyes of any neutral observer. Only he could see the tall, athletic blonde frame beside him, stretching her hands in a very distracting fashion.

She was perhaps the most "unique" piece in his collection. He had captured her by forcing her to retreat from Tanya's mind, only to trap her with Blob. He had expected her to be utterly furious and swearing enmity for life, but instead, she had acknowledged her defeat and accepted her new place as a member of his inner-world.

Don't I look good? she asked, posing, making Lukas wonder whether logic and common sense had vanished from the world when he wasn't looking or it was just him.

"Uh, yeah," he said dryly, wondering why the former Empress had decided to do a California blonde impression, complete with khakis and a turtleneck. Technically, she could appear as anything or anyone since she didn't technically have a soul.

Your world's fashion is rather interesting. Not very optimal for warfare, but certainly more . . . liberating.

"I'm glad you like it," he said.

Lacking a soul, Meynte couldn't use any of her Skills, despite her wealth of experience at wielding Everfrost. And his inner-world had nothing remotely similar to a yuki-onna, so Meynte couldn't even draw on her true powers. And even if it had, he doubted she could have, regardless, because, by Frost's own admission, one Everfrost user could exist at a time.

Memory or otherwise.

Of course, that was only valid for the real world outside and not his inner-world, which, for all intents and purposes, counted as its own separate reality, so technically, it might have been possible to replicate Fimbulwinter within it as well. But Lukas knew better than to let the End of Potential take root inside his world and destroy everything within it.

Not that it would have worked, but still, why take a risk?

"I think I might have a himthursar prototype somewhere."

Absolutely not, scoffed Meynte. *I refuse to be reborn as one of those vile beasts.*

"You realize they're just prototypes. Just Skills, body, and instincts. Perhaps with your memories . . ."

No, she said stubbornly. *I refuse.*

Lukas sighed again. He had developed a habit of doing that a lot recently.

We've been floating in this endless Haze for quite some time now, Soulcrafter. How long do you wish to go on? Even your world can only siphon so much energy before it burns out.

"I'm trying to figure something out."

I've heard, said Meynte. *But do you know what you're even looking for?*

"I am creating . . . correction, *discovering* the structure of this vast Haze from when it was a proper realm."

And to what end? The Ikai is fragmented. The worlds within it are in disarray. The Yggdrasil and the borderlands are spread along many planes, and all that remains is this dead zone of energy.

Meynte was right. It was a dead zone for people—or yokai, he supposed. Even for kami.

But for an anomaly such as he, it was a relic of a bygone era that he could connect with. Understand.

"The Haze isn't dead. It's still there. We . . . . *I* just need to know how to interact with it, without . . . uh, getting blown up."

Gosh! I'd never have thought of that myself, Soulcrafter.

Perhaps American fashion wasn't the only thing Meynte was absorbing from his memories.

"You can just call me Lukas, you know."

I can, yes.

There was no need to make that failed argument for the umpteenth time. Meynte was bound by the same laws that every monster adhered to—to be utterly obedient to the anomaly to which it was bound. Granted, most monsters didn't exactly share the quirkiness that came with being an advanced lifeform, either.

"I guess it's the anomaly in me that keeps treating it as . . . well, as kin. I'm scared shitless of the kind of power it has. I'm awed and jealous of what it was, or *is*—even in this state. And there's also that part of me that just wants to destroy it."

Great, Meynte deadpanned. *All that remains is for you to actually decide what to do, and we're set.*

"Less insult, more analysis."

I would, but I'd have to actually learn things from you to even begin analyzing.

Lukas rolled his eyes. He was trying to understand how the Haze truly functioned, hoping to reverse engineer some of his findings and apply them to his inner-world. He was approaching it from different angles, applying a lot of different theories and mental models developed from piecemeal information he had collected from a variety of places: Frost, the texts in Solana's library, trivia from Inanna's fragmented memories that rose up into his subconscious from time to time, and, of course, his private discourses with Meynte about the nature of Truth and Taboo.

Much like mathematics, you could get to the same place through a lot of varied lines of theory and reasoning, with none of the processes truly right or wrong, only different, with some of them more *useful* than the others.

But the crux of the matter was, like all sciences, the existence of worlds lay in certain pre-established Rules. Rules that might be beyond what the mortal mind could process but Rules nonetheless. The Origin was not some divine being playing an ineffable game of his own devising with the Universe. It was an entity that followed its own protocols and operated on a level so far above Lukas's own that it was impossible for him to grasp.

The idea was to study the Haze and figure out how it behaved: its structures, its limits, its foundations—study them, experiment with them, and test his theories on them, all with the intention of finding a way to reverse engineer a lost goddess.

Or at least, that was his intention in opening a portal to the Haze and stepping through, leaving Tanya's education to Solana, and Frost to protect her just in case the skinwalker bitch tried something sinister.

I still think you're wasting time with this silly project of yours.

"Silly project, is it?"

Of course, said Meynte, flipping her ponytail. *Anyone who has spent too long in the presence of divinity knows that the gods never care much about mortals. Trust me, the best you can hope for is to be remembered as a footnote.*

"I'm not her worshiper, I am—"

Are what? A World? Her bastion? You're barely able to keep your head on your shoulders. What do you think will happen when a goddess takes charge of your world and dominates it with her Truth? What will you and your ragtag army of brain-dead monsters do against her?

Her words tore at him like barbs. But he didn't react. After all, it wasn't her fault. Meynte simply didn't know. Didn't understand.

Even with my Everfrost, I was able to fight just one goddess and almost bring her down. But now? I'm just a memory. No soul, no Skills, nothing. Mark my words, Soulcrafter. You will rue the day you resurrect her.

"You think . . ." said Lukas softly. "You think a goddess can triumph over a World? You think that the world is just a bastion for a higher being, created to spawn followers to do the divine being's bidding, is that it?" He smiled. "Let me correct your ignorance."

Opening Nexus
Transferring Consciousness from Prime Host to Anomaly State

The next second, he gasped as he was submerged in startlingly cold water. The cold pierced him like a thousand sharp needles, and all the air was thrust from his lungs. He lost all feeling in his arms and felt his vision flicker in the dark, unforgiving cold of the water.

Despite his shock, he didn't make the slightest attempt to get out of the stream, whatever it was. The current pushed him straight into a ball of bright light, and suddenly Lukas had an idea of what infinity looked like. His eyes shut tightly, and there was no saying if he was standing or falling or if he could even fall at all. Gravity deserted him, leaving him in a multichromatic vacuum that shattered him into a million pieces, only to be re-formed in countless permutations in all sorts of dimensions and—

—and then it was over.

And before him lay . . . *That.*

The base was a swirling mandala, with shoots arising out of it, contorting into itself in all sorts of ways that defied Euclidean geometry. Calling it looped into itself would be inadequate, because there was nothing inside—or was it upside down? Sideways went upward and inwards vanished into nowhere. It was pulsating like a beating heart, firing waves of energy enough to destroy Worlds with the frequency of nerves firing, and at the same time, it was dead and the least organic thing he had ever gazed upon. Back when Inanna had shown him the Origin, he had been unable to see it all, take it all in, so all-encompassing as it was. Now, he faced the exact opposite situation.

Having achieved a nexus, Lukas was sharing this massive cosmic entity's awareness. An omnipresence and omniscience hundreds—no, *thousands*—of times greater than what his mind could fathom was being forced through his brain cells. It wasn't astral projection, as he had shared so many times with Inanna. It wasn't some kind of extrasensory cognizance nor telepathy that connected him to a system far greater than himself. No, instead it was like he had become . . . *more*. Like he had transcended into an elevated life-form, one past the boundaries of reality, time, and space, beyond the reach of any monster, demon, king, or god. How maddening that, when granted the knowledge of *everything* all at once—to see all, to know all—he was completely and utterly immobilized due to the fact that every action had endless potential outcomes, and each of them had equally endless outcomes and . . .

What . . . What is that thing?

Meynte had turned white. She was trembling and staring at the image before her as if she had never seen anything more terrifying; as though she couldn't bear to be near it; as though it frightened her to her very core. Sweat was beading on her forehead, which made absolutely no sense since she was a mere illusion. Even more so, she was a being of Frost. Seeing her sweat like a human being—

Was this how Lukas had looked while gazing at Inanna's memory of the Origin? Granted, the Haze—or rather, the Ikai—was far less complex than the Origin, but it mattered little. For what difference did a two-story building or a mountain make to an ant? Still, she couldn't have—

SPLAT! She exploded into shards of energy.

Memory Prototype MEYNTE disintegrated
Creating new Instance . . .

A new "Meynte" popped into existence right next to him and—
What is . . . that—

Memory Prototype MEYNTE disintegrated
Creating new Instance . . .

Shit! He hadn't seen this coming.
Soulcraft—

Memory Prototype MEYNTE disintegrated
Creating new Instance . . .

And on and on it went. An endless loop. And every time her consciousness broke apart, his inner-world created an exact copy of Meynte, complete with the memories of the previous one until the point of its own disintegration, and again, and again, and again. Lukas hastily severed the connection to the nexus, and he was back in the colorful mist of the Haze, and then—

Creating new Instance of Memory Prototype MEYNTE . . .

WHAT! said Meynte, looking absolutely haggard, like someone who had been brought to the brink of death half a dozen times, only to be brought back at the last moment. Which, to be frank, wasn't far from the truth.

What was that, Soulcrafter?

"That," said Lukas, smiling and meeting Meynte's eyes, "Is a World. Or the remnants of one."

But . . . She gasped. *The Ikai is gone. Destroyed. All that's left is the Haze and it's—*

"Is what you just witnessed. A remnant of the past, yes, but it's also a macrocosm of infinite possibilities. One that's magnitudes greater than the Empire, greater than the pantheon, greater than the politics of mortals and the divine. *That*, Meynte, is a World. Gods come and go, but the World forever expands."

For that one moment, Lukas was back in the Awareness; the feeling of being in oneness with the Haze infused within him. Every single time he had formed a nexus, he had access to every single borderland within the Haze: terrains burning hotter than lava, and worlds where the ice had iced over; singularities that gave the impression of a perfect knife's edge, and worlds where the ground was rusted metal and dust storms reigned in the sky; borderlands that were essentially underwater, and those crafted out of sentient, cube-like metallic forms.

Lukas had swum through the Haze's awareness, shifting from world to world, borderland to borderland—sensing, feeling, seeing, hearing, and most importantly, *comprehending* exactly how vast and endless it was.

Had he been just another inhabitant, his perception would have been limited to the world he was born in. But he wasn't. He was an Outsider, and more importantly, a World. At some level, he was kin to every single borderland within the Haze. At some level, the shattered remains of the anomaly within him shared a mutual understanding of what it meant to be destroyed.

It was hard to explain it in words. The more he understood the Haze, the more beautiful it felt, a true wonder to behold. But Lukas felt no joy at the sight of it. Instead, his eyes watered and his vision blurred as an emotion he could neither name nor understand swelled in his chest. For a reason that he still couldn't grasp, his soul ached.

Inanna had called it a remnant of a Has-Been, but, frankly, he doubted even Inanna ever truly understood what it meant. Where it came from. She might have stared into the Origin, but did she know its story?

Its thoughts. Its feelings. Its *history.*

But that . . . said Meynte, still fumbling for words after that soul-wrenching experience. *That is*—was *the Ikai. You are just* . . . you. *Surely your world is different. Smaller. Less.*

A thin smile flickered on his lips. "You say that I am just me. Compared to the Ikai, or even what is left of it, I am but an individual. Perhaps you speak true. I am smaller, with lesser reserves, lesser resources, lesser power . . . But to say that I am *less?*"

Are you claiming that the World within you is as great as the Ikai?

The smile was now beginning to hurt.

"No," said Lukas. "It's *bigger.*"

He held her gaze for a full ten seconds. Truthfully, he wasn't sure why he was so insistent on making his point known to the entity before him. After all, she was a part of his World and nothing she said nor believed in should have made a pint of difference to him. But Meynte was an empress—someone with decades, perhaps *centuries* of experience, and most importantly, was a Taboo vessel in the past. At her greatest, she was his antithesis, and only by knowing her could he truly understand the nature of Fimbulwinter. And if he had to teach her a few things about himself and the World she was part of in the process, well, it was an acceptable loss.

She wasn't going anywhere, after all.

"The Ikai Realm was fragmented, not destroyed, and whatever remains is this Haze. But the world I come from? It was more, *so much more.* That which you call my inner-world, the one that holds you and every single prototype I have siphoned; that so casually denies Amaterasu's Eternal Light and exerts its own Rules and carves its own domain—it's just the ruined part of my World's omphalos. Think. What will you find when I actually get my World to *work* again?"

But— Meynte's voice quivered only a little. *If that's how it is, why did you have trouble fighting me?*

"Because you weren't wrong," said Lukas, still smiling. "I'm a World, but I'm *also* an individual. And as an individual, I need to grow. And in this Haze, we will find *hundreds* of prototypes. Monsters with Skills I can assimilate and make my own. Creatures to kill, Experience to gain. Level up while I study the Haze."

Monsters like the Ifrit King?

Lukas let out a hollow laugh. "Just getting close to it will vaporize the fuck out of me. No, I'm looking for something that bridges the gap between Level 3 and Level 4."

Locating Rifts . . .

Something like that?
An image rushed into his mind.
"Are those giant cockatrices?"
I thought you wanted to start small.
Lukas laughed and thrust his hand out. The next moment, he was gone.

CHAPTER 1

The Zwaray Keep was at war.

The stench of blood and death filled the air as Ultaf Shimizu and his army of spiritists, warriors, and monsters tore through its outer defenses. The svartalfar pillars—massive structures of an unknown metal which were said to be able to guard against the finest of armies—now lay in melted pools of sludge.

"Give up and open the Well for us," said Ultaf. "Or you'll die like . . . Well, him."

He cackled madly as his soldiers lynched a svartalfar, not seeming to care if they actually would give up.

"You crazy bastard! The Well is damaged. WE DON'T KNOW WHERE THE GIRL—"

The shouting soldier literally exploded.

"Tell me," Ultaf cackled madly. "Does anyone else not know where the girl is?"

The air screamed as aeromancers summoned pulsing spheres of compressed wind at the towers. The svartalfars' response was disorderly, pointing their weapons from the tops of the towers and mostly missing. As a whole, they weren't ones for long-range combat.

"I . . . I surrender." An old svartalfar who seemed to be one of their leaders came to the front. "Please don't kill me."

"So, you'll resist to the end?" Ultaf sneered. "Summon my Tier-3 kami!"

"W-wait. That's not what I said!"

"Filthy animals, eh?" He turned and patted Zuken on the shoulder.

Zuken for once had no words. This was not how one waged war.

Ultaf wasn't taking prisoners. He was nominally asking for Tanya, but he was also more than happy to slaughter them regardless of their answer. There was no purpose to this and the depraved smile on Ultaf's face made Zuken wonder if he needed to worry about his own safety.

Ultaf wasn't particularly bright, and Zuken had been contemplating his escape based on that. This massacre was a reality check that showed him that that could very well backfire. Plans were always made on the basis that the opponent wasn't crazy.

The keep that had once stood proudly now lay in ruins with only some large fragments among the rubble to hint at its former size and grandeur. The broken walls, the shattered cantonments, dead svartalfar children. An ingenious civilization dismantled by a tempest.

It was hard not to feel bitter and useless.

An image rose in Zuken's head. His mother. Himself. Standing at the gate of their capital city. Her final words to him:

You have no power, no talent with mana, your Soul Capacity is pitiful, and your faith in the pantheon is a flickering flame. The Earth King's son must be strong, but you are weak.

Even his mind—his greatest strength—was worthless here.

Still, all was not lost. He was alive, as was Elena. Tanya was safe with . . .

He frowned.

Tanya was safe with—

Zuken smiled as the name escaped him. It might not do anything in the long run, but small acts of resistance made him feel better despite his situation.

But was this really the most appropriate reaction?

Ultaf's army destroyed his castle, captured him, and decimated his hill. His psion raped his mind, found whatever was useful, and came to the svartalfars, demanding they hand over the Well. His only solid way to gain true power—featherglass—was now in shambles.

Wasn't he supposed to be furious at having been tortured? Shouldn't the fact that all his developments and research were gone and he was back at Square One have crushed him?

Perhaps he had just become so accustomed to his own suffering that he felt it was inevitable.

The mind was a strange thing and difficult to comprehend. Perhaps it had endured too much and therefore simply decided to stop caring.

He closed his eyes and took a deep breath.

Despite the fact that his brain was screaming at him to give up, there was a persistent underlying itch that pushed him in another direction.

He had overcome being thrown out of his clan. He had dealt with numerous political opponents. Losing to this buffoon . . . The sheer indignity of it would push him forward.

Any kind of negotiation with someone insane brought with it the risk of death, and he would never match Ultaf in power.

But could he make him weaker?

That felt more reasonable. Weakening the enemy wasn't necessarily dependent upon your own strength. Ultaf lacked neither power nor authority. Having a warlord and an entire army underneath him, along with the status of being a member of the Sacred Eight, did all of that for him.

That left two options.

The first was to use his fear against him.

And the second: use his pride against him.

Fortunately, Ultaf had both in spades to spare.

"You know, my grandfather always preferred the bitch," said Ultaf.

Another strange quirk. The girl. Bitch. Lowborn. Traitor. Creature. Ultaf called Tanya anything but her given name.

"A Soul Capacity so high, she was given a goddamn Tier-5 kami. *My* kami." He grabbed Zuken hard. "You see? That's why I need to get her back. I'm stronger now, and the kami will see that too. And anyone who dares stand in my way will end up like that."

He pointed to a pile of dead svartalfar. "All that in less than an hour."

Zuken stiffened but refused to show any fear. "Do you—do you realize what you're doing? Svartalfars are endangered. And they're the only ones in the Empire that can forge Wells."

Does he truly not understand how much he is escalating matters here?

"Then they should've just surrendered the Well in the first place. These insects should know better than to test the resolve of one of the Sacred Eight." Ultaf smiled. The madness of being drunk with power shone in his eyes. "They need to learn that actions have consequences."

Such pointless malice. Zuken thought. *It's like he has no goals beyond just making everyone grovel before him, and he doesn't care how many enemies he makes in the process. Had Mujin Shimizu intentionally ruined his own grandson?*

"Always attack the enemy's weakness," said Ultaf proudly. "That's the secret to victory. Your compassion is your weakness. Their population is theirs."

Threats were powerful as leverage—a gentle pressure to get what one wanted. To show that you were serious, people often made some grand overtures such as a kidnapper cutting off a hostage's finger to prove that he was willing to cut off their head.

It was as if someone had taught the oaf basic concepts but without any ability to use them practically. Attacking the enemy's weakness was important but at the same time, who the fuck did that in public?

His shoulders squared.

Do you really understand what sort of reprisal you're inviting right now, Ultaf Shimizu?

"Banksi," said Ultaf, with the air of a grown-up asking a toddler to take a first step by himself, "you said you know them, yes? Make them give me the Well. Try to get information about the girl, too."

Zuken stared at him. Did he really think negotiations were possible after burying over half their population?

"Oh, and don't tell them I'll kill them after they hand the stuff over."

"..."

The news of the massacre spread like wildfire. While Haviskali was a fringe city and therefore not of interest to most, the svartalfars were the ones who crafted the Wells that connected to the other side, where the people would gather their kami.

They were given a pseudo-amnesty to live on the fringe of the desert and, in turn, forged all the required needs for the Asukan Empire.

The first to bear the brunt of this was Lord Naowa.

The glass of wine dropped from his hand and tumbled across the floor. "He did WHAT?"

Several confirmations and multiple headaches later, he was still stuck in this bad dream where Ultaf Shimizu randomly waltzed into the svartalfar colony—the only one in the entire Empire—and chosen to eradicate them.

If it had been anywhere else, he would have eagerly watched the flames burning between the Empire and the Shimizu Clan, who he was quite sure had no future after this. Unfortunately, it happened in Haviskali. Which meant that this entire mess was his problem. The bastard would be lynched, no doubt about that. But he wouldn't come out smelling like roses, either. For another Sacred Eight clan to just waltz in, butcher the endangered species that held amnesty even from the army and were one of the prime contributors to the commerce in his kingdom, would be portrayed as weakness at best and incompetent at worst.

There was blood in the water, and the sharks were coming.

"Sir, Strogen is calling from the Empire."

"Put him on hold," Naowa replied curtly. This was the sixteenth message in the past twenty minutes from nobles asking for confirmation of the news and, more importantly, trying to figure out if Mujin would take the fall for it and the subsequent gap in political capital that would be left in its wake.

"Lord Straff wants to know if this is true. He says it's urgent and is demanding—"

"Later."

A few minutes passed.

"Sir, we have received another urgent—"

"I said PUT IT ON HOLD, GODDAMMIT. I can't deal with this now. I need to figure out what happened, and these stupid politicians are something I cannot handle at the moment."

He needed to figure out who to assign blame to and what actually happened. In that order.

"Well?" he asked his staff member who was standing at the threshold, hesitantly. "Just tell them I'll call them later."

"It's the Emperor's brother, sir. The Fire King."

Lord Naowa put his head in his hands.

CHAPTER 2

From above, the town of Haviskali looked like a set of ever-moving blocks—stone for the commoners and glass, wood, and precious metals for the wealthy. The moving platforms ran all over the town, with uniform-sized shops on either side of them, separated by spiral monolithic keeps that housed the aristocrats.

But up close . . .

"Don't even think twice! This is the finest ether in the land!"

'Yes, of course." Tanya's fake smile had been plastered on for so long now, her face hurt and she wondered if she'd ever be able to smile normally again afterward.

Maude looked genuinely interested, but, given this was the thirty-second person who had stopped them in the last two hours to peddle their wares, she likely just had a far better poker face than Tanya did.

He was selling ether crystal and was exactly the same as all the other peddlers. If there was anything particularly distinct about him, it was his mustache. The man was getting progressively more excited as he described why his ether was the best by far, compared to all the frauds around him who were selling inferior and low-quality products.

There were two types of towns in the Llaisy Kingdom. The first were towns that were considered "useful," providing valuable materials from anomalies, and unique minerals and resources. This usually led to military might as well, with both nobles and adventurers gathering where the wealth was.

The other kind were those that sold ether, which everyone needed for quick, easy manacrafting and didn't require any particular skill to manufacture. Rather, it was just the compressing of raw mana into feldstone crystals, which were present in abundance throughout the kingdom. It only required time, and therefore, everyone was doing it.

Moving away from the salesman who had now picked a fight with the man who had set up a stall next to him, Tanya stood in front of the massive edifice of pure, white tefelvane stone looming over her. This was the Grevane, a citadel that both served as the administrative center of the town, the offices for the Cobalt Army, and the official premises for most bureaucratic activity.

Most nobility unlucky enough to be delegated in Haviskali ended up living here, a show of wealth against the backdrop of the surrounding ether factories. The area was marred, however, by the conspicuously missing hillock upon which once rested Zuken's mansion.

"Feels weird, doesn't it?" Tanya murmured. "Just less than a year ago, we were so excited to be working for the nobility for the first time. And now . . ."

She trailed off, staring at the ugly, misshapen, charred land that contrasted with the surrounding whiteness.

"I wonder how it felt when Zuken saw it getting destroyed before his own eyes," said Maude. "Must have been intense, no?"

And there it went again. Ever since the change, Maude was different. She had all the memories and abilities of the old Maude, but there was a cruelty about her that was so unnervingly casual.

"Almost makes me wish I was there to see it happen. Zuken was never one to display strong emotions. It would've been so . . . *stirring*."

Maude had been doing this throughout their journey. Despite her assurance that the old Maude was still in there. And yet she seemed to view humanity with an eye of curiosity akin to a child poking an ant nest with a stick.

"Do you . . ." Tanya hesitated. "Do you feel happy that this happened to him?"

Maude's lips twisted into something that was almost but not quite a smile. "I . . . don't know. Zuken was good to me, but he was also an intruder to the yurei. And yurei cannot feel. Vanir . . . feel a lot. I just wonder how exquisite that pain must have felt. Seeing his life turned upside down before his very eyes . . ."

She looked at Tanya with an almost-hungry look.

"Are . . . I mean, should I still call you Maude?"

"Maude knew suffering, struggle, and strife. She spent her entire existence cultivating and building and working towards something. Malon guarded the corridors of the anomaly ever since its conception. Guarding, creating, killing—that is all it has ever known. And one day, both woke up and found that their existence—their memories—had been given to someone else. To have your entire life's accomplishments and purpose snatched from your grasp and given to an identical twin you never knew existed . . ."

"Me," Maude said after a moment's pause. "I'm not Malon. I'm not Maude. I'm . . ."

"An oni," said Tanya, looking at her warily.

Oni were not something overly talked about in the Asukan Empire. There were records of Arpen, the first oni to be captured around four hundred years ago—the first-known true fusion of bremetan and yokai since the war. Because of its tremendous power, they tried to weaponize it, but it had gone out of control. Something had happened because, a month later, not only was it executed but everyone who had anything to do with it had vanished as well. After that, any research on the subject was banned and the word 'oni' had gradually faded from common use.

"Mmm."

Whatever she had been about to say had died in her throat. Tanya stared, bewildered, at the large twenty-by-twenty banner floating high above their heads. On it, above the sigil of the Shogun, was printed in bold, glowing letters:

**ALL SVARTALFAR WARES ARE HENCEFORTH CONSCRIPTED BY THE GOVERNMENT!
TRADING IN SVARTALFAR WARES DECLARED ILLEGAL.
TRESPASSERS WILL BE FINED 5,000 MEZALS.**

There was the insignia of Lord Naowa, the Shogun himself, along with the signature of Bezu Carvein, the Cobalt Army general, and Joran Axelson, the army captain of the Phalanx, posted in Haviskali.

Now that she looked, none of the shops that traded in svartalfar wares were open. The shutters were down, with bills stamped with the Cobalt Army's seal on their doors.

"What's going on?" she asked. Svartalfars were anal-retentive, bloodthirsty weaponsmiths with a fetish for beheadings, and ferocious sticklers for privacy. They also loathed the Asukans with a passion, and that went double for their nobles. They were notorious for only trading their wares through third-party agencies or the government. Additionally, they had some kind of deal with the Empire that gave them access to a particular borderland in Haviskali, a fringe territory bereft of Eternal Light, and a form of pseudo-amnesty from the Cobalt Army so long as they didn't break sacred protocol.

"'Aven't you 'eard?" coughed a peddler from the street. "Shimizu killed them all. Keep's gone. No more magic metal, no more weapons. Gone."

Tanya couldn't believe her ears. *Gone?* The Shimizu had killed the svartalfars? What nonsense—

"The big guns up there are furious," said the peddler. "Army's gathering all their wares. Me son was dealing with those bitches at the Keep. Told 'im, don't. And now this."

But Tanya was no longer listening. She and Maude had come to Haviskali to find out what had transpired at Zuken's place and visit the Zwaray Keep in order to contact the svartalfars and fabricate a story of their return through the Well. Solana had enough pull with the greedy bastards to make them play ball.

But if the svartalfars were gone, then . . .

"Well, this is interesting," said Maude, looking at a cheap item at a stall to her right. A bundle of tiny balls with Eternal Light glowing and reflecting within. "Does it come in black?"

Tanya suppressed the urge to growl. "Interesting, my ass. This fucks up all our plans! Stop mucking around with—"

And for the second time that day, Tanya froze, staring at the stall owner's face, or rather, his eyes. The last time she had seen those black orbs, they had glittered with savage laughter, surrounded by fierce features, shoulder-length hair, and someone with the build of an experienced soldier. It was a face to dominate or fight, never one to patronize or pity. Like a wild animal trapped in a cage too small.

Now? The eyes looked glassy. His hair was no longer perfectly styled but rather bedraggled, his skin pale and his cheeks sallow and sunken. He looked like he wanted to leap and maul anyone he could reach with his grasping, talon-like hands, only to be held back by an ironclad confirmation that he would lose.

". . . Olfric?"

The hawker froze and looked at her with a mixture of fright and shock. The light of recognition filled his eyes, and he croaked out, ". . . Tanya?"

"And that's how Elena and I escaped. We've been in hiding ever since," said the mustache.

It was brown and long and, while the color matched his hair, its shade was slightly different, and Tanya couldn't take her eyes off of it.

"Is it real?"

"Sorry?" asked Olfric, bewildered.

"Is it real?" she asked, edging closer. "Did you paste it on? Or grow it naturally?"

Tanya had many questions bubbling through her mind, and none of them had anything to do with Olfric's story. She was no mustache connoisseur, but there was something about it that fit Olfric's face to a tee. It was furry, almost worm-like, and moved left and right in a manner that made her want to poke it. It just looked so right that she wondered why Olfric had never worn one before this.

It took him a moment to realize what she was talking about. "Does it matter?"

"Err . . . no." Tanya blinked twice and pulled back. *I really should have Lukas grow a mustache,* she thought.

They were sitting inside Errol's Tavern, a dull, dim, drafty sort of place. Tanya had often visited here when she'd first started out as an adventurer.

It was where you could get good beer for cheap, along with under-the-table deals—dirty jobs that paid a lot of mezals upfront but with no guarantee for later. Thieves, assassins, abductors, spies, Feelers serving the Empire, undercover agents serving the Cobalt Army . . . you found them all here.

Basically, her sort of place.

They were sitting at a side table—Maude next to her, with Olfric on the opposite end, his back facing the wall. He had an Eternal Light trinket held tightly in his left hand, and he kept glancing warily at Maude, half-expecting a demon to tear its way out of her and eat him alive.

"I'm not going to bite you, Olfric," said Maude saucily. "At least, unless you want me to."

Maude had been going out of her way to antagonize him. And watching her wearing the face of a former comrade was taking its toll on him.

"Stay away from me, Demon, if you know what's good for you," said the former aquamancer, reaching for his sword with his right hand.

It was larger than she remembered it, to the point that its large size actually impeded its ability to be wielded effectively. It was how Olfric dealt with trauma. Every time he went through something difficult, he would come back with his sword a size larger. His arranged marriage had fallen apart after he had been cast out of his clan, and his sword seemed at least twice as large since the last time Tanya saw him.

Maude gave him a rather sad, gentle smile. "Look at you, poor man. A trinket and a sword. Did Father not give his son a new kami after he lost his?"

Maude's face showed such genuine concern that had she been looking at the scene from the outside, Tanya would have believed that she actually cared.

"You and your kind are to blame for my loss, Demon."

Maude smiled with a shade of mockery so faint that no one who wasn't looking for it could possibly have seen it. It was just enough to make sure that Olfric knew that she was rubbing it in his face.

She probably practiced it in a mirror.

She didn't stop there. She kept goading him, trying to bait a reaction, and Tanya didn't understand why. Something had changed in Maude beyond a simple fusing of memories. And she wasn't sure what Maude's angle was . . . or if there even was an angle.

The old Olfric would have most likely attacked by now. Instead, he simply took a deep breath and ignored her.

Turning to Tanya, he asked, "Can you help us out? Elena and me?"

Of all the things he had said, this surprised Tanya the most. Olfric was always a headstrong man—stubborn bordering on arrogant, self-righteous, and absolutely set in his beliefs. His definition of right and wrong was rigid, inflexible, and unbending, like the trident of the storm god he worshiped. For him to put his ego aside and ask her of all people—someone he had always looked down upon—for help spoke volumes.

"Do you realize what you are asking?" she said. "I *can* help you. But you'd have to join me and the yokai."

"The yokai . . ."

"Or you can go and hide as a hawker," said Maude. "Seems to come naturally to you."

The air between them seemed to get physically colder, which was . . . *impossible.* Olfric didn't even have a kami. Tanya saw the slight curving of Maude's lips.

"Think carefully," said Olfric, grinding his teeth, "before you call me a coward."

His strong, blunt features were unreadable. He must have wanted to scream. To fight. Instead, he gave her an angry glare and sighed, looking down at the glass of liquor on the table and downing it in one go. Mirroring his action, Maude took hers and made it vanish without twitching an eyelash. Meanwhile, Tanya took a polite sip and looked at the other two, amused.

"Say I agree . . ." he said at last. "What's the plan?"

Tanya beamed.

The so-called plan was split into three parts. The first was escaping the city, which was now crawling with guards and added security after the destruction of the svartalfars. There was no doubt that Shogun Naowa would deny the Shimizu any and all access to the Cobalt Army, but that didn't mean her grandfather didn't have spies and abductors all over the place.

The second was to locate Zuken and Olfric and to regroup with Lukas and the yokai.

The final part of the plan was to rescue Zuken.

It is worth mentioning that Tanya was not a strategist.

"That's not a plan," Olfric roared. "You just listed exactly what I told you needed to be done in three points."

"No, it's fine," Tanya argued. "I've been on the run for a long time, and it's always worked out for me."

It is worth mentioning again that Tanya was not a strategist.

"Perhaps," said Maude, "we should contact the Leader and discuss?"

"Leader . . ." began Olfric as Maude left the table and walked off to the counter.

"Think of all the demons your daddy told you stories of as a kid," said Tanya. "The wicked spirits, the evil body-stealing demons, the vile nameless things that live in the shadows." She grinned savagely. "Solana gave them *lessons.*"

Solana was the heavyweight champion in Yokai Territory. Whether it was in direct, face-to-face mayhem or acting through defensive wards, there were relatively few people in the territory that could face her and win.

"And . . . you want me and Elena with you . . . close to her."

"She's a monster, yes, but the monster I know. We'll be fine."

Solana would limit casualties, not for the safety of innocents, but because their deaths would draw attention to and complicate her own operations. She would agree to peace—not to protect others but to ensure her own kind weren't getting killed as well.

As Maude returned with a saucer-like bowl, Olfric asked, dumbfounded, "And you're going to contact her using . . . that thing?!"

"Mind filling this up with some water, Olfric?" asked the oni.

A pained expression flitted across the former aquamancer's face as he poured water from the jug. Maude waited for the water surface to go completely still before placing her palms over the bowl, channeling energy into it. A single ripple formed on the water's surface, and a reflection of a pair of eyes appeared in it. While they were beautiful, they were cold eyes, alien, filled with intelligence and desire but empty of compassion or pity.

And then Solana's voice said, quite clearly and from within, "Report."

It was possible to communicate with the wicked Leader of yokai through still water, but the process involved channeling ethereal energy in a fashion Tanya had yet to learn.

Maude recounted all that had happened in a dull drone that bordered on mockery, but the yokai leader didn't react. She also insisted on wearing clothing with colors that were an inverse of Solana's attire, which wasn't very subtle.

Despite the fact that Lukas had bullied Solana into handing over the reins of the yokai to him, Tanya felt irrationally spiteful toward her.

Or perhaps it was completely rational, seeing as the bitch had set her up to be a vessel for someone else's soul.

"The Shimizu destroyed Zwaray Keep," Solana said in a quiet voice. "Who survived? Can you contact Dvalinn?"

Dvalinn was the de facto spokesperson for the Zwaray Keep, and a member of the Svartalfar High Council. He was the one who Lukas had spoken to and the one who had coordinated the trial-by-combat from which Lukas had emerged the winner.

"Dead," said Tanya. "The Keep is gone. As is the Well."

"This . . . can be used in our favor. Lord Naowa is unlikely to turn a blind eye to this. The Llaisy Kingdom was responsible for the protection of the svartalfars. For the Shimizu to walk all over them like this and destroy the Keep . . ." A long moment of silence passed. "Can you contact the Outsider?"

"Yes," said Tanya. She was still a little miffed at her lover for leaving her like this, but she understood his obsession with resurrecting his goddess. If nothing else, he had left her an option to contact him, but only if the situation was dire enough.

"Do so, then," she said. "We will need to change our plans to adapt to the situation. Actually, there is another possibility . . ."

Solana paused thoughtfully.

"How would you like to become the next Lady of Shimizu?"

Olfric was lucky that she wasn't drinking at the moment, because she would have surely turned to spit on him. Tanya considered drinking some and doing a spit-take regardless because nothing else could sufficiently convey just how ridiculous an idea it was.

"And how," she asked Solana, "do you plan to do that? I mean, we can always try asking nicely and see how it goes, but somehow I doubt it will turn out the way you think."

"You leave that to me," said Solana with a confidence that she had no business having, given how spectacularly her previous plans had failed. "For now, we need information on their movements."

For the first time, she turned to address Olfric. "You said you were being hunted, no?"

Three days later, they made their move.

"Are you really a Shimizu or is this more demon trickery?"

This was the seventh time he had brought up the topic. The shock of the fact that Tanya wasn't of common blood had allowed him to temporarily forget his own misery, as well as the fact that he, an Omnyoji, was now allied with the yokai. He had taken them to the solitary ramshackle hut that functioned as their temporary hideout, where Elena was hiding, and gotten her onboard.

"Let's survive the day and I'll tell you."

Following Solana's suggestions, they had dressed Olfric up in rich-looking Asukan robes, fitted with his atrociously long sword. Olfric had then been spotted at a number of locations all over the town—the Otamba Bridge, the destroyed mound where Zuken's mansion once lay, and an official appointment with the overseer, the request for which had been filed through the proper channels at the Grevane.

Not a single person stopped him as he and Elena went to meet the overseer, submitted a formal request to look into Zuken's capture, received empty platitudes in return, and walked out of the Grevane with a pouch of mezals after cashing one of Zuken's cheques.

No cries of alarm. No tromping of soldiers. No attacks by mercenaries. Nothing.

Tanya stuffed another one of the little peaches into her mouth, chewing with satisfaction, as she stood on the roof of the adjacent building, watching them walk out of the Grevane with that giant pouch of mezals.

"What do you think?" asked Maude.

"Oh, they're quite good," said Tanya. "Elena's always had excellent taste in fruit."

"About *them*, Tanya."

A lazy smile spread on Tanya's face. Even from this far, she could clearly feel the subtle movement in the crowd. The shifting eyes. The looks on certain faces. Six men had been following Olfric and Elena for the last thirty minutes. The duo crossed the street and moved into the alley on the right. Tanya casually stepped off the roof, and the next moment, she was overlooking the alley.

No signs of wards that interfered with manacrafting. Then again, direct interference like that was rather easy to detect and they probably didn't want to risk getting caught.

There was a person hiding by one of the building's windows to the right. They weren't stupid enough to stand right next to it and risk getting caught, but nobody would be there in a seemingly empty alley for no reason.

The pole to Olfric's left was more interesting. Tanya couldn't tell if they were spiritists, but there was at least one person capable of veiling their presence.

Likely a psion.

That alone told her that these people were working with limited resources. Mana interference was easier to set up than mental interference, but it was a double-edged sword and would prevent the abductors from using mana as well, leaving no option but to fight using fancy weapons and physical mediums to enact their spells.

They were honestly pathetic when compared to the people her grandfather sent to pursue her. She sighed, more out of disappointment than anything else. These idiots weren't being subtle in the slightest. Sure, they were playing to their strengths, but it would have been more effective if they had waited to enact the wards after some time.

The six from earlier surrounded Olfric and Elena while two more shot out of the ground from behind.

"Your grandfather has gotten sloppy," said Maude.

It was true. The fools didn't even question why two adults suddenly turned into an alley right after they were being followed. Anyone who had been in this kind of game long enough could smell when a situation had become too convenient.

Her right hand shot forward, and a silver whip extended out, ripping through any and all magical protection like toilet paper.

Two of the men were executed before they could even blink—and then they promptly exploded. The whip shattered, forming shards of twisted metal, each of them tearing through the air, following independent trajectories, tearing through the bodies of the eight other mercenaries, chopping off their legs right above the knee.

"What was that?" asked Olfric.

"Just a little gift from my boyfriend."

Tanya whistled, and the metal projectiles zoomed back to her, reforming into a thick aqāru wristband for her right arm.

"Now then," she said, "I'm Tanya, the granddaughter of the man you work for. I have some—"

"We know nothing," one of them cried. Tanya's eyes flashed, and an invisible blade tore through the man's torso in a zigzag fashion, splattering blood all over the cobbled street.

The man was dead before his body hit the floor.

Tanya gave the others a smile that she tried to make as reassuring as possible. "The way this usually works is that I ask you a question, and *then* you tell me a lie. If you give me a dishonest response before I've had the chance to ask the question, it offends me."

The other mercenaries shook their heads in quick, jerky spasms.

"Now," said Tanya, "exactly what is my dear grandfather up to?"

The interrogation was surprisingly short. However much her grandfather was paying them wasn't enough to buy their loyalty in the face of death.

"Arghh!" cried another, after five minutes of torture. "Just . . . just kill me."

Then again . . . she mused as Maude tore another fingernail off the man in front of her, cackling happily.

No amount of money was worth that.

"That's enough. He's told us everything."

Even Olfric looked uncomfortable.

"So?" asked Maude.

There wasn't any more information to be had; she simply wanted to hurt them.

"So leave them be." Tanya extended her arm and Blob followed, killing the remaining men.

She knew Maude had been mentally unstable ever since the merging, but this was unsettling—far worse than she had ever been before. Maybe there was a reason oni were forbidden.

Pushing aside her misgivings, Tanya tossed a bag at Olfric.

"Clean clothes. Take off anything that had blood on it and throw it in a pile."

She stepped back and away from the bloodied garments before tossing Blob right in the middle of them.

"Eat."

The silver Blob shriveled and then expanded, covering the clothes, the bodies, and all the blood. It pulsed once and then compressed. What was left behind was a polished alleyway that looked even cleaner than before the murders.

"Always leave a place cleaner than before you used it."

Nobody could accuse Tanya of not having good manners.

"Alright, you can rest for a few minutes, and then we'll head out. I've contacted Lukas and we'll meet him with Solana."

"Where did you manage to hide in Haviskali?" asked Olfric.

"Not Haviskali. We're going to the desert."

CHAPTER 3

The only thing that stopped it from being a graveyard was the lack of bodies.

It should've been, what with the large monoliths arising out of the dreary, sandy terrain like upturned coffins. Every few yards, there was a mound of translucent, pale crystal, and inside it, a recumbent, shadowy form. Some of them held figures no larger than a regular-sized dog. Others were the size of multi-storied apartment buildings. Together, they ran across the endless terrain, an infinite number of headstones heading towards a horizon that wasn't there, all the while reflecting light that wasn't coming down from the pitch-black canvas above. Even the air itself had a leftover, reheated feel.

In the center of the fake graveyard stood a cat.

It had to be a cat for it was cat-shaped.

There were some cats which, when you met them, reminded you that, despite the thousands of years of human evolution, they only needed to mew and blink their eyes at you to turn you into a gooey mess of affection.

This could be that cat. It had the eyes for that.

And then there were cats that had embraced Darwinian evolution to become agile hunters with sharp claws, powerful teeth, and unparalleled speed to take down even the largest, bulkiest prey quickly and efficiently. A combination of striking beauty, lethal strength, and adaptable, stealthy, predatory instincts that would make even the most fearless man freeze in fear.

This cat would even make that stealthy, apex predator hide behind a boulder and pretend to be extremely preoccupied with its fluffy tail.

It was already meowing, even though said meowing came out less like a purr and more like a plug of hot iron dragged over asphalt. It took a few steps forward and sniffed the sullen air.

Its ears flicked up.

There were voices a long way off. A voice that came from a different World that was outside this World. A voice that spoke to its ear and sought to seek its master, the center of its universe. It could sense another itself in that World, many Worlds away, an itself that its master had left back.

"*Lukas,*" said the voice. "*Find Lukas. I need him.*"

The cat gave the feline equivalent of a shrug and immediately lost interest in the voice. Instead, it began looking for its master, who was somewhere inside this World. A World that was nothing like a certain underground network of tunnels with a pit of featherglass and aqāru in the center. A World that was also nothing like an expansive galaxy with a multitude of planets, stars, asteroids, comets, meteors, and everything in between.

Every single monolith here shared a history that did not exist, yet the cat remembered it all. Every single monolith contained within it a prototype— a monster with instincts that was unique and untouched but felt strangely familiar.

"*Find Lukas,*" said the voice again. "*Bring him back.*"

It purred softly in a question.

Multiple copies of It existed. There was the It that existed with that [PREDATOR] that was and was not its exterminator in the past. There were also several large Its in the same World, and one *very* large It that was growing in a different World that was different from the World [PREDATOR] came from. It did not quite understand how that contradiction really functioned, but such trivial issues were beneath its notice compared to the command its master gave it.

It was It. They were It. That's all that mattered.

It looked around, sniffed, and instantly located its master. He was . . . up there.

But how to get there? An idea came to mind. It was very un-catlike.

Lukas ran his hand across the surface of a crystal mound growing from the ground and felt oddly giddy as he did so.

This wasn't the first time he had been to this place. No, that honor belonged to the Crypt's omphalos, back when he had been stuck in a tug-of-war with its awareness as it tried to subdue his rational human thought with the dranzithl's instincts and protocols. He had received a vision, an eventuality, an outcome so impossibly weird that even the gods themselves would have ignored it. A fusion of two anomalies—one born in an environment that harbored a grudge against anything alive, and the other, a revenant splinter of a Lostbelt cut off from the Origin. Lukas had also momentarily accessed this place when he had activated Warmonger Protocol for the first time to sort through prototypes faster than the speed of thought.

The Crypt hadn't lied. Together, they could be great, but even now, the fusion was incomplete. Staring at this endless graveyard of soul prototypes made him feel like the Crypt staring back at him—so different, yet so similar. Fused, yet distinctly separate. He had its potential, its near infinite reserves, and its history, but the chasm between them was as vast as the terrain and the sky.

In this case—*literally.*

And there was a long furrow creasing across the length of the land. Far away into the horizon, one could see a fracture in the sky canvas.

Soulcrafter? Meynte called.

Lukas didn't immediately respond, standing on top of a small hillock, looking at the jet-black night sky with a wistful expression. "It's fine. This place isn't ready yet. But it will be. Soon. I can feel it."

This was the first time he had voluntarily manifested both Meynte and Blob inside his inner-world. Meynte was a memory, consciousness given form, but in this desolate reality where Lukas presided with utmost authority, even the shade of the empress could not willingly manifest without his express permission.

Blob was an accessory that was simply an extension of this inner-world in outer reality. Watching it react to this place that was both "It" and not, was rather amusing.

That's not the point, she uncharacteristically snapped at him in genuine anger before swallowing heavily and going silent. There was a minor itch at the back of her mind, but somehow, she was unable to finish that thought.

If Meynte had been in full control at that moment—something that never happened while she was within this place—she would have noticed that, whenever she tried to think about the world around her beyond a superficial level, her thoughts slipped away like water off a duck's back.

Lukas smiled. Not even Meynte could wrest herself away from that feeling of contentment that came from not knowing, not being, not having to care for anything at all. One could call it a curse, except he didn't know the conditions that set it off. He wasn't sure of the length and breadth of this mystery, and he was the source of the damn thing.

MEOOOW!

The sound of a massive air horn imitating a cat threatened to tear his eardrums apart. Lukas wasn't sure, but it was somewhere in the vicinity of 130 decibels, practically the same as a small passenger jet taking off. The sound exerted pressure against his skin and hurt his ears. If not for the recent Level Ups he had gained by fighting powerful species over the vast multitude of borderlands floating in the Haze, he'd have been rolling on the floor, bleeding from his nose and ears by now.

Inner-world be damned.

He looked up.

And up.

And up.

It was a reptilian monster prototype, there was no doubt about that. But to call it merely a "monster" seemed the equivalent of calling a wolf a "puppy" or a tiger a "kitten." It was dark gray, clothed in thick sheets of crimson and purple flesh, all crafted out of varying layers of aqāru. The massive two-legged lizard had a row of thick spines beginning at the neck and running down the back to its hip region, extending all the way down to the end of its tail. Its teeth were the size of a crocodile's, unevenly jutting out of its lipless mouth, which could have swallowed Lukas whole.

This was a giganotosaurus. One of the largest dinosaurs known to mankind. One of the most destructive monster prototypes from Lostbelt Earth—finally available to him. It was as long as a city bus and easily spanned thirty feet in height and, given how even the terrain sank with its every step, weighed its value as well.

Sometime before leaving for the Haze, Lukas had collected a large quantity of aqāru, not knowing what kind of danger he might run into while traversing it. This also meant the chance to explore larger monster prototypes, now that he had access to an impossibly large collection of those.

So far, it was proving less of an experiment and more of a headache. For Blob the Giganotosaurus lowered its massive maw and let out another roar.

MEOOOOW!

He sighed.

Form shaped nature. Certain behaviors were appropriate to cats. You couldn't just become a cat and mew around and hope to stay unaffected—eventually a certain cat-ness would permeate your very being.

It showed in the way Cat-Blob kept chasing around rodents like it was the most enjoyable experience in its life. And how it had attempted to stand off against another feline by standing on all six of its limbs, raising its fur, and yapping loudly.

Lukas understood that. What he didn't understand is why it kept meowing even after transforming into something big and terrifying like a dinosaur.

A headache for another time. He instantly synchronized with its dinosaur-like cat-brain, a task that was easier than it sounded. And with it came a message—a voice from far, far away.

"_Find Lukas,_" floated Tanya's voice. "_I need him. Bring him back._"

A call to return this soon? asked the shade of the empress.

Lukas frowned, wondering the same. He had left a tiny portion of Blob back with Tanya before jumping into the Haze. Blob, by some mystery that he was still unable to fathom, didn't care when multiple copies of it existed. All of them were capable of carrying out functions that he had installed in them independent of each other and, at the same time, were a single, shared existence

that answered to the name Blob. The closest way to describe them were perfect clones, and when you introduced concepts of scrying to them, that's when
things turned . . . *exciting.*

"I told her to call me back if things really went south," he said, frowning.
He was still far from done. There was still so much to know, to calculate, to
understand before he returned. He . . . he shouldn't have to go back, not so soon.
He should've had a few weeks at the very least before he was made to fight
again.

He swallowed the bile rising up in his throat at the thought.

What are we going to do about this?

"There is no option," said Lukas, jumping down from the hillock. "I've
learned all I could. I've a theory, and it's got a fair chance of working. We might
as well try it."

And if you fail . . .

"Oh, I'm exceptionally skeptical that everything will go smoothly," he
admitted with a slight grimace. "I've conjured all possible potential worst-case
scenarios of what could go wrong, whether it be rewriting a past reality, or the
Haze being incompatible or reacting in an unconventional manner, the possibility of me being unable to resonate her Truth with the Origin, or even me
dying in the process . . ." He looked up. "The chances are one in three."

One in three? whispered Meynte. *You realize manifesting someone that doesn't
even belong to this reality is paradoxical. So, one in three . . .*

"If I sacrifice my soul to serve as the creation fabric, eight out of ten chances
are it will work."

Then you will die.

Lukas almost smirked at the note of tension in Meynte's words. "You forget, Empress, I'm not just an individual. I'm a *World.* And Lukas Aguilar is a
soul prototype, like the hundreds and thousands of others in this terrain. If it
kills me, which I am quite certain it will, the World will simply create another
Me."

But you will die!

"Yes," Lukas deadpanned. "That's what killing me means. Don't worry, the
next Me will be just as fine."

But it won't be you. *You will be dead—*

"I died back when I tried to absorb the Crypt's omphalos into myself.
Inanna might have kickstarted the process and fueled it with her divinity, but
the original data that was Lukas Aguilar was there inside the omphalos. Inside
this terrain. Her sacrifice of her own divinity merely elevated my soul into
something so significant that the omphalos chose it as the Prime Host and
brought me back to life. So, by your logic, I'm just a thing that believes itself to
be the same individual. I'm not Lukas Aguilar. I'm a clone. A *lie.*"

You don't know that.

"Only because I don't remember dying," said Lukas drolly. "And, trust me, I won't. My World will install all my memories until before the point of death."

He knew it would. It always did that for the monster prototypes. And Lukas Aguilar, Prime Host prototype, was no different.

Meynte didn't respond. She didn't need to. Her displeasure made its way clear onto her face. Lukas wondered if he should tell her that she herself had died eighteen times while witnessing the true nature of the Haze. That she was the eighteenth—no, *nineteenth*—copy of a copy of a copy of the original shade of Meynte that had been siphoned into his inner-world.

How . . . are you going to do this? she asked.

Lukas smiled and closed his eyes.

It took them a couple of days just to go through the potential worst-case scenarios all over again. Not because Lukas was afraid—which he was—but because Meynte had an absolute, all-consuming fear of being erased from existence. It was hypocritical behavior for a former wielder of the End of All Things, but Lukas knew better than to voice it out loud.

And finally, they were ready.

The borderland he had chosen for the ritual was rather beautiful as far as borderlands went, if a little too hot and humid. The forest around him smelled fresh and rich, the heat burning his skin through the shadow of the gargantuan trees looming all around. He wanted to bask in the glow of another fine morning, he really did, but he couldn't allow himself to be distracted from his goal. There was finally light at the end of the tunnel, and it was shining brighter and brighter every day, for he was getting close to reaching the climax of this multi-world trip.

Performing it in the Haze itself would have been easier, but Lukas chose an isolated setup over having more energy readily available. Precision was the name of the game, after all.

The first step, as always, was a circle. A layer of complete isolation from the rest of the world, where he could perform his craft without any disturbance. Meynte had taught him that almost all rituals required a circle, augmented through the use of props that provided physical as well as symbolic parameters to the circle. An Asukan would favor the Eternal Light as the ideal prop, while the yokai preferred the boundless Haze, using it to envision the pathway for energy influx, their manipulation, and so on. Props also served as a mnemonic device—you attached a certain image to the prop inside your head and every single time you saw the prop, the image was packed along with it.

In theory, it was simple.

In Lukas's case, however, the props wouldn't work, for the simple reason that they were all part of the mortal world and the Haze, and what he was trying to summon was anything but.

Instead, he'd have winged the whole thing through pure imagination, concentration, and arrogance.

Use the abstract to summon the abstract onto the real.

"Territory Creation," he commanded. "Set boundary. Ten feet. Expansion. Set Isolation Matrix."

A wave of anomalous energy erupted out of his body, expanding in a massive circle. This was the Isolation Matrix, and it would prevent anything from the outside tainting the interior where he'd perform his forging. When Meynte had demonstrated it in person, she had used the structure of a pentagram, its five points representing five elements—fire, wind, water, earth, and ether. The inner pentagon and the circumcircle acted as constraints that filtered the innate power of the yokai coming from within and safely conducted it into the possessed host body.

A prison within a soul.

But that structure would not do. Not in this case. Instead, he drew on a different structure, one that Inanna herself had shown him back in the anomaly. Anomalous energy erupted further, moving in straight lines, only to change directions and then move straight again, until he stood in the eye of a pentagon, the outer circle touching its vertices in perfect symmetry.

Inanna's symbol of Order. Five points. Five sides. Five elements. The circle represented his hold on the spell crafted within, molding it to obey his orders.

Force within restraint.

So, you're actually going to go through with this . . . Meynte said flatly.

"Don't have much of a choice." Lukas shrugged. "If we don't test my theory, we can't progress any further. If we don't test it out, we can't progress any further."

You don't even have a physical part of her to cast the Truth into.

A non-issue. Gods were spiritual entities, not unlike yokai. The soul reflected on the body, so the more esoteric components that were added to the soul, the stranger and further from physicality it became. And a Truth was so far into the abstract that its wielder would, sooner or later, shed their physical forms and assume a spiritual existence, since physicality and faith didn't go together. That didn't stop divinities from crafting a physical shell to interact with the world around them, but it would be little more than a false construct conjured out of ether, only far stronger. They would be completely indistinguishable from mortals—they could eat, sleep, drink, breathe, carry on physiological functions, have memories, feel the senses, the entire shebang. And yet, those bodies would be little more than puppets operated by the soul.

So, no, it wasn't the lack of a physical body that made any difference.

To bring Inanna back, a total of five different ingredients were needed:

First, a template to craft her identity from. A blueprint.

Second, the materials to create her form with.

Third, a forge.

Fuel was the fourth.

The final step was to anchor the spiritual entity into the world, allowing it to manifest.

The blueprint would come from Inanna's own divinity that resided within Lukas's own soul. The materials—physical and spiritual—would be created out of pure anomalous energy. As an omphalos, Lukas himself was a forge of the perfect quality, and the fuel would be supplied from energy he would draw from the Haze.

And finally, the anchor would be her own relic—the pendant currently hanging on his neck.

Using all five elements, he would likely be able to manifest a proper version of the goddess. That was the theory, anyway.

He closed his eyes.

"Metaforge."

Spells happened within the mind of the caster, and if something went wrong, it could fuck a lot of things up. For that reason, it was always better to insulate it by giving it a name, a state of mind, and a phrase to lead oneself into that particular mindset. With how he was attempting to act like a World and not a human, the presence of an insulation barrier separating the two was even more essential.

Searching optimal Rift channels along periphery
Opening Rift . . .

For a second, everything went completely silent.

Then, there was a dull disturbance in the air as a sinister crimson sheen began forming in the air around him. The circle's power grew like a tidal wave as it met it, the periphery touching, vibrating, expanding, contracting, and deepening as endless power from the Haze poured through the rift into the spell.

His heartbeat was torturous. The mere act of breathing sent jolts of pain down his spine. His arms, his chest, his *everything* burned.

Finally, after what felt like an eternity, the Screen displayed a notification.

> **Forging Circle complete**
> **Power Levels holding steady**
> **Initiate Metaforge?**

"Yes."

The fuel was pouring in. The forge was ready. The blueprint was next.

"Scan soul prototype: Lukas Aguilar. Filter. Access divinity."

> **Prime Host accessing DIVINITY**
> **Breaking existing conventions**
> **Safety Off!**

An alien rage lit up his mind. Like a white fiery blade, it cut into his conscience, threatening to overpower reason and undo the tranquility within. He struggled to wrestle it back. But it was a living thing, this anger. The more he pulled, the more it fought against him. It would not be extracted; it would not be twisted. It was something beyond his mortal soul.

> **DIVINITY ACCESSED**
> **Maximize Sympathy Ratio**
> **SCAN Initiated**
> **ANALYZE Initiated**
>
> **METAFORGE Initiated**

The gates of his mind blew open and the anomaly within him broiled under the strain, waves of power magnitudes more than it could deal with rushing through his body. He could feel it surging within, the rage saturating every inch of him. It was all he could do to prevent it from leaking out.

What seemed like an eternity passed when it couldn't have been more than a few seconds. The volatile emotions gradually abated. The pentagon around him writhed in power, achieving a balance between the anomaly within and the Haze without.

A small smile floated along the edges of his lips.

The pendant on his neck began to glow, and with that, the fifth element was added into the mix.

"Now," he whispered, and yet his voice resonated across the entire terrain. *"Give her back to me."*

A dazzlingly bright light erupted out of the pentagon and rushed into the pendant, forming a human-sized silhouette around it—white, translucent, and unmistakably female. The form shimmered, a haze of blurred imagery. The face was exactly how he remembered, yet there was no emotion in it: blank, featureless, wiped clean by the neutrality that was death. Like the rest of her form, it was a transparent thing, and in the moments where the hazy energy solidified, it shone like quicksilver.

Lukas felt his knees weaken. He funneled lifeforce into them to keep them steady.

It was time for the last element to be added.

Identity.

Accessing Host Memory

He reached into the depths of his consciousness. Flooded it with everything he knew of her. Her good parts and her bad parts. His mental image, his understanding of Inanna. Piece by piece, the information flowed. Power coalesced. Not wrathful like before. Calm. At peace. It surged through him like water through a broken dam.

The body began to turn corporeal.

Lukas knew he was breaking rules. Defying laws. The spiritual form had appeared, brought into existence through sheer will, spitting in the face of all accepted rules. The power was coming from the Haze, but it was creating something that did not exist before.

For potential never followed rules. Instead, it merely shaped them to its will.

The omphalos within him laughed in approval at what he was doing. The borderland he was on . . . didn't. It screamed and whined as he broke the laws of the universe with impunity. The creatures in the borderland screeched and roared and attacked him from all sides, filling the air with power and sound. Even the monsters knew what he was doing, what he was so close to achieving, and, in desperation, they selected him as a target.

But Blob was protecting him, so they failed.

Like his hearing, Lukas's vision too had become a former mockery of what it once was, but he could still see. In flickering imagery burned into his mind, he saw the monsters all around him, meeting their deaths as Blob tore them apart, passing on their Experience directly to him.

Lukas didn't give it a second thought. Fires roared within him, seeping from his bloodied, grimy skin as drops of white-hot liquid fire. His eyes burned and shriveled in his sockets, only to heal almost instantly and be burned again, and his hair caught fire. For a split second, the little semblance of conscious thought that Lukas had left idly noted that Inanna was right. His greed would be his death.

The pain was only bearable because, to an extent, his body was merely a shell. Worlds weren't meant to feel pain.

The very molecules that made him human shuddered and quaked as something otherworldly settled upon them, crafting a place within his body for itself. He didn't know how long this went on for, as he lost meaning of time, but it occurred to him at one point or another that this massively overwhelming presence that threatened to tear his mind and soul in half was very familiar.

Still, this would all be worth it as long as he could bring back Inanna.

> **WARNING!**
> **Truth rejected!**
> **Aborting . . .**

"WHAT?" Lukas yelled. "No. The body's forming, isn't she? It has to—"

This was a roar of pure, unthinking rage, brought on when the area beneath his right knee disintegrated into motes of dust, followed by his left. The anomaly within him screamed at the suicidal behavior of the Prime Host, as his flesh began to dissolve and tendrils of white began to worm their way through the rest of his body.

The pentagon wavered, and his face cracked, motes of white light exploding out of his face. His skull was crushed like a tomato under a sledgehammer. The half-forged form of the goddess shattered, and Lukas prepared himself for oblivion.

> **Metaforge aborted**
> **You died!**

After everything he had been through, Lukas had begun to believe that his inner-world would never let him die. Even if his soul disintegrated, the World would create a perfect copy of it and resurrect him as good as new. Even his body and soul disintegrating at the same time made no difference.

> **Error detected**
> **No vital signs found for anomaly body**
> **Soul Prototypes cannot be utilized**
>
> **Troubleshooting . . .**
> **Host Prototype exists. Anomaly body does not exist**
> **Incompatible**
>
> **Attempting failsafe protocols . . .**

> **Divinity Identified in Host Prototype [LUKAS AGUILAR]**
> **Converting Host Prototype to PRIME HOST**
> **Initiating reconstruction of anomaly body based on Prime Host's**
> **configuration . . .**

Somewhere inside the borderland, an identical copy of Lukas Aguilar was born. The copy did not feel any different, but he was still a copy of him and, thus, thought like him and understood that he was dead.

Why? Because the copies (instances) were installed the moment the previous instance was deleted, complete with memories until the point of death. But with the body destroyed, that was no longer the case.

The copy knew this, and even though the omphalos had crafted a perfect replica of his body using anomalous energy, the copy understood that it was just a copy.

A brief Scan and Analyze told him that.

The copy of Lukas Aguilar opened his eyes and sat up, looking around, slack-jawed for what seemed like an eternity. Finally, he roused himself from his stupor and made his way to the place where he had performed the resurrection spell. Inanna's pendant—good as new—had fallen on the ground, pulsing with power. The self-analysis also told him that somehow he still had Inanna's divinity in his soul, exactly how it was before he had begun the ritual. Despite the fact that he was a copy, the core of his soul was also preserved. As were his memories.

So, was he still a copy?

The copy decided that now wasn't the time for such complex thoughts, and looking around at the devastated borderland around him before finally speaking his first words after getting his new life:

"SONOFABITCH!"

CHAPTER 4

By legal definition, a clone was an identical or near-identical copy of an individual who was not birthed but made, be it through technological, supernatural or systemic means. Following that logic, the soul prototypes stored inside Lukas Aguilar's inner-world were clones, or, as the Screen referred to them, *instances*, created and destroyed right after they had fulfilled their tasks, their memories and any alterations to their spiritual data filed away for the creation of future instances.

They weren't alive nor dead. They weren't part of reality, but they interacted with it. And even if they perished, the world outside would not register them.

They were *forgotten*.

When Inanna had reforged him by sacrificing her own divinity, she hadn't resurrected the true Lukas Aguilar. No, she had activated an instance that knew and thought of itself as Lukas Aguilar, and merged her own divinity with it, elevating him to the status of Prime Host and taking over the anomaly system.

And then that instance of Lukas Aguilar had manifested an instance of Inanna—one that had all her powers, her Skills, her Truth, and had helped him escape the wrath of the Ifrit King.

Talk about being poetic.

That instance of Lukas Aguilar had perished. His mind had perished. His soul had perished. His body had disintegrated.

He was dead. And gone.

But instance-Lukas was just a projection of Lukas the World. Rather than referring to himself as Lukas with an inner-world, it actually made more sense to think of him as a World with an outer Lukas. As long as the World existed, no matter the destruction of his body and soul, his inner-world would craft a body that perfectly matched his own in every respect.

An instance of his soul prototype was pulled out of his inner-world, complete with his memories, all the way until and past his death. Much like the one that had perished in the Crypt of Fiendish Worms, this one, too, was forgotten.

As would *every* Lukas Aguilar, every Inanna, and every single twisted Creation that arose from his inner-world. A blind spot in the Origin's design.

It was such a lopsided, trippy concept that even Lukas himself had trouble understanding it. And he was the source of the damn thing.

Mulling over his thoughts, Lukas opened his eyes and stared at the sky above. But then the Screen intruded into his vision.

Status	Prime Host
Type	Human
Deciphering Spiritual Constitution . . . Decoding . . . Rendering Complete	
Spiritual Core	Divine
Level	26

Why was it showing this? From what he could see, everything was fine.

. . . Or perhaps not.

Reconstruction of anomaly body has left a nonactivated feature **Activating . . .** **New protocols are now available** **[Association Protocol]** **Confirm for activation . . .**

"Elaborate."

Elaboration denied. Confirm for activation . . .

"That's not how it works, and you know it."

[Association Protocol] Activated **Calibration commencing . . .**

And then Blob climbed all over his body and engulfed him like a cocoon.

Calibration complete

When he finally woke up, Lukas found himself wanting nothing more than to remain lying down and ignoring the rest of the world. That or take a force blast to his head to get rid of the massive headache he was experiencing.

"Ugh."

I see you've finally graced us with your consciousness, Soulcrafter.

"Empress." Against his body's protests, the Outsider pushed himself up and rubbed his eyes in exhaustion before remembering how everything had been before he had blacked out. All at once, his body went stiff, and his eyes darted around at full attention.

He was still in the borderland with Meynte hovering over him. She was, of course, a spectral entity that was otherwise invisible to others. Meanwhile, Blob was . . . somewhere.

Calm yourself, said Meynte. *Everything is fine. The moment the ritual broke down, the borderland stopped attacking us.*

"And?"

You failed.

Lukas paused before turning to his comrade. "But . . . I survived. And Inanna's divinity is still intact. Within me. That shouldn't have happened."

Meynte arched an eyebrow. *Do you make it a point to question good fortune?*

"Sometimes."

She shook her head. *Obviously, something occurred that we didn't consider. The World rejected the goddess's divinity right away. I imagine your World utilized that divinity to re-create a copy of your soul and reforged the body accordingly.*

Lukas had figured as much. Scratching his head, he said, "But why reject divinity in the first place? Previously existing or not, divinity is divinity. Every Truth is born at some point in time. Even if we assume that Inanna's past was removed from history itself, nothing explains why the World would reject the chance to assimilate a new Truth."

I recommend considering that before attempting another suicide.

She clearly didn't take any joy at seeing his face scowl. The smug look she had on was merely a trick of the light.

I imagine my rebellious descendant demands your attention. As it is, it has been over two days since the ritual.

Lukas fumbled with his words for half a minute before giving up. "Two days?! You let me waste two entire days sleeping?"

I didn't. I just didn't argue with that metal monster who did.

With that, Meynte discorporated. Grumbling, Lukas pushed himself up and offered his arm to Blob.

"Come on, it's time to get back."

With almost unconscious effort, Lukas opened a rift into the Haze, connecting the borderland to the natural rift inside Solana's office. Despite his best attempts, however, he was unable to replicate Meynte's rift technique and needed to physically open a rift and step through. On the other hand, sharing an awareness with the Haze, however temporarily, allowed him to locate every single Well and borderland connected to it, allowing him to navigate far better than Meynte ever could.

Now, if only he could manage it without tumbling through Solana's room and crashing into the wall.

Blob entwined itself around his body, reminding Lukas for the nth time that, without his increased strength from the constant Level Ups, it would've been impossible for him to remain standing while wearing body armor that weighed as much as a small car.

He stepped through, tumbled into the room, and crashed into the wall.

Blurry impressions of an annoyed skinwalker pulling him up, and Tanya's voice in the background. Opening his eyes, Lukas found himself lying on his bed in his room. Groggily, he pushed himself up and made his way to the bathroom, where he unceremoniously fell to his knees and emptied the contents of his stomach into the toilet.

Being reborn was far more exhausting than he had imagined.

Flushing the unpleasantness down the drain, he stood up and walked to the single jagged piece of flat glass in the tiny room. The yokai had no need for mirrors, so Lukas had had to alter rock into glass for that purpose. His reflection in it was not a pretty sight. Bloodshot eyes on a sunken, pale face stared back at him. He pointed his palm at the bathtub and filled it to the brim with a torrent of water from his hand and modulated the temperature a bit to make it lukewarm.

Stripping, he soaked himself in the tub, closing his eyes. As memories of the past day returned, an intense feeling of rage and disappointment surged through him. At least the previous time, he had managed to raise a shadow of Inanna, albeit temporarily. His eyes fell on the pendant, which was still glowing iridescent blue, just like it did when Inanna was communicating with him.

"Inanna?"

Nothing happened.

"Inanna?"

Still nothing.

He tried scanning it for more but to no avail.

And yet the glow didn't fade, so he had to have done something right. But then why didn't the ritual work? What had he missed?

He knew that Inanna's divinity was acting like an autonomous system with protocols that were fully capable of resisting his and the omphalos's attempts until he fulfilled certain criteria. The last time, it displayed nothing but a prompt claiming that the information he was seeking had been redacted. This time, that divinity was churned out of his soul, used in an incomplete process, and then reused to forge his soul all over again.

His theory had been right. So far. Those five components could resurrect Inanna, and maybe they would have, but he had failed in getting the World to accept Inanna's Truth. Despite everything he knew of her, despite all his memories, the system had classified them as inadequate.

Why? He had no idea.

Even more confusing was the anchor part. Inanna's reflection had stayed in the pendant—a relic—for who knew how many millennia, and even this perfect vessel had fallen short.

He was missing something. But what? A sixth element, perhaps?

Divinity was a complete set. An extremely defined, esoteric set but a set, nonetheless. And somehow, this fact had been emphasized exponentially to the point that it was almost a mystery in itself.

To use an analogy, it was like five different chemical constituents. He just needed to find the right stimulus that, when applied in the right manner, could cause them to react in the right way. Whether that stimulus was a sixth variable, a condition, or something else was the question.

His fingers closed on the pendant.

I've come this close. I'll find a way to get you back, I swear.

As always, silence was his answer.

Closing his eyes, he relaxed in the tub. His thoughts went to Tanya, and he wondered how his little weapons were faring. Hopefully she'd give him some glowing reviews about their performance after she'd met him. Knowing her, she was probably training with Solana right now.

Which was fine. For now, he just needed a long soak.

And, of course, someone decided to walk into the bathroom right at that moment.

"May I join you?" asked Tanya, closing the bathroom door behind her while holding her towel in front of herself with the other, but the way she was holding it, the cloth did little to conceal anything.

For some reason, Lukas felt a little self-conscious. "Tanya? Uh, what are you doing? Wait, I'm almost finished. If you'd only give me a minute—Aaah!"

Tanya had thrown her towel right at his face, obscuring his vision and making him fall back inside the tub. When he had finally gotten it off his face, she already had one leg submerged in the water.

"What are you doing?" he asked, but instead of answering, she just turned her back on him and sat down between his spread-apart legs, leaning against his chest.

"This feels nice." She sighed, snuggling further against him. "I missed this."

"And me?"

"Mmm," she murmured. "Did you have a fun trip?"

He thought back to the feeling of dying. The excruciating agony at feeling his body disintegrate. Being reborn with an ironclad confirmation that he was a copy of the original.

"Yes, I suppose it was."

Tanya grabbed his arms and put them on her belly, sighing as his fingers began crawling all over her front.

"How are you?" he asked.

"Fine," she murmured. "Now that you're back."

"I'm glad to be back too," he said.

Tanya giggled and kissed him on the lips, putting her arms around his neck and cocooning herself against his chest. They stayed like that for a while.

"We should get going," said Lukas at last. "Or else Maude might come looking."

Tanya grumbled. "Maude is getting on my nerves. And honestly, it's driving me crazy. You and Maude get along quite nicely. Even Solana stopped being a bitch after you left. I'm not sure how you pulled off that miracle, but she seems almost . . . nice."

Yeah, he might have had something to do with that.

"I guess Maude and I just understand each other. Makes it easy to get along."

She frowned. "It took us ages to understand each other and get along."

"What can I say? You were being rather obstinate," he teased. "Who knew a round of sex would make an honest woman out of you?"

"Dog!" she retorted, and bit him on his right earlobe.

Lukas hissed and tried to grab her, but Tanya was already pulling away, squealing. He grabbed her by her waist and pulled her back, tickling her.

"Please!" she squealed. "Stop! I can't—Oh, I can't breathe!"

He stopped, and she relaxed on top of him.

"So . . ." he said at last. "What brought this on? Not that I'm complaining. It's just unexpected."

"Well, for all I know, you're gonna plunge right into whatever new craziness you've thought of next. When else am I supposed to spend time alone with you? I mean, we had just gotten together, and then you decided to vanish into the Haze and leave me all lonely for another nineteen whole days. Not that anyone's counting."

Nineteen days. That was surprisingly brief, compared to the amount of time he had spent inside the Haze, where time flowed differently. It was also the reason behind his reaction when Tanya had walked into the bath without a care in the world.

"I'm sorry," said Lukas, tightening his hold over her. Tanya pushed herself into him and rested her head on his right shoulder. "It's just that it still doesn't come naturally to me to think that anyone would like to spend time with me."

Tanya whirled around, coiling her hands around his neck as she glared at him. "We're in your tub, wet and naked. We spent an entire week making out every single chance we got. And I've already promised to be on your side in whatever madness you decide to take part in. Take the fucking hint."

She snorted. Their noses touched. Finally, she spoke, almost apologetically. "Sorry. I'm just new to this kind of thing. All my life I've only had people use me or attack me. Sometimes I wake up and wonder if it's all going to go away tomorrow."

"You know I'll always acknowledge you."

"I know, and you did. Right from the very first day. I'm not sure why but every time I looked at you, I had this urge to jump your bones. It didn't help when you took my side against Zuken and the svartalfars and everyone else."

That was probably Inanna's doing. But there was no need to mention that.

"You're welcome," he said. "If it helps, I found you utterly captivating as well."

Tanya gave him a mocking grin, before she shifted again, entwining her legs around him.

They stayed like that for some time, basking in the warmth of the water and each other's bodies. As he sat there, more content than he had been in a long time, Lukas thought that even this, the way he was now, was not a bad way to live at all.

It was almost a shame it wasn't going to be his life.

Nobody spoke for a while.

"Lukas?"

"Mmm?"

"This is the moment when you tell me what's bothering you."

"Is it?"

"Yes."

"Okay, fine. It's a long story, though," Lukas said thoughtfully and began narrating his experiences in the Haze, how he had traversed a multitude of borderlands, fighting, growing, leveling up, experimenting, and learning all sorts of secrets of the Ikai Realm and the universe. He conveniently avoided everything having to do with Meynte and his inner-world, choosing to only allude to the latter, ending with his failed resurrection attempt, minus feeling what true Death felt like before being recreated with all of his memories.

"There are holes in your story," Tanya pointed out. "Many, many holes."

"All boring parts, I'm afraid."

"And no doubt important parts as well."

"You asked for a quick description, not a documentary."

"You're telling me that you just wandered around the Haze and you got answers to the secrets of the Haze that Asukans and yokai were unable to gain in thousands of years?"

"I had . . . help."

"And resurrecting your goddess?"

"The help gave me some more help."

"You're being deliberately infuriating, aren't you?"

"Believe it or not, I was born like this."

"Lukas . . ."

He exhaled. There was no avoiding it. "It's just . . . I was so certain that this would work. I took into account nearly every single thing I could think of, but I . . . I failed. All that time, all that effort, everything that I did, and it led to absolutely fucking nothing. And I . . . I died."

Had he been looking at Tanya, he'd have noticed that she had turned white.

"I died. Again. Just like back when I killed the anomaly. And then I was resurrected by my inner-world, because . . . because I guess it just won't let me die. I guess I'll just chalk it up to my dumb luck and be done with it, then." He grinned. "No point in worrying about this mess."

Apparently, that was the wrong thing to say.

"No point? *No point?*" Tanya hissed, grabbing his shoulders so tightly that, had he been a normal person, she'd have drawn blood. "Have you seen yourself in a mirror lately? You've changed *so much* since I first saw you in the anomaly. Back then, you were this lean, pale thing with a bag of tricks. Now? Your body has gotten heavier, your eyes have permanent flecks of green in them, your skin's a darker tan . . . Hell, even your soul is an eldritch abomination. You've changed from a lifeforce warrior to a World creating shit out of your bare hands. It doesn't even matter that you've practically regrown your organs several times over during the last six months. Why? Because you *BLEW YOUR-SELF UP!* Even Solana's scared shitless of you. Am I missing anything on my list of horrible alterations that you've inflicted on yourself?"

Tanya was trying not to get overly emotional, but she had started to tear up again as she went through the list. Her voice was forceful, but her usual strength was lacking. It was clear that she hadn't had a peaceful night's sleep recently.

"I . . . uh, may have suffered multiple aneurysms."

The muscles on her neck strained, clearly revealing her inner thoughts. "How many?"

"Thirty-seven?"

"Are you asking me or telling me?"

"I don't know. Maybe? At least? Is it hard to count them when you're having them multiple times every other day? I was fighting monsters there in the Haze."

"And may I ask how many monsters you siphoned off there?"

A number fired off in his head instantly. "I'd say about 753 different species. If you're counting each individual one, maybe 6394 . . . Damn it, Tanya. That doesn't matter, and you know it."

She dropped her head into her hands in exasperation. "I'm stuck between making a snarky reply to your paltry excuse and being stunned at the number you gave me."

"I'm sorry?"

"No," she said. "That's just it, Lukas. You shouldn't be sorry. You're too messed up to be sorry. You've put yourself through too much for others' benefit to be sorry. You shouldn't have had to suffer through whatever Solana put you through. The Crypt shouldn't have been able to possess you. Using the memory of your destroyed World to kill the Crypt in a suicidal moment shouldn't have had to happen, either. The svartalfars, the borderland, facing those bylestyrs and muspels, the king, your impossible task to resurrect your goddess, and all the shit that Solana and Meynte put you through—none of that was your fault. There was literally no reason for you to have to take responsibility for what happened."

She touched his cheek with one hand.

"That's not true," Lukas said. "I did all of that because I—"

"*Don't*," she said, her viciousness shutting him up. "Just don't."

She stayed silent for a few seconds. He let her.

"It's just . . ." she began again, struggling for words. "I've seen how far you push yourself when you set your mind on something. I remember what happened with Meynte, and what you did back then. You could've died, Lukas. You could've died several times. Meynte could have killed you many times over, but you didn't care. And all of that for me."

"Which should tell you how important you are to me."

She frowned. "Yes. But I also remember what you said. You told her that you wouldn't fight for me but for my freedom to choose."

Lukas blinked. "Tanya—"

She shook her head. "You fought for my right to choose because you would also fight for your own right to choose. And this goddess Inanna—it's obvious she holds you in a great debt by sacrificing herself. And I understand that. But I'm afraid. I'm afraid you'll go too far in trying to get her back and I'll lose you, and I'm not sure I can bear that."

Her eyes were glistening.

For once, Lukas fell short of words. He had never considered how it might have appeared from her perspective. "You're angry with me for jumping into the Haze."

"No," she said, vehemently shaking her head. "I'm not. I can't be. I'd be a hypocrite if I tried to stop you from following your own desires after you fought so hard to protect mine. But I'm afraid I'll lose you. Every time I leave you alone, I can't help but wonder if it's the last time I'll ever see you. You vanished into the Haze just like that, and none of us—not even Solana—knew if you had a way to come back. And to know that . . . You have no idea what you do to me, Lukas Aguilar. You have no idea how it feels to wake up in the middle of the night, dreaming that years had passed since you've left. Dreaming about how I'd never see you again. Dreaming about you not even recognizing me the next time you saw me, because I'd grown so old."

She pulled him tighter and began to sob.

Lukas felt bitter inside. He didn't want to hurt Tanya, and he knew where she was coming from. But he also knew what he wanted and why it was necessary.

"You know what?" he said, grinning, pulling her closer. "After all this is over, let's go out on a holiday. I've seen some really charming places in the Haze. It'd be a nice vacation."

Her eyes brightened. "Promise?"

He kissed her on the lips. "Absolutely."

She giggled, and, not for the first time, Lukas noted that despite all she had been through, she was still very much a young woman experiencing romance for the first time. He'd have to keep that in mind.

"I visited Haviskali while you were gone. Me and Maude."

He blinked. "Solana let you?"

Tanya giggled. "We didn't wait for permission. I wanted to see what had happened to Zuken's mansion with my own eyes. And when we got there, we found that my brother Ultaf and his army had destroyed Zwaray Keep and ended the svartalfar race for good."

". . ."

"I swear you can't make this shit up."

And what followed . . .

Lukas wasn't sure what to call what followed. It seemed like something from a B-movie.

"And Solana wants you to become the next Shimizu Leader?" he had to ask, and Tanya nodded.

"Ultaf has already stepped on too many toes, and Grandfather will care even less for what he does now that the Shimizu are about to lose their Sacred Eight status if they cannot find me in another month."

"That's good news," said Lukas. "You just have to avoid getting noticed until—Oh, I see."

She nodded. "If he loses the Sacred Eight status, he'll have no reason to keep Zuken alive. He's desperate, and that makes him dangerous." She paused for a breath. "Lord Naowa, the Shogun of Haviskali, dragged the issue to the emperor's court. The Earth King helped Grandfather secure a forty-five-day grace period. Obviously, this is just a formality. Unless they find and capture me, they'll lose it all. And I know Grandfather. If that happens, he just won't care."

Lukas frowned. "But if he kills Zuken . . ."

"It *doesn't* matter," she stressed. "Nothing matters. The moment he loses it, he is a loose cannon. He'll kill Zuken, even if it means throwing the Llaisy Kingdom and Eaborid Kingdom into a war. Even if it means his own death, or the extermination of the clan."

"That's . . . that's *madness.*"

"That's *Mujin Shimizu.*"

Lukas sat quietly, feeling her taking small breaths against his chest. "So, if we want to save Zuken, it has to be within a month. Too soon, and we risk him taking action. Too late, and Zuken's dead. And we can't let him find out anything about you being alive. And we can't face him, either. Which makes the day of this Shogun meeting the best time to rescue Zuken." He looked at her pleased expression. "So, what's the plan? I imagine you have something to go on. Or else you wouldn't have summoned me back."

"Well," said Tanya brightly. "I discussed it with Olfric. Escape the city, which is crawling with guards, locate Zuken and regroup with you, and then rescue him from wherever Ultaf is hiding him."

Lukas blinked. "That's not a plan. It's a list of things you want done."

Tanya faltered for a second before beaming. "Yes. That's exactly what I told Olfric."

CHAPTER 5

———

It was Lukas's first time watching someone bind a kami.

Tanya and Olfric had run him ragged through the entire Shikigami Ritual back when he had been an earnest student at Zuken's place. With Inanna gone and Lukas exclusively focusing on his own survival in an alien land, he had jumped at the chance to learn whatever knowledge he could gain with all the grace of a starved animal. By the time he was done with those texts in Zuken's library, each book had at least six creases in it.

Naturally, none of them ended up making a lick of difference since he ended up siphoning any and all kami the old way, but that was another story.

That said, this was probably the first time in the history of yokai that an Asukan, not to mention a former clan heir, was performing a Shikigami Ritual in front of yokai. Given the kind of crowd this had gathered, Lukas imagined that seeing a fellow spiritual creature be caged within the soul of a traditional enemy garnered a morbid fascination similar to how the natives flocked to watch prisoners of war being subjected to the guillotine by the colonizing administrators in the late nineteenth century.

Olfric was standing in the center of the large circle that was mostly reserved for settling debacles through trial by combat. Not long ago, Lukas had been subjected to a similar trial against a kasha called Quonnan. He had vexed the fiery devil to the point of self-immolation, only to siphon it into himself, an act that cemented his position as the vaunted Outsider of legend.

There would be no trial today. Instead, Olfric was standing close to the periphery with Elena next to him. Behind them was a barrier separating him from the yokai crowd outside the circle.

"All this just for a kami binding?" he asked.

"Not just a kami binding," said Solana from beside him. The two of them were standing on a balcony overlooking the circle. Solana was an ancient skin-walker who had been there for at least six centuries and still had enough vanity to make herself look like a young woman in her late twenties. She was the de facto leader of the yokai, and a persistent pain in Lukas's side.

It was hard to blame her for how she treated him. After all, he shattered her six-century-old resolve to pieces.

"The Shikigami ritual always takes place at a shrine, Outsider. Within a territory cursed by that usurper's Eternal Light, they drag a kami out, weaken it in every way that matters, and seal it within their soul, subjecting it to a lifetime of imprisonment."

Pot, meet kettle, Lukas wanted to say. But irritating Solana would get him nowhere.

"But there is no Eternal Light here." Her teeth showed, and Lukas was suddenly reminded of how she looked beneath that flesh-mask.

"And here in the desert, there is no Eternal Light," he reasoned. "So Olfric has to face the kami at his own peril and subdue it."

"Exactly."

Okay, he was looking at this the wrong way. This wasn't a crowd expecting a guillotine death. This was closer to the Romans sitting in the Colosseum watching gladiators being thrown to lions.

Then he was struck by his own lack of discomfort at this.

He really had made some bad choices in life.

"If Olfric subdues the kami, he demonstrates his fortitude, and you know he'll be a useful pawn. If he loses and the kami takes over, you'll still have a useful pawn. Either way, you win." He cocked his head. "And Tanya agreed with this?"

"She didn't. The changeling did. So long as she was allowed to help that Asukan."

Lukas narrowed his eyes in Elena's direction. The changeling had always stuck out on his weird-ometer; while she was a capable psion, something about her abilities rubbed him the wrong way. Gathering anomalous energy within, he shaped it into a metaphysical lance and hurled it at Elena. It was a new trick he had learned, allowing him to exercise his anomaly functions outside his range, and Elena was the perfect guinea pig to test it upon.

So color him surprised when, instead of a Screen unfolding before his eyes with Elena's details on it, he suddenly had the oddest feeling in the back of his brain. It was almost like a kaleidoscope coming into focus, only the point never arrived and it kept spinning and spinning without ever providing the expected insight. Even more disturbing, Lukas realized, was the feeling of déjà vu, a certainty that he'd experienced this sensation before, though for the life of him, he couldn't recall when.

Thankfully, something else happened right then to distract him. A large, stone coffin erupted from the ground before dispersing into sand, revealing . . .

A demon.

Lukas hurled another mental lance, and the Screen flickered into existence.

JAAN (LEVEL 3)
Spiritual Parasite. 97% spiritual similarity with MARID species. Lack of physical body. Energy core employs water and ether.

It was a serpent, there was no doubt about that, easily fifteen feet in length, its body as thick as an oak tree trunk, with a large draconian face and protrusions erupting all over its body up to its tail. It was a twisted combination of a snake and a porcupine, crafted out of water and held in place by ether.

To call it a mismatch would be a laughable understatement.

Every single one of its motions was akin to the deadly beauty of a hawk in flight. Not as deadly as Meynte or some of the other things he had faced recently but certainly far, far more than Olfric could possibly face. In fact, he nearly died at the first strike.

Meanwhile, more information flooded into Lukas's mind.

SKILL	LEVEL
Possession	2
Water Creation	3
Water Manipulation	1
Pressure Modulation	3

He arched an eyebrow. A kami that had a natural facility for Level-3 Pressure Modulation and Water Creation? Where had this gem been hiding this whole time?

His understanding of kami was that they were spiritual parasites, most of them limited to Level 1 or Level 2. More importantly, they didn't gain any Soul Capacity or Level Ups, and hence, required a host to possess, using their Soul Capacity to do so. Asukans exploited this dependency to entrap them within their souls through the Shikigami Ritual, forcing them to do their bidding.

And then, from time to time, there came along some kami that were born at a higher level.

Like the bylestyrs.

Or the Ifrit King.

Also, something about this creature set him on edge. It was strong, but nothing like he hadn't faced before nor could he crush without exerting himself. No, instead there was this feeling of *nothingness* that exuded from it. A numbing, empty void that seemed to make the world around it smaller with every pointless, meaningless, mechanical movement it cared nothing for.

It was hideous. Disgusting. A beast that had no intention to bond or grow. Just a butcher's tool that wanted to cleave the object in front of it.

That would be Olfric.

"That thing is . . ." he began.

"You feel it, don't you?" whispered Solana, and Lukas noticed a mad light in her eyes. "Its name is Uwabami, and it's a true demon. One of the most dangerous beasts I've ever faced in my lifetime. It has devoured the lives of sixteen Asukans to date during the Shikigami Ritual. I consider myself lucky to have been able to get my hands on it before the soldiers of Baramunz could kill it."

"Why are you doing this?" asked Lukas flatly. "Olfric will die, and Tanya will hate you for this."

"Oh, not necessarily," whispered the skinwalker, her hungry eyes fixated on the former aquamancer. "I admit I was most vexed when the brat brought the Asukan and his pet changeling into my territory. But I've seen what festers within him. Something tells me this will be no inane battle."

Lukas would've disagreed, but seeing the former Asukan battle this monstrosity made him falter. Olfric was using the aqāru weapon Lukas had crafted for Tanya—a condensed band of the metal with a memory function installed within it, allowing it to take the shape of whatever weapon the bearer could think of, and currently, it was in the form of a curved scythe connected to a cylindrical hilt ending in a long chain that connected it to another weighted hilt on the other side.

Basically, one of those weapons that should have had a "Don't try this at home, kids" tag.

The scythe cut through the serpent's liquid body with deceptive ease, only for the watery form to regrow while the monster tried its best to tear Olfric limb from limb, instead of trying to possess him and twist him into a mindless host.

"I've studied his soul," said Solana with the air of a scientist discussing a lab rat that survived a particularly brutal experiment. "That one is a former aquamancer, and houses the Skills of his previous kami. Water Manipulation Level 3. Together, they could be great."

"Together, they'd be a rabid dog I'd have to put down on sheer principle," said Lukas, scowling. "Even if Olfric somehow survives its onslaught, he can't hope to control the kami without Eternal Light. And that beast doesn't look like the kind to follow orders."

As if his words had been a portent, Olfric slashed through the beast's head, dropping the severed slab of meat into water, only for three heads to grow back in its place.

"I suppose the two of them will just have to surprise us then," said Solana.

Lukas frowned. He hated when he missed the subtext.

The kami's three new maws lashed out. None of them were alike. One had a dozen small, snapping jaws, the second, the fang-lined pit of a lamprey, and in the third were a hundred, jagged, grasping finger-like appendages. All they had in common was that each one was large enough to hold a man of Olfric's size comfortably inside it before crushing him to sticky paste.

Olfric charged, ducking under the first head and stabbing upward, dragging his weapon along its neck and splitting it open in a single, smooth motion, leaping back in midair, and swirling the weapon in a circle, slashing the second head off its neck. He landed lightly on one foot and snapped the weapon behind him, letting the third maw impale itself head-on. The beast drew back, shrieking in rage with such force that Lukas could feel his bones vibrating from the sound. It flailed its tail around, grabbed Olfric by a leg and slammed him down to the ground. The water condensed, forming a singular head, which reared back, and Lukas prepared himself, ready to halt the beast before it hit the Asukan and—

Someone pushed and leaped between Olfric and the serpent and raised both arms up, as if to use her own body as a shield.

"Stop!" said Elena.

Lukas would've found it rather sweet if it weren't the single stupidest thing he had ever seen in his life. For starters, the kami was just going to stomp through her—she was no shield at all. The incongruity of the situation nearly made him laugh out loud, if he wasn't painfully aware that he needed to intervene at any moment, and the serpent maw was already descending . . .

And stopping?

What the hell? thought Lukas. The serpent stopped in its tracks, its jaws halted roughly an inch away from Elena's face.

"Don't attack us!" Elena yelled. As if the monster was going to simply listen to her. "Stay right there!"

To Lukas's utter surprise, the serpent paused and stared at the changeling like she had grown a second head.

"What are you doing?" asked Olfric, pushing himself back up.

"Giving you time, you moron!" snapped Elena. "Prepare the circle, quick."

Lukas had to give the man points for not wasting any time as he instantly pulled out a trinket and released Eternal Light from within, channeling it to conjure a perfect circle around the kami.

"I had almost forgotten," said Lukas. "Olfric was an Omnyoji."

Circles were a kind of screen or barrier, a way to trap spirits, make a shield, or prevent something ethereal—or even raw power—from escaping. And then there were props to help improve focus, and sigils, runes, or whatever you wanted to call the important-looking squiggles inscribed within the circle, to direct the power and make it work in predetermined ways.

For Lukas, who never had to deal with power limitations, it was all about enacting his will on the universe. For Olfric, it was also about finding the right amount of power to get the effect, no more, no less. Lukas was willing to hazard a guess that more experienced casters were able to estimate just how much power any given spell would need just from experience, taking the complexity of the different symbols, and being able to factor them together to figure out a precise number.

Kind of like algebra—only algebra that might blow up if you don't divide and then add in the right order.

The serpent hissed and tried to escape the circle, which was already constricting around him, while the crowd all around were getting agitated and howling at Olfric, his actions no doubt fueling their hatred for Asukans.

The Eternal Light he'd unleashed wasn't enough to subdue a monster like that, even with whatever strange effect Elena was enacting upon it. It would paint Olfric and, by extension, Tanya in a bad light, but . . .

But it was too simple.

The Solana he knew wouldn't waste her time on something this inane. He glanced at her out of the corner of his eyes and found her staring down with undivided attention.

What game are you playing?

A second circle manifested around Olfric, this one smaller and constricting around him. Lukas saw the familiar sigils of the pentagon taking shape, the spiritual and elemental restraint materializing around him. The serpent hissed and screeched but never once did it try to shatter the constraints or physically attack Elena, who was standing between it and Olfric, glaring at it and shaking.

"You see it, don't you?" whispered Solana. "That changeling. Her lifeforce is pitiful, she has no mana, and yet, she commands an ethereal form to obey her every command . . ."

"It's not Olfric you were interested in seeing do battle," Lukas reasoned. "It's *her*."

Her teeth showed. "You've always suffered from tunnel vision, Outsider. Both of us can see beyond the physical. You tell me, what's going on?"

Curious, Lukas settled his stare on Olfric. The Screen listed him as boasting all the Skills that his previous kami—a Level-3 marid—had. Combining them with this beast would indeed make the two of them greater than the sum of their parts, but there was something more . . . something odd.

Mutated Soul Architecture Detected
Spiritual Resonance Detected

Mutated, not damaged. Every single bremetan possessed by yokai revealed damaged Soul Architecture. And Spiritual Resonance? That was only possible when—

His thoughts vanished as Olfric raised his hands and motes of energy began to condense around him. His arms grew larger, almost claw-like, and extended outward to grab the serpent's head in its iron grip.

"That's . . . Metamancy!" Lukas almost yelled. Olfric's previous kami didn't have any metamantic ability, and Olfric was a bremetan, which meant he couldn't use mana without a kami. This was freaking impossible.

He watched with a mix of fascination and disbelief as those claw-like arms shattered the serpent's form, and for the first time, the water droplets weren't re-forming back into the snake but instead were being drawn towards Olfric, snaking around his arm and merging into him as immense hissing noises escaped the remnants of the spiritual beast.

Lukas looked to his left. Solana was a slender, pale thing, her eyes bright, jet-black, narrowed, and watching the former aquamancer fall on his knees as the Eternal Light Circles dissipated.

Then it happened.

The ground shook, and Olfric threw his head back, letting out a monstrous roar—his eyes bright blue, his jaws open, power rolling off him in waves. And around him, erupting out of his very skin, rose a massive volume of water. It contorted and condensed, forming into a familiar serpentine form, twisting around his body, arising out of his arms, its head reaching ten feet into the air before looming downward as if daring everyone to fight it.

And then it dispersed, and Olfric collapsed.

The Screen flickered, revealing new information.

SYMBIOTE	
SKILL	**LEVEL**
Possession	2
Water Creation	3
Water Manipulation	3
Pressure Modulation	3

A complete collection of Level-3 Skills in Aquamancy. Enough to make all but the most powerful monsters out there stop and take pause. Even Solana would be hard-pressed to defeat him.

Still, no mention of Metamancy. So, where had *that* come from?

"Show's over," said Solana, a small smile playing on her face. "And he even managed to save his soul."

"His soul is resonating with *something*," said Lukas, freezing Solana in her tracks as she turned to walk away. "I'll wager it has something to do with the possession back in the anomaly. Mizo—she was the one that possessed him and failed. Wasn't she?"

A corner of her mouth ticked up. "Mizo has always been talented as a reiki."

"Level-3 Metamancy," said Lukas, still not moving from his place. "That incomplete possession left something behind, didn't it? A slow, but guaranteed mutation in Olfric's soul. I bet something similar is happening with Mizo and you wanted to test how deep the connection went." He narrowed his eyes and looked at the skinwalker. "What are you expecting? Another oni?"

She gave him a tiny snort. "Even after thousands of years, we yokai have no idea what conditions allow the transformation of a yokai and a bremetan into an oni. They are rare, unique mysteries and, if you believe the legends, heralds of change. That Asukan over there is different, but being different is not some free pass to surpass the natural order. Something slightly unique, perhaps, or at least with a set of fairly amusing tricks. Whatever he ends up being, it should be interesting. Same goes for the girl."

Lukas considered that. "You want to watch both of them develop? Then you need to help Tanya rescue Zuken Banksi."

Solana spun around. "I refuse. The Shimizu have shot themselves in the foot by annihilating the svartalfars. They are on the verge of losing everything, and they are lashing out. And when they lose, they will kill that man, and the Shogun of Llaisy Kingdom will lash out. The Eaborid Kingdom will be stuck in a rebellion, the armies of Lord Straff facing the might of Mujin Shimizu. The Earth King will try to bend the scales in Mujin's favor, as he always has, and Lord Naowa will escalate things."

Something wild shone in her eyes, and her smile widened to inhuman proportions. "And just like that, the entire Southeast will be devoured by war, and we yokai shall feast upon it. And all I have to do is . . . *nothing*."

"Tanya told me you wanted to make her the next Lady of Shimizu."

Solana clicked her tongue. "She will. Once the entire Southeast lies shattered, Tanya will rise up bearing the Wind King's kami and resurrect the Shimizu. Even better, she will start her own clan. And through her, the yokai will rule over the entire Southeast, without any opposition."

"Because they will be dead."

"Exactly."

The worst part? Lukas found himself agreeing with her. He had killed his fair share of beings during his time in this cutthroat world of murder and mayhem. With the southeastern side of the Empire devolved into chaos, Tanya would be safe, and that was all Lukas cared about. It would also give him enough time to focus on resurrecting Inanna and fulfilling his promise while letting Tanya come into her powers without any threat to her life. Inanna would applaud this solution.

All he had to do was let Zuken die.

"You know as well as I that I am right, Outsider," said Solana, giving him a look of pity. Or possibly contempt. "Yes, you can defy me and choose to protect that Asukan for whatever obligation you feel for him. I'm certain that the changeling and our newest symbiote will join you and Tanya in this mad quest. But what will you gain from it? The wrath of a warlord and attention on Tanya. You know perfectly well that Tanya isn't ready to face that kind of challenge. Not yet. Without you supporting her, she will give up. *Make her give up.*"

Lukas closed his eyes. Solana was right, as much as he hated admitting it. Yes, she was suggesting an easy way out, but it was also the safest bet and came with the greatest rewards. But . . .

Easy did not turn wrong into right.

"What if we can save Zuken and *also* let things play out the way you want? Let the world think that Zuken is dead and have things devolve into war between kingdoms?"

"An interesting suggestion but risky. Why should I spare it any thought?"

"Because if you do, then it will go a long way to building bridges with Tanya. Olfric and Elena joined hands with her to save Zuken. You help them do that, and you have them under your thumb. But none of that really matters, because I'm going to give you something that can change everything in the eventual war that happens between the Asukan Empire and the yokai."

"Which is?"

"A goddess," said Lukas, meeting her eyes. "The goddess that beat Everfrost into submission and did so with her hands tied and eyes closed. The Supreme Queen that—Empress Meynte claimed—shone brighter than Amaterasu. A monarch that tore pantheons down and sat on a mountain of corpses of kings and emperors. A dictator, a tyrant, a killer of gods and beasts—that is the goddess I am willing to give to your kind. The goddess that I want to bring back."

"Bring . . . back?"

He pursed his lips. "She is no more. She sacrificed herself to save me."

Solana snorted. "A goddess dying to save a mortal? Now I have heard everything."

Lukas did not laugh.

"You're serious," said Solana, flabbergasted.

"Because it's preposterous that she did it. She . . . she was something else. But that is what I offer as an incentive, Solana. I'm not going to sugarcoat it. You used me and you betrayed me. Several times over. And when you lost, you tried to break Tanya again by destroying her old relationships. Even half of that is enough to make me want to sic Blob on you and slowly consume your soul, make you feel the exquisite agony your kind loves to share with hapless bremetans. And, yes, I've reached the end of my patience and so this is how things are now."

"And what is that?" she demanded defiantly.

"Help me save Zuken. Grant me all your six centuries' worth of connections and knowledge to find a way to get my goddess back. And in return, I will give you a chance to take back what is yours."

"And why would I believe you?"

And there was the clincher. This would make or break it.

"Because Meynte wasn't the only one that became an empress through a Taboo."

Solana stilled.

"My goddess wasn't the Supreme Queen for nothing. First, she became an empress with a Taboo. And not a half-assed effort like Meynte. No, a true Taboo-wielder. One who massacred entire pantheons in her wake. And then she ascended with her own Truth, as the Supreme Queen of the Heavens and the Earth."

"Tell me something," she demanded, her eyes affixed to his. "This goddess . . . If she was this powerful, why is it that I have not heard of her?"

And that was the crux of the matter, wasn't it?

"Tell me, do you remember that tale you told us, about how the war ended?" he asked conversationally. "About how Meynte was winning, how your gods Fujin and Raijin had slayed Tsukuyomi? And then . . . they *hadn't*? Instead, Fujin and Raijin were dead, and Tsukuyomi was alive?" He met her dark eyes. "Do you remember how you described it to me?"

Solana gazed at him inscrutably. "Like someone who didn't like the story that came to pass and tore the page out to rewrite it. But what of it?"

He smiled. And it was a bitter one. "Once upon a time, there was a girl. A slave girl. She didn't have fancy soulcrafting powers like me, nor was she an ancient skinwalker like yourself. A plain, vanilla mortal with an ambition. A lust. A desire so great that the entire world—no, the entire universe—wasn't enough to accommodate it."

"A desire for what?"

He smiled. "*Everything.*"

He looked down at the trial circle. It was empty now.

"She was a slave. She had nothing. No identity, no power, no ornaments, nothing she could claim for herself. Rock-bottom was her reality. And from there, with nothing but sheer diligence, willpower, and treachery, she arose. She tricked, hustled, betrayed, and tortured her way to power. She was to murder as maestros are to music. She was to war what oil is to flame. Her footsteps left behind mountains of corpses. Entire clans, nobles, kings, even emperors—she conquered them all. And then, when faced with the might of a god, with her greatest power no longer enough, she turned to something that even the Great Progenitor would shrink away from."

"A Taboo?"

"A Taboo," Lukas said. "She became its wielder. Butcher of Gods and Beasts, they called her. She destroyed multiple pantheons, taking her acolytes with her, stepping over the broken thrones of the dead gods, and upon that hill of corpses, created her own Empire. Akkad. And if that wasn't enough, she ascended through a new Truth and became a goddess of her new pantheon, ruling as the Supreme Queen of Heaven and the Mortal World."

"Akkad . . ." murmured Solana. "In all my years, I have never come across that name. I imagine it predates Crooked One-Eye and the Nordic Pantheon."

He let out a bittersweet chuckle. "It does. But I'm certain even your Crooked One-Eye, if he's still there, somewhere, doesn't know of it. No one—" He sighed. "—No one knows of it."

". . . Why?"

"Because," said Lukas, "something happened, and it erased all history of the goddess—her journey, her legend, and her pantheon—from existence. As if someone didn't like the story that came to pass and tore the page out to rewrite it."

Solana staggered. "You—do you think—"

"I do."

"But—But how can I—"

"The question isn't if we can defeat the Empire, Solana. Nor is it if we can survive against the Asukan Pantheon. The question is what if we managed to do all that, only for this story to be rewritten yet again? *That* is the enemy that I want to defeat. And I need the true power of Everfrost and every single bit of help you can give me. The question is, *will you?*"

Solana remained silent for a while. When she finally looked up at him, her eyes were like granite.

"Sometimes I wonder if killing you back then would have been the better option."

Lukas snorted out a quick laugh. "Let me know when you've made a decision."

"I believe I can take you to meet Ultaf Shimizu. In person." A small, grim smile crossed her face for an instant and was gone. "Say, how do you feel about a field trip?"

CHAPTER 6

*W*e *should've just flown,* thought Lukas, frustrated by the slow pace, sitting inside the carriage drawn by the gargants, which seemed to be distant relatives of oxen on Earth, only they had six pairs of limbs and moved at speeds that would have made deer green with envy. Unfortunately, the mists had engulfed the town after sunset, and with the reduced visibility, the gargants' speed had crawled down to a point where he could've walked faster.

Unfortunately, walking was for commoners. A noble pedestrian was an irregular sight in town, especially with the mists around, and he couldn't afford to appear conspicuous. And—as Solana had drilled repeatedly into his head—tonight, he was a noble. Or at least, the enforcer for one.

They passed a large square with a large fountain in the middle of it dedicated to the storm god Susanoo, depicting him in a dramatic pose, subduing Fujin and Raijin, the yokai gods of wind and lightning. He could hear beggars calling out from the sides of the street. The gargants trudged on.

Three streets over, he found another square, again with withering beggars and malnourished children lying around on the sides of the road. Reflexively, his hand reached for his purse.

"Don't bother," said Solana. "They are vagrants, Aguilar. People who have either been driven from their homelands by Asukan clan-lords, or worshippers of the Old Folk forced to convert to the Empire's doctrine. Or worse, half-breeds caught by the Cobalt Army."

He raised an eyebrow.

"Does that surprise you? No dalliance between Asukans and other breeds is allowed under the Holy Eternal Light." Solana threw her head back and let out a wicked little laugh. "Naturally, it happens all the time, so long as Asukans clean up after their messes."

"I . . . I didn't see anything like this in Haviskali."

"Lord Naowa's father, the former Ether King, rose from common blood. The Llaisy Kingdom is rather welcoming to every race out there. Had this been, say, Luthar, there'd be bodies of young boys and girls floating downstream into the Sea of Mone after Asukan Lords had their way with them."

A beggar woman let out a most piteous whine as the carriage passed them. Solana took one look at Lukas's face and threw a small pouch of mezals out the window. The sounds of coins jingling reverberated into the night.

"I'll have a platoon of yurei visit this place tomorrow."

"So, they can possess them?" Lukas asked, annoyed. "How is that any better?"

"Their lives mean nothing, Aguilar," said Solana. "Not even to their own kind. At least their bodies would be of some use to us, and when we overthrow the Empire and rid the world of the accursed Eternal Light, future generations shall reap the benefits."

"Still doesn't make it right."

"You'd better keep that attitude in check," warned the skinwalker. "You're about to meet a Sacred Eight member, and that lot are bloodhounds when it comes to this. I cannot have my enforcer seen harboring negative feelings about the Empire."

Lukas rolled his eyes.

"And don't forget, always refer to me by my moniker."

"Lady Kandra," Lukas intoned. "The Whore Mistress of Balthagor, the Mother of Skulls, and the Exarch of the Baramunz Kingdom."

Lukas had reacted to the revelation that Solana, the six-century-old skinwalker and yokai leader, was secretly an information broker feeding intelligence to various clan lords in the Southeast in exchange for mezals, resources, and favors, with a mixture of hilarity and incredulity. From Shoguns to businessmen to adventurer guilds to the Sacred Eight, Lady Kandra was a name that penetrated all but the highest echelons of the Empire. Whether Lady Kandra was a single individual or an organization working under that name was subject to speculation, and Solana knew how to use their doubts to armor herself.

The fleeting amusement died down as the stench of death flared against his nostrils; he didn't hear anything this time, not even the scrambling sounds of beggars. The thin, dark alley was clogged from the other side, and he sensed twelve—no, *thirteen*—individuals around them, every single one of them boasting a lifeforce rivaling a Level-3 muspel, along with the distinct sense of pressure that he had come to associate with Tanya.

Aeromancers.

"We've arrived," said Solana.

Following protocol, Lukas got down first to gauge his surroundings . . . and froze.

The cobbled street in front of him was littered with corpses, their twisted limbs shadowed by the mists. The sight was haunting in the dim light. The people hadn't just been killed; they had been torn apart. Limbs lay separated from torsos, with sticky, dark blood splattered everywhere. A stench arose as three large, hairy beasts gobbled their way through bremetan flesh without a care in the world.

Igriotts, Lukas realized, suppressing the urge to tear them apart. Monstrous creatures illegally bred by the Shimizu to slaughter enemies. Each of them was slightly larger than the average ifrit and easily twice as long. But to set these beasts free on weak, hapless beggars . . .

What kind of person would order something like this?

The door on the other side of the carriage opened and the person who stepped out looked nothing like Solana. Instead, she was brunette, with glossy curls running down either side of her face. She was tall, even without her high heels, and her eyes carried a deep, cunning intelligence with strength of will enough to dominate any man. Slender waist, flared hips, long, shapely legs— she looked ready to enthrall with her beauty, an ethereal conjuration over dead flesh.

"You look lovely, Lady Kandra," said a man, stepping out from the mists with three bodyguards positioned behind him. Brown-haired with Caucasian looks, the twenty-something man wore an attitude that screamed that the world was his to command. From the destruction this man had supposedly caused, Lukas had expected someone with Solana's ferality with the silent strength of Zuken Banksi. Instead, what he found was . . . disappointing. He looked more like a politician than a warrior, though he certainly carried himself like the latter. Lukas would wager he was a nightmare at office meetings. He was an aeromancer, with power levels far beyond where Olfric presently was.

"Ultaf Shimizu," said Solana in a lazy, smoldering tone. "My apologies for keeping you waiting for so long."

"I was expecting you to not show at all," said the man. "It is a rare occasion that the elusive Lady Kandra appears by herself."

"I am never just by myself, Lord," said Solana curtly. "My enforcer is always with me."

Ultaf gave Lukas a lazy look. "One man? I don't see how he'd make any sort of difference."

"Trust me—" Lukas smiled. "—you *won't* see it."

Ultaf then did what Lukas half-expected the poor fool to do and looked up at a certain spot behind him.

Then, without even turning, Lukas conjured a transparent ether blade and launched it at sonic speed, impaling the sniper leaning out of the window on the third floor of the building behind them. It pierced his abdomen while missing the vitals. Another pair of blades decapitated the igriotts in front of them, splattering purple blood everywhere.

"The next time you want to position assassins, do try to find some less-obvious perches," droned Lukas. "Now if you'd be kind enough to withdraw your men from the tower to my right and the ones that are veiled right above the building above us, we can get this farce done with."

"You dare kill my igriotts? For this, I could—"

"Do nothing," said Lukas. "I am my Lady's blade. If anything, blame yourself for positioning your men in such unsafe positions."

He matched Ultaf's dirty glare with his own cool indifference. After all, the man Ultaf was glaring at had bright red hair with a goatee and gray eyes.

The benefits of a Level-3 Conjuration Skill.

Solana snorted. "I'm sorry, Lord Shimizu. My enforcer has trouble keeping his worst habits in check."

That took the metaphorical wind from Ultaf's sails. With a huff, he crossed his arms and shook his head. "Fine, let's dispense with the usual song and dance and get to the brass tacks, as they say."

"Indeed."

What followed proved to Lukas that no matter what World he was in, if there was something that aristocrats could be relied upon, it was the ability to waste an ungodly amount of time making doing nothing sound important.

Two. Hours.

They had spent two goddamn hours simply going over all kinds of trivia. As a student of the law, he knew the importance of various minutiae, but without the right context, they were gibberish even to the most attentive listener. It didn't help that Solana was the one asking, and Ultaf answering. Whatever the bastard wanted in return must have been important enough to make him play ball like that.

Then, finally, they got to the main point.

"It was Banksi's fault," the man growled. "He must have poisoned the svartalfars' minds. The wretched creatures chose to destroy their well over saving their miserable lives."

"And now Lord Naowa has even more arsenal to act against you," concluded Solana. "Things were dire enough for your clan already without this. You should have exercised restraint, My Lord."

"Well, it's hardly *my* fault I can't accept no for an answer."

Lukas blinked. Even Solana looked flabbergasted at that response.

"And now Grandfather is facing opposition from the other Shoguns. Banksi's lucky grandfather wants him alive or else I'd have gutted the bastard. His brain and heart would have been left intact, and I'd have made him go through eternal torment for his transgressions. And the worst part? The traitor has his memories obscured, and not even my finest psion can undo it."

"Obscured, you say?" asked Solana, tilting her head with interest.

"My psions believe that the girl he employed might hold answers on that front. But they are in hiding, and none of my abductors in Haviskali can find them."

"A changeling, if I'm not wrong," murmured Solana.

"Rumors of your networks aren't exaggerated, I see."

Solana let out a small, refined snort. "Merely friendly with the administration, I assure you. And Zuken Banksi is a famous name in Haviskali."

"If I could get my hands on that girl and undo the Obscuration, we would get all the evidence we need," said Ultaf. "Everything would be solved."

The urge to clench his hands around the bastard's throat and make him squeal out Zuken's location rose in Lukas, but he calmed himself down.

"Get me the girl, Lady Kandra," said Ultaf Shimizu. "Alive and before the Shogun meeting happens. And, in return, all you want shall be yours. Trust me, there is no number you can quote that's too large for me to pay."

The rest of the meeting went surprisingly well. Ultaf seemed to trust Lady Kandra. And Lukas was simply too busy reeling from one single fact: Elena was the one responsible for obscuring Zuken's memories.

The realization brought with it both elation and disbelief—elation, because his status as an Outsider wasn't compromised; disbelief, because it turned out that Elena could obscure memories, copy them, and implant false ones.

The Asukan Empire, as Solana described it, had banned all research into memory-altering psionic abilities some four centuries ago but later developed improved versions of memory alterations for bureaucratic usage. From the way she described it, it was quite common for people working in the upper echelons of the government to have their memories obscured, if not erased, for their own protection or that of the others. The psions capable of this art were called Obscurers—one of the most prestigious careers out there. You had to be a practicing Level-3 psion for at least five years and get a clearance certificate from the Cobalt Army before you were eligible for a license to serve as an Obscurer for the Empire, and you had to swear vows limiting your ability to use the power, making it nearly impossible for you to teach it to anyone who wasn't licensed.

It was no doubt similar to Inanna's Veil of Ignorance or the way Solana had sealed away the knowledge of the yokai legend from her conscious thoughts.

Not for the first time, Lukas was reminded of what a strange world he had fallen into, one where people sometimes felt the need to give themselves amnesia to forget dangerous truths.

There was also the matter of how Elena, whose Soul Capacity suggested she could do nothing beyond Level-2 charms at best, was able to obscure memories with such perfection. But that was a headache for another week.

"This isn't his first rodeo," said Elena, giving Tanya a look of half-condescension, half-pity. "Zuken can't go through a year without stepping on some bigshot's toes or falling into a trap or being kidnapped by insurgent groups or being forced to help assassinate an entire clan overnight, or . . ."

"We get the idea," said Lukas, raising his hands in surrender.

Elena scoffed. "Zuken knew he'd be attacked. The moment Ultaf Shimizu showed up, I instantly ran. I always do. Only this time, I had to grab Olfric as well."

"I resisted," Olfric said defensively. "But then—"

"I'm hard to say no to, I know," Elena said quickly. Too quickly. "Don't worry. Without the right mnemonic trigger, Zuken can't access those memories. Nor can anyone else."

Given that Level-3 psions failed to do anything, Lukas was willing to cut her some slack. "Where do you store these memories?"

Elena grinned. "Away."

That meant featherglass. There were very few naturally available substances that could store memories, and given how Zuken was obsessed with featherglass economics, that had to be the answer. And if that was the case . . .

A plan began to form in his head.

"Say . . ." he began, his eyes glinting with what Tanya would describe as the herald of something crazy and dangerous, "how difficult would it be for you to get something from those stashes for us?"

Elena reached into her pocket and pulled out a tiny shard of featherglass, holding it in her hand. "This is all I have with me. If you need more, I have to go to Haviskali. But what do you plan to do with it?"

That Elena was so freely trusting him with something like that showed how desperate she had become.

"I'm . . . not sure. But I have an idea. This memory belongs to Zuken and is invariably connected to him. I'll just try to link it to Zuken himself and then make the spell give us an indicator of some kind, so that we might tell which way it's flowing."

"Which way it's flowing?" demanded Olfric, agitated. "Zuken is in a different kingdom. Are you telling me this spell can reach all the way there?"

Lukas decided not to share the fact that Inanna had planned to use her scrying spell to search for her real body across the entire universe.

"I'm . . . not exactly sure," he said, looking at Tanya, who had found the floor surprisingly interesting just that second. "But I have an idea. The last time someone did it using my power, it didn't work, but that was because the object didn't exist. But I know how to do it, or at least, how it *feels* to do it, if that makes sense."

"Should I be worried that you're apparently the brains of the operation and yet you're clearly just making things up as you go along?" asked Olfric.

"I don't know. Should I just leave you here with the yokai while I take the rest with me to go find Zuken?" Lukas shot back. "Listen, this is the first time

I'm gonna try this, so I'll just do what I can. And if we can do it without anyone talking, we'd all be happier."

Olfric scowled, but Lukas didn't care. The aquamancer was easy to rile, and doing so made his inner child happy.

"Now everyone, step back, please."

Closing his eyes, Lukas began to work. He might be new to this World, but he had more than enough experience at maintaining his concentration as well as building complex images in his head. Lines of anomalous energy exploded out of him in different directions, moving in straight lines, only to change directions, and then go straight again. Meanwhile, a thin strand of light spun in a circle around him. As the spectacle slowed, he stood in the eye of a pentagon, with a circle touching its vertices in perfect symmetry.

He was deep in concentration by now, the kind of focus that he usually maintained when attempting some sort of complicated ritual that could kill him if he messed up, like resurrecting a certain goddess. By reducing his focus to a single spell, practice had made it almost second nature by now. He dug the kinesthetic memory of Inanna casting the spell through his body from his inner-world, and submerged himself into it.

And then a deluge of violence blanketed his world.

After a small eternity, Lukas opened his eyes, as well as his right hand, and met Elena's eyes. Slowly, hesitantly, she held out the featherglass crystal, walked ahead, and, careful not to step into his circle, gingerly dropped it in his hand.

Taking a deep breath, Lukas grasped the memory crystal, pouring in more power.

The next instant, a connection was made, and close to a thousand miles away, a man's eyelids snapped open. The color in them was not a soft brown, as was usual, but rather an ominous green.

CHAPTER 7

Common myth suggested that a truly brave and courageous man could resist the agonizing pain of torture and refuse to give the torturer the pleasure of screaming. The torturer would grow angry and apply more and more punishment in which the victim would just smile in victory and pass out at the right moment, denying his captor the satisfaction of breaking his victim.

Zuken called bullshit on that one. Torture hurt. It really, really hurt. It especially hurt when the torturer was a being that held a penchant for misery and a sadistic edge that made sociopaths look like naughty kids. When he was being tortured, Zuken considered it a smart move to avoid what pain he could over puffing up his pride. Ultaf didn't need any more incentive to hurt him.

He was distantly aware that he was screaming in agony, but it didn't matter to him. He was above pain, beyond pain, his mind hovering just far enough from his body to be aware of its actions. Every bit of his mental concentration was being used on an ancient psionic technique he had learned from a recluse in the Baramunz kingdom that could safely transfer his thoughts and memories away from him, yet with a metaphysical link that he could later use to get them back without frying his brain. It was as if he could see his own body before him, his skin all frostbitten and blue from the freezing air and his digits missing, reddened frozen stumps where fingers and toes once were. He was also missing all the hair on his body, and that made him feel a tad queasy; he couldn't have that.

Any loss of concentration and he'd come rushing back into his battered body.

It had happened a few times before. Zuken would like to have claimed that it took hours for Ultaf and his men to break his mental hold, but he was kidding himself. In less than a minute, the psions had reached into his head and dragged him back into the agonizing world of real life—and *fuck*, it hurt so badly. Ultaf was playing with him, testing and prodding him like a small child might do to an injured bug before squashing it.

He became aware that his screaming had stopped, and so he immediately had to divide some of his consciousness back to focusing on Ultaf. His torturer didn't like it when he asked him a question and received no answer and would demonstrate his displeasure accordingly. Immediately, his vision swam, the walls of the prison fading in and out of focus and his entire body throbbing with pain. It was agonizing but still only a fraction of what he really should have been feeling. He took deep breaths, one after the other, in and out, in and out as his turbulent emotions swam to the foreground. Panic, fear, and unbridled rage assaulted him from all directions to the point that he was barely aware of his body thrashing about.

And then the strangest thing happened: a weird energy surged from the back of his head into his chest, and his muscles went limp. A feeling of utter exhaustion, fright, and at the same time, euphoric exultation filled him, the various emotions dancing upon threads of his will, demanding his complete focus and attention. He choked and wondered if he was about to die.

It's me, said a masculine voice that he didn't recognize. *Don't fight me.*

A sudden warmth flooded into his body, and his lifeforce suddenly blazed up like wildfire. The lifeforce-suppressing manacles could not restrain it—or perhaps they were simply unable to. The power doubled and then doubled again, seeking to cool and comfort, but behind that was something different, yet equally familiar. Not merely soothing but *healing . . .*

And then his eyes snapped open.

His neck moved of its own volition, and Zuken didn't resist. His eyes took in his surroundings: his own broken, tormented form, the torture chamber he was in. His thoughts turned to his recent interactions with Ultaf, though after flickering through several memories of him listening to the man's boorish self-righteous tones as his men tortured him, other memories rose to the forefront of his mind, memories connected to his current condition by tenuous threads he didn't immediately understand.

He remembered asking Elena to obscure his memories as always and to entice Olfric into following her. He remembered the psions discovering information about Tanya being stranded in the borderland owned by the svartalfars, and Olfric's flaming, mindless rage at the svartalfars that provoked them to destroy the Well and bring wrath upon the Shimizu. He remembered his meeting with Ultaf in his own office, refusing to accept that Tanya was the same Shimizu princess Ultaf had paid him to search for. Finally, the strange presence withdrew, and Zuken reasserted his mental shields while simultaneously suppressing the sudden burst of anger he felt at this strange presence wandering through his mind.

"It has been quite some time now," came Ultaf's voice.

Zuken shuddered in fear. Had that presence been . . . Ultaf?

No, whispered the voice. *Where are you?*

Meanwhile, Ultaf slid into view, his eyes gazing upon Zuken's battered form almost fondly. "I'll admit, Banksi, your perseverance is rather . . . endearing. I'm enjoying this."

He leaned forward, his rotten breath in Zuken's face, and smiled. "It is all for nothing, Banksi. I know that the girl houses all your secrets. You think that, so long as she is out of reach, I cannot kill you. But guess what, I hired the best of the best to find her. Lady Kandra herself. She found out about the creature, didn't she? You went through so much to keep her safe, but to what end?"

He grabbed Zuken's chin tightly, twisting his fingers into the raw wound splitting his left cheek. "She has found the changeling. They are bringing her to me as we speak. Just watch, Banksi. After she has undone her obscurations, I will strangle her myself. I have won, Banksi, and there is nothing you can do that will change that."

Zuken couldn't help himself. He laughed. It hurt and it felt wonderful.

"You're—" He coughed. "You're lying."

Ultaf went very still and took a step back. Fire flickered in his eyes, cold and angry. ". . . What?"

A sense of satisfaction surged through Zuken. "If you had Elena, you'd have her in here with you; you'd rip my mind apart and be done with it. Not stand here boasting like a fool."

"Has your stay here taught you nothing, Banksi? Do you wish for death? I can inflict horrors upon you that people will speak of for decades to come."

Zuken didn't flinch. "I think you've got too much on your plate already, Ultaf. Lord Naowa won't stop until he has your head. You exterminated a race that crafts our Wells, you buffoon. And you *still* don't have a clue about Tanya. Not even my blessed Father can help you now." He spit out blood as he laughed. "My family threw me out because I was weak. But look at me now— without lifeforce, without mana, imprisoned and tortured, and yet, I set things in motion that brought down the end of a Sacred Clan. Thanks to you, Ultaf, I have become strong. And that's how I know . . . *I have won.*" He met Ultaf's eyes. "And that's why you're lying to me about Elena. Because you're a coward. Because you're weak. Because you're afraid someone will break into this place and free me."

"Free you from *here?* This is the *Peak,* you fool. Forget saving you, no one can even get in here alive without my permission."

"Really?" asked Zuken. "And why is that? Go on, you've got to tell me, Ultaf."

"I do?"

"It's tradition," Zuken managed with a tight grin. "Whenever the hero . . . gets captured by the bad guy . . . the bad guy always tells them about how nobody will find them . . . so that the good guy can find a way out and escape."

Ultaf stared at him, and Zuken waited for the pain he would surely be inflicting upon him. But, to his surprise, Ultaf simply tossed his head back and laughed.

"You are amusing, Banksi. Just this once, I will entertain you. This is the Peak, my grandfather's stronghold. The heart of Shimizu territory in the Northern Dominion, protected by my grandfather's invincible army. To come here *is* to die." That infernal grin again. "Now then, you have our location. I eagerly await your attempts to escape."

And with that, Ultaf turned around and walked away. Had he looked back, he'd have noticed that his prisoner's eyes weren't their usual brown but an unearthly green.

To say that Lukas was pissed would be like saying that Everfrost was cold.

As soon as he was done, Lukas held out his hand, conjured a shard of featherglass, and closed his eyes. The shard glowed an eldritch blue before returning to its normal shade. He handed it to Tanya and stood up. No more words, Instead, he just walked past everyone but not before glaring at the skinwalker, who made a point of staying a certain distance away from him lest she accidentally provoke him into an unfortunate course of action. She was fully aware of how unsettled Lukas looked and her own role in the current state of affairs.

That wasn't to say that Solana was in fear for her life. Far from it. Maybe a lasting injury or two or perhaps genuine permanent damage, but even that would have been absolutely pointless. She had crossed more lines with her plan involving Tanya, and Lukas hadn't killed her then. He wouldn't lose his cool and try to kill her now for helping Ultaf Shimizu.

But that didn't mean she'd go out of her way to make things worse.

She crafted a three-dimensional conjuration of the memory, much like she had done with the attack on Zuken Banksi's mansion earlier. Not a single one left the room until the memory had finished playing, only for them to stare at Solana with various degrees of apprehension and animosity.

"So . . ." said Tanya finally. "You told Ultaf about me. You're responsible for the attack on Zuken."

Solana met her glacial eyes with her dark ones. "I have dealt with various groups in the Empire for centuries. In return, I gain knowledge of places where I can access food and resources for my kind. It helps us plan attacks, sometimes directly, other times by proxy."

"That's just ridiculous," said Olfric.

"Reality is stranger than fiction, Asukan."

"Why did you attack Zuken?" asked Tanya.

"It was just a side bet, to be frank," said Solana unrepentantly. "I expected that, with the Shimizu after you, Banksi would no longer choose to get involved. Honestly, the moment the Outsider entered my lair with you, that plan became unnecessary. I certainly didn't expect the Shimizu to attack Banksi's mansion."

"How are we going to get Zuken back?" the changeling asked.

"Zuken made him say it, didn't he?" asked Olfric. "The Peak. In the Northern Dominion. It's close to the border between the Eaborid Kingdom and Baramunz, and a no-trespass zone."

"Because it's Shimizu property?" asked Maude.

"No," growled Tanya. "Because it's *dangerous*. A world of icy chasms and crevasses, perpetually cocooned by a massive, constant snowstorm. A place where layers of mysteries and illusions are interwoven more delicately than embroidery, and every single step assures you that you are moving to your doom, your eyes and instincts always fooling you, death traps lying in wait for you to make a single mistake. It's like one giant anomaly in itself . . . It may even literally *be* one. All we know is that the Wind King sealed the entire area from outside interference. And it has himthursars, abominables, frostwolves . . . you name it. And that's ignoring the most dangerous monster of all—*my grandfather*."

The room was dead silent for well over a minute as its occupants digested the information. Even Solana, who had been pale to begin with and now looked practically cadaverous.

"Well—" Olfric was the first to speak up. "–shit."

Elena turned to Solana. "How are we going to save Zuken?"

"I personally believe it's worth playing the long game here," said Solana. "Ultaf Shimizu will not kill your friend until they've lost everything. And that means we still have enough time until the Shogun—"

"Solana," Tanya cut her off bluntly. "I understand the situation, and I understand what your intentions are. And yes, I also know that Lukas wants you alive for some reason. But I want you to know that if you ever try this shit on me again . . . I *will* kill you."

It wasn't a threat. It was a certainty. Regardless of how vast the difference in skill and experience between them and how much time it took, the girl *would* bring that to fruition should Solana push her luck once more.

The skinwalker felt the slightest, meager facsimile of a chill running down her spine. And then she smiled. Despite the girl lacking in fortitude or direction, despite her past and her dependance on the Outsider, it appeared that the Outsider had been right, after all.

This girl *could* be the next Queen.

"I assure you, girl, I know better than to doubt your dedication and your vows."

Tanya didn't say anything, maintaining her stare for several more seconds before huffing and closing her eyes once more.

"Maybe I should get Aguilar to come—" began Olfric, but Tanya cut him off.

"Don't," she said. "Let him be. I fear his ire has peaked to an almost unmanageable level. It's . . . concerning."

Pissed off to the point that even the girl herself was worried. That was not a good sign.

"Why?" asked Olfric, frowning. "I mean I'd understand if the Shimizu had abducted *you*, but this is Banksi. He and Banksi were . . . associates, at best."

"At face value, that's the case, yes," said Tanya despondently. "But you're overlooking one critical detail: Lukas saw into Zuken's memories and what he did to keep our identities secret. There's a debt, and Lukas will cross every line to resolve it."

"Shit. He's really going to try and break Zuken out of that place, isn't he?" Olfric paled, coming to the worst, most likely conclusion given the circumstances. And Solana agreed. If there was one thing even she could count on the Outsider for extreme situations like this, it was having tunnel vision, a hyper pinpoint focus that allowed him to bear through her own machinations and win an unwinnable fight against herself and Empress Meynte.

"He's probably doing that now for all we know." Maude lazily waved her hand, only to pause as everyone else in the room began to pale. "Eh . . . I was joking."

"By Wind, he is planning on breaking into the Peak and assassinating my grandfather as we speak," Tanya muttered as if coming to terms with a cold reality that she didn't want to believe was true. "We've got to stop him before he does anything reckless."

"I'm pretty sure you can stab him with Everfrost all over and paralyze him temporarily until he's calmed down enough to act logically," Solana suggested, deadly serious.

"Won't work," said Maude with an equally grave expression. "The empress tried that. He just burned his frozen arm off and regrew a new one."

"You're right," said Olfric. "He did that in the anomaly too. Perhaps take him out completely?"

"I can paralyze him," suggested Maude. "He wouldn't even know what was happening."

"We're *not* stabbing him with Everfrost or paralyzing him either," Tanya snapped, pretending to ignore the slight pang of childish disappointment from Maude.

"I'd heal him back."

"Please be serious about this," said Tanya. "Why don't we just try talking to him before deciding to do something ridiculous? We know where Zuken is, and we know they are going to keep him alive—"

"Suffering horribly every waking moment but alive," Maude pointed out.

"Not helping," Tanya muttered. "Can we not . . . you know, pass this information to Lord Naowa? He's the Shogun, and the Shimizu are on slippery ground as it is. Maybe if he can get permission from the Empire, they can get him out?"

Before any of them could say anything, a subtle chill went up their collective spines, as Lukas Aguilar entered the room.

Solana was impressed with the raw desire to murder that flooded the room. It felt less like something a person could possibly produce and more like a genuine, malicious curse, not unlike the one emanating from the desert above.

"We need more of those memories," said Lukas Aguilar. He looked at Elena. "You are coming with me and Tanya tomorrow. I need every bit of information about the Peak if we're to take it by storm, and I'm not content to let Zuken suffer until then. So, tomorrow, Tanya and I are going to meet the Shogun of the Llaisy Kingdom and use what we know to our benefit."

He looked at the faces around him and sighed. "I see, you've arrived at the same conclusion then."

"To the Zwaray Keep," said Solana.

Lukas paused and looked at her. "The Keep? But I thought—"

"The svartalfars are gone, yes," said Solana. "And ever since then, Lord Naowa has been staying there, with the rest of his entourage. Rumor is, they are doing their best to reactivate the Well. If you want to meet the Shogun, that is the place you've got to be. I can . . . set things up, if you want."

"Don't think this changes anything."

"I wouldn't dare," said Solana coolly.

Lukas glared at her for another few seconds before he turned around and left.

CHAPTER 8

The rumors about the Shimizu's massacre of the svartalfars had spread through Haviskali like wildfire. Gossip was the language of the common folk; people living ordinary lives reveled in talking about people of a higher status. Giant banners floated across the marketplace and above the floating platforms, boldly blaming the Sacred Eight Clan and accusing them of destroying Haviskali's commercial avenue. As a town that relied on commerce for its day-to-day activities, the attack on Zwaray Keep was nothing less than disastrous to its economy, and the local populace wasn't shying away from demonstrating their discontent.

"Uwah, his grandson is a murderer," said one.

"He eats little kids, you know?" said another.

"I've heard he sent his grandson to kill the svartalfars for an evil sacrifice . . ."

The rumors grew more and more imaginative with every iteration. And most did not even doubt it despite the complete and utter lack of proof. But when did something so irrelevant as proof matter when it came to public opinion?

At least, those were the thoughts running through Lukas's mind as he stared at the large banner featuring the warlord's face, with negative annotations printed all over it. He knew that, sooner or later, he would have to fight this man, and knew that even the thousands of Skills he could draw upon would fall short before this maniac.

He idly wondered how much these protests would affect Mujin Shimizu's political power. If the man was half as unforgiving as Tanya made him out to be, he'd have already killed his grandson by now.

"We're holding a public protest calling for his imprisonment," said someone from the street. "That clan is a curse for Haviskali. They must be punished."

"Absolutely. Never liked him," said Tanya to no one in particular.

Lukas rolled his eyes.

After that attempt at connecting with Zuken using Inanna's scrying ritual—which was a really inappropriate name for whatever long-ranged, half-assed possession he had ended up doing—the group had spent the rest of the day and night picking apart whatever all of them could share about the Peak like vultures. The more they learned about its protections and enchantments, the more likely it seemed that Ultaf was more correct than they wanted to believe.

The Peak was actually cocooned by an enchanted snowstorm crafted by the Wind King himself and held in place as a permanent mystery courtesy of the ley lines in that area. The entire place was akin to a large anomaly, given how the normal rules of geography fell apart once one entered the zone. Somewhere in the middle of it was an enormous fortress atop a massive mountain, which those in the know knew as the Peak.

It was just the tip of the iceberg.

The Peak, according to Tanya, could be best described as a twisted mix of several garrisons, most of which were actually hidden from the senses thanks to the innate enchantments of the area. There was technically no center to speak of, but that didn't mean that all its resources were evenly distributed through the individual bodies that made it up. Somewhere deep within was a ward chamber that was directly connected to the ley lines going through the area, granting the Peak access to infinite amounts of energy to keep the enchantments and protections active and at full power forever. According to Tanya, not even a king's most destructive attack could shatter its defenses.

If there was a way to get Zuken out without having to attack the Peak (and die horribly in the process), it was worth considering.

That was why she was accompanying Lukas to Zwaray Keep to meet with Lord Naowa. Solana didn't know why the Shogun was so concerned over a single Well when there were thirteen more in the entire kingdom, but whatever the reason, it was significant enough for the Shogun to order his terramancers to bring the destroyed svartalfar fortification back to livable conditions while his men worked day and night to reconstruct and activate the Well.

It took them several hours to reach the destroyed Zwaray Keep. The last time he was there, the entire complex had resembled a futuristic industrial belt, with massive, floating stone pillars fencing the inner territory from the rest of the town, while dozens of buildings—composed of the moving-block architecture—seemed to be laid down in blocks that went for miles on end, with gigantic machinery exuding bursts of steam and purplish light from various exit points.

Now? It looked like a ruin. A couple of pillars were still floating, but the ward line had been utterly destroyed. Smoke hung over the decapitated belt like a blanket. A repulsive blanket. Buildings were crumbling and sinking to the ground, covered with massive craters and chasms, smeared with dried blood. A demolished building next to him was still emitting smoke, and an awful stench arose from the carcasses of several unfortunate svartalfars—their features unrecognizable, their bodies trapped under the crumbling buildings.

He felt Tanya fall to her knees. "This . . . this is madness. Why would anyone . . ."

Lukas would have said something, but his eyes caught sight of a familiar face. Under the bloodstains, he could identify the facial features. Pupilless, pitch-black eyes, her jaw torn out of her face and lying a few inches away from it.

"Mo . . . Mori . . ." Mori, the extractor he had been to the borderland with. The one who had given him a glimpse of what sensing the terrain truly felt like. The one who had offered him a place at the Keep, much to Tanya's annoyance.

He knelt down, his hands slowly inching their way toward the fallen form, until the dried blood touched his skin. The anomaly within him reacted.

Boundary set. Creating territory with 100-foot radius.

"Lukas?" Tanya asked, feeling the waves of energy rolling off him. "What—what are you doing?"

But Lukas didn't answer. Anomalous energy was radiating off him, creating a massive territory, while the omphalos ran complex calculations and scanned the biological tissues within the area. The Screen kept listing how he was scanning the genetic structure, residual imprints of their mana patterns, and schematics of potential skill use by reverse engineering their physiological characteristics. Everyone knew that the soul was imprinted on the body, which was why one's physique always reflected one's Skills, but when viewed from a different angle, a deeper, more curious question could be asked: If the soul was imprinted on the body, and the body was studied in absolute detail, could it be possible to reverse engineer it to create a soul? One that wasn't born naturally but forged through the memories of a previously existing entity? And if so, would it be possible to know the difference?

The Screen blinked with one final message.

**Genetic structure of 114 svartalfar specimens analyzed and preserved.
Spiritual schematic construction underway . . .**

Lukas smiled and got up. Maybe this wasn't the end after all.

"Lukas?" Tanya asked again.

"Nothing," he said at last. "Let's go."

It took them a while to reach the newly constructed premises. It was a dull, dim, drafty sort of place. Anyone that had seen the original could guess that the terramancers had done a hasty, patchwork job, copying the existing enchantments to create a rough facsimile. The result was a maze with various offices located in different sections, the walls covered in carvings of depictions of what Tanya described as the Great War, the Glorious Ascension, the Bath of Illumination, the Gate of Might, and so on and so forth.

Not only was it large but it all looked the same too. Checkpoint after checkpoint, all with the same droll paint. It felt like they had been walking for hours and, at the same time, hadn't moved anywhere. Luckily, the medallion Solana had handed him for the journey opened all doors.

Different worlds. Same rules. Connections got you everywhere.

Finally, they approached a large statue, one that provided contrast to their surroundings. A man in a simple tunic raising a crystal of ether—the one and only Ether King and Lord Naowa's father. Interestingly, he was of common blood. Without an affinity to anything in particular, he rose through the ranks with a notably weak kami and, before anyone had realized it, stood at the top of the continent.

Opening the door, they stepped inside and found themselves being introduced to the Overseer of Haviskali. The overseer was the same stocky old man he had encountered back at Zuken's mansion—easily past fifty, clean-shaven, dark-skinned, with tattoos engraved all over his body, starting from the tip of his scalp and running all the way downward. His strong, blunt features were smooth and unreadable, but the light of recognition in his eyes was anything but.

"You," he said, his tone filled with surprise. "I remember you. We met at Banksi's mansion. And . . ." His eyes flickered at Tanya. ". . . I believe you were there as well."

Lukas sensed Tanya tensing beside him.

The overseer gave him a confused look. "Forgive me, I was told that Lady Kandra sent her representatives to discuss something immediate and profitable. But you . . ."

"Are one and the same," said Lukas.

"I see," said the man. "Very well. Come with me."

The man took them to a different room and made introductions.

"Lord Naowa. They are here."

Lord Naowa was huge, but there was something about him that suggested agility and grace. It was like looking at a tiger. Sure, it might look all calm and relaxed at the moment, but you knew that at any second, it could surge with speed and terrible purpose and that it wouldn't give you any warning before it came at you and snapped your neck. He had black and gray hair, a dark beard, and terrifyingly intense eyes. He wore standard noble attire, albeit slightly anachronistic. They were also black as the darkest night, matching the black fractals that were wrapped around either wrist. Lukas became painfully aware of Blob imitating his original pair of black fractals.

"Interesting," said Lord Naowa. "I don't believe Lady Kandra has ever sent either of you here before."

"I met these two when they were working for Zuken," said the overseer.

"I didn't think you would remember us, Lord Overseer," said Tanya.

The man let out a hearty laugh. "You would, too, if some vagrant had demolished one of your best security staff like a grown-up caning a child."

"That may be a generous assessment. As for why we are here, it's like you said. To discuss matters most immediate and profitable."

Lord Naowa let out an amused snort. "Fine, I'll bite."

He raised a single finger above his head and twirled it around, a tendril of gray lagging behind as his finger completed a circle. Lukas felt a flicker of the man's will as he released power into the circle, expanding it outward, raising a thin, enclosed barrier around all of them—a sudden, silent tension that was almost entirely impregnable to eavesdropping.

He waited in the pregnant silence. Something like this required a degree of precision and careful wording rather than the blunt force approach he'd have preferred. Tanya's words, not his.

"I suppose I should start by introducing myself," said Tanya. "My full name is Tanya Shimizu, beloved daughter of Yanric, half-sister of Ultaf, and the original heiress of the Shimizu Clan. I am an aeromancer and the wielder of the Wrath of the Wind King, his Level-5 kami, Ezzeron."

His eyes twitched.

Both men stared at her like she had grown a second head. Lord Naowa was the first to recover.

"I hope that you have proof to back up your claims."

Tanya looked perfectly at home. "I could tell you about how my half-brother attacked Zuken and took him captive to get to me. I could also tell you that he attacked the svartalfars because Zuken told him that I was on a borderland mission for them, and they refused to allow Ultaf access to the Well to fetch me out of there. But I'll just say that I have an eighty-seven percent ECR. I am not going to insult anyone's intelligence by assuming you don't know what it means."

ECR. Experience Conversion Ratio. It was the secret to power in this world. Representing how much Experience gained was converted to Soul Capacity while leveling up, a person's ECR was fixed from birth. For most bremetans, it didn't cross the thirty-five mark. Occasionally, there would be someone with an ECR in the lower forties and they would end up becoming a master spiritist within a decade of training and work experience. The only people who boasted of ECR values in the fifties or low sixties were kings.

But *87%?*

"That's . . . impossible," claimed Lord Naowa.

"Feel free to verify it then," said Tanya coolly. "It's why Ezzeron chose me. I was young, but I had the greatest chance to unleash his potential."

And Naowa did verify it. Lukas watched as the Shogun ordered an entire setup to be installed and performed a live scan of Tanya's vitals.

Level 32. Five Level-3 Skills and two Level-4 Skills. Which was two more than what he had—apex-tier Kinetomancy, be damned.

And he definitely wasn't feeling jealous. Not at all.

"I've a quandary, Miss . . . Shimizu," said Lord Naowa. "Your family has wronged me twice. First by capturing my trusted advisor, and second, by destroying one of my kingdom's prime sources of revenue. What's stopping me from capturing you and sealing you away and letting the Shimizu crumble before my very eyes?"

Lukas and Tanya shared a glance. It was time for him to interfere.

"You could," said Lukas. Briefly, he took note of the sheer number of wards running in and around the room. There was no way in hell he or anyone else would be able to get away with anything inside this place, let alone understand what half of the wards did for that matter.

"A lot of things could happen, Lord Naowa. For instance, you could choose to attack and subdue us, and Tanya could choose to unleash Ezzeron. It would be interesting to see how the Shogun of the Llaisy Kingdom survives after being at point zero of the impact of a Level-5 kami. You could also ask your terramancers right below our feet and the ones above the ceiling to take us by surprise, or ask the six standing outside to barge in. You could also gesture to the group hiding in the veil there—" He pointed to his right. "—to take us by surprise. You can also ponder how we know Lady Kandra, and why knowing what Tanya means to the Shimizu, she would willingly walk into a hostile situation demanding your aid."

He smiled. He might as well have pointed a blade at the man's throat.

"You are either too sure of yourself or too stupid to commit such brazenness, young man," warned the overseer.

"My grandfather has a saying," said Tanya. "If violence doesn't solve your problem, you're not using enough of it."

It was a stalemate. The false calmness before the storm. Lukas noticed the deep worry lines forming between the overseer's hard, steady eyes. Lord Naowa rested his large, blunt-fingered hands on the table, and Lukas could see scars on them—the graffiti of violence. If those two decided to attack, he'd have to make sure the results would be sudden, precipitous, and damning.

Part of him wondered if he had fallen for Solana's deceit yet again. He wouldn't put it past the ancient bitch to trigger a situation where he made

Tanya and himself enemies of the Shogun of the Llaisy Kingdom, cutting off every possibility of the two of them leaving the yokai.

"Do you really think it's wise to antagonize me in my place of power, young man?" asked Lord Naowa softly. His expression never changed, but the way his fingers tensed slightly spoke volumes. Lukas could feel the obdurate, adamant will that drove the man and made his power the reigning center of the entire kingdom.

"You've already lost Zuken and now the svartalfars. Can you really afford to antagonize the wielder of the Wind King's Wrath in such close quarters, Lord Shogun?"

When standing against a powerful foe, it was a very, very dangerous thing to stand still and appear like easy prey.

Lukas pulled on his power, lifeforce surging through his body. Mana flooded in as well, mana as hot as the fires of the bylestyr. There was anomalous energy, too, to form, give shape, and render his attacks far more potent than they otherwise would be. A layer of anti-motion formed around him, micro-thin, yet coating every inch of his body. His vision molded to include potential motion trajectories. The next second, he crafted a territory around all four of them, sealing them off from the world around them. Instantly the spiritists rushed at them from all sides but failed to penetrate Lukas's motion barrier.

"Earlier," Lukas growled, "you said that there was nothing stopping you from trapping and stealing Tanya away. Tell me, what's stopping me from killing you before any of your men can even get to us?"

No one said anything for several seconds. The Shogun stared at him with greater intensity than he had since the start of the meeting, and Lukas met his gaze without hesitation.

"What do you want?" he finally asked.

"What I want is for Zuken to be released, and for Tanya and me to be left alone for the rest of our lives—but we don't get what we want, do we? So, instead, we are here with an offer that could be to your benefit and ours."

"I'm listening."

Lukas tilted his head at Tanya and let her take over.

"Before we tell you what we want, I want to let you know two things. First, Ultaf will kill Zuken the moment the Shimizu lose their Sacred Eight status. Luckily, we know where they have kept Zuken captive and are working on a way to get him out."

The Shogun said nothing.

"The second thing you need to know is that we plan to kill Mujin Shimizu."

No one missed the fact that she said "we" and not "I."

"And . . . what has that got to do with me?" asked the Shogun.

"We want you to sponsor my candidacy as the next Lady of Shimizu after I kill my grandfather."

The man's lips ticked up in one corner. "And why should I do that? In case you've forgotten, girl, I am Lord Naowa, son of the Ether King, and the Lord of one of the Sacred Eight. Unlike other lords, I do not grovel before your might."

"Perhaps not mine," said Tanya with a cold, cruel smile. "But you certainly do before the Earth King."

And just like that, the mood of the room shifted instantly. Naowa's relaxed look morphed into a grave expression.

"Oh, the truth hurts, does it now?" asked Tanya. "The Earth King may be a friend to my grandfather, but everyone knows how he advocates against the loss of the Sacred Eight clans. About balance. Surely you know all about that, Lord Naowa?"

That, more than anything else, unnerved the man, and Lukas wondered what this was about.

"Make no mistake, sir," said Tanya, her voice drolly unapologetic, "I will end my grandfather for the wrongs he has done against me, with or without your help. You might not benefit from the Shimizu's survival, but the Earth King will. With his support, I will rule Cyffnar, and Lord Straff will have no option but to bend before the Earth King's command. And seeing as you did nothing to help me save your advisor, I think we both know whom Zuken Banksi will choose to serve next. Oh, and you'll still be here, bereft of your trusted advisor."

Ultimately, it was just one big game of chicken.

"Those are big words for someone that has been hiding from her family all her life," said Lord Naowa.

"Gotta start somewhere," said Lukas.

"I see," said the man. "And what if we support you?"

Tanya beamed. "If you support us, then we can end the constant fighting between the two kingdoms. Let's face it, sir, both of us know perfectly well why the anomaly in the desert was destroyed."

Lord Naowa froze for a second and angrily turned to the overseer.

"Not his fault," said Tanya. "Zuken hired me for that mission. In fact, my record as a sinner for destroying a Class-2 anomaly was scratched off just so that I could serve the Llaisy Kingdom by sinning again." She snorted. "The hypocrisy of bureaucrats, I swear." Then she regarded the man evenly. "My grandfather taught me to split people into three categories. The first are the people you can manipulate who never realize they're being manipulated. Those are just tools. The second are people who, when manipulated, realize they're being manipulated and disrupt your goals. Those are enemies. And the third are those who realize they're being manipulated and turn it around to gain the upper hand on whoever is manipulating them. Those are called allies."

Lord Naowa frowned, lost in thought.

She met his eyes. "I'm done being a tool, and you don't want me to be your enemy. Guess the only slot left is ally. I understand my clan has done a lot to hurt your kingdom and be declared enemies, but personally . . . I'd like to be friends."

"Friendship is not done through coercion, Miss Tanya," said the man gravely.

"No, it is done through actions," said Tanya.

"Your clan has permanently harmed my kingdom by annihilating the svartalfars. No gesture or action on your part can undo that."

"I don't understand," said Lukas. "The svartalfars are one of several species from the Time Before. Why would their presence mean so much to an Asukan kingdom?"

The Shogun gave him a conflicted look and sighed. "Come with me."

CHAPTER 9

———

The construct in front of them looked just as alien as the first time Lukas had gazed upon it. Peaked spires and metallic pillars arose like dark talons, varying in thickness and jutting towards the sky. It had a twisted, off-center symmetry, an almost-balance. Ash-black, something about it gave the eerie sensation that it was sucking away something fundamental from his body. In the middle of that behemoth was a roughly oval construct crafted out of several feet of thick stone—an archaic archway and, in its center, the familiar bruise floating in the air.

Just like he remembered it.

Or . . . almost. Something was missing, but he couldn't put his finger on what.

This was the svartalfar Well, the same one through which he and Tanya had stepped into the Lava Ridge borderland. The only difference was that the last time, they had a legion of svartalfars around them, with Mori and Kradir accompanying them for their journey. This time, there were a legion of Asukan builders running tests on the archway. He and Tanya watched as a marching band of armored soldiers came stepping lightly from behind, quickly catching up to them. Suddenly halting, the legion bowed before the Shogun.

"Continue," said the Shogun offhandedly, the legion's captain barked out another command, and the band moved marching ahead. Far away, he could see more workers constructing new equipment and repairing the existing ones and putting them back in place.

"Svartalfar technology is very different from our own," said Lord Naowa. "Our terramancers are nowhere near as capable of refining metals to the degree that the svartalfars could. And that goes double for spiritual alloys. This massacre is a great blow to the entire Empire, and the Shimizu have only begun to feel that."

Lukas glanced at Tanya, who looked around solemnly.

"The Empire doesn't advertise this fact, but Wells are a svartalfar creation. Their unique metalworking, their runecraft, their ability to merge the physical with the spiritual is a skill that Asukans have longed to acquire for centuries but failed at again and again. There are clans out there that have tried to illegally breed svartalfar-Skills into their bloodlines by forcing them to impregnate Asukan women, or vice versa. And now, with them extinct, no more Wells can be created. Worse, we will be helpless if any of the existing wells malfunction at any point in the future."

"Is that why you are here?" asked Lukas. "Trying to repair this Well, hoping for a miracle?"

The man's face fell. "Unfortunately, even miracles fall short here. Not even the Eternal Light can refine spiritual alloys like svartalfar runecraft can."

Lukas said nothing. The Screen had long since reported the successful completion of the reconstruction of svartalfar genetic structure and prepared an amalgamated spiritual rendition, using Hreidmar as a blueprint. His inner-world now boasted a hybrid svartalfar prototype that had seventeen different Level-2-to-Level-3 Skills, including metalsensing, extraction, metalmind, runecraft, and many others.

He glanced at the stone archway and finally realized what was missing.

"The runes," he murmured. "The runes on the archway are wrong."

"Well, obviously they're wrong," snapped the Shogun. "The craft makes no sense."

Lukas suppressed a chuckle. Mori had once given him a cursory introduction to svartalfar runecraft back in the borderland in her attempt to entice him into joining the Keep. The closest analogy Lukas could find was a programming language, but instead of zeroes and ones as its base or even something as complex as the twenty-six letters of the alphabet, they decided to go full-on crazy and use hundreds of unique characters instead.

What made it worse was that the system it operated under was a nonsensical mess. It had no rhyme or reason. No clearly defined laws that one could understand, and the few rules that he somehow managed to wrap his head around didn't make a lick of sense. Like the fact that lines from different sections shouldn't ever overlap, except, of course, for the dozens of exceptions, when they should. Oh, and for some reason, the same rune could convey thirty-something different meanings all at the same time, and the resulting outcomes got weirder and more diversified as more runes got added into the mess.

Simply put, it was something that only the mind of a raving lunatic could fully comprehend.

Or someone that had been blessed by an arcane skill to do exactly that.

Unfortunately, there were no svartalfar gods alive, and now with the race rendered extinct, there was no one capable of understanding their peculiar runecraft.

No one except . . .

**Rapid installing [SVARTALFAR] prototype
Activating memory sequencing and recognition . . .**

Analyzing related alien Truths and adding them to System Tray

"The line there is too short," he blurted out, pointing to a spot on the archway. "See there? It's supposed to reach this line. Not touch it, but almost. You are supposed to stop just a hair's width away. You are supposed to invoke a prayer to the World and let it fill in. Not the entire amount, just the tip. But this . . . is almost double that. You're demanding the World do your job for you. Don't be so greedy."

The builders around him gave him varying looks of incomprehension.

"You . . . Can you read this?" asked one.

"How?" asked another.

Lukas shrugged. "I don't know . . . How *can't* you?"

"That's not an answer and . . ." began a builder, but the Shogun stopped him short. "Young man," he said, giving Lukas an apprehensive look, "you're certain you recognize what's wrong with this?"

Lukas shrugged again. A feeling of stark indifference was filling him. Looking at these builders, at the way they were butchering the metalcraft in the half-broken machinery, he couldn't help but wonder what idiot had the gall to call these morons "terramancers."

"Yes," said Lukas softly. "Everything. Everything is wrong about this."

"Excuse me?" asked a builder, affronted.

"Yes, you are excused," said Lukas uncaringly, a passive annoyance bypassing his usual polite demeanor. He looked at the Shogun. "Get them out of here. If you're paying them, do it for something constructive."

"And . . . why would you say that?" asked the Shogun, tilting his head, studying him with great interest.

The first stirrings of annoyance flooded through Lukas's being. What was this ignorant Asukan doing here, anyway?

"Fine. I'm going to say this once, so pay attention. Runecraft is the focused application of power, inscription, form, interpretation, definition, and execution to get something done all at once. It doesn't matter if you know how to write the word if you don't know how to read it. And even if you do know that, it's just as pointless if you don't know the rules behind it."

"Lukas." Tanya all but hissed. "What are you doing?"

"Commenting on a shit job," he answered honestly. Really, these people were putting too much power into their half-assed attempt to copy runecraft. It was causing the lines to get distorted in several places. If they were planning to etch anything more than four or so letters, they could just forget it.

"You're lucky the Well not working is the only thing happening here. Honestly, I'm shocked the entire facility hasn't blown itself apart in your faces already."

"Are you saying that you understand this?" asked Naowa. "Can you repair it? Make it work?"

"As it *was*, maybe. But after your people contaminated it . . . I'll have to see." Tanya slapped her palm to her face.

"Lukas . . . That is your name, correct?" asked Naowa. "I'm sorry, I just realized I don't know anything about you. Where are you from?"

"I—uh, I'm from Maluscion."

"Maluscion," murmured Lord Naowa. "A terramancer who can construct barriers, and with extraordinary sensing abilities . . . and a runecrafting Skill."

Lukas frowned briefly in confusion for a moment before the realization hit him like ice water. The shock was enough to shift his consciousness back to himself. He glanced at Tanya's frozen expression and nearly smacked himself for the oversight.

Naowa had mentioned how other clans tried to breed svartalfars into their bloodlines to gain their runecrafting Skills.

And he had just demonstrated the ability to not just understand runecraft but also claimed to have repaired the damaged svartalfar machinery. And if he could do that then the jump to becoming a bremetan-svartalfar hybrid wasn't nearly as outlandish.

The man's previous demeanor was gone, replaced by a surprisingly impassive mask. "To my knowledge, even svartalfar-bremetan hybrids are incapable of runecrafting. And yet, here you are."

Lukas cursed to himself. He had just revealed an ability that was, to a great degree, alien to this world. He had gotten careless. If he had a time machine, he'd use it to go back five minutes and slug himself in the face for this.

The question was, *what now?*

"It seems," said Lord Naowa, "that the clans in Maluscion have been hiding a lot from the Empire. Tell me, Lukas . . . are you, perhaps, a deviant?" His eyes fell upon Blob, who was imitating a pair of black fractals on his wrists. "And a skilled metamancer to boot. You are a man full of talents. No wonder Banksi got his hands on you before anyone else."

"I'm just a vagrant," said Lukas, letting himself relax slowly. He had forgotten the other kind of reaction people had to finding out something impossible.

Rationalizing it away until it made sense enough to ignore completely.

"Indeed . . ." said Lord Naowa. "Tell me, Lukas . . . do you think you can help reconstruct this Well? And perhaps, the entirety of Zwaray Keep? If you are indeed capable of performing runecraft bordering on the svartalfars' level, there are ways in which we can be useful to each other."

He glanced at Tanya and then back to him. "How would you feel about taking over the Zwaray Keep?"

Lukas blinked.

The next day, Lukas and Tanya left the Zwaray Keep, idly watching two floating platforms carrying massive mountains of metal ore into it. He had to hand it to the man—when Shogun Naowa gave his word, he damn well kept it. Every single staff member was leaving the massive structure, leaving behind the furniture, machinery, and other resources for Lukas to start using. There would be more platforms floating in, carrying more ore, and the security posted outside would keep away all trespassers until Lukas took over and got the earlier security system up to snuff.

"Well, that was profitable," he said, grinning.

"Hmm." Tanya made a disagreeable sound. "It was a master stroke to acquire the entire Keep for yourself in return for runecrafted equipment and repairing the Well, but I can't help but think you could've bargained for more."

"More?" asked Lukas, giving her a look of exaggerated disbelief. "Now I've got a *job*. It's all I've ever wanted."

"Forger," said Tanya, rolling her eyes. "How apt for the guy that is a walking-talking World in and of himself."

"I probably could have pushed it more if I tried," said Lukas, "but it would cost me goodwill for future negotiations and might have damaged the possibility for future business. And he is also getting me everything from books in advanced Terramancy and Metamancy to smithing and energy manipulation. And I've had all these resources and, most importantly, this vast estate all to myself."

Tanya shrugged. "It's just land."

Lukas decided not to explain about real estate back in the United States, or the cost of even renting a two-bedroom apartment in Manhattan. By a rough estimate, the entire zone he was being handed over was a little over six hundred acres.

"Look," he said, "it's a place to shack up away from the desert. That alone makes this a good deal."

He'd also have a massive workshop for himself once he figured how to establish a permanent territory connecting to his omphalos. One that could exist without him having to be physically present at all times.

But those were happy problems, and best reserved for the future.

Fortunately or unfortunately, the Keep wouldn't officially be his until the next Shogun meeting, which conveniently fit in with his plans to infiltrate the Peak, break Zuken out, potentially kill Mujin Shimizu, and get Tanya set up as the next Lady of Shimizu. She would take office there in Cyffnar, while he would set up shop at the Keep, making runecrafted weapons and enchantments as the official Forger of the Llaisy Kingdom, which conveniently ensured that Tanya could never entice Lukas to leave the Llaisy Kingdom and join the Eaborid Kingdom.

Again, assuming both of them didn't die trying to kill Mujin Shimizu via whatever harebrained scheme they were cooking. In which case, Zuken Banksi would obviously die and Lord Naowa would ensure that the Shimizu lost everything and perished. It wouldn't help his kingdom, but at least he'd get his vengeance.

Lukas just loved it when there was a bright side.

"What's next?" asked Tanya. "We know that Ultaf has Zuken imprisoned at the Peak. We know that Lord Naowa can keep Mujin busy during the Shogun meeting and delay him by an entire day at best. I really hope you aren't planning on visiting the Peak and trying to hammer through its defenses like a caveman."

"Of course not," said Lukas quickly. "That would be stupid, after all."

Four days later, he stood next to a glaring Tanya while doing his best to pretend everything was hunky dory.

"I can't believe I let you talk me into coming to the Peak to hammer into its defenses like a caveman."

In hindsight, Tanya really had good instincts.

Of the five people on the mission, one looked nothing like Lukas Aguilar, another looked nothing like Maude, a third looked nothing like Olfric, and a fourth looked just a bit like Solana—if the notorious skinwalker had brown, shoulder-length hair, instead of her natural dark tresses. The woman who looked a bit like Solana was distinctly unhappy to be wearing Asukan clothing.

Alas, the burdens one must bear when searching for vulnerabilities in the impenetrable fortress that was the Peak.

The fifth person looked *exactly* like Tanya in all-white Asukan attire, her white hair pulled back in a ponytail—as she honestly thought that the others were simply being paranoid and that such subterfuge was unnecessary.

"Oh come now, Tanya," said Maude. "You need to learn to be comfortable in uncomfortable situations. And you don't get to complain, Miss Yuki-onna."

Lukas suppressed a laugh as Tanya scowled at her acquaintance-turned-healer-turned-enemy. Maude exaggeratedly grabbed his arm closer to her chest as if to stave off the cold, despite being covered in several layers of monster hide. He knew enough of Maude's shenanigans now to not be surprised anymore, though given how Olfric was intently looking away, he knew towards whom this behavior was directed.

"And you can just stop showing off," scoffed Tanya.

"Who, me?" asked Lukas, who was wearing a sleeveless jacket and a pair of trousers, happily ignoring the wintry plume around them. "I'm just channeling fire mana. Letting the fire burn within is more than enough to ignore this weather."

He glanced at his snow-laden clothes which had begun freezing at the edges.

". . . Almost ignore the weather."

Technically, he had access to a himthursar prototype that could have helped him utterly ignore the cold, but when it came to the elements, he would always hold fire as the all-time best. Besides its pure destructive power, it also had the ability to purify everything tainted. Plus, there was just something primal and deep inside every person that made them unconsciously fear fire, to flinch from it, knowing that if they got too close, they'd be burned.

The Northern Dominion was a sterile sort of place. The ground had vanished under who knew how many feet of snow, with towering mountain peaks in every direction looking bleak and hateful, wreathed in mist and snow. The wind moaned and blew frozen crystals into everyone's faces and then sank into a temporary lull.

"This is really the farthest I can get us, Lukas," said Tanya, reading his thoughts. "Any farther and we risk getting detected by the perimeter wards."

"Why?" he asked. "I can't even see any checkpoints here. Or soldiers. Can't you just rift us past the perimeter?"

"That's not how wards work," said Solana. "A ward isn't just a barrier you step through. It's an enchanted volume that extends from one ward-line to another, in this case, from one checkpoint to another. The moment we rift in the middle of it, the ward will sense intrusion and react, and it won't be nice."

"Not . . . nice," repeated Olfric. "What kind of wards are those?"

"The kind that only lets people in that are completely loyal to Grandfather but would kill everyone else," said Tanya drolly.

"I gazed at a soldier once. Just *once*. He had come after me on Grandfather's orders, and I tortured him and penetrated his mind. I didn't know why they were so loyal to him and I wanted to know, to *understand*. I looked deep into his psyche and what I found was . . ."

She swallowed.

"It's a process Grandfather calls the Initiation," she said distastefully. "In the name of psionic training, his people insert a matrix in their minds that creates a malleable copy of the true personality. Grandfather fears that giving them any degree of autonomy would create an escalating danger of them eventually breaking free. So, instead, they are bound deep within their own subconscious, while a completely subservient copy remains in control of their shared body."

"Trapped within one's own mind," whispered Olfric.

"The man had a great deal of empirical knowledge of matters ranging from Aeromancy to combat training to the command structure of the Peak to . . . *'how best to please Ultaf Shimizu.'*"

Her expression hinted at how distasteful she found those memories.

"He knew nothing about the intervening period, except for what he could absorb through osmosis from coexisting with the artificial personality created to control him. He had absolutely no emotional context for anything he did or was done to him during that gap."

"And . . . what happened after you sought out the original personality?" asked Lukas.

"Nothing," said Tanya, meeting his eyes. "The moment I left his psyche, the false personality took over. I couldn't destroy it. And when the other persona took over, I just killed him on sheer principle."

"But—"

"No buts, Lukas," said Tanya. "They are utterly loyal, absolutely obedient, and only move to follow their Lord's will. They cannot be bought, bullied, reasoned, or negotiated with. There is nothing they will not do. No act too vile, no Sin too dastardly, no crime too reprehensible for them. They are fanatics and Mujin Shimizu is their god."

Lukas frowned but stayed silent.

"Wards that only let you in if you're loyal and horribly kill you otherwise," said Olfric. "What kind of enchantments can we expect from them? And how do you get around such protections?"

Solana sighed. "The possibilities are, well, limited. But fairly broad. Perhaps we should adjourn to the Territory for some research?"

"Wonderful," Lukas griped. "I might as well be back at school."

They returned empty-handed that day. And the next. And the next. Sometimes it would be the entire group but mostly it was just him and Tanya. Lukas would have her rift into different locations adjoining the outer perimeter, and he employed Blob—infused with multiple prototypes—to infiltrate the ward barrier. Half the time it ended with the ward pressing Blob down with a hideous vacuum-based technique that would have crushed any living person to paste.

Still, it wasn't completely useless. By the eighth day, they discovered an igriott-drawn coach rushing out of the snowstorm, seeming to have appeared out of nowhere. Despite the urge to interrupt it, they let the coach pass unbothered, and then two days later, another coach came through again.

And finally, it was time.

One moment the coach was screeching across the dangerous terrain. The next moment, an invisible wall of inertia gripped it, paralyzing it in space. Elena stepped forward and charmed the two beasts into falling asleep, leaving the soldiers unable to escape interrogation.

"What good will it do?" asked Olfric. "The moment you let him go, the false personality will take over."

Lukas grinned. "Not quite. Tanya kills the soldiers because she doesn't have the means to defeat the false personality. I do. I have a Skill that has no other purpose other than to utterly destroy a mind."

Activating Monster Prototype Dranzithl
Initiating Consciousness Shift
Enact

The first indication that something had changed was when Olfric stepped back, recognizing in the soldier's eyes a look of glimmering insanity—the unforgiving desire to kill, to destroy, and to violate. A hiss of steam oozed around him, the magnified body heat causing the hoarfrost to instantly evaporate.

Lukas's eyes went hard and cold as he looked into the soldier's eyes and peered into his soul.

"W—what are you?" A strangled whisper was all the soldier could get out. The man had gone fully pale. Sweat was beading on his forehead. He was trembling and staring at Lukas like he had never seen anything more terrifying, as though he couldn't bear to be near him—as if he was frightened to his core.

Inanna had once described the dranzithl as a monster so antithetical to life that even its proximity would cause a living being to wither. To feel its presence within one's mind, therefore, was sure to have grave results.

"Get it away from me!" The soldier was thrashing, flailing his arms and legs around, an animal move that paid no mind to the way the dagger-sized icicles were stabbing his legs, holding him down. "Get it away! Get it away! GETIT-AWAY! GETITAWAY!"

"What's happening?" asked Olfric, but his words were drowned out by the soldier, who just then let out a wail accompanied by an intense blue light that burst out of his eyes and mouth, illuminating the area. After a few seconds, the scream abruptly died off.

"You—you didn't kill him, did you?" asked Elena.

Still crouched down, Lukas regarded his two companions. Olfric was a potential comrade, one who he could rely on in the hunt. So long as he stayed out of his way, he could share in the prey. The woman, Elena, *was* prey. She would be slain, but later.

"And *shift*," he declared, forcing the dranzithl instincts back down with the ease of long practice.

The sounds of the soldier's heavily exhausted breathing told them that he was still alive. The man slowly opened his eyes to look once more at the people looking at him. He blinked repeatedly before his eyes met Tanya, and his brow furrowed in consternation.

"Princess . . . Tanya?" he asked in puzzlement. "When did you get so . . . *old?* And why is your hair white?"

CHAPTER 10

E veryone in the War Room was doing one of two things.

They were either focusing on the large table with the ether projection of the Peak, which had been pulled out of the soldiers' minds, complete with little statues placed in seemingly random locations.

Or they were watching Lukas as he did the former.

Walking around the table, his eyes were never still. His gaze kept darting back and forth between the road joining the perimeter of the first checkpoint, and the largest fortress where Ultaf's office was supposed to be. Small bands of different shades that represented what appeared to be the different kinds of soldiers were scattered all over the place. He kept moving the small statues representing those on his side from one location or another, then back, as he second-guessed each decision. More often than not, he'd turn to the bulletin board that was also covered in notes in order to either write something down or look up a fact.

He had also started his simulated attacks more than a few times, clearly not liking where each led in his mind. Enough that most of the group there had given up trying to keep track of the number of times.

"Why did you abandon that approach?" asked Olfric as Lukas silently gave up on his latest strategy. "It has a good chance of getting us into the interior without facing the outer defenses. We could overwhelm them and get into the lower floors."

"Bad idea," said Lukas, taking the marker and putting it in a different spot. "We cannot let Ultaf think he's facing a strong force. We don't know for certain how the army will react to our offensive, so we'll be charging in blind."

Pouring in more ether, he expanded the projection, highlighting every single path that led to the inner fortress.

"The only way to get into the Peak is through the igriott-drawn carriages; trying to brute-force our way in will only prove detrimental. There are thirty-one checkpoints, nine towers, two bastions, and a drawbridge before we enter the actual territory. The actual fortress has seventeen buildings, all of them protruding at different spots, so the real construction is likely within the mountain. And we have no clue how many ward-lines exist between the perimeter and the inner courtyard to encourage a frontal attack."

"Basically, we need a way in without triggering an offensive from Ultaf," he finished. "So . . . any suggestions?"

"Blow up the perimeter wards," Solana suggested. "Apart from being the first line of defense, it's also a trap designed to hold back and separate as many intruders as possible. But if you could take them down . . . perhaps by employing the technique you used against me?"

She was referring to that one time when he had converged all motion trajectories around Solana to come crashing down, creating a massive implosion that obliterated her barriers and hacked her physical body apart.

"That was that, and this is this," objected Maude. "These wards are empowered by ley lines, Leader."

"I . . . could destroy them," Lukas admitted, ignoring the looks that everyone else was giving him. He was a little uncomfortable with all the admiration and awe that people were throwing at him recently. As far as he was concerned, he was just conveniently suited to take down barriers and wards.

"But I won't," he said. "Or rather, if this was a normal siege, that may have been the right approach."

"Oh?" Solana's eyes glinted with anticipation. "If this is going where I think it is, you're being really cruel . . ."

"I don't get it," said Olfric, frowning. "If you can blow up the perimeter then—"

"Because Solana is right," said Lukas. "The perimeter wards are designed to keep as many people away as possible. So long as it's there, Ultaf will stay confident. In contrast, if we get rid of it with minimal damage, his hope for victory will be massively reduced, and knowing the guy, he'll panic and take unreasonable actions."

He ran his fingers through his hair. The more he studied the situation, the more he was convinced that the best way to lay siege to this impenetrable fortress was to attack alone. He could use his anomaly powers to negate the effects of the wards, slip in, and lay waste to the Peak's inner defenses, kill Ultaf Shimizu, and get out.

There was only one glaring problem.

He needed someone to go save Zuken while he was busy dealing with the army. And the only two people competent enough for that were Tanya and Solana. The former was simply too risky to reveal so early in the battle, and the latter was . . . well, a wild card who avoided physical combat with a passion, despite how good she was at it.

There was also the Eternal Light to take into account, as well.

"There is one way," said Solana softly. "But it will put your Asukan friends in danger."

"Oh, I have considered that," said Lukas offhandedly. "I just decided it was too brazen and unpredictable."

"Wh—what is she talking about?" asked Olfric warily.

"She's suggesting we go through with Ultaf's request," said Tanya softly, her eyes never leaving Solana. "Isn't that right?"

The skinwalker nodded. "He was willing to pay us substantially in exchange for getting these two to him. And he hasn't been noticed in Cyffnar at all, so I imagine he is living behind the protections of the Peak. If we go through with the deal, he'd be letting us walk through the perimeter ward without anyone being the wiser."

"It's a risk I'm not willing to take," said Lukas, crossing his arms and glaring at everyone else as if daring them to try to contradict him.

"Well, I am," said Olfric. "The only reason I joined Tanya was to help Zuken."

"As did I," Elena chimed in.

"Yes, yes, all this posturing makes you look real brave," scoffed Tanya. "You two were hiding from abductors. The soldiers at the Peak? They make those abductors look like unruly children. And even then, he only wants Elena. Olfric would just die needlessly."

"What if they offer to sell Tanya's location away?" asked Maude out of nowhere.

"Excuse me?" asked Tanya, affronted.

"That's the main reason behind Zuken's capture, isn't it?" asked Maude. "To get to you. What if Olfric and Elena sell you out in exchange for Zuken's safe return?"

"So, a deal with Lady Kandra opting for negotiations with Ultaf Shimizu in exchange for Tanya's location?" asked Olfric, quickly catching up. "Yes, that might actually work."

"Yes, if you're looking to die," Lukas snapped. "Can you guarantee Ultaf Shimizu's gonna stick to his word, because I sure can't. If he captures the two of you, he'll get Tanya's location either way, bargain be damned. Plans can be made against opponents who think rationally, not a bastard with a head full of cats."

"He has cats inside his head?" asked Elena.

"Yes," Lukas told her, feeling very much like slapping his face with his palm at the moment. "Because that was the relevant point I wanted to discuss."

"Perimeter wards, headcount bordering two thousand, and an unpredictable bastard," Tanya summed up pretty nicely. "And the moment he has you two, he also has my location. However you put it, the situation's fucked."

"But we need to do *something*," pleaded Elena. "We can't just let them kill Zuken."

Lukas took a deep breath, closed his eyes, exhaled, and walked away in an attempt to clear his head. Elena was right. Regardless of the circumstances, they needed to stage a rescue attempt, and it had to be soon.

You're not allowed to give up, he told himself. *You have to find a solution. Compartmentalize and conquer, Lukas.*

It was like being back at the university. Legal problems were, more often than not, intricate and not able to be solved all at once. There was always a larger, overarching question—the big target. But if he obsessed over the enormity of it, he'd lose focus.

Like he was right now.

The trick was to start small. To focus on what he could answer. Build some ground to stand on. And after he had put in some of the work and *if* he was lucky, the mystery of the overarching problem would become less intimidating and more solvable. Almost like stepping back from a tree to look at the forest around it.

Right now, there was only one factor that he could control and that was *passing through the perimeter wards without having to fight the army*. Ultaf Shimizu was an unpredictable son of a bitch, but he was also a noble, so factoring his arrogance into the equation, the only thing he could say for certain was that they wouldn't be ambushed *until* the deal was done.

And then it clicked.

"I agree," he said. "The three of us—Olfric, Elena, and I—will go meet Ultaf Shimizu, offering a bargain under Lady Kandra's banner, to reveal Tanya's location in exchange for Zuken's safe return, as well as ours.

"I don't think so," said Tanya. "That's a lot of risk you're taking—"

"I'll protect these two—" Lukas began, but she cut him off.

"I was talking about *you*, you idiot," Tanya snapped. "This is my problem. Don't think I didn't notice how you're keeping me in the least amount of danger possible, and yourself in the most."

"It is the only option," Lukas countered. "We can't risk you in the initial stages of this operation. Olfric, Elena, and I will get there. Olfric will sign an Eztli contract in advance, stating the bargain, reinforced by his faith in the Great Goddess. Surely that's enough for Ultaf Shimizu to not doubt the veracity of our claims?"

Solana, on the other hand, didn't seem to agree. "That's a lot of risk you are taking with my people."

Lukas met her eyes with an uncaring gaze. "It's called a risk for a reason. Or am I to just risk my own, and Olfric and Elena's, lives on the mere chance that Ultaf Shimizu will play by the rules? Have you gotten too used to playing as the House to remember that? Higher stakes come with higher risks. And I don't see what the big deal is. And even if the information gets passed to his grandfather, it only plays in our favor."

"Uh," interrupted Elena. "What is he talking about?"

"He wants to lure Mujin Shimizu into the desert." Maude's mad smile widened.

"What?!" asked Olfric, shocked. "Are you crazy?"

That Tanya hadn't so much as reacted to Maude's statement spoke volumes.

"Facing Mujin in the desert has advantages over striking him at his territory. Here, the yokai have the home base advantage. There's also the psychological advantage of the Desert's Curse. The shadows. The lack of Eternal Light."

"Aguilar," interrupted Olfric. "Mujin Shimizu is a warlord. Psychological advantage means nothing if he can just snap his fingers and destroy everything within a mile. And in the Desert, he wouldn't even have to hold back."

"Yes, but neither would Tanya."

The aquamancer looked at Tanya in surprise. "You think you can fight a warlord?"

Before Tanya could speak, Lukas cut her off.

"Whether she can or not is irrelevant," he said. "Because Mujin would come for her either way. This won't stop until he has her, or she kills him. And mind you, she won't be alone. All of us will make sure that Mujin Shimizu is at his weakest."

"You actually sound scared of him," noted Solana, a knowing glint in her eyes. "After defeating the empress, I'd have guessed that battling a warlord would be easy for you."

Lukas smiled. He didn't need to be a psychologist to see through her taunt. She was poking at his pride, expecting him to act out. Unfortunately for her, he had little need for pride. His strength had always come as a side effect of his being an anomaly. Whatever little battle experience and training he had gotten paled in comparison to that. So, unlike others, he was not above believing in his own imperfection. They were after all, facing a being who was powerful enough to decimate all of them singlehandedly. Prudence was necessary.

"As much as I hate to agree with her, she has a point," said Tanya. "You shattered her barriers. You faced the brunt of the Ifrit King and survived. You defeated Meynte herself. And if firepower is really the issue, Ezzeron can bridge the gap."

Lukas shook his head. Tanya was being difficult. That or she just didn't want to feel powerless. Not that he could blame her. After all that she had suffered because of that man, the last thing she needed was for him to point out how weak she was.

He steepled his fingers in front of his hands. "I'm being pragmatic here, Tanya. The more firepower we use against them, the lower the odds of success. Not because you're weak, but because the more people that attack him, the more seriously he'd be forced to fight."

"So, if he thinks there's a genuine chance of losing . . ." Tanya murmured.

"He'll refuse to allow it and fight with his fullest strength. Hence, our chances go down even further."

"I concur," said Solana.

"Is anyone else creeped out by how well those two are getting along?" asked Olfric.

"I thought I was the only one," said Maude.

Solana scoffed. "I have no intention of getting along with anyone. We share a common goal, and I stand nothing to gain from antagonizing the Outsider. While I feel no real gratitude to him, I can appreciate the reality that being uncooperative is counterintuitive to our operations. Nothing else."

Lukas just gave them a half-shrug. "Either way, the fact is, we cannot defeat Mujin Shimizu head-on. We need a game changer. Elena . . . I need a list of everything you can charm out of the captured soldiers. Every step into the castle, the defenses, the processes—everything. You and I will also use the other memory crystals to connect with Zuken and see if we can get any intel. Olfric, I need you to make a list of everything that Asukan soldiers tend to use in battle—strategies, weapons, enchantments, the lot. Solana, I need you to prepare the yokai here to defend against Mujin's assault when it comes. I also need you to set up a meeting with Ultaf Shimizu on the exact day of the Shogun meeting. I have a hunch that Mujin will keep his grandson safe and protected, and that is where we want to meet him. Tanya, you and I need to discuss the rifting ability you've been working on."

"*Discuss,*" drawled Maude. "Is that what they're calling it nowadays?"

"Yes," said Lukas evenly. "Maude, you . . . can stay and make sure the soldiers survive the interrogation. If that's all . . ." he said and walked out of the room with Tanya, leaving a perplexed group behind.

"Wait, how did I get elected nanny?" asked an annoyed Maude at their retreating forms.

"More importantly," said Solana, "who put him in charge?"

Alone in his room, Lukas was dealing with an entirely different issue, one that was much more difficult than facing down the rest of the crowd. With everyone else, he could just firmly state his desires and expect them to follow along—but not with her.

"You want me to do *what?*" she asked, frantic. "I thought—I thought you destroyed that featherglass shard in front of Solana. By Wind, why would you think that allowing her to survive was a good idea in the slightest?"

"Because it's something I can control and predict . . . to a degree." He shook his head. He hadn't thought it was a good idea either, but it was a necessary one.

And because unlike you, Descendant, the Soulcrafter knows my worth, came the familiar, feminine voice as a figure arose from the floor next to her. Tanya all but shrieked and jumped aside, as the floor erupted in a half-molten rock construct, morphing into a humanoid form. The newly formed female, complete with rock-carved eyes, ears, and lips, spoke with a clear voice that felt less like it came from her mouth and more like it was projected from elsewhere.

My felicitations, Soulcrafter. I believed you could only corporate me through that metal.

"It's a work in progress." Lukas shrugged. Turning to Tanya, he said, "No matter how much Solana cooperates with us, we cannot trust her. So, I need to place you in more trustworthy hands."

Tanya gave the rock construct a look of deepest loathing. "In *her* hands? Are you sure this isn't the anomaly in you trying to kill me?"

I wish, said Meynte before Lukas could reply. *I cannot emphasize enough what sort of threat you will be now that Everfrost is slowly creeping into your soul. You represent the greatest threat the Soulcrafter will ever have to face. A true monster of his own making.*

"No," said Lukas coldly. "The moment Tanya dies, Fimbulwinter will find another way to manifest in this reality, and this time, we won't have any control over it."

Do not lecture me about controlling Taboo, Soulcrafter. This is why you should have allowed me to take control of the girl's body.

"Or," said Lukas, "you could stop sulking and help her learn the control you once had."

It's a foolish game you play, regardless. She has my instincts, but her power and control are tentative at best. A tempting lure, yes, but even this insect you call a warlord is an almost-insurmountable opponent for the likes of her.

"Stop talking like I'm not even in the room!" snapped Tanya in irritation. Being seen as frail and worthless was getting on her nerves. She had grown exponentially stronger in the last several months and yet, when it mattered, she fell short. "Mujin Shimizu is my problem, and regardless of how 'insurmountable' you think he is, I'll still deal with him myself."

"And then what? Get captured?"

Tanya wanted to snap, but one look at his eyes and she stopped short. There was no fear or uncertainty in them. Just a steel-cold resolve.

Neither spoke for the next few moments.

"Tch . . ." With a heavy shove, Tanya pushed him to the side. "Fine. I'll go along with this ridiculous idea of yours. Let's see if you survive the disastrous operation you've planned for the Peak."

With that, she turned around and left, probably towards her room.

She is rather cross with you.

"With due cause," said Lukas, exhaling. "I made an unreasonable request this time. And at the last second, no less."

I doubt being forced to deal with me is what has gotten her this distraught, observed Meynte. *Foolish and weak she may be, but she is committed to you. I know loyalty when I see it. This one would walk till the End of Time with you.*

Lukas frowned. "I know. I take it you are not particularly fond of my plan."

I would be a poor confidant if I said I was. I understand what you're aiming for, and agree with it to an extent, but the unnecessary risk you place on your shoulders . . . But I've known many who ran off to accomplish unreasonable tasks.

"Just another thing we have in common then, I guess."

Thump.

"Ngh?!" Lukas staggered back from the quick jab to the side of his chest. He grunted, hunching over toward the floor.

Meynte ignored his distress. He was fine. He was still standing.

Be honest. What are your odds of success?

"Mmm . . ." Lukas picked himself back again, rubbing his now-tender side. "It depends. If it's a matter of simply dealing with Ultaf Shimizu to some degree, I'd say . . . one in two. Not the best, but not terrible. If I can't do that, everything else is pointless, regardless. And if I do, the odds of the next time working in my favor increases drastically. A domino effect. The real question is, are the pieces ready and in place to topple?"

CHAPTER 11

The dreaded day had finally arrived. The day when the fate of the Shimizu would be decided in front of the entire Shogun Court. A series of events that had snowballed from the moment Ultaf had arrived at the Peak with news of the Creature not just alive but bonded with his father's kami, Ezzeron.

And the worst part? Mujin knew he was walking into a trap. Despite that, he stepped through the front door of the Shogun's mansion.

He loathed admitting it, but the Earth King had pretty much saved his ass in front of the emperor. Despite the overwhelming evidence against him and his clan, the Earth King had convinced the emperor to give him a forty-five-day grace period to tie up his loose ends. Trestan Banksi had offered his own services for the position of judge for the upcoming Shogun Court, but it was strikingly obvious that the emperor had seen through his ploy. After all, it would be tough for the prosecution to successfully argue their case if the judge himself was on the side of the accused.

No wonder the emperor himself had added the extra clause—prove Zuken Banksi's transgressions and provide enough evidence that the girl—his so-called granddaughter—existed, and had strong compatibility with Ezzeron, and had enough potential to be a future claimant for the Wind King's position. If not, the Shimizu's status as one of the Sacred Eight would be called into question.

And Trestan himself would have to be the one to sign the Shimizu's death warrant.

Well, thought Mujin glumly, *it's not like that matters anymore. Not after the brat gave Naowa yet another dagger to impale me with.*

It felt like his grandson was shooting himself in the foot whenever he looked away. As if assaulting Lord Naowa's wetworks man and destroying his mansion hadn't been enough, Ultaf had attacked the Zwaray Keep, home of the svartalfars, and wiped the race out of existence. If there were still any left in the fringes, they were already underground.

Literally.

There weren't enough words in the six languages he spoke that could describe the sheer idiocy and irresponsibility behind those actions. Ultaf's response: Tanya was stranded inside the borderlands, and the svartalfars weren't bowing down and accepting every word that left his mouth as gospel.

He should've known better than to hand over control of his army to Ultaf. The brat had spent too many years playing lord in Cyffnar to understand what real power meant. Despite his attempts to shape the brat into a worthy heir, it had all ended in dismal failure. Ultaf had grown into his twisted facsimile and hung on Mujin's own power, wealth, and status as a warlord. Worse, he acted as if that power was already his. Mujin's spies had confirmed that.

If not for the fact that Ultaf was his sole remaining heir, and that he was too old to even consider procreation, he would have slaughtered the bastard on the spot. Really, there were moments when his mind wandered over the possibility of raising that creature as his heiress instead. Despite the taint, she definitely had his cunning, his pragmatism, and his penchant for violence. She had escaped their attempts to capture her for all these years, and the fact that she wielded Ezzeron only proved the potency of Asukan blood within her. Truly, imprisoning and torturing her back then was proving to have been a most costly mistake.

A mistake he could no longer correct. Even as a child, she was oddly resistant to the Initiation. An effect of her yokai heritage, no doubt.

Hearing a guard addressing him brought him out of his musings.

"Lord Shimizu?" said the guard. "You're expected in the Great Hall."

Of course I am.

Maintaining his aura of quiet dignity, Mujin walked into the hall and found himself facing a familiar audience. The entire Shogun Court—all thirteen members—were present. Naowa hadn't pulled his punches in getting the full set to witness the Shimizu's denigration.

Mujin's friendship with the Earth King was no secret. But there was a difference in standing in support of his friend from a position of strength, and facing the might of the entire Southeastern Council. None of the Shoguns could match the amount of power or potential Trestan had in his little finger, but demonstrating bias in front of their collective political presence was something not even the Earth King would dare to risk.

Especially because the emperor and the other kings would hear about it after.

Silently, he walked over to his right and took the empty seat next to Lady Akiha Troyl, the least politically powerful person in the room, and one of the most dangerous. Maluscion was one of the smallest nations in the Empire, a coastal territory a staggeringly high crime rate. Smugglers, abductors, thieves, spies, deviants—Maluscion was a hub of everything that the Empire officially looked down upon. Quite naturally, it was also the place that most influential people reached out to whenever they needed something done under the table. Officially, the Maluscion government was known to be one of the weakest, but Mujin had a sneaky suspicion that the illegal hub was actually a parallel government run directly by Lady Troyl herself.

"Lord Mujin." Lady Akiha curtsied as their eyes met. "Looks like the start of a bad day. Lord Straff looks especially excited."

"Of course he does!" grumbled Mujin. "That dog probably thinks this is his ticket to becoming one of the Eight."

"I think he'll be happy with the Shimizu's fate just as well," said the woman. "Then no one will challenge his dominion in the kingdom."

"Yes, he'll turn it into a wasteland. Useless waste of sperm that one was."

"Are you not worried?"

"Should I be?" asked Mujin. He was on the verge of a political defeat, but he'd be damned if he showed weakness. "This is hardly the first time I've had to defend my throne from usurpers."

"I hear it's different this time around," she murmured.

Yes. Naowa had summoned all the mice together to fend off the cat. That just didn't happen. When the cat came out to play, the mouse would run and hide in fear.

It was a rule of nature.

"I spoke with the others," said Lady Akiha. "Lord Naowa was furious when the Earth King demonstrated indifference to his son."

"Indifference?" grunted Mujin. "He ordered me to send the brat back to Naowa."

"Only because of the precedent it would have otherwise set," the woman countered. "I haven't worked with the young man before, but I know of his reputation. Very skilled and connected in micromanaging under-the-table deals, yes?"

His scowl deepened. As much as he disliked it, the woman spoke the truth. Zuken Banksi was practically a mini-Maluscion. An individual power broker unconnected with any of the major powers, who had risen to become the invisible left hand of Shogun Naowa.

"Then he should have known better than to breach a contract made with the acting Lord of Shimizu."

Not that it made any difference.

"I've been wondering . . ." murmured the woman. "Just what is it that happened between your clan and your heiress? Surely she has a reason for hiding from her own heritage at this point?"

"As I said before the court, there are certain misunderstandings between us."

"You had forty-five days to solve it. People are wondering just how complicated this 'misunderstanding' is", she said with animated fingers, "that the heiress and potential claimant of the Wind King's throne would rather remain in obscurity than take her place. Many are wondering if she's even alive, and if all of this has been a mad ploy to squirrel away more time from the emperor."

His eyes flashed. "Did you just call me a liar?"

"Absolutely not," she said, flapping her eyelids at him. "I only say what I hear."

And what you think will tempt the other into reacting. Mujin scoffed and looked at the room at large. "Wolves don't concern themselves with the opinions of sheep. It is, as I said, classified."

The woman smiled. "Somehow, I doubt it will remain as such."

"What do you mean?"

She gave him a cozy, knowing smile. It made him want to clench her throat in his hands and squeeze the life out of her. Then her expression transformed into a calculating, composed smile. "Lord Naowa took the Earth King's indifference to his wetworks man's life and importance as a personal insult. Whatever this Zuken Banksi must have done to gain such support, it must be significant. It's almost *disgustingly* loyal."

Mujin suppressed the urge to spit. *Loyalty!* Bah! Loyalty was enforced, not won through sentiment.

The woman brought her dainty hands to her mouth and laughed softly. It was almost enough to fool him.

Almost.

Inwardly, he wondered why Lady Akiha was trying to cozy up to him. That woman was a scorpion.

"I believe Lady Menasse had something she wanted to discuss with me," she said and stood up, her seat instantly sinking into the floor as she walked away with a parting smile. Mujin pursed his lips, inwardly seething. Something about this whole conversation felt . . . off.

Straff could whine as much as he wanted, but the truth was his clan was just a bunch of layabout espers and middling spiritists who held enough political influence and physical resources to bind together to form a clan. Even the Bergotts of Llaisy Kingdom were far better, and the greatest level they had reached was warlord. Compared to that, Mujin was a standing warlord at the height of his power. He might not have been king-class, but he was definitely head and shoulders above any of his esteemed colleagues.

The next forty-five minutes of the meeting had been nothing but pleasantries, introductions, pandering, and official babble that in all honesty was done for show and had nothing to do with the situation in the first place. Given the identities of the guests, Mujin wondered why Naowa was taking such an elaborate, time-consuming method. Perhaps he wanted to bore him to death?

He knew he had handed over the acting Lordship to Ultaf for a reason. He was too old for this shit.

He gazed at the Earth King and found the usual calm, cool indifference in them. Unsurprising, for he was the presiding judge. Still, there was something in his expression that felt wrong.

His thoughts screeched to a furious halt as Naowa stood up and took to the central dais. "Lords and Ladies, back at the royal palace forty-five days ago, the Shimizu claimed that the wanton destruction they caused in Haviskali was a rightful display of personal vengeance against the actions of Zuken Banksi, my personal advisor and confidante. I would ask Lord Mujin if he has any proof behind those wild accusations, but honestly, it's unneeded. Ultaf Shimizu, Acting Lord of Shimizu Clan and perpetrator of the attack in Haviskali has demonstrated how little he regards law and justice in the Empire."

Naowa took a moment to stare at every single face in the hall.

"For those of you who do not know, I'm referring to the genocide of the svartalfar race in Zwaray Keep by Ultaf Shimizu and his army. Because of his despicable actions, the Empire is now devoid of svartalfar enchantment. Without them, the technology fueling the Wells is lost forever."

Mujin tried very hard to ignore the looks he was getting from every single presence in the room.

When the whispers died down, Naowa spoke again. "I formally apologize, Earth King. As per the emperor's decree, you were tasked to judge this trial. But this has become a matter of interracial relations, critical damage to my kingdom's economy, *and* a significant threat to the Empire's commerce. Such a travesty could not be blithely ignored. Hence, I had to contact the chief administrator of interracial matters—"

Mujin's blood ran cold. No. Not *him.*

It wouldn't end well for anyone if it did. If that man entered the picture, then—

"And he so very graciously agreed to join the judging panel. It is my great honor to host a council meeting with him present, and I thank my ancestors for making me worthy to bask in his presence. He, whose name alone is enough for me to instantly genuflect and pay our obeisances before his might."

He smiled and extended his arms wide and spoke in a ringing voice.

"SECOND-BORN OF THE GREAT GODDESS. BROTHER TO EMPEROR NINIGI. COMMANDER OF THE OBSIDIAN GRIP."

Two platoons of soldiers—all of them wearing mithril-plated armors walked into the room, with gold-plated fractals on each hand and wearing flowing crimson robes. An army of fifty individuals, their faces were covered in hoods, enchanted to allow them to see through them without disclosing their identities. Every single one of them was a Gold-class adventurer—the most powerful private battalion in the entire Empire. They moved as one, worked as one, and fought as a singular unit, the commander's personal brigade, called into action only against the strongest of enemies.

Mujin furiously glanced in Naowa's direction, but the bastard didn't even notice him. Instead, a small, crafty smile played on his smug face.

"DEMIGOD. FIRE KING. WIELDER OF SUZAKU, THE MIGHTY PHOENIX."

Easily seven feet, taller than the emperor himself, the newcomer walked into the room, with every single person instantly standing up and bowing in respect. This man . . . he didn't have the lion-like charisma of his esteemed brother. No, he was like a bear—broadly proportioned shoulders, huge in size, yet something about that physique suggesting inhuman agility and grace. He looked calm and relaxed, but also as if at any second, he could surge forth with terrible speed and purpose without the slightest warning.

His forearms were nearly the size of his biceps, and he had the kind of thick neck one usually saw in abductors and thugs. Most of his body was hidden behind mail crafted of a metal Mujin didn't recognize, but he could see scars all over his hands and face, all of them faded away to ancient white lines. His hair was crimson, shaggy, and flowing down the nape of his neck like a mane. His eyes shone like lumps of smoldering flame, and the temperature in the room seemed to automatically rise just by the simple action of him entering it.

"LORD JIMMO ASUKA!" finished Naowa with pride.

Every other member of the court was busy genuflecting in the Fire King's presence, but Mujin only had eyes for the Earth King. It was as though a switch had been flipped, and a wave of madness seemed to pour from his very being. Red bloodlust flooded from the man's gaze, and something utterly malicious flickered in his otherwise composed features.

The moment lasted for barely a fraction of a second.

"An injustice has occurred," said the demigod, sharing an odd look with Trestan. "And in my mother's name, I will not allow a single blemish to fall upon those laws that hold the foundation of our Empire together. Is the accused present?"

"Lord Mujin Shimizu is here," said Naowa. "He is representing his clan for the duration of this council meeting, My Lord. As are sixteen Shoguns of the Southeast Dominion."

"Very well," said the Fire King. "The requirements of the quorum have been met. With that, I call the council to order."

A cold knot formed in Mujin's stomach.

Countering the Earth King using the Shogun Court's political power was one thing. Using the utter lack of evidence and the wanton destruction of the svartalfars, even that he had seen coming. But to bring the Fire King into this madness and force Trestan Banksi to play ball like this practically screamed insult. Naowa wasn't just flirting with insubordination, he was grabbing it round the waist and kissing it so deep that he was massaging its tonsils. Did he really think that Trestan would forgive this insult? Or was he just that arrogant that he thought that the support of the Fire King would protect him? Did he expect his own status to rise amongst the other Shoguns in the Southeast because he caused the fall of Shimizu?

Did Naowa truly understand what sort of reckless game he had inadvertently started? Taking a risk like this just for publicity?

No. That would be the actions of a fool, and Naowa, to his knowledge, was no fool.

Just what are you planning, Naowa? What do you know that I don't?

It was a question that would haunt him for days to come.

—————

Like all great plans, Lukas's current scheme began with willingly walking into enemy territory.

The day was finally here, and Lord Naowa, true to his word, had held the Shogun meeting in Pinefell, a city on the other extreme end of the Llaisy Kingdom, bordering Thornblandt and Luthar, which meant Mujin Shimizu had left early and would be stuck there for quite some time.

"Remember," said Olfric, "they probably don't know about the deal, so they can refuse entry. Just try not to lose your mind, and be diplomatic. We need them to authorize a carriage for us to step through the perimeter wards."

"Sweet," said Lukas, as the trio stood outside the first checkpoint. The moment they crossed the ward-line, half a dozen guards accosted them, their enchanted blades pointed at their vital parts, while one of them approached, spine rigid, shoulders squared, and manners relaxed with the lean athleticism of youth and the weather-beaten edge of experience. A quick analysis pointed out some strong enchantments on those blades, increasing their sharpness and strength by a magnitude. He was sure each of those swords could easily deflect a Level-2 elemental attack with ease.

Interesting, but nothing fancy.

"Can I help you, sirs and lady?"

He didn't even bother with a friendly smile, or the kowtowing reserved for noblemen, not that any of them counted as one.

"Swordsmen," Lukas commented, a thin smile spreading across his face as the swords in question shifted slightly in his direction. "Inside a mana-disrupting ward no less. Someone sure is paranoid."

The man shrugged. "Can I help you?"

Lukas gave a quick look at Olfric and Elena. "I'm Lady Kandra's representative. I believe I'm expected along with . . ." Lukas gave a quick look at Olfric and Elena. ". . .these two."

"We have no information about a prior appointment with the lord."

"Really?" Lukas gave the soldier his best condescending look. "Shows how much he values you, doesn't it?"

Both Olfric and Elena went pale.

Lukas sighed. "Look, Ultaf Shimizu contacted my lady for her services. About getting these two—" He grabbed Olfric by the collar, pulling him next to him forcibly. "—to your big guy. I told the lady that he's going to try to weasel out of paying us. I know a weasel when I see one."

The blades edged closer.

"*What are you doing?*" Olfric hissed.

"We're gonna die," said Elena, sighing.

Lukas was unfazed. "Pick a fight if you must, but I'll tell you this: if Ultaf Shimizu doesn't get them today, you lot won't even have a job to come to tomorrow."

At least one of them had some sense, pulling his sword back and rushing to the camp. A few anxious moments later, he walked back out with a peeved expression on his face.

"Prince Ultaf wants to meet them. Now."

But the swords did not move away.

Instead, the man doing the interrogation pulled out a small vial from his pocket and uncorked it.

"Your names?"

"Lukas Aguilar," he said. "With Olfric, formerly of Bergott Clan, and Elena, a changeling."

"Your palm, please?"

Lukas eyed the vial but said nothing.

"This is Okuninushi's Resolver," said the man. "We need to confirm that you are who you claim to be and not some imposter under enchantment. Security protocols, I'm afraid."

Tanya was right, thought Lukas, as he gauged the soldiers. *Nobody can tell if they're enthralled, charmed, or otherwise.* Not even a quick analysis of their souls showed any difference, which was more than mildly annoying.

"Your prince might take offense at this delay."

"Then he'll have to take that up with the lord," said the man offhandedly. "You can refuse, but then I'd have to deny you entrance."

What a load of crap. If they resisted, it would automatically raise flags and they'd be all over them before Lukas could cry foul. He would have been impressed by the man's steadfastness and loyalty if not for what he knew about the Initiation.

"Alright," said Lukas, pushing Olfric first. "Whatever gets you off."

"I'll pour a single drop of this elixir into your mouth. Kindly remain still for another ten seconds. I wouldn't want any of my men to become alarmed at some furtive movement and slice your head off. We do not follow the Empire's rules here."

The guard poured a single drop of the resolver on Olfric's tongue, while looking up at a pocket watch. Olfric stood perfectly still, save for shivering before the man finally put his watch away.

"All clear," said the guard into what looked like a receiver. "Initiating interrogation."

Olfric swallowed.

"Who are you?"

"Olfric . . . formerly of Clan Bergott."

"What is your reason for coming here?"

Lukas observed how Olfric had gone all stiff, his throat constricting, and when he spoke next, it felt like someone had forced an answer out of his mouth.

"I am here to negotiate with Ultaf Shimizu for Zuken Banksi's safe return."

Lukas exhaled. Softly. They had prepared for this. Okuninushi's Resolver was an elixir that enforced the compulsion upon the drinker to speak the truth. It was standard procedure to drink one drop of the elixir before finalizing deals between kingdoms, wealthy individuals, and corporations. Unless he was woefully wrong, their conversation was being observed by personnel inside the camp. He didn't have the slightest doubt that "All clear" and "Initiating Interrogation" were key phrases without hidden commands within them. Had the guard said anything else, a force of aeromancers and more would be upon them.

For that reason, Lukas had to play his cards close to his chest. It had been funny, seeing Olfric work on believing that his sole job was to meet Ultaf Shimizu, negotiate with him, and do his utmost to get Banksi out. He would not be taking part in the infiltration, nor physically or magically try to harm anyone within the compound. In fact, he was supposed to surrender just in case Ultaf tried to imprison him. Knowing what they knew about the man, the chances of that were at least 60%.

Watching Elena obscuring Olfric's memories and implanting false ones was, frankly, terrifying. Doubly so when she had done the same to herself.

Yet again, Lukas took a moment to remind himself that he was in a strange world where people sometimes felt the need to give themselves amnesia in order to forget dangerous truths.

It was Elena's turn next. As per the plan, Lukas would tell her a mnemonic password that would undo the obscuration once they were inside, and she, in turn, would utter the password that would restore Olfric's memories, and they could get things rolling.

It made him wonder. If Elena could self-obscure her mind to this extent, then who was to say that her bubbly, somewhat airheaded personality also wasn't the result of some self-obscuration? And if that was the case, just what sort of person was Elena truly beneath all of that?

Finally, it was Lukas's turn.

The guard poured one drop upon his tongue, and Lukas felt it burn his insides for a second and then—

Living Anomaly Resisted Alien Truth

He couldn't afford to smile, so he just waited for the customary ten seconds before the guard put his watch away.

"Name?"

"Lukas."

"Where are you from?"

Lukas remembered the cold, impersonal manner in which Olfric had answered the questions. "Maluscion."

"Objective?"

"To meet Ultaf Shimizu, collect my payment, and offer him a new deal on behalf of my employer."

That raised some eyebrows.

"Who is your employer?"

"Lady Kandra."

And that was that.

"All clear," said the main guard again into the receiver. "No signs of enchantments. No immediate signs of mental resistance, no immediate signs of hostility. One security personnel and three approved visitors will accompany me to the fourth dome. No action unless ordered otherwise, or if there is a Level-3 or higher deviation from protocol. Security code SINK - FIVE - ORDEAL - SEVEN - BLACK! CONFIRM!"

The man turned to them. "All of you will have to go through the rest of the checkpoints on your way to meet the prince." He smirked at Olfric's look of false dismay. "Security protocols. I'm sure you understand?"

They passed through the rest of the checkpoints. At some point, the guards checked his and Olfric's fractals for proof. His original pair had gotten damaged during the fight with Meynte, so he had gotten a fresh pair from Haviskali. It wasn't the same as the ones Zuken had gifted him, but it did increase his mana production by 30%. Not that he needed it, given his capacity, but not having a fractal would likely attract attention; make it too expensive, and it would attract a different kind of attention. Blob was conveniently ignored as body armor was draped on all three of them.

Even then, they were made to wait for another fifteen minutes while a whole range of enchantments did all kinds of cursory scans of their bodies, and for all he knew, their souls.

Again, not an issue. A bremetan prototype had done the job. After all, they had been studying the Peak's defenses thoroughly over the last two weeks. Their plans demanded it.

At a closer look, the Peak was closer to an army camp, only with large stone-walled constructions instead of tents. The place was infinitely old and infinitely horrible, full of dark passages, high ceilings, and cobwebs. That it was so brightly lit with not a single shadow to be seen only brought forth the utter alienness of the edifice. Between the sigil-carved stones and the rotting smell of corpses from the other side of the walls, this was precisely the kind of place where all kinds of Gothic nightmares came to life.

Only a tad brighter than one might have expected.

Lukas and his crew had followed the guard into one of the buildings, slowly descending into the heart of the mountain and the festering madness within it. A single stone slab, eight-by-eight square, slid down to the lower levels—Friction Manipulation at work. There were no sudden stoppages, their descent occasionally punctuated by the occasional scream or plea for mercy from beyond the walls, which only made it feel longer. It was like walking through a murder scene *while* said murder was being committed.

His fingers twitched, an urge to burn this place to the ground surging within.

Finally, they were down to the fifth floor, which had several rooms filled with enough weaponry to win a minor war. Racks of metal spears stood side by side with long, double-handed great swords, quivers filled with sharp arrows, and other weapons. Lukas reminded himself to do a quick scan of this place before he went back to his plan of burning it all down.

"Guess your Lord Shimizu likes being prepared for an attack."

The guard smiled with only his eyes. "This is the fortress of a warlord. You would be foolish to attack it."

"Oh, you know," said Lukas as casually as possible. "Just curious."

"Don't be. It will get you killed."

He snorted. "I agree. Back where I'm from, we've got a saying: Curiosity killed the cat . . ." He noticed Elena stiffening from the corner of his eye. ". . . and satisfaction brought it back.'"

Elena opened her mouth to say something. But then she paused suddenly, blinked her eyes repeatedly, and slowly closed her mouth. It was the passphrase meant to click something within her changeling-brain and remind her of what she had chosen to forget.

Neither of them looked at each other after that.

Finally, they were led down through a winding, almost serpentine tunnel that led to an open, spacious foyer with a humongous chandelier hanging above and large, arched doorways marking the periphery of a massive, circular hall. Lukas counted twelve guards, all of them wearing different shades of fractals. He didn't risk analyzing them, but it was safest to expect they were Level-3 and skilled at their jobs and would barge into the room the moment they sensed the slightest hostility inside.

Inside sat Ultaf Shimizu, just as arrogant and disappointing as Lukas remembered. The aeromancer's eyes widened instantly at seeing Elena before his eyes darted to Lukas.

"You're almost late," he said in a tone so dismissive that he absolutely had to have practiced it. "Lady Kandra has gotten sloppy."

Lukas decided that it took a special brand of conceitedness to look down on someone who had saved their life.

"It was a rush job," said Lukas. "Also, Lady Kandra asked me to offer you a deal."

Ultaf lifted an eyebrow. "A deal. I hope it's worthwhile, Vagrant. My guards will be most displeased if I find you've wasted my time."

"Hmph," Elena frowned at his tone. "How rude," she murmured.

Ultaf sneered, and Lukas couldn't help but wonder at the source of his confidence. True, he was in a room surrounded by guards outside, but surely he couldn't have been moronic enough to think that it meant he was safe from all harm . . . *Right?*

Putting his hands inside his pocket, he focused on creating a tiny orb of lifeforce. Nothing useful, just enough to serve as a test.

Nothing happened.

He wished he could say he was surprised. But at least it proved that Ultaf was more than just an arrogant moron.

Let's see. What exactly does the ward inside his office interfere with?

The passive flux of lifeforce within his body was still there. He had half-expected these guys to chain them up in lifeforce-restraining manacles or at least interfere with him actively using lifeforce—that or take away their fractals. Then again, such direct interference was easy to detect and was more likely to piss off potential clients who came to meet Ultaf here.

So, if his inner functions weren't being hindered, then there must have been something that was hampering the execution of a lifeforce-based Skill or attack. His lifeforce must be being disrupted from casting somehow, preventing it from taking proper form and concept. Normally this would be an easy workaround for him since it did nothing to keep him from using mana or just raw anomalous energy, but that was neither here nor there.

At the same time, this ward acted like a double-edged sword that would also prevent Ultaf from using any lifeforce-based attack. Which was why Ultaf had those enchanted tools and weapons, just in case things got messy. Objects with a physical medium to enact their enchantments.

Amateur.

Oh, well. It wasn't like he was going to call him out on it like a brash idiot.

"Look, I know why you've been hunting Elena," said Olfric, without wasting time. It was one of the things Lukas liked about the guy—he recognized his own lack of diplomacy and never claimed otherwise. For someone with a stick so far up his ass, Olfric was surprisingly genuine.

No wonder Banksi kept him around. Finding hardworking employees was difficult. But hardworking employees that weren't yes-men? Rare.

"You want her because you think she can help in unobscuring Zuken's memories. But I'll give you a better deal: Let Zuken walk away with us, safe, and in return, we'll tell you where Tanya is."

Ultaf threw his head back and laughed. "Your bluntness is refreshing if a bit crude. I was surprised by your letter. Bold of you to walk into my garrison and demand things of me. I still haven't determined if it's bravery or stupidity."

Lukas agreed with the sentiment. Well, mostly. He too couldn't determine if Ultaf Shimizu was being brave or stupid. So far, the more he spoke the more Lukas leaned towards the latter.

He glanced at Elena and found an obvious look of hostility on her face, a narrow-eyed glare leveled at Ultaf. Her expression was a trap, an illusion to keep him from noticing what she was really doing.

"Tell me," said Ultaf, "where is she?"

Olfric stood his ground. "Not until I have Zuken. And Lady Kandra promised—"

"Lady Kandra isn't here," said Ultaf, sniffing in disdain. "It seems you don't understand the situation you've found yourself in." His smile turned smug as he continued. "You are at the Peak. Just a gesture and my men will relieve you of all your heads."

"I'm hoping that your men know how to extract memories from decapitated heads, then," Olfric retorted. "For I ain't saying a thing until I see Zuken."

Ultaf sighed. "Pity. A little humility could've gone a long way for you."

"It's easy to talk of humility when you're surrounded by guards and protected by a mana-interference field. But I suppose that's the only way the Shimizu have been taught to behave."

"You dare . . ." Ultaf began to stand up.

"I'm sorry I simply cannot admire people who stand on others' shoulders and call themselves tall," Olfric retorted. "You brought your entire army, in the dead of the night, to attack my friend by surprise. That's the coward's way."

Ultaf bristled.

"But I'm not here for that," Olfric continued. "I want nothing to do with you or this woman Zuken's so intent on protecting. Let Zuken walk away with me, and I'll give you Tanya's location. As promised. For once in your life, try being a little honorable."

Ultaf took a moment to regain his voice, caught slightly off-guard. "*Honorable?*" he spat out. "Banksi has lied and kept information from me."

"And you've destroyed his mansion, slaughtered his people, and imprisoned him," Olfric shot back. "I think as far as transgressions go, yours is much worse."

"Have care how you speak to me, Banksi's Dog!"

"I'm no one's dog. I just have no patience for cowards and backstabbers."

"Big words for a man without a family name to call his own."

"Better to be confident in one's power and stand alone than play a king while clearly being a jester."

Despite how placid Lukas kept his face, his mind had been frantically scrambling since the moment the altercation between the two spiritists had begun. Olfric's bluntness was a natural grindstone to Ultaf's arrogance. It was one of the reasons why he was chosen to do the talking. That he had passed Okuninushi's Resolver before getting here only made it further confusing for Ultaf, because he clearly knew that Bergott wasn't planning some kind of surprise attack.

He glanced at Elena from the corner of his eyes and found her softly stroking her thigh with her fingers. She was already done allaying the guards. They weren't asleep or anything, merely distracted. *Perfect.*

"Could you just move this along?" he interrupted. "I don't care whether this deal is accepted or not. But I do care about getting the payment for my lady's services."

Ultaf lazily picked up a small envelope and slid it across the table toward him. Silently, Lukas grabbed it. A brief analysis that lasted no longer than a fraction of a second indicated that there were no spells of any sort within; the only thing inside was a piece of paper. Ultaf didn't look like he was going to speak anytime soon, so Lukas slowly opened the envelope.

It was a check for his "hard work," and given the sheer number of zeroes that followed the numeral on the left, he had a good idea why Solana had targeted the Sacred Eight for her information-broker business.

"Thank you," he said, replacing the check in the envelope and placing it inside his pouch.

"Now, get lost," Ultaf said, absently. "The guards will show you the way out."

"I will. There's just . . . one more thing."

His eyes flashed green.

Ultaf's body spasmed as his entire nervous system went haywire. After all, the human body—the bremetan one as well, for that matter—was run by electrical impulses traversing through countless nerves connecting every end. Manipulating that electricity into acting oddly was enough to paralyze the man within two seconds of contact. He opened his mouth to scream . . .

But no sound escaped his lips. Instead, when Lukas let his hand go, Ultaf collapsed back into his chair, opening his mouth in vain; nothing save gurgles escaped his throat.

"Yeah, don't bother," said Lukas as he pushed the chair back and moved towards the fallen man.

"*Aguilar!*" Olfric hissed. "What are you doing?"

"Just accelerating some parts. That's all."

"Yu—bsss—trd!" Ultaf tried to speak, only for the pain to overwhelm him. He paused as he felt Lukas's steel-like gaze crushing his windpipe. He looked up and met his furious eyes.

"Now then," said Lukas Aguilar. "What were you saying?"

CHAPTER 13

The first thing that Ultaf felt was pain. Immense, horrendous, stabbing pain. He looked down at his hands which by now should have been conjuring intense blasts of power against his enemies, like his grandfather had taught him.

Instead, a feeling of despair flooded through him.

My hands. I can't feel my hands.

They weren't broken, yet he couldn't move them. His entire body looked as it always did, yet it refused to obey his commands. The moment the vagrant released his hands, his body collapsed like a stringless marionette.

Ultaf screamed. No sound came out. That's when the aeromancer realized his windpipe was being crushed. He began choking for air. He locked eyes with the vagrant.

By the Goddess! The wards should have disrupted all mana and lifeforce activity. So how had this happened?!

"I've paralyzed you for now. In case you're wondering, this just a fraction of what I'm going to put you through if you don't tell me exactly where Zuken Banksi is."

Ultaf frantically drowned in an ocean of agony, incapable of even remembering his own name at this point. He desperately attempted to call upon his lifeforce, but at this point all it could do was the bare minimum of keeping him alive. Worse, it was flaring his nerves, adding to his misery.

The smile on the man—no, the *monster's*—face grew.

"Ah, right," the vagrant said. "I almost forgot. You can't speak properly. At least until your lifeforce heals you. Which should take *days* if I'm not mistaken. But then there's the chance that you might say or do something . . . inconvenient, in which case I might just start damaging some of your nerves. And by some, I mean like . . . *half* of them. Oh, rest assured, I'll keep the main parts intact. Just your arms and legs. It can be really hard to avoid your heart and spine, but I think I can manage a decent job. Wouldn't you agree?"

Ultaf tried to speak but all he could do was gurgle.

"Shit," said the vagrant. "That must have been the damage to the windpipe. Or perhaps nerve damage? Grandpa told me so many times to take that anatomy course in school. For fuck's sake, I even audited the damn thing. But *noo!* I had to decide to be a lawyer! Then again, lawyers don't go around electrocuting others like professional hitmen, do they? You know how the saying goes, 'Man proposes, God disposes' and all that . . ."

Ultaf almost wet himself in fear. Who was this madman, speaking all this gibberish? And what did he want with him? And where were the guards? Why weren't they here already? They should have sensed the mana—

Wait. Mana? He couldn't have done it using mana. He couldn't have broken the wards. Surely someone must have sensed something! Anything! He desperately tried to move his hand towards the table. All he needed to do was press a little button and all the guards would be there, raining down on this bastard. But he couldn't. He—he needed to shout!

"GHHH!" A pathetic grunt escaped his throat, and Ultaf fell back limply as his nerves flared, fear tearing through his mind. His throat felt like someone had shoved a brick through it. But it had to have been worth it. His guards had to have heard it. They'd come! They'd all come. They'll surround this bastard and absolutely butcher him and—

Nothing.

No one was coming. Ultaf tried to divert his lifeforce into his auditory receptors. It hurt like Hell but—

Still nothing.

Wait. What was going on? Why weren't they coming? *WHY WEREN'T THEY COMING? COULDN'T THEY HEAR HIS SCREAMS? COULDN'T THEY HEAR THIS—*

"*Urk!*"

Ultaf looked down in horror at his chest, where the stranger had just poked him with a finger.

"Don't bother wasting your breath on screaming. You don't exactly have much left. That poke I just gave you shattered a rib right above your left lung. Just one little push and it'll puncture the lung and you'll probably have a minute or two before you suffocate and your heart stops, assuming you don't die from the pain first." The monster paused and gave Ultaf a friendly smile, which filled him up with fresh horror. "Unless I poke you again, at which point, your right lung will be punctured, and the broken ribs will be buried in your heart. You have exactly one minute before I do that."

The clinical, almost polite tone in which these words had been delivered chilled Ultaf to his very core.

"But you can't speak, can you? In that case, I guess you'll just have to *think*. See, Elena here—"The man animatedly gestured towards the girl standing by him. "—is an expert Obscurer. You know what those are, right? I don't know how she does it, but we all have our talents, don't we? Yours is, I think, idiocy."

"Can idiocy even be a talent?" Olfric Bergott asked from behind. Ultaf would have thought that the man was just being a condescending bastard, but the confusion in his eyes painted a different picture.

"Eh, who knows? The world's a big place. Now, Idiot here is going to open his mind wide to Elena and let her see whatever she wants. Aren't you . . . Idiot?"

Ultaf shook his head vigorously. He watched with growing dread as the girl—no, the *changeling*—walked up to him, noticing the slight hesitation in her gait. She wasn't used to working like this—or rather, working with strangers. Same for Ultaf. Whoever this stranger, this vagrant was—they were working for him! This was a planned trap!

How had he failed to notice?

The changeling crossed her arms across her chest, her fingers paused in a particular hand gesture, before she uncrossed them, both hands parallel to each other. Despite the simplicity, Ultaf had a growing sense of foreboding, that some kind of lock was opening and that whatever was about to emerge was something not of this world.

"*Shokan!*"

Suddenly something fairly anthropoidal with squid-like features and large bright, iridescent blue eyes appeared before him, and his world exploded in agony. Blood erupted out of his nose and lips and his vision faded to darkness.

When he awoke again, he was still sprawled across his chair. He had no idea how much time had passed; given the room's lack of windows, there was no natural light to tell the time.

His body ached, and he felt no connection to his mana. Ultaf immediately knew the position he was in. How could he not? It was, after all, something he took great pleasure in doing to others.

He was a prisoner.

"This is just a waste of space," a voice spoke from behind him. "Wind Creation, Wind Manipulation . . . All of this is just fucking Level 2. Pressure at Level 3, I'll bet he's just touched it recently. Is this really the kami of the lord of the Shimizu clan? All this time I had been expecting a warrior and instead I got a loudmouthed politician. At least he isn't fully perpetuating the stereotype and potbellied as well."

"Why would he be potbellied?" a female voice responded.

Ultaf forced his heavy eyes open. And then froze.

Above him, held by strange ethereal chains arising out of the stranger, was his kami, Sigrun. The ethereal wind-type marid was screeching and trying to escape in vain, but the shackles wouldn't let it get away.

"Are you going to kill it?" asked Bergott.

"No, I'll just let it go. It's a big world out there. Maybe it'll find someone better."

Ultaf watched, flabbergasted, as his kami vanished into the air, a translucent ripple the only sign of its passage.

"Oh, look, you're awake!" said Aguilar cheerfully. "Good for you. Elena knows where to find Zuken, so they're off doing that now. Guess that leaves you and me."

It was that polite, friendly tone again, Ultaf decided. It was like listening to someone simply making conversation with an old friend he had not met in a while. It told him that if this Aguilar wanted to kill him, he'd be finished off with no fuss whatsoever, not unlike squishing an ant.

"So, uh, the guards," asked Bergott, "why aren't they coming to help him?"

"Occlusion bubble," said Aguilar. "And Elena might have allayed them a little. Just enough to keep them distracted while we talk." He turned to Elena. "Where are the wardstones?"

"Seventh floor, downwards. They surround the Well," she said. "They're used to power both the wards and the rift. If you can destabilize them, then . . ."

"The entire system cascades to one massive failure," Aguilar muttered. "I'm almost annoyed at how disgustingly easy that is. It's like they're asking for someone to come damage their property. How are you going to get to Zuken?"

The changeling smirked, walked over to the left end of the room, and pressed her palm to the mirror. Ultaf stared in horror as his secret escape door opened, revealing his private elevator system. How did she—*wait*, she had attacked his mind. But he hadn't felt any psionic intrusion. All he had seen was . . .

A wave of static threatened to overwhelm his vision, and suddenly, it hurt to think.

"Awesome," said Aguilar. "Get Zuken out. Send the signal if you need help. Or wait for my signal. Whichever comes first."

"What's the signal?" asked Bergott.

Aguilar smirked. "Don't worry. When it hits, you'll feel it."

"What are you planning?" The changeling frowned and shook her head. "Never mind. I don't want to know." She looked at the door. "We're going to need a distraction, though. Too many guards otherwise."

"Distractions, my dear," said Aguilar, looking at Ultaf, filling him with fresh horror, "are a sort of specialty of mine."

And then, before Ultaf realized what was happening, the monster grabbed him by his collar and hurled him out of the office like so much trash. He gasped and whimpered as he landed with terrific force, and then bounced, flipped, skidded, and rolled nearly twenty feet. The first *snap* was merely surprising. By the fifth, he was becoming alarmed, wondering if he would even survive the day. His body smashed against the wall on the other end, and Ultaf fell, vomiting blood all over the floor.

His only saving grace was that he was outside, and the majority of the guards were now rushing towards him.

"Sir? What happened?"

"They're inside," Ultaf croaked through his damaged windpipe. "Don't let them flee."

He heard the guard captain yell, ordering his men to take down the vagrant like the worthless piece of trash he was.

Multiple wind orbs—each of them easily Level 3—wind blades capable of piercing through walls, and a fireball the size of a small igriott were hurled at the intruder and exploded with a thunderous detonation, followed by an explosion that all but blinded Ultaf. He strongly doubted that his office had survived taking the brunt of that attack, but the feeling was squashed by the sense of triumph that now coursed through him. An attack like that was enough to send an enemy flank flying. No doubt the vagrant had died a horrible death.

Ultaf blinked.

Standing between the man and the attacks was an offending layer of shiny metal, easily fifteen feet high, covering the entire doorway. Its surface rippled into an undulating formation and looked absolutely no worse for wear.

The wind blades ricocheted against it.

The pressurized blasts and fireballs exploded against it, yielding no results.

The warriors barged into it, only to be thrown back.

The swords shattered against it.

And all through it, the metal wall remained, fluttering like a curtain, keeping those behind it safe.

"What is that thing?" asked a guard. "Did we get the bastard?"

"Oh, I assure you," came Aguilar's voice from the other side, "the bastard is quite safe and sound."

Ultaf watched with widened eyes as the curtain cleaved in the middle, allowing the vagrant to walk through. He looked utterly dispassionate as if oblivious of the danger around him. It was as if he truly believed he wasn't in any danger here. Ultaf wondered how a single man could ever be so foolish.

No matter. It would only bring his end faster.

"Redirection of force," said the vagrant. "Nifty, isn't it? Why the sheer number of applications—"

"DIE!" roared one of Ultaf's warrior personnel, rushing at him with a great sword. The monster casually grabbed his hand mid-swing, and the next moment, a headless body fell upon the floor, the head rolling all the way to where Ultaf lay fallen.

Aguilar threw the sword away and looked down at the decapitated corpse with a scowl.

He's toying with me, Ultaf realized with horror. Aguilar had thrown him away just so that he could tear through his guards, then claim him again. Like an igriott playing with its prey.

"Where I come from, it's considered bad manners to interrupt someone while they're talking."

Ultaf blinked.

"Whatever." The monster sighed, examining his fingers, and frowning as he noted the blood splattered all over them. A tiny burst of wind escaped him, and the blood vanished.

"Much better . . . Say, what would you say to a ceasefire? Just let me walk away with Banksi and these two. That way you don't have to fight me, and I don't have to kill you."

"KILL HIM!" roared a soldier.

Aguilar sighed. "This really doesn't need to be that difficult."

He snapped his fingers, and the chamber exploded, followed by an earth-shattering detonation. By the time Ultaf's vision returned in blotches of rear-ranging color, it was already too late.

What . . . he thought as an icy feeling settled within his chest. *What by Amaterasu is that demon?*

The ornate pillars, the enchanted walls, *everything* had crashed. And in the epicenter of the blast, a colossal black form loomed. Taller than the eye could see. And it was still forming.

Its jaws were metal, its flesh as dark as the accursed shadows themselves. Horns sprouted out of its crown like demented protrusions. Blood-red eyes glared out of sunken sockets, the light in them something maddeningly primordial.

Slowly, the demented beast's full form took shape. It took a single step, and the floor gave way, the enchanted stone shattering in the wake of this beast's power, the slabs rising like upturned coffins, ready to swallow every single living being above it.

Another step.

Ultaf saw its reptilian form, its tail thicker than three bremetans huddled together.

It lifted its maw and *roared.*

Those closest to it instantly dropped down unconscious with blood trickling down from their eyes and noses. Ultaf didn't fare any better, his heart throbbing against his broken ribs and his body shaking as his skin felt like it was being pierced by thousands of sharp needles as a hammer blow of pressure slammed into his face.

Whatever remained of his guards now stood rooted in shock. Their attention was riveted by the beast, but Ultaf only had eyes for the lone figure standing next to the massive destroyer—small and seemingly inconsequential compared to the giant next to him. It didn't help that there were a dozen guards lying on the floor, their bodies charred to husks, and their kami exploding out of them and escaping into the very air itself.

The reptilian being moved, and then all around him, the guards began to die.

As much as Lukas Aguilar scared him, there was a part of Olfric fascinated by seeing him cut loose and mean it for once. He had heard tales of Lukas's exploits in the borderland and then against the yokai leader and a wraith of a certain yokai empress, but there had always been a line Lukas hadn't crossed with them.

So, when he saw Lukas hurl Ultaf out of the room like so much dead meat, with guards swarming into the room like flies, Olfric knew he had to *duck*.

The former Bergott heir grabbed Elena and hurled himself to the ground.

The guards attacking him held no such compunction. They were elite warriors, spiritists, and monster tamers. They were part of one of the most powerful brigades in the Empire and didn't have the flexibility to understand what was about to happen even as it was happening. They rushed towards the door, mana swirling in their bodies as they prepared for the assault.

Until the first of many of them were decapitated without so much as a word from Lukas.

And then the world around them shattered as Aguilar's black metallic sludge erupted, morphing into that nightmarish beast. Olfric couldn't even see the head from his vantage point, but its muscles were so massive and corded that they bordered on the grotesque, exuding an aura of sheer, mindless, impossible power. Its two hindlimbs ended in a massive tail, which tore Ultaf's office apart with a single swish before it moved forward.

It was like standing in front of an oncoming hurricane, frozen in fear and awe by the unimaginable destructive potential and the prospect of certain death.

A monster? No, this was a *destroyer*. A being whose only purpose was the obliteration of life, its only goal to choose a target and attack, attack, attack with relentless fury and unstoppable force until that target was nothing but dead meat inside its massive jaws, and then to choose another target and another and another until there was nothing in its vicinity but blood and gore and death.

Like moths to a flame, scores of guards rushed in from all directions. They were met with the sight of this ginormous beast and a single man standing next to it, looking practically lackadaisical as he welcomed them with a smile.

"Tanya told me you were a disagreeable lot," Lukas said and Olfric heard the annoyance in his tone. "I was really trying to keep you alive. But that's fine I guess." Blob *roared*.

A single slap of the tail brought the walls down. The guards jerked and twisted, firing elemental attacks as the demonic beast found them. Blood fountained into the air. Limbs were torn from shoulders and hips. Bodies crumpled, then came apart as giant openings larger than the size of their heads formed on their bodies, the rest of their organs slipping through them and splattering all over the floor.

Olfric stared at it. His stunned mind had finally begun to process the information in detail. The giant reptilian beast striding unflappably through the chamber, tearing down droves of soldiers with the air of a wolf hunting rabbits, was one of Lukas's creations, crafted at the spur of the moment and brought into existence to do his bidding. It shouldn't have been possible to create sentience out of nothing, but he supposed nobody had told Aguilar that.

Suddenly, Zuken's musings about Lukas Aguilar being an actual demigod began to make a lot more sense. And if he really was one then—

He was interrupted by a distressingly strong hand slapping him across his face.

"Elena?" he muttered, flabbergasted.

"I yelled your name out four times," she chastised him, while also rubbing her palm. "And what's your face made of—*iron*? I felt like I was slapping a metal door."

"I always knew you were a hands-on kind of girl, Elena," said Lukas, grinning and seeming to ignore the fact that they were currently cornered by enemies inside a warded enemy fortress.

Elena stuck out her tongue at him. Then, she turned to Olfric. "We need to find Zuken. Let him deal with them."

Olfric blinked. Elena had it backward. It was the soldiers that would have to deal with Aguilar, not the reverse. Still, there was one question he felt that he absolutely needed to ask.

"Uh, Lukas," he said tentatively, "how many do you think we need to kill before they surrender?"

The man's smile didn't reach his eyes. "Ask me again after this is over."

CHAPTER 14

Shock was always the most important aspect of warfare. From ancient to modern history, it had always been the crux upon which battles changed from utter defeat to overwhelming victory. In medieval times, it was provided by the cavalry arm of each faction. Armored lancers astride massive horses, thundering down upon the poor, unfortunate souls that made up the infantry line. The initial impact of thousands of pounds of horse flesh and armored rider inflicted such horrendous damage—such psychological shock—that entire formations of men would break and run.

It would be followed by volleys of arrows shooting from the sky, aiming for the escaping soldiers.

The modern world had changed from cavalry and archers to fighter jets and missiles. A single detonation of the first atomic bomb had ended the war. Biological weapons, nuclear warheads, terrorist sleeper cells—the methods had evolved but the psychology behind them remained the same: Shock the enemy into inaction.

When Lukas hurled Ultaf out like a dishrag, he had inflicted shock on the protectors standing guard in the antechamber. They were in the heart of Shimizu territory, surrounded by powerful spiritists and men of power. Never in a hundred years would anyone expect a metal dinosaur exploding out of the walls and tearing them apart with its jaws and fire.

Twelve men. Dead. Just like that. Blob swirled its large tail around, leaving a trail of bifurcated corpses in its path. Wherever its body swung, cloven body parts fell around it in a rain of gore.

Back when he had found himself in the anomaly, such a thing would have paralyzed him—the idea of killing other people and *relishing* in the knowledge that their deaths made him just a little bit stronger. But back then, he wasn't aware of just how dire the situation actually was.

That was before he had rampaged through the Crypt of Fiendish Worms.

Before he had traveled across dozens and dozens of worlds, murdering monsters, collecting Experience, and, if he found them interesting enough, siphoning them into his inner-world while on his path to finding strength.

Even then, it had been easy to justify. *Those were monsters, not people.*

But didn't monsters, too, have lives? Didn't they also have dreams, plans, a family to call their own? Did they also not seek to grow? When he had committed genocide on several borderlands in his attempt to grow stronger, had he not killed the chances of their species' ability to uplift themselves? What right did he have to cut them down like so much dead meat, when being asked to kill something that looked like a fellow human being caused him to hesitate?

He was an anomaly. To an anomaly, all creatures—monsters, demons, gods—were prey.

Soldiers killed other soldiers on the battlefield. Religious fanatics butchered in the name of their god. Twisted, yes, but at least they had something to pass the blame to.

Lukas had no one. Unlike on Earth, humanity wasn't the apex of the food chain here, and these people weren't human, no matter how much they may have looked it.

They were *bremetans.*

And he was an anomaly. Their natural predator.

There will be time for morality once you reach the apex, Inanna had once told him.

He paused in his line of thought and snapped his hand down, cutting a man into two, vertically. Two equal, diametrically perfect halves flopped to the ground.

You have crossed the Threshold Barrier
Level-Up Initiated!

And immediately after . . .

Level-Up Delayed until PRIME HOST is in Stand-By

The ironic thing about the Peak was, for all its defensive fortifications, Mujin Shimizu was its greatest power—its main deterrent against invasion. Very few people would want to infiltrate a place so powerfully warded only to find a bloodthirsty warlord residing inside. Not that the protections were weak, but compared to his overwhelming might, they felt like a complementary addition at best.

Getting Mujin away, even if it was only for a few hours, was a deciding factor in this plan. Shogun Naowa had taken care of that, and Ultaf's own ego had opened doors to an onslaught he couldn't possibly have ever imagined happening even in his worst nightmares.

More guards had arrived and reacted, but it was too late. The fear and confusion had set in. Their power was halved by their utter loss of composure as they shouted and ran around in general confusion. The more experienced ones were attacking while their partners were busy defending them with shields of force and metal, attacking Blob with weapons that didn't even scratch his outer shell.

The key was to layer shock on top of Blob's already imposing stature. To build a sense of invulnerability around this beast of fire and metal while tearing down the opposing side's confidence. To inflict so much psychological and physical damage that the enemy would be fundamentally incapable of continuing the combat.

That is why he had derived Blob's physiological baseline from the giganotosaurus while adding some extra physiological characteristics, such as the infrasonic roar of the neothelid, adjusted to a frequency that instantly impaired the sympathetic system and worked perfectly with the massively strong vocal cords of the dinosaur prototype. The bylestyr's ability with fire and Blob's own anti-mana constitution only made things worse for the soldiers. The result was a deadly combination that any army would hesitate to take on, even on a good day.

The soldiers were finally doing what they should have done to begin with. Aeromancers were casting shields to protect themselves and hurling precision attacks to penetrate the metallic hide, and pyromancers taking control of Blob's flames to conjure their own attacks—but the shock had clearly gotten to them. The sheer horror of what was being done to them had turned their ability to reason logically upside down.

What should have been precision missiles materialized as brittle things hitting all over the place. Meanwhile, the pyromancers' attempts to manipulate the flames were sloppy, and they gave little care as to how their actions might impact the other spiritists.

Lukas himself was the final piece of the puzzle. He stalked through them like a perverse predator. A man wielding a large axe came running at him. He grabbed it mid-swing, spun it around, and hacked the man through the abdomen, walking through the space as the two halves fell to the ground, all the while smiling at Ultaf who looked like he would have fainted had his mind not been paralyzed by the horror he was witnessing.

Gathered +2141 Experience

The shock in the man's eyes represented a vital question:

Why was he doing this?

He could have told himself it was to free Zuken and to take vengeance for his sufferings. Ultaf was a madman high on power, who had massacred the svartalfar race. Surely that was enough grounds to kill him and level his army.

Or perhaps it was about Tanya. Tanya who he loved, and who had been mercilessly hunted for years by Ultaf and Mujin. He could have sold himself the story that he was humiliating this bastard and giving him a taste of his own medicine—that by destroying his men, wasting his castle, and leaving him an utter wreck, he was making an example out of him. Showing the other people in power that having power didn't make them immortal or above justice.

But he wasn't there for that, either.

Tanya had told him how Mujin had turned his soldiers into flesh puppets that followed his will to the letter. For Lukas, who valued freedom over all else, who had rejected the goddess Inanna's offer of vassalage several times in the past, who had spat in the face of yokai, monsters, anomalies, and the shard of an empress because they had wanted to dominate over another's will, such an existence was absolutely abhorrent. It sickened him.

By killing them, he was bestowing upon them an act of mercy. It would not be painless. They wouldn't even know why he was doing it. They would think of him as a monster until their dying breaths. But . . .

They would be at peace. In death. The only peace they would ever know.

Lukas could have sold himself that story as well.

But he didn't.

The truth was that he was a man seeking power. He wasn't there to save Zuken nor to humiliate or possibly kill Ultaf. He wasn't there for Tanya's vengeance nor for inflicting justice upon the Shimizu for their vile actions. And, despite how much he would have wanted to say it, he wasn't there to bring relief to those tortured souls serving as the protectors of this fortress.

No, he was here for power. Somewhere deep in the darkness of his heart, a voice was telling him that the Peak housed more than two thousand men, plus legions of beasts. That even if he slaughtered a fraction of them, the Level-Ups he would gain would be significant. Easily enough to bridge the gap between himself and the warlord.

Even if it meant he was committing deliberate, calculated murder.

The least he could do was own it.

Like Inanna said, he'd have all the time in the world to deal with morality once he was at the top. And whatever he needed to do to get there, he would do it.

So, he slaughtered them. And just killing the enemy wasn't enough. He needed to systematically rearrange the landscape to send a message. He needed to make the opposition know that there was no place in this world they could hide where he would not find and annihilate them. Blob kept slashing and gobbling up multiple attackers while smashing through the stone pillars and ornately carved architecture of the garrison.

Killing the enemy was good. Killing the enemy in the most brutal ways possible was better. The shock factor grew exponentially.

Meanwhile the toll kept rising further.

Gathered +7741 Experience
Gathered +12867 Experience
Gathered +8894 Experience

And on and on.

He needed to drive the point home that he was the most dangerous and overwhelming force these men had ever faced. He had to inflict a horror so terrible upon a relative few that the rest would immediately lay down their weapons and surrender.

He watched several soldiers whipping blades of intense pressure at Blob's giant reptilian form. A single hit from even *one* of those could cut a stone wall in half. A bright red beam of intense flame careened towards the towering figure; a warhammer-wielding warrior capable of knocking his target senseless for a week with a single blow came for it.

The blades slashed against the beast's neck. The red beam hit through its jaw. The hammer slammed against its knees.

The slashes melded into fluid, metallic skin.

The red, half-molten jaw re-formed.

The hammer was pushed back with equal force, flinging the warrior back.

Lukas watched in morbid fascination as his dinosaur snapped off the upper half of a man's body and ate it in a single gulp, leaving the remainder spurting blood, painting the floor red. One of the soldiers tried to stick a flaming sword into the beast's gut, only for the sword to be pulled into it.

Claws wreathed in flames cleaved through him a second later.

Blades of wind, torrents of flames, and overpowered bursts of raw power struck it but could barely manage to halt it for half a second before a loud roar caused almost half the warriors to fall down to the ground, grabbing their heads and crying in agony.

"It's a demon! Summoned from the pits of Yomi by that madman!" yelled a guard. "Kill him and the demon will die."

"Please," Lukas said. "Believe that with all your hearts. It will only make ending you easier."

The guard roared and came at him, warhammer in hand. He leaped at him midair, only to pause, as if frozen. Then, the guard crumpled down to the floor, unmoving.

"Why are you in such a hurry to die?"

Lukas took a moment to register the irony that, for someone who went out of his way to avoid a fight, he ended up taking up the mantle of executioner more often than not. First the Crypt, then the borderland and now this . . .

Despite being racked with guilt at the realization of what he was about to do, despite the fact that taking another life was absolutely antithetical to everything he stood for, the moment he had started massacring the soldiers, lifeforce had blazed through him. More than anything else, it just felt *right* to be the one slaughtering, cutting through hordes of armies, tearing through them apart without care or concern. Was this what felt like to be Inanna?

His eyes scanned the crowd and found Ultaf gone. Clearly some of the guards had escaped with him. No matter. He'd find him soon enough. Speaking of—

Level-Up Delayed until PRIME HOST is in Stand-By
3 Level-Ups in sequence

"Blob," he commanded. "Come to me."

Blob the dinosaur roared again, unleashing a sea of flames from its open maw, killing several dozen more of its prey, before dispersing into liquid metal, and flying up to him, cocooning every inch of his body, melding with it—a fluid suit of armor concealing him from head to toe.

Aqāru was an excellent conduit for lifeforce and mana, and with his ability to alter its chemical constitution, it could be harder than titanium, as long as he could keep it powered. It channeled the power directly from his omphalos reserves and powered up his body to epic proportions. And the weirdest part? It felt strangely *alive.*

It was just like the Crypt's omphalos had predicted. Lukas supposed it was a cruel irony that, after rejecting the Crypt's offer to fuse and become a greater entity, he was on the path of accomplishing the same.

I am not the kind to go gently into the night.

It had told him so in its last moments.

I am becoming you. Becoming us.
I am you. You are me.
We are the future.

"Really," said Lukas, laughing, "I hope you're watching this, Crypt."

He closed his eyes.

The metal flesh rippled and warped, flexing and changing colors from steel gray to a hybrid gold to an intense burning crimson and then back to steel.

> **Maximize Sympathization Ratio**
> **Accessing monster prototypes based on desired Skills**
> **Altering and repurposing structure while maintaining integrity**

The first time he had put on the suit, it had been a lot easier to deal with. Especially because there was no downside to it all. Killing monsters was fun and mindless. He was siphoning new prototypes, traveling through borderlands, and gaining levels. But the more he used it, the more he felt schizophrenic. On the one hand, there was the logical part. The anomaly, Blob, the suit. He saw scans, patterns, and sequences. He made calculations based on raw information and probability—cause and effect. On the other hand, was the illogical part—Lukas, the human. He saw hopes and dreams, people of faith, creatures fighting to save their kin even if they ended up getting slaughtered. Those two sides were at constant war with each other, fighting over what to do next, who to save, who to spare, who to kill. He wanted to be the best man he could possibly be, a beacon of hope who could make a difference. And then there was the part of him that whispered that the good human was just an illusion, that the best man he could ever hope to be would tear everything down and start everything from scratch. Rebuild the world in his vision—fair . . . cold . . . inhuman.

The part that whispered that the fates of the hapless soldiers weren't his to worry about. He wasn't there to grant them salvation nor to save them. Victory was meaningless. As were the deaths. They were all a part of the process that he had to undertake to reach his desired end.

He was no soldier, fighting for his nation. He was no fanatic, fighting for his god. Here he was, committing endless slaughter, but neither blessing nor bane would touch him. Sin couldn't latch upon him either. Every step of his growth, every trial he underwent, had no individual meaning, yet they continued to shape the World within him.

He was a tyrant. He was an invader. A World that took from others and made itself more.

Executing and Forging complete.
Enact.

War came to the Peak.

There was no mercy in any of the weapons or attacks fired all over the castle—even if it was an entire army trying to kill one individual—and neither was there any victory when said weapons shattered and the attacks exploded uselessly, missing their target. Endless sprays of mana-fire perforated the air, piercing endlessly in straight lines chasing an errant flicker of steel. Slower but more noticeable were the blasts of fire, mana, and lightning that seemed to track the target's movements to the point that one could see them automatically correcting their paths mid-flight.

The sounds of beasts and the warriors fighting with weapons were loudest. The percussive impact of their launches and detonations were powerful enough to scramble a normal human's organs from anything short of a hundred meters away.

And yet, their target didn't fall as it flew and flailed through the air, partially due to the massive castle and its interiors serving as obstacles for the projectiles, and partly because none of them seemed to reach him at all.

Walls crumbled. Pillars shattered. Ceilings collapsed.

Nothing hit the target.

And that wasn't for lack of trying. The soldiers' constant barrage of spells and attacks was rearranging the entire terrain, but none connected with him. The himthursars came at him, oversized, frost-coated weapons in hand, a sharp contrast to the crude tools the muspel used. No doubt part of the Shimizu monster-breeding program.

"KILL HIM!" the soldiers yelled. "Attack him from all sides!"

Each of those beasts were easily ten feet tall, with massive, fur-lined bodies and gnarled, muscular limbs, stag-like horns growing out of their heads and thick, sharp fangs sprouting out of their jaws. Unlike their fire-breathing counterparts, himthursars were quite docile to begin with. However, they could also become furious when provoked, and that was when everything changed. Run away from them, face them head-on, beat them, bind them, get defeated by them . . . it didn't matter. Everything simply seemed to provoke more and more anger in them, strengthening their madness into unbridled, unrestrained, raw rage. And if that wasn't enough, the angrier they became, the more lifeforce they used and the stronger they got—at the cost of their sanity.

A true berserker.

The only peace an infuriated himthursar would ever find, was in death.

The least Lukas could do was get them there quickly.

Altering Skill Sets
Accessing svartalfar prototype

Body function was altered. New Skills were rising to the forefront, altering his fighting technique to suit the new targets.

Disappearing in a flash, Lukas appeared right in front of one of them, and drove his hand in their face. His armor extended into a sharp blade and tore through the creature's eyes. He spun around, slicing the neck of another creature to his left before sending a burst of raw force aimed for the knee of a third, blasting it off.

"You cocky bastard!" someone yelled. "You won't escape this place. We'll—"

It was quick to follow its compatriots in death soon after.

The time for restraint was gone. It was time to end it. After all, if he held back now . . .

Increasing Lifeforce Output by 120%
Increasing Mana Output by 270%
Removing Limiters . . .

. . . then when?

Seventy-six shards of aqāru shot out of his armor, altering themselves mid-flight into the shape of thick daggers aimed at the himthursars.

Asserting Anti-Friction
Altering chemical composition to vatuatil
Setting predetermined constant velocity
Setting predetermined targets

"Oh, you dirty little shit—"

"*Fire.*"

As though a cannon had gone off, the seventy-six nigh-indestructible daggers fired en masse and tore into man and monster alike, indiscriminately. The blades in themselves had little weight to them, but vatuatil was the sharpest substance he had ever come across, able to cut through bone like a hot knife through butter. With the anti-friction lining, and Kinetomancy powering their initial momentum to move at a high speed, regardless of external factors, their onslaught faced little opposition.

Gathered +48923 Experience!
Large number of prey located within scan radius

Lukas whistled. An entire contingent waiting on the other side? What kind of guest would he be if he kept his hosts waiting?

"Index and ring fingers," said Solana, looking at the dispersed stone remains. "The Asukan and the changeling have rescued Banksi, and they need help, and the Outsider is busy elsewhere . . ."

"Of course, Olfric's the first one that got in over his head," snapped Tanya, as she looked at the army behind her. "How soon can we move in?"

"Not as quickly as you think," said Solana, frowning. "Nihil and his group were supposed to have at least an hour to open a tear through the wards. Aguilar was supposed to deactivate the ward stones first."

"Don't have that much time on our hands," said Tanya. "For all we know, someone alerted my grandfather. We're on a time constraint, so I'll improvise."

"Improvise?" demanded Solana, annoyed. "You can't rift before Aguilar clears the central courtyard for you to rift *through*."

"Won't be rifting," said Tanya. "I'll tear my way through the wards. Tell your people to get ready to move in."

"Don't be stupid. The wards are powered by ley lines. Without shutting down the wardstones, nothing short of a Level-5 hit can affect them."

Tanya smirked. Two weeks ago, she would have been in complete agreement. But Empress Meynte had shown her a different technique. Without bothering to explain, she raised both hands forward. Between her palms, a sphere of devastation appeared—an orb of tremendous pressure, held in place by madness just as deadly.

She couldn't have explained to anyone what she did. She wasn't sure that she understood it herself, at least on a conscious level. She simply *gathered* the essence of Everfrost and fed it to the Wind core in the center, grinning as it began to take it in, becoming more and yet *less* at the same time.

The shot she lined up was perfect. If her father were there, he would have praised her. Her stance, mental draw, and release were fluid and perfect.

"*WIND SHEAR!*"

The aerodynamic implosion missile cut through the air, and only after it had been gone for half a second did the noise of its passing actually meet their ears, a strange warbling howl as it twisted through the air, spinning with impossible intensity, the force of its turning so great that just its passing struck the area around it like a physical blow.

It took six more seconds for Wind Shear to cross the distance between her and the ward barrier, the missile arching upward on a parabolic path that took it far above the highest peak in the area, and then it began its descent, howling its belated war cry as it homed in on its target.

There was no thunderous detonation. No flames reaching towards the skies. Nothing.

Instead, a ripple of *something* spread from the epicenter of the blast and then—

"There is a . . . rupture in the ward," whispered Solana, her intense gaze on her face. "And . . . it isn't closing."

"This is inconceivable," Maude murmured, shaking her head slowly. The perimeter ward was still up there, but there was a tiny crack where the missile had struck. It wasn't enough to let even a single person pass, but the fact that the rupture remained was more than stupefying.

"I only do one thing," Tanya said softly, preparing her next shot. "But what I do, I am the best at."

"I see," said Solana. "From the empress's memories?"

"Something like that," said Tanya, smirking.

"You've got to be quick, Tanya," said Maude. "Aguilar is strong, but he can only hold on for so long."

Tanya snorted.

"You think he's too strong?" asked Solana, little flickers of annoyance in her dark eyes. "He defeated the empress, yes, but don't forget that she was held back by your body's limitations."

The top left portion of the fortress erupted violently with a flash so bright that it would have put a bolt of lightning to shame. Layers upon layers of protective wards sprung into existence, trying to block the power from escaping— a classic case of an unstoppable force against an immovable object, the shockwave from the collision blowing the rooftop into splinters.

And then it exploded again.

And this time the wards didn't just intercept the might of the attack, they *detonated*, silvery flames roaring upwards, leaving a sickly, grayish void in the sky.

An army of several hundred soldiers met Lukas's assault.

The battalions around him were spread resourcefully in camps, surrounding him from all three sides. The first five rows of soldiers held spear-like things nearly twenty-feet long that required two hands. Lukas had faced them before so knew that they could shoot energy blasts out of the pointy ends and were this world's equivalent of guns—heavy and not easily maneuverable, but the sheer firepower made up for the lack of flexibility. Analysis told him that the only thing protecting them from any wide-area attacks were the remarkably strong defensive enchantments on their scale mails.

That is, assuming someone could get past their suppressive fire and reach them. Then there were the spiritists—pyromancers with flaming arrows aimed at him, aeromancers with vacuum missiles arched and ready, swordsmen dressed in chain mail from head to toe, rows of igriotts and their tamers. And that wasn't counting those outside his range of vision, attacking him from afar.

Number of Prey within Scan Radius: 917

Overwhelming through quantity? No doubt they had come up with this after watching him battle. The strategist in him approved.

"We've been waiting for you, Vagrant," called out Ultaf Shimizu from behind the safety of his armored vehicle. That he was able to talk so soon spoke volumes about his healing skill. Or maybe he had had some healer rejuvenate him. Didn't matter either way.

"Darling," said Lukas, "we must stop meeting like this. This is how rumors get started."

"Surrender," yelled the Shimizu prince. "You face the might of the Shimizu army. Surrender and your death will be quick."

"That's not much of an incentive, is it?"

For someone who had been crying like a child earlier, he does sound awfully confident, mused Lukas. Inwardly, he was already scanning the entire area, analyzing what it was he was about to face and what he could work with.

The floor is thick. Too thick. Warded against Terramancy, and the energy source is . . . on the other side. I doubt they planned it for me, which means . . . There's something interesting over there.

He ran a deeper Scan.

Energy Drain Sources detected
Downward distance: 40 feet

In Screen-speak, "energy drain sources" could only refer to one thing only—wardstones. If he could access them, he could deactivate the perimeter wards and let Solana's forces in.

But digging through forty feet of reinforced stone would take time. Doubly with him having to throw every bit of his strength into defense should the army around him attack him all at once. He was pretty sure his motion barrier could hold them off for five seconds, but it wouldn't be enough time for him to smash his way through the floor to the other side.

Plus, it lacked style, and . . .

He paused and reconsidered what he had just learned. The more he dwelled on it, the more the discovery took on newer meaning and purpose. Options that he hadn't seen before were now available. He could work with this or not. It would be a nasty thing, and the part of him that still differentiated between right and wrong would be devastated by it but . . .

. . . this could be a game changer.

He held out his right hand and Blob lazily slid away from his entire body, forming a thick metal staff that he clenched his fingers around. Spinning the heavy staff a couple of times, Lukas then smashed it down into the floor and left it there.

The army took it as a sign of surrender and eased up just a little.

Set boundaries, Lukas inwardly commanded. *Neutered Earth. Six-inch radial diameter. Downward expansion.*

Interesting thing about wards. They were quite effective when used right away but once you figured out their limitations, they were also quite easy to work around. The anti-Terramancy barrier would instantly dissipate any and all earth mana employed within the warded surface, but it would do nothing if he proceeded the mundane way.

And it didn't make a distinction if said mundane way was done by hand or through a living metal operating as an extension of a walking, breathing anomaly.

He regarded Ultaf. "I don't suppose you're up for a five-minute break, are you?"

Despite himself, Ultaf's eyes twitched in frustration. "A—are you mocking me, Vagrant?"

"I just took out 114 of your guys without breaking a sweat. It's a legitimate question."

The funny part was, he actually gave this fifty-fifty odds. The arrogant noble type like Ultaf never paid attention to the subtext. He'd refuse the break time and instead mock him and engage in meaningless banter that would cost him the same amount of time.

It took a while for Ultaf to get past his indecision. Lukas didn't know if it was because he was rooted in fear or if he was just stunned at the proposition.

"Do you take me for a fool, dog?" the Shimizu snapped with a growl. "It's obvious you're on your last legs. Fighting my legion of himthursars had to have wasted all your mana. Do not think you can fool me into giving you the chance to recuperate."

"Yes, because someone who wanted to recuperate would willingly land in the middle of an army and plant his weapon in the ground."

"I see," Lukas rasped out disapprovingly. It wasn't hard to fake, considering how put off he was with his own plan. "You think I'll just give up and surrender."

"You have no choice," said Ultaf, his usual smugness returning with every passing second. "Give up. Your associates are already captured. Surrender, or they'll be cut down like swine."

Liar, Lukas thought. Olfric had sent a signal through the gemstones, and Tanya was already on his side of the fence.

But Ultaf didn't know that.

He was clearly the kind to grab a mile when offered an inch.

"Captured, you say?" he asked. "And Zuken?"

"Still in his prison. Where else?"

"And . . . if I surrender, you'll set them free?"

"*Of course*," he said in an oily tone of voice.

Liar, thought Lukas again. The Screen flickered right then.

Energy Drain Source detected
Establishing connection . . .

About time.

"You have some power in you, Vagrant," said Ultaf, his voice reverberating across the arena. "You are young and powerful, but serving under me could make you stronger. You could become one of our most formidable fighters," he said softly. "There is almost nothing that would be denied to you."

Lukas feigned a moment of consideration.

"Nothing you say . . ."

"Absolutely," Ultaf purred. "Whatever riches and facilities the changeling promised you and Lady Kandra, I can match it and more. Wealth, property, weapons, Skills, coin. We are one of the Sacred Eight, after all. You would be welcome among my elite ranks."

"And I'd get all that by serving you?" Lukas asked doubtfully, tilting his head as he examined him.

Ultaf smiled and spread his arms. "Yes. Absolutely. All I need you to do is surrender."

Another notification. Blob had already bloated up to 70% of its capacity. *Just a little more . . .*

Lukas tapped his chin and pretended to consider that. "Tempting, but I believe I have a better option."

The smarmy smile on the man's face twisted into a frown of consternation. "Which is?"

"I can just kill you."

The soldiers tensed, their resolve shaken by how casually a single man they had surrounded had thrown out that ultimatum. Ultaf's eyes narrowed, a sneer forming on his face even as Lukas said, "In case I wasn't clear, that was a threat. In exactly one minute from now, you and your little hunting party will become the prey. Now, based on past experience, you couldn't manage to subdue me even when I held back. I'd recommend you heed my warning."

Initiate Reverse Shift.

And right then, the World seemed to be trying to contort itself, as though it were being sucked through a black hole with no discernable point even while gravity remained unchanged. Lukas himself almost swore as he experienced vertigo a dozen times over in an instant, and he wasn't even the target of the Reverse Shift guzzling through the raw energy of the World.

Judging from the way the entire structure around him let out a hollow, almost mechanical groan that shook the hallways and the floor itself, it felt it, too.

"Well, gentlemen," said Lukas, offering his hand as if for a dance, "shall we?"

The army took that as provocation and responded with deadly force just as he grabbed his Blob-staff.

It was over in an instant.

Scores of wind blades, dozens of fireballs and flaming arrows, lances of lightning and sharpened blocks of stone were thrown at him. Their attack came from every angle, leaving no room to maneuver or escape. There was no hesitation or imperfection in their forms. Their coordination was perfect as well—impossibly so.

It didn't matter.

Before any of them could so much as blink, a bloody mist erupted into the air, painting the floor crimson as the bifurcated corpses of the front row of soldiers fell to the ground, their attacks exploding before they even reached their midpoint.

Gathered +17738 Experience

He could understand their confusion. Hell, his staff was still rooted to the floor. Before any of them could respond or comprehend what had just happened, Lukas thrust his free hand in an arc, and flames began randomly erupting around soldiers, scorching and burning them to ashes. They weren't exactly as potent as the dranzithl's white flames but enough to critically injure those whose physical strength and endurance didn't exceed that of the average Level-2 muspel. It threw the soldiers into a frenzy. Unprepared, they couldn't decide whether to step away from each other and break formation or attack him and risk being immolated.

Ultaf let out a bellow of rage and pointed a dagger at Lukas, a bolt of furious energy leaping out of the weapon and shooting towards him. It hit the edge of his motion barrier and fizzled out like a wet firecracker.

"Wow," Lukas drawled. "I knew you were kinda weak, but you didn't have to go so out of your way to prove me right."

"YOU—" the man bellowed. "When I get my hands on you, I'll . . . I'll . . ."

"Do nothing," said Lukas coldly. "Because there's nothing you *can* do." He smirked at Ultaf's flabbergasted expression, the man's impotent fury trying to get past his fear. "So listen to my words carefully. Look around. Look at the snowy peak, this falling fortress, the dying men, the blood, the fire . . . Take in these sights. I assure you, they will be your last."

The army greeted him with a wall of spears, encircling and trapping him within its unforgiving embrace. They left no gap in their ranks, no weaknesses that could be exploited, and allowed no attack to slip by their guard, while they kept firing elemental blasts from the tips of their spears. Lukas instantly crafted a motion barrier around himself to deflect the incoming barrage from all sides.

Their strategy was clear: They would close in on him step by step, shrinking whatever little space he had until he was forced to defend himself with his fullest might: any attempt to attack would cost him his defense. The ground was warded against Terraportation, so he'd be forced to either fly into the air, where he'd be vulnerable to attacks from the spiritists ready to snipe him from all sides, or remain on the ground and be skewered by the spears. Either choice would lead to his doom.

It should've been a flawless strategy, simple in both plan and execution.

Lukas smiled. They really should have run when they had the chance.

Rapid-Installing monster prototype DRANZITHL

"Maximum Boundary Limit. Use Decay Effect. Expansion."

And a little over *four hundred* soldiers of the fortress's army were robbed of their lives in an instant.

---

417 Prey Eliminated!
Gathered +4,59,754 Experience!
Host Body Placed in Stand-By
Number of Level-Ups: 10

Tanya didn't so much as blink at the pain searing through her arms as she exposed herself once again to the antithesis of Potential that was assaulting her body and mind, squirreling just a tiny amount of it away into Reality. Her blood was both freezing and boiling at the same time, the Taboo punishing her very being as she shot it out in the form of another missile.

Just like before, no sound, no explosion. But the rupture enlarged. This was her third hit, and it already looked large enough to allow two people to pass through it at a time. And the best part? The hole remained despite the rest of the wards staying up and active all around.

Accumulation of Aberrance. That was how Meynte had put it. The more exceptions to a Rule of the World existed in one place, the more magnified their effects became.

Such a lopsided thing Everfrost was. When applied to a living being, it sucked its lifeforce and consumed its potential. When exposed to mana, it acted like a natural counter to it, regardless of the element involved. And when facing the tyrant that was the raw natural energy of the World, it acted like an insulated brick—allowing nothing to pass through it, and instead deflecting it in a better direction.

Overall, it was pretty boring compared to the kind of explosions her lover was causing inside, but Tanya was happy to contribute in her own way. The presentation needed work, but in the end . . . All that mattered was results.

She breathed in and out slowly, her arms feeling like someone had replaced them with heavy metal clubs. Her ears were popping and protesting from the violent pressure, and it even hurt to keep her eyes open.

She didn't pay it any mind.

"Are you alright?" asked Maude.

Tanya took a moment to breathe, seeing the yokai army enter the hole into the impregnable fortress. "I . . . I need to go help Elena and Olfric." She looked at Solana. "Make sure to grab everything you want and get out before Lukas gives the final signal."

"Anything I should take care of?" asked Solana.

"Tell them not to get in Lukas's way."

"Your faith in the Outsider's abilities will someday bring you ruin, girl."

Tanya chuckled. "My grandfather had a saying: 'Encountering people of extraordinary power changes people. Fighting them, surviving them, even more so.' Lukas, more than anyone else I know, has lived through that experience in a very short span of time. Less than a year ago, he'd have perished from a single stab to his neck. And look at him now."

As if to emphasize her point, the entire mountain housing the fortress groaned. Nobody could tell if it was stronger or louder than the previous explosions as the standard eardrum wasn't designed to take in such violently chaotic sounds at this range, but it struck hard all the same.

"This is just the beginning, you know," said Tanya, smirking as she prepared to shoot into the sky and join her lover in battle. "From here on, Lukas will only grow more dangerous and terrible. And his opponents will try even harder, and he will only be more dangerous and more terrible for it. If you all have the sense, and I know you do, you have seen it. You have felt it. I might be the one to wield Ezzeron, and I may be the future Lady of the Shimizu after all this is over, but make no mistake, it will be Lukas who'll have defeated my grandfather in battle, shattered his bones, torn his kami away from him. I might be the one to strike the killing blow, but the deed will be his."

"Are you claiming he's a threat to us?" asked Solana.

"I'm saying no such thing," said Tanya. "Lukas is a kind person. Too kind for the shit he's dealing with. To the point of being a flat-out fool at times. But he isn't unreasonable, and he likes to help people if they ask for it, without expecting anything in return. You have tricked and deceived him from the start, captured him, forced him to fight for his life, bound him in unreasonable, and tricked me—someone he cares for—into being possessed by Meynte. And yet, he's being civil with you. That's just the kind of person he is."

Solana glared back at her with irritation.

"We both know how he was when he first arrived in our world, Solana. And in these few months, he has battled more things that most people face in their entire lifetimes. Yes, he has his own priorities, which he will go to the end of the world and spit in the face of monsters, yokai, Asukans, bylestyrs, emperors, kings, even *gods*, to achieve. They are not unreasonable, immoral, or unrealistic, at least for him. But that hasn't changed the fact that he faced everything he did, passed through every impossible obstacle that this world threw in his path, just to stay true to his goals. *And he won.*"

She smirked at the skinwalker's caustic expression, as her feet left the ground. "Food for thought."

Above all else, choose victory.

That was the motto Mujin Shimizu had taught Ultaf as a child.

There was no honor in defeat. No triumph in one's destruction. Honor died a dog's death, drops of blood smeared onto grass from the enemy's blade. It helped that the number of people capable of challenging him, telling him to reign it in, and didn't discover their heads being cleaved from their shoulders a moment later were few and rare.

Unfortunately, the person standing before Ultaf was one of those rare few.

And Ultaf wasn't his grandfather.

He watched as a single spell, a single wave of tumultuous power, and multiple flanks of soldiers dropped dead.

Just like that.

"D-demon . . ." he slurred through shocked lips. "Demon . . ."

Said demon swayed drunkenly; the only thing keeping him from falling over was his iron-clad grip on his metal staff. He looked like a broken, battered doll, his eyes glassy and staring from their sockets, wide open and burning with such intensity that he couldn't possibly be bremetan.

Anyone else would have taken advantage of the situation and speared a lance through his back.

Except for these fools he called soldiers.

Ultaf inhaled. "ATTACK—"

And then his mouth clamped shut.

An overwhelming feeling of sheer power crashed upon his shoulders, and he fell to the floor. Gravity multiplied itself a hundred times and he was unable to lift his face upwards to figure out how this was even possible. His chest burned in his lungs, and he realized his lips couldn't move. His teeth chipped against each other, biting his inner cheek and leaking copper upon his tongue.

He barely registered what followed. The world swam in his vision, a shockwave that propelled him forwards. It took him another moment to register that the raw, unbridled power saturating the atmosphere wasn't exploding outward, it was flowing *in*. It was rising from the floor, pulling away from the castle defenses, the wardstones, dragging through the pipelines into that metal staff impaled in the floor, and through it, into the demon. It defied physics, the titanic, writhing power compressing inward on itself, drawn in by a force so strong that nothing could escape it.

Perhaps in the most literal sense.

And then, it was over. The demon lifted his head and a death rattle ripped free from his throat.

Every window that was not already broken now shattered, pulverized by the sonic boom, atomized into fine powder. Cracks appeared on the floor, splitting the very ground. They ran like wildfire over the terrain and up onto the walls of the courtyard. Chunks of Terramancy-reinforced masonry peeled off and fell down. The nearby soldiers shuddered at the noise and then *burst*, their bodies coming apart in ragged explosions of gore. Steaming offal landed all around them, splattered on the ground like pieces of rotten fruit. Swirling blemishes of color twisted their way into existence, and the sky suddenly became cloudless.

And all Ultaf Shimizu could think of was death, emanating from the demon in front of him. As much as he wanted to address the rest of his army right now, all of his senses were preoccupied by the *horror* in front of him.

Everything else was insignificant.

No previous experience, not even standing in front of his grandfather, came close to the sheer terror invoked in him by this embodiment of destruction standing before him. It was simply something he couldn't comprehend, that screamed into the core of his being that it could not be defeated, fought, nor even touched.

His soldiers—whatever remained of them—were shouting, screaming, and running around in general confusion. Half of them had already deserted their flanks to escape, jumping off the courtyard to save their lives.

Ultaf couldn't blame them. There was nothing wrong in fighting an opponent you couldn't beat, but one you couldn't *understand,* that was another matter. And then there was that smile playing on the demon's face as he stood up, one that told him that what awaited the survivors was something far, far worse than death.

"Who . . ." he ventured in a broken voice. "Who are you?"

The demon smiled. "Judgment."

Ultaf sighed in resignation and looked up at the sky.

It was, as the demon had said, quite beautiful.

CHAPTER 15

They had kept Zuken inside a ritual chamber. Its roof jutted with spires, their exteriors adorned with ornamented windows. Its tallest point was capped by a bronze-hued dome, a portrait of the goddess Amaterasu etched onto its metallic surface. The hallway that led to its arched entrance was well-kept, and the effigies placed along the wall were pleasing to the eye.

Which made Elena a little sad, as she stared at the absolute destruction around her. Everything in the vast chamber was crushed, fractured, split, splintered, or otherwise annihilated.

She and Zuken were crouched in one corner, with Olfric standing before them, a massive watery serpent, easily fifteen feet long, coiling around him, attacking everything else with vindictive fury. The hottest flames, the lances of Eternal Light, the hardest stone, the strongest winds—the ferocious kami was keeping everything at bay.

It helped that the opponents were limited to a couple of spiritists and Omnyoji. It was difficult to send reinforcements to secure a prisoner when the impregnable fortress was crashing and burning like a house of cards around them. Whatever Aguilar was up to, it was *working*.

"You know," Zuken rasped, coughing as he did, "I expected a negotiation. Maybe even tricking Ultaf or applying political pressure. I didn't expect . . . this . . . suicide mission."

Yes, thought Elena. *A suicide mission for those trying to stop Aguilar.*

Her mind was still reeling from what had happened earlier. She remembered the power she had sensed from that metallic monster, the overwhelming amount of mana crammed into such a tiny amount of metal that she had *worn* for the Goddess's sake, that she could hardly even believe it.

It shouldn't have been possible to craft a weapon more powerful than you were, but it appeared no one had bothered to tell Lukas that.

"If Aguilar is here," rasped Zuken, "then Tanya . . . where is she? Have you heard from her?"

Heard from her? Elena wanted to laugh. What would she say? That Tanya was the leader of a yokai contingent living beneath the Desert, or that she and Lukas and that skinwalker were playing the two kingdoms? Or that Lukas had used several of Zuken's stored memories to spy from afar?

Finally, she opened her mouth. "Yes, I have."

"And—"

The rest of Zuken's words died in his mouth just as a sickeningly sweet sensation crawled up Elena's spine. If the scent of decaying bodies and corrosion could be converted into a tangible feeling, then would have been its closest analogy. The next sensation came shortly after, not that Elena could feel it, because she was too busy grabbing her head and screaming.

"Elena—" Zuken cried.

"I'm . . . fine," she half-hissed, half-growled. "That insufferable Outsider. He's already begun Stage Two. We have to hurry."

"You have a Stage One *and* a Stage Two?"

Elena's dry stare told Zuken what she thought about his quip. "This entire place is about to blow up. Don't ask me how. I don't know, and I don't care. Olfric," she yelled, "we need to get out. Send the damned signal!"

"Already did," Olfric called back, slashing an Omnyoji with poisoned water before stabbing him in the chest. The paralytic poison took effect instantly. "But Tanya cannot enter until someone brings the wards down."

As if things weren't bad enough, the ceiling above them caved in right then, and Olfric hastily raised a wall of water to stop it, just as a terramancer took that window to tear a gash through his stomach. Olfric barely managed to drag the watery shield all around himself to cover Elena and Zuken, but it pushed him completely into a defensive position. Olfric grunted and went down on his knees as the spiritists kept bombarding his defenses relentlessly like raging lumberjacks. The shield kept fracturing and exploding in several places, with blades of wind and fissures of steam exploding out of corners aimed at Zuken and Elena, who were doing their best to crouch down.

"Damn it!" he cursed, throwing in every bit of mana he could procure to hold the heavy weight above them while also trying to find a way to squeeze out. "God Susanoo, I know I have committed blasphemy recently, but you know my intentions were pure! I only wanted to save my friends, and both of them deserve better than to die here! Please, show us a way out!"

And then, abruptly, the wall behind his attackers exploded and was instantly hollowed out by a burst of furious wind, a massive tremor that pierced into the heart of the stone colossus, telling everyone that a feral storm had arrived. The explosion flung the caved ceiling high into the air and sent it crashing down in the opposite direction.

"I—I thought Asukan gods weren't so literal," Elena choked.

Olfric exhaled, and the water barrier dissipated, his dust-stained face breaking into a brief smile as he took another breath. "Are you complaining?"

"No, no way," began Elena, only as she realized who was standing in front of them and what that explosion had really been.

"Tanya . . ." choked Zuken. "You look different."

"And you're . . . alive," chirped the aeromancer. "Sorry I was a little delayed in getting here. Had to deal with those annoying Omnyoji first. Sanctimonious sons of bitches tried to trap me in Eternal Light." She paused and looked at Olfric. "No offense."

"None taken," said Olfric dryly.

Elena let Olfric act as Zuken's support. "Aguilar's gone crazy. Are we still heading for the Well?"

"Well, you need to. The others . . . Oh, excuse me!" She jerked her head and a soldier that was aiming at them from atop a pillar instantly lost his head, his body unceremoniously falling into two halves.

Elena hadn't even seen Tanya hurl anything at him.

"I can see why you were trapped," Tanya said. "This place is practically infested with soldiers. Fighting so many at once must have been troublesome."

"I . . . yes," said Elena. "You clearly look troubled."

Tanya giggled, filling Elena with fresh horror. "Well, I didn't say I was upset by it. Just noticing that it isn't effortless. I must confess, I was actually looking forward to adding my own two bits of carnage, but obviously Lukas is being a meanie here and grabbing all the fun for himself. Still . . ." She sighed. ". . . there are enough soldiers running around for me to enjoy myself a little."

Elena and Zuken looked at each other. Not for the first time, she wondered about the strange dynamic between Tanya and Lukas. Yes, they were lovers now, but even from the very beginning, they had seemed to connect on a deeper, more primal level. Even their manner when it came to approaching war was similar.

As was their insanity.

Birds of a feather flock together, as the saying goes.

"Erm," said Elena, raising a hand, like she was asking a teacher at the Shrine for help, "do you know exactly what Aguilar is up to?"

Her grin widened. "He's indulging himself."

"And . . . that means?" asked Zuken.

Tanya giggled again. "Whatever. Let's get out of here. I'm already pissed off that he got to face an entire army and didn't think of inviting me."

I was right, Elena decided. *Birds of a feather, indeed.*

Dragging Ultaf by his leg, Lukas walked through the scene of absolute carnage that awaited him. Toppled pillars. Upended furniture. It looked like a hurricane had swept through this place and he knew exactly who said hurricane was.

The yokai army had rushed in, killing whatever people were left alive and possessing those that weren't, and could now be seen rushing through the snowy terrain downhill, carrying large trunks and floating cargo with them, loaded up to the brim with looted mezals, artifacts, weapons, and grain. In retrospect, Lukas was surprised just how efficiently an army of yokai-possessed bremetans could pillage an entire fortress when sufficient motivation was applied.

He moved down the stairs and stepped into the ward chamber.

It was barren, save for a large Shikigami Ritual circle in the center, enough to hold a trial by combat within it with room to spare. He actually felt tiny standing near the giant thing.

As he stepped inside, he noticed the large rocky obelisks dug into the floor. There were five of them, placed at the vertices, each one possibly representing a different element—Elemental Constraint, as Olfric called it. There was a sixth obelisk, cut exactly into the shape of a pentagon, and placed at the center. The Spiritual Constraint. The entire ritual circle was crafted out of carquane, an alloy of silver and vatuatil that held—

"Eighty-three percent efficient at conducting natural energy?" Lukas muttered with a chuckle. "Looks like we've got something that's way better at channeling natural energy than you, Blob."

"*MEAAAOW!*" growled Blob, currently in the form of a bylestyr.

"Oh, don't be like that." Lukas laughed, getting an in-depth analysis of the alloy. Blob's own efficiency at conducting natural energy was somewhere around 29%, but on the other hand, carquane was absolutely shit at everything else.

It wasn't good for storing energy.

It wasn't good for storing spiritual data.

And it definitely couldn't come "alive" like aqāru.

It was a superconductor, plain and simple; as far as natural energy was concerned, it could hold it in it for thirty-four seconds, at best, before the energy diffused out of it. That made it useful as a wardstone but good for little else.

Though, in the right hands—meaning his own—it could become something else. Depending on how vulnerable it was to alteration.

Something to consider in the near future.

The rest of the room was fairly simple. There was, as expected, the tiny rupture in the air right above the obelisk in the center—no doubt the Well through which the Shimizu were able to penetrate some borderland to harvest kami and other monsters. Even if he were to demolish the entire castle and destroy these wardstones, the rupture would still be there, but Mujin would no longer be able to use it.

In one stroke, everything he owned would be gone.

Just like that.

Inanna would've gotten a kick out of that.

"GUH!" groaned Ultaf.

"Let me guess, you're wondering if this is where you die, right?"

"GUH!"

His lips thinned. "Believe me, after what you and your grandfather did, I'd like nothing better than to kill you with my bare hands. Squeeze your throat and all that. But I'm afraid I can't."

"GUH?"

"Oh, I'm still going to kill you," he said, smiling like a shark. "But first, I'll give you a taste of your own med—"

He paused, as the sounds of footsteps grew louder and louder. The door opened, and Tanya and the rest entered. Before he knew it, Tanya had crossed the distance between them and caught him in a hug. Lukas might have squeaked in surprise, but the undignified sound was muffled by her mouth, suddenly glued to his own. The world vanished into irrelevance, her lips tasting like victory.

When she pulled back, Lukas noticed the intense look of satisfaction on her face—she was hungrier and more dominant and alive than he had ever seen her. He was as aroused as he was intimidated.

"Someone's going to get really lucky tonight," she promised. As she said that, her eyes shone a brilliant white.

Olfric cleared his throat.

Tanya backed off, but not even Olfric and the others' presence could quell the emotion shining bright in her face. Lukas smirked and glanced at Olfric and Elena, who both looked like they had seen several miles of bad road, and Zuken . . .

Zuken looked broken and battered. He had dozens of wounds, many still dripping with blood. If not for the intensity of his gaze, Lukas would've thought he was looking at a corpse.

"Banksi," said Lukas, "they did a number on you, huh?"

"And then some," said Zuken with a tired grin. Those potions Solana got for Elena must have been *something* for this man to be able to talk now without effort. "I heard you had a harrowing experience yourself."

Lukas laughed. "You could say that. But first, let me introduce you to our guest."

"GUH!"

"Hello, Big Brother," said Tanya. "Heard you were looking for me."

"GGGUH?" Tears were flowing down Ultaf's cheeks. A pathetic sight.

"Eh . . . he's having a little trouble speaking right now. I might have accidentally broken his neck bone."

"GGGGHHHH!"

"Right. Sorry. And his arms, legs, and rib cage."

"Accidentally?" asked Elena, bewildered. "How could you have done that accidentally?"

It was Lukas's turn to look sheepish. "I, uh . . . I just wanted to break the bones in his arms and legs, to be frank. You know, just in case he was stupid enough to try anything. I guess I underestimated how weak he is and might have squeezed a bit too hard."

"And somehow you broke every bone in his body?"

"I might have squeezed really, really hard."

No one in the room looked like they believed his excuse. Sighing, he said, "Look, he won't die of those injuries. But it will take him days to heal from them, even with healing spells. And he won't be able to speak until then."

Tanya snorted. "Nothing he doesn't deserve." She looked at Lukas. "I'm guessing the plan's still the same, right?"

"More or less." He shrugged. "Say, Ultaf, think your grandfather will mind terribly if I total his castle?"

"GUH?!!!"

"Right. Got it."

"He really can't understand him, can he?" asked Olfric, looking at everyone flustered.

"Who cares?" muttered Elena. "I just want to be done with this."

"Yeah . . ." Olfric murmured, looking no less flustered. "You know, it's not even four hours, and half the time was spent at the entrance."

"What's your point?" asked Tanya, curious.

"Four hours . . ." the aquamancer repeated. "We just infiltrated one of the most well-defended fortresses in the entire Empire, massacred their entire army, freed Zuken, captured their lord, and are about to destroy the fortress and get away with it clean. And all of it in less than four hours."

He rubbed his head in exhaustion, looking at Lukas for answers.

"And?" Lukas asked.

"It was a well-planned smash-and-grab." Tanya nodded, though now that Olfric had pointed it out, she seemed a little disturbed. "In and out."

"But that's just not the way this kind of thing goes!" Olfric shook his head furiously. "This is the fortress of a warlord! It just went so well! *Too* well! How often do you do this kind of thing, Aguilar?"

"Actually, it was my first time," Lukas admitted with a shrug. He really wasn't able to see what the big deal was. They had planned for everything, and they had simply gotten lucky that none of the Shimizu soldiers were able to overpower him—and that Ultaf was an obnoxious, arrogant son of a bitch.

"It was a very impressive victory," Tanya agreed. "I can't wait to see how Mujin reacts to it."

"Probably by bombing the Desert," Elena quipped.

"GUH?" Ultaf added his two bits.

"I'd have said experience matters," said Zuken. "But clearly you don't need it."

"Whatever . . ." said Lukas. Now that the adrenaline rush was wearing off, he was beginning to feel the aftereffects of the constant exhaustion. His powers had grown, yes, but he had channeled far too much lifeforce through his body and the consequences were starting to show. Acting as a direct conduit to all of that natural energy through the ley line hadn't helped matters either.

There was also the accumulated number of Level Ups that he needed to take care of. But before that, there was just one last thing left to do.

"I—I need to destroy this place."

"And how are you planning to do that?" asked Olfric. "By blowing it up?"

"Yes," said Lukas absently, glancing at the carquane crystal outgrowth. His head was still pounding. Between channeling the natural energy, the dranzithl's decay, dealing with a shitload of Level Ups and now Elena's mindfuckery, he really needed a couple of days of sleep just to feel normal again.

The wardstones there were nothing but chunks of carquane, 83% efficient at conducting the natural energy of the world. Fantastic as wardstones but pants at storing energy. Barely 4%. But if you altered the vatuatil percentage down from 71% to 64% and increased the silver past 29%, the conduction efficiency dropped down to 59% but the storage shot up all the way to 37%.

Unfortunately, the increase in silver made the alloy unstable. If he was lucky, the entire thing would at best hold for ten seconds before shattering.

The Screen popped in front of his eyes.

Territory Creation Active
Altering material composition and functionality
Reducing key limiters . . .

The wardstones around him were slowly morphing.

As was the ritual circle. Instead of the Asukan matrix that constrained power and let it out in controlled amounts, he altered it into Inanna's pentagram, applying the principle of harmony to it. Too bad the stones would be shattering too quickly to even attempt that.

Set
Alloy Alteration complete

Blueprint saved and stored in Anomaly Database
Initiating Charge . . .

Every single one of them felt the wards vanishing instantly.

"Get them out quick," he snapped at Tanya. "I'm nearly done."

That spurred the girl into action. She grabbed Elena and disappeared as if going behind a wall he couldn't see. She appeared a moment later behind a flabbergasted Zuken and grabbed him, vanishing again shortly after.

"I swear I'll never get used to—" Olfric began, but he was grabbed away before he could finish.

Blob and Ultaf were next.

And then she reappeared, looking absolutely haggard.

"It . . ." She inhaled and exhaled heavily. "It takes . . . a lot! Out of me . . ."

"You can do one more, right?"

"Yeah . . ." She panted. "Just give me a second."

Lukas smiled. And right then, the Screen displayed another message.

Charging complete
Reaching critical limit . . .
Full discharge in 10 seconds . . .

"NOW!"

Tanya gritted her teeth and grabbed Lukas, and he felt something tugging at every inch of his body as if he was being pulled in every direction, before his feet touched ground again and he found himself on the opposite mountain with Solana, Olfric, Elena, a gobsmacked Zuken Banksi, and the rest of the yokai staring at each other in apprehension.

"Barriers up! QUICKLY!" he commanded.

"Six . . . five . . . four . . ." Lukas muttered, inwardly smiling at what was about to happen. Natural energy was an absolute demon to control. Once you pulled it out of the World, the Haze, or any other World-level entity, there was no hope of trying to put that genie back in the bottle. And even less hope of taming it.

He could only hope that Solana's barriers would hold back the impact.

"Three . . ."

So he hadn't bothered with controlling it. He was betting on the energy being unleashed into the sky and back. It wasn't about harnessing the power;

it was about dissipating it all at once in one massive explosion. And with the wardstone chamber being connected to everything else, there was only one way in which the massive surge of energy could be liberated.

Meanwhile, layers upon layers of dense energy fields and barriers were forming all around them. Solana's craft at work.

"Two . . ."

A wave rushed through the air, and Lukas smiled at what was to come.

"One . . ."

BOOOM!!!!

The explosion of light that followed would have put a nuclear explosion to shame.

If left unobstructed, the dense, unfiltered energy would probably have shot upwards towards the heavens until the carquane that had been channeling it had disintegrated. But if there was something in its way . . .

Such as the wardstones channeling it into the very walls of the castle. Into the layers and layers of wards placed to control and channel that energy. Dozens of enchantments, hundreds of defenses, all of them prepared to hold it in place.

An unstoppable force against an immovable object. The two titanic powers erupted against each other with such might that the entire mountain shook, the waves from the collision creating avalanches on surrounding mountains, the sonic boom nearly shattering everyone's ear drums, as the castle—every pillar, every wall, every enchantment—was blasted away in every direction in one cataclysmic detonation. Solana's barriers held the shockwaves back, but even she had to grit her teeth and nearly dropped to a knee, despite being at least a mile away.

By the time that the light and smoke died down, the entire top of the mountain had vanished, leaving a vast crater in its place, with shattered stone blocks—no larger than small boulders—littered all around. And those were the most identifiable pieces of the mighty fortress that stood there a moment ago.

"He . . . blew it up," muttered Olfric. "He just . . . blew it up."

Tanya shared an amused look with Lukas and grinned at Olfric. "Well, he did say he would, yes."

"Yes, but . . ." The aquamancer trailed off, unable to think of the words to properly describe his thoughts. But he didn't need to finish; they all understood what he meant.

"Yeah," said Elena, nodding her head dumbly.

Silence filled the area for a moment.

"What happens now?" asked Olfric, giving the fallen Ultaf a kick in his ribs, eliciting a groan from the man. "And what about him?"

"We'll take him with us," said Lukas. The comfort of a bed was calling for him. "I have questions for him."

"Lukas," interrupted Tanya, "Grandfather is the real power behind the throne. Ultaf's just a placeholder."

"Placeholder or not, he's been playing Lord for quite some time. I want to see what we can squeeze out of him. Pretty sure Elena can help us there."

The changeling scowled. "Trust you to come up with the most vulgar requests, Aguilar. Fine, but after all of this is done, you're going to owe me a favor."

"What?" Tanya interrupted. "What for?"

"Fine," said Lukas absently. He just wanted to be done now. Hit the bed, and prepare for Mujin's reaction. In that order. "The Peak is destroyed, we've saved Zuken, and for all Mujin knows, Ultaf is dead. Makes him the best kind of captive."

"But the warlord—" began Olfric blearily. "We just totaled a warlord's fortress. A member of the Sacred Eight."

"Not a member anymore," Tanya reminded him confidently. "Don't worry, Olfric. The hard part is over. I expect everything will go smoothly from here on out."

CHAPTER 16

As soon as Lukas woke up, he immediately regretted it.

He could tell his body was healed and upgraded to the latest Level Up, but he had neither fully acclimated to the changes nor gotten enough rest.

"You're up."

This only made matters worse when he heard Tanya greeting him politely.

Without him realizing it, his eyes flashed green, and the entire room froze in place.

Cursing, he exhaled, and blinked twice, attempting to control his newly upgraded power. Time be damned, he was in no condition or mood to welcome the world right now. Much less what the world would likely throw at him in the next few days.

Wait . . .

"Tanya," he said, and mentally canceled the Impedance around Tanya. Impedance? How had he known what it was called? Tanya both sagged and went alert at the same time, violently coughing as the air left her lungs. Lukas slowly pushed himself up and put a hand around her back in apology and concern, taking care not to exert his powers by mistake.

"Wh—what was that?" She coughed.

"A nuisance I clearly have to deal with sooner rather than later," he said. Looking around, he found he was in his room; nothing appeared amiss. By the color of the light in the room, it was still daytime. When Tanya came closer and kissed him lightly on the lips, his hands went up to her hair. In response, she deepened the kiss. Only when he relaxed did she pull back, a smile on her lips.

"Better?"

A small chuckle escaped his throat. "That was to make me feel better?"

"Among other things," she said airily. "I had big plans, but someone just decided to sleep the entire thing off."

Yeah, having ten consecutive Level Ups to get through would do that to a guy. He was lucky he had receded into his inner-world, shutting off all sensory reception as his body was violently altered from within to reflect his drastically altered spiritual constitution. But before he could reply, she held a finger to his lips. "But we owe our victory to you, so I'm willing to cut you some slack this time."

He barked out a slow laugh. "We won, huh?" He paused and looked her in the eyes. "No issues whatsoever? No traps, no deadman switches? No Cobalt Army?"

She shook her head. "If there were any, they exploded with the Peak."

A slow exhale escaped his lips. And he turned his attention to his hands as if expecting something there that wasn't. He had lingering flashes of channeling the raw energy from the wardstones into himself and amplifying the Dranzithl's lethal power at the army closing in around him. He remembered altering those wardstones, feeling the raw power brushing against him again as he set the stones to unleash the energy from the ley lines directly into the fortress, blowing it up. He had some flashes of Tanya warping him through space to safety and the image of something intensely bright and blue blowing up on the horizon, a feeling of triumph surging through his body. But most of all, he remembered intense, emerald eyes gazing at his soul as his body was forced to go through ten intense Level Ups all at once, his inner-world drastically changing.

But what was most surprising was that Kinetomancy—not the half-assed, broken fragmented version he had been pulling off up to this point but the *real* thing, the original Level-4 apex Skill—was now sitting within his inner-world.

His world didn't work like that.

Whatever was stolen from the outer World was analyzed, comprehended, and sorted into prototypes based on soul, memory, and a whole bunch of other factors. Steps could be skipped when it came to manifesting them through the rapid install process, but the initial examination was practically unanimous with the end result of processing information and details of the Skills to the utmost limit.

And Inanna's Kinetomancy—which arose from the divinity that lay at the base of Lukas's soul—was no exception.

He would have understood if his World had altered his own soul prototype, reflecting the addition of the apex Skill to it. Instead, Kinetomancy had itself somehow skipped that rule to purposefully stick inside his inner-world by itself, like some kind of black box that ignored his world's attempts to understand, much less replicate. And it did so in a way he couldn't even begin to comprehend, much less explain.

Without having a soul prototype.

Or a memory.

Or an identity.

How? He didn't know. And it unnerved him, but there was nothing he could do about it now.

"—kas?"

Tanya's words shook him from his reveries. "Err."

She gave him an amused look. "How many levels did you ride over in one go after the attack?"

She laughed at his flummoxed expression. "You think you're the only one who had to hold back Level Ups while clearing hordes of enemies in one strike?"

As if answering her question, the Screen flickered before his eyes.

Status	Prime Host
Level	36

So close.

"Ten," he said slowly. "Ten levels."

"Mmmm . . ." said Tanya in a half-amused tone. "The last time you went through a consecutive Level Up in the borderland, you ended up destroying Nidhogg's Lair. Should I be worried about the territory crashing down?"

"Not unless someone decides to pull something over me."

"I doubt that will happen," said Tanya, flipping her hair. "Everyone's scared shitless of you, and that includes Solana. Really, Lukas, first you defeat their empress and the Leader in one go, and then you massacre an entire legion of Asukans, obliterate a warlord's fortress, despite king-class enchantments protecting it . . . How's a girl to keep up? Any more and you'll be a threat to my queenship."

"Tell your kingdom that this Outsider will always be in service to their queen," he said with a mock bow.

"Drat!"

The entire yokai territory was active like never before. Tanya had led Lukas through the entire territory, showing him the drastic change in the place and the people that had taken place while he happily slept for the last two days. The entire yokai war engine was churning again. Their army was mobilizing, weapons were being forged, and it wasn't just the yurei patrolling the corridors of the yokai territory. Nearly every yokai capable enough to possess or manipulate an element was training again. Their entire underground living area was being fortified. Several of them had seen their new queen break through wards using a technique that had baffled their Leader, while her compatriot and confidant, the Outsider of legend, had obliterated the warlord's castle until nothing save rocks and pebbles remained where a massive and nearly impregnable fortress had once stood.

In a way, the destruction of the svartalfar race had served as a wake-up call for several subdued races. Muspels, himthursars, dokkalfars—those who held second-class status in the Asukan Empire and were forced to live on the fringes were slowly voicing their resentment. Even the ljósálfars, who had enjoyed plenty of privileges, were being forced to reconsider their beliefs since the svartalfars had also had diplomatic immunity, and yet all it had taken was one arrogant noble to destroy their entire race. Even bremetans who followed the old religions were taking note of the change and observing closely.

There were, of course, those who were apprehensive about the yokai colony in the Desert taking an offensive stance against the Shimizu warlord—one of the most frightening figures in the entire Southeast—and were shying away from supporting this suicidal move. The surprising part was the amount of sincerity and conviction with which Solana was leading the charge. Something about the ambush on the Peak had changed her views drastically, she was now actively voicing her support for the Outsider even if that meant supporting the new queen as well. She had called in other skinwalkers from who knows where; platoons of yokai were entering through her office, which had been turned into a makeshift door to the yokai from other regions of the Empire.

"Honestly, I don't see why Solana insists on fortifying this area," said Tanya as she led him towards the chambers where Maude and Elena were taking care of Zuken while he recovered. "It isn't like Mujin knows anything about who attacked the Peak, and even if he did, he'd have no idea where we are hiding."

Lukas shook his head. "Maybe, but we led an ambush, and who knows what kind of triggers we stepped through? We might've made mistakes and left plenty of evidence for Mujin to discover."

Tanya raised a skeptical brow. "You sound ridiculous and hypocritical, you know that, right? You speak of caution in the same breath as you do your reckless feats."

Lukas laughed. "How else did you expect I survived everything? I've significant evidence to prove my luck usually works against me."

"On that I have little doubt." She was not amused, but she refrained from speaking her mind any further and instead let out an amused snort. "And here I thought gaining ten levels would make you a warlord's equal."

That stung. Tanya was right. Gaining ten levels should have unlocked plenty of abilities from Inanna's Level-4 apex Skill, but it seemed like the box would remain closed until he passed that Level-39 threshold. Like there was some kind of abstraction, a black box that refused him access until he passed that milestone.

It didn't make any sense to him, but he just chalked it up to it having arisen from a goddess's divinity.

But the most surprising twist had been the letter Lord Naowa had sent to Lady Kandra, to be forwarded to a certain "Lukas Aguilar."

Inside, was an engraved invitation, welcoming him to a private meeting in two days, granting him a private audience with the Fire King—the original owner of Zwaray Keep before it had been indefinitely leased to the svartalfars in exchange for certain benefits. The letter claimed that Lukas would be granted a similar setup with the Keep and the Fire King was hinting at the conditions of whatever new arrangements they wanted to rope him into.

"What does it say?" asked Tanya, noticing his frown. "I tried to open it, but Solana forbade me to. She said it's enchanted to combust within minutes of opening it."

Lukas laughed. "Just another example of the people in power roping the less-fortunate into their elaborate plans.

"They said that I was going to get the property, and now they're claiming it's a lease instead. Which means they can snatch it from me the moment they think I'm an issue. Just when I was thinking I could do without . . ." He trailed off.

His voice wasn't confident. Instead, it indicated acceptance bordering on apathy. Like he was genuinely at peace with whatever came next. Tanya snatched the letter from his hand and managed to peruse the contents just before it spontaneously combusted.

"It's standard protocol, Lukas," Tanya enlightened him. "The Empire owns the world, and everything that comes within the Eternal Light's dominion. Only the Sacred Eight are allowed to own land; everyone apart from them leases it from the Empire."

"I'm seeing why being Sacred Eight is such a big deal," Lukas said. "Almost makes me wonder if they have a bigger duty than just being entitled assholes."

Tanya opened her mouth to respond but then thought better of it. "Still," she said, "if it's the Fire King, you have it better than most. Out of all the existing kings, Jimmo Asuka is perhaps, the sanest."

"Wait . . . did you say Jimmo *Asuka*?"

"Yeah," said Tanya, flipping her ponytail. "I thought you knew this. Jimmo Asuka, the Fire King, is the elder brother of the emperor himself, son of the Great Goddess Amaterasu. A *demigod*."

Demigod. That was the title Zuken had used to describe him during their very first meeting after Inanna had resurrected his soul.

Son of the Goddess Amaterasu. He wondered if he was going to meet this World's version of Heracles (only one with complete mastery over flame). His mind went back to the casual way in which the Ifrit King had twisted and turned the borderland with his very existence, and this man . . . he was a living embodiment of that power.

Two days later, he and Tanya had gone to Haviskali. Thanks to her improved facility with rifting under Meynte's tutelage, they were able to shift all the way to Haviskali without encountering any of the Cobalt Army checkpoints. For everyone else, them showing up at the Keep would only indicate that they had been living in Haviskali all this time, an illusion they were happy to allow to propagate to their benefit. The guards outside the Keep quickly let them inside, and the stark difference in the Haviskali overseer's behavior was notable.

It was obvious he had no doubts about who was responsible for the devastation of the Peak, and no matter what World you were in, that ability to get shit done earned you respect.

Tatun Kinosu led them to the innards of the gargantuan chamber they had visited the last time, and even Lord Naowa, who had done his best to appear intimidating the other day, now looked completely at ease, perfectly content, not unlike a child who had been gifted with a brand new, expensive toy. But nothing—not the warm welcome, nor the ease in the Shogun's features—could compare to what came next.

"Lord Asuka, might I introduce you to . . ." began the overseer.

"You must be the famous Lukas Aguilar!" said the Fire King enthusiastically.

And just like that, Lukas found his internal tension skyrocketing.

The Fire King knew his name.

This was his first time meeting a real power in this world, and he *knew his name.*

"Yes," he said, trying to conceal his unease. "That would be me."

"I was most distressed by the fate that befell the svartalfars," said the Fire King lightly. He casually grinned as he tried to meet Lukas's eyes, and Lukas instantly focused on his nose to avoid a direct gaze. "Lord Naowa here had much to say about you. Claimed that there was a true bremetan-svartalfar hybrid out there. It's a shame that such a gem had been hidden from us all along."

Lukas didn't know whether to be flummoxed or elated, so with a deep breath, he chose a course of action.

Smiling politely, he regarded him. "Trust me, I'd have to come to the Llaisy Kingdom far sooner if I could. However, those damn soldiers . . ."

The look on the overseer's face was priceless.

Yeah, he was a smart-ass. Lukas had no problem admitting it. He had mouthed off to everything from monsters and ancient skinwalkers to quite literal goddesses and empresses.

The overseer's eyes twitched.

Lukas had actually been expecting the same sort of reaction from the Fire King, but it only lasted for a moment before the man blinked and his smile widened.

"Well, now you're here. I'm sure the Cobalt Army will not hinder you any longer. They are sticklers for rules, but they're good at what they do. I'm more interested in how you managed to get the svartalfars to share their lore with you. You'd think after leasing them land and resources, they'd be a bit less . . ."

"Anal-retentive? Sticklers for privacy?"

The Fire King seemed taken aback, blinking at him in surprise. Lukas tried not to show how tense he was. Mouthing off to creatures like this was always a risk.

You could tell a lot about a powerful entity by the way it responded to a one-liner. A lot of regular people too, for that matter.

So when his smile widened, and he threw his head back and guffawed, Lukas relaxed, if only slightly.

"Yes," said the man heartily. "Lord Naowa also mentioned a queer spell of yours that trapped motion around you. Don't suppose you want to talk about it? I am always interested in learning new things."

Lukas gave him a small, easy smile. "Sorry. Union rules. Never reveal all your tricks. You know how it is."

The Fire King was talking about his ability to understand runework and the svartalfar's metalworking. It seemed that they assumed his ability to be just a particularly well-designed spell.

That misconception meant he still had an edge.

"Lord Fire King, sir," said the overseer, frustration evident in his features, "this here is Tanya Shimizu, granddaughter of—"

"Bearer of Ezzeron, the Wind King's kami," finished the Fire King, as he regarded Tanya. "And the closest substitute we have for Wakamura. My, how you have grown. The last time I saw you, you were just eight, I believe."

Tanya blinked. "I . . . I don't believe we've ever met, Lord . . . err, Fire King."

The man tilted his head quizzically. "I see. You don't remember. That's unfortunate but not unexpected. Regardless . . . I cannot say I was friends with your great-grandfather, dear child, but he and I respected one another."

Ah, Lukas had almost forgotten. Jimmo Asuka had just celebrated his eight-hundredth birthday last year. That was the kind of trivia you could get from an ancient skinwalker-turned-information broker.

"I know of your peculiar issues with your grandfather, and your little deal with Lord Naowa. Be advised, child, while I do not interfere in familial disputes, I must say that I do not think much of your grandfather."

"If you will forgive the impertinence, sir," said Tanya, "I don't think much of him either."

Lukas took a moment to examine the man as he exchanged more words with him.

Jimmo Asuka was tall, topping his height by several inches. His crimson hair fell down from his head, ending at his shoulders, giving him an aristocratic look. Dark eyes shone out from a handsome face, filled with such joy and kindness that—along with his cheerful smile—made you instinctively want to trust him and grin right back. It was a smile that seemed to have your best interests at heart. A thin scar ran down one side of his chin, but instead of blemishing his appearance, it added to it, giving him character.

It was hard to believe that this was the face of the Lord of Flame, but Lukas knew better than anyone what he was. This was Jimmo Asuka, the Fire King, and one of the strongest Asukans alive.

Just having been reforged by a reflection of Goddess Inanna had been enough to classify Lukas as the Prime Host by his omphalos. And this was a person literally born to a goddess.

A demigod.

The Fire King gave a hearty laugh. "Disputes over the lord's mantle are always fun to watch. That goes double when it comes to one of the Sacred Eight. It's unfortunate we couldn't host a battle arena between your forces and your grandfather's. The Empire is in dire need of an entertainment upgrade."

Lukas heartily agreed. Not with the battle arena idea but with the latter.

Solana had informed him that everyone had been speculating about the Peak's destruction, and the general consensus was that the Fire King had something to do with it. Rumor was that, as Head of Interracial Cooperation, Jimmo Asuka was absolutely furious with the Shimizu's massacre of the svartalfars. There were rumors that the entire Shimizu affair was quickly becoming a power play between the Earth King and the Fire King, and the svartalfar massacre had angered the Fire King something fierce.

That the entire mountain top was blown up like that suggested that it couldn't have been the act of a Water, Ether, Wind or Earth spiritist, and the only known Fire Warlord was far away in the Northern part of the Empire, completely unconnected from Southeastern politics. That the Fire King was the one who had ripped Mujin Shimizu a new one in open court only added greater fire to the rumors, and for all everyone knew, Jimmo Asuka could've obliterated the Peak as an example of his displeasure.

Naturally, no one was stupid enough to accuse the emperor's brother of destroying the fortress of a disgraced clan.

For this was a creature of power, one of the rulers of the Empire. In a world where Might made Right, where people killed each other and other species to grow stronger and rise in hierarchy across decades and centuries, a murder-world where mortals could rise to become gods—this man was sitting close to the very top. Unlike the Ifrit King, this magnificent entity somehow held his control with the ironclad grip of a swordsman wielding a blade.

Lukas noted the way Tanya seemed to shrink just a tad in his presence.

"*What do you think?*" he asked Meynte, who he knew was looking through his eyes right then. The Fire King looked at him almost instantly, and for a moment, Lukas feared he had heard him, but instead of surprise, hostility, or contempt, the Fire King just seemed curious for a moment before returning to his conversation with Tanya.

I would advise you to speak with great caution, to mind your manners, and to endeavor not to offend this creature, Meynte spoke in his mind. *But since I know you too well, Soulcrafter, I'll simply remind you that this territory is very flammable and that this creature is far better at blowing things up than you.*

"*What do you rate the chances of this being a meet-and-greet by a cheerful, altruistic guy who just happens to be one of the Empire's big guns?*"

Somewhere between zero and three percent.

"*So, theoretically, it could happen, right?*"

Whatever you say, Soulcrafter. Just maintain your guard.

"Pardon my rudeness," said Tanya carefully, before Lukas got a chance to probe any further. "I do not have any . . . forces to face my grandfather as you put it. It's just the two of us, and we'd rather have the advantage of secrecy if we can help it."

Of all the things Lukas had expected the Fire King to do right then, bursting into laughter had not been one of them.

"Of course," said the man, still chuckling. "Even without the power levels, I'd keep him as far away from the limelight as possible if I were in your place." He looked at Lukas, not in the face but at his chest. "How long has it been since we've had a Pathforger in the Empire, and one unregistered with the Empire Archives, at that?"

The Fire King was still looking at him now, smiling, and much to Lukas's consternation, he couldn't figure out if the man was being genuine. "No wonder you got past the Peak's defenses."

Every single person in the room stiffened this time.

"Er—Lord Fire King," began Lord Naowa, "I think you're—"

"Mistaken?" asked the man, his affable gaze never leaving Lukas's chest. "I think not. I have to commend you, Pathforger. Walking in this brazenly, wearing that divine pendant around your neck, yet expecting me not to take note? Especially one this potent and . . . old, so old . . ." He peered at him. "Wherever did you find it, Lukas Aguilar?"

Shit. Shit. Shit, cursed Lukas.

This was rapidly approaching the worst-case scenario.

You cannot win, warned Meynte.

Against a demigod? thought Lukas. *Just getting out of here alive with Tanya would be winning.*

"I'm a follower of the old religions," he said at last. "This relic has been passed down to me by my grandfather."

He wasn't quite sure if gods or demigods knew when they were being lied to, so he decided to err on the side of caution, lying by omission.

"Your grandfather," murmured the Fire King.

"Yes," said Lukas. "He was a collector. He claimed that the key to our future is hidden in our past."

"I see," said the man. "May I see it?"

"Ah . . ." Lukas said. He swallowed hard, trying to calm the flood of adrenaline within him and think reasonably. After a moment of consideration, he pulled the pendant out of his Blob-vest. If the Fire King noted any irregularities with Blob's material or spiritual constitution, he made no comment on the fact. Instead, his eyes were affixed to the iridescent aquiline radiance emanating from within the lapis-lazuli orb.

"Will this suffice?"

"Very much." The man inhaled, eyeing the pendant with a sense of clear wonder. His hand slowly reached toward it but stopped inches away. "Millennia old . . . and still as flawless as the day it was forged. I can feel its power like an echo in my mind. Like a song forever being sung without anyone to hear it . . .

"Do not sell it," he said. "Do not give it away to anyone. Think twice before you even show it to anyone, and think it over three times again before you reveal it as a relic. Treat it with respect, for this is a thing of power."

For a moment, the man gazed at the pendant wistfully, and then he looked up at Lukas. "I do not know what Truth of the Universe hides in that blue iridescence, for I am not worthy . . . You, however . . . Tell me, did this relic choose you?"

Lukas couldn't help himself and started laughing. At the man's curious expression, he replied, "Chosen?" He snorted again. "On what basis? Brains? Talent? I doubt I have anything that comes close to even a measure of divinity. Perhaps I activated it by mistake. Or perhaps it just activated by itself and I just happened to be wearing it at the time."

"Just what we needed," muttered Lord Naowa. "A *humble* Pathforger."

"And unrepentantly honest and blunt too," said Tanya, with the façade of helpfulness but clearly finding joy in stirring the pot further.

"Whose side are you on?" Lukas complained. But the moment he met her eyes, he noticed a spark in them. She knew something he didn't.

Then he looked back at the Fire King, whose face was grave once more.

"I will not hold your caution against me, Lukas Aguilar. We must do our best to remain wise. You did not know me. And in truth, there are many in the Empire who you would do well not to trust. Perhaps even some you call associates."

Lukas narrowed his eyes. Had he just—

"This changes things. Not only are you our last hope to rekindle the svar-talfar craft, you're also an aspiring Pathforger. I will not insult you, but I might ask, do you think it wise to side with the lady here, knowing that you face the might of a warlord?"

"Yes."

"He's empowered by the might of the Earth King."

"Won't stop me."

"Your valor does you credit, Pathforger," said the man. "But the outcome of this battle remains the same. The Shimizu have lost their status as a Sacred Eight and will remain as such until a new bearer of the Wind King's kami presents herself before the emperor."

He glanced at Tanya from the corner of his eyes, before refocusing on Lukas. "So when you face him, keep in mind that you face the stand-in for the Earth King. And the Earth King has never known defeat. Not once."

"Hasn't stopped me before," said Lukas.

"Big words," said the overseer. "You don't lack in spirit, do you, Lukas Aguilar?"

"Intentions are meaningless, if you do not have the power to back it up," said Lord Naowa. Well then, condescension—the staple of just about every creature he had come across who thought they were better than humanity. "Pathforger or otherwise, you still have a long way to go. Perhaps in a few decades . . ."

Lukas restrained the urge to grit his teeth. These people were looking down on him. On *him*, who carried within himself a World that eclipsed their own. A World whose very last memory was enough to render any of their brains to mush within but a few moments of exposure.

He wasn't being taken seriously at all. Even with them recognizing him as a Pathforger, he was still just an "interesting" person, who would help them bring back the svartalfar runework. A curiosity but not an actual player.

Even if he ended up killing Mujin Shimizu, things wouldn't change to any substantial degree. He might get a seat at the table, but it would be the kid's seat, and the adults had no problem talking over him.

It was irksome and dangerous.

Meynte too had taken him the same way at first. Even after he had defeated her, she had maintained her opinion until he had finally given her a glimpse of what the Haze truly looked like. Just a brush against the true mysteries of a broken, shattered realm was enough to kill the empress eighteen times, and only after that had she begun to appreciate what Lukas was, what he contained, and where he stood in the World hierarchy.

But here, he was back to Square One. If he didn't want to deal with the small fries again, if he wanted some credibility, he was going to have to do something risky.

"*Empress*," he began, taking a deep breath. "*I'm about to do something reckless and potentially stupid.*"

My goodness. The Soulcrafter doing something irrational? The surprise has rendered me speechless, she declared in a dry tone. She continued, more seriously now: *Soulcrafter, are you certain? What you are planning . . . it might pose great danger to you.*

"*I'm banking on the fact that it can't be worse than dealing with you or Everfrost.*" Then he closed his eyes and exhaled. When he reopened them, they were an intense emerald green.

Then he opened his mouth and jumped into the deep end.

"Tell me, *Jimmo Asuka*, do you know what it means to be strong?"

A cold draft spread through the room. From Tanya's expression, she wasn't sure if she should freeze or grab him and rift far, far away before things turned worse. Both Lord Naowa and the overseer looked utterly outraged at his casual utterance of the Fire King's name, as if he were a peer.

"Of course you do," said Lukas before anyone had a chance to reply. "You were born strong. Son of the goddess Amaterasu. A demigod by birth. Talent, intelligence, Soul Capacity—you have it all. You were destined to be strong from the moment of your birth. A natural-born genius. An existence completely different from someone like me." He shut his eyes and took a deep breath. "But let me tell you about someone else. Someone who was born with none of that. No talent, no bloodline, not even an arcane Skill. None of it. She was a slave girl. Weak. That was all she was called for as long as she could remember. She thought it unfair. Why were others born strong while she was not? Why were some blessed with talents and Skills while others like her had nothing? Why could even ordinary people who had never trained a single day suddenly gain immeasurable power by offering themselves to a god's mercy, when she had none? She envied them, she wanted what they had. Wanted it all."

He opened his eyes. "That woman was my teacher. And she cursed me. Cursed me to never lose my selfishness nor my defiance. To stay true to myself no matter how many dreams of others I trampled upon. Be the invader that she was. The monster. The conqueror. I am not allowed to pretend you are merely a survivor, not anymore. And if that means I must stand atop the corpses of the mighty, warlords, kings, emperors, even . . . I won't think twice."

One could have heard a pin drop in the silence that followed his declaration before everyone was suddenly shaken from the stupor. Tanya was the first to do so and hissed like a feral cat.

"*Lukas!*" she half-yelled, half-whispered. "What are you doing?"

Lukas ignored her. He only had eyes for the Fire King, his eyes, now mostly emerald-green, shining with a confidence upon which the universe itself could rest.

"You are the Lord of Flame. Surely you understand what I mean when I say, 'only a fire may devour another'?" he asked. "The nemesis that I have claimed for myself is someone so far, far beyond me, that in comparison, the Earth King is merely a bump in the road—at best."

Just one phrase, but the weight behind it was insurmountable.

Bump in the road. That was what he had called the Earth King. Someone in the same league as the Fire King himself.

It was a significant and risky thing to do, and every single entity in the room took note of it.

"I . . . see," said Jimmo Asuka. "Must be a formidable enemy to make a king look petty by comparison."

"Someone once told me," said Lukas without skipping a beat, "that no mortal power, no matter how great, can eclipse a god."

The Fire King froze, and for a moment, Lukas had the feeling he was staring at a cornered animal. An absolutely lethal predator but a cornered one, nonetheless. Then Jimmo Asuka straightened slightly, wearing one of the most astonished expressions Lukas had ever seen on another living being.

"A god?" he asked, and Lukas thought he saw wonder in his eyes. "You want to challenge . . . a god?" He paused again, glancing at Lukas's vest that hid the pendant behind it. "You . . . Of course. Remarkable! Remarkable indeed!"

He rubbed his chin thoughtfully, a tiny smile forming on his lips. His previous words had been spoken quietly, but what followed was loud and clear. "However, if you think that a king's throne can be so easily reached, then allow me to rectify that misconception."

That's when Jimmo Asuka, the Fire King, stopped hiding his power.

In a blink of an eye, every single person in the vicinity, including the members of the security task force that had been hiding under veils as well as Tanya and Lord Naowa fell silent and dropped to their knees, forced down by the oppressive pressure that now filled the air, their feet no longer able to support their own weight. It was so powerful that it felt as if the hand of a giant was crushing down on his shoulders.

Without lifting so much as a finger nor speaking a single word, Jimmo Asuka demonstrated his full might to everyone who stood before him.

And Lukas knew that even *this* was but a fraction of his real strength—that in his true form, he was *much* stronger. And while the Fire King continued to smile benevolently, his eyes told a different story as flames hotter than hell flickered in the backs of them, hinting at the madness that gripped his soul.

It was like staring into the pit of a frothing volcano.

Only, the volcano was staring back.

Lukas managed to stand under the strain, tall and proud. A bead of sweat had broken out on his brow and spilled down his face, but he'd be damned if he'd let his confidence waver even for an instant.

The rest was taken care of by the Living Anomaly function.

"It's because it's so hard to reach that it makes it worth it," he said.

At his words, the Fire King cut off his power so quickly and thoroughly that it almost caught him off-balance.

Living Anomaly - Neutered Earth - Deactivated

Living Anomaly was truly a lopsided omphalos function. It didn't grant him any special abilities like creation, alteration, or regeneration. Hell, in a battle against an opponent, Living Anomaly was all but useless. It did only one thing—create an environment where the Truths of his home planet, Lostbelt Earth, held true, and everything else was canceled. Because neither lifeforce nor mana existed on Earth in his time, he was able to exert that condition within his created territory, which could include the world around him, like he had done at the Peak, or just be limited to his own body.

It meant that any and all effects of lifeforce and mana would have no effect on his person during the period of its activation, but neither would he be able to do anything in return. During that time, he was, for all intents and purposes, *human*.

Lukas exhaled and tried not to shiver as lifeforce flooded back within him. The Fire King had absolute authority over the Fire element, which meant he could alter the emotions of any person within his vicinity to a massive degree without even exerting himself.

And Lukas, neither a fellow king nor even a warlord, but rather a budding Pathforger, had stood against that power and resisted, even if for just a little while.

His point had been made.

Even Tanya was staring at him as if for the first time.

"If you understand, then there is no reason for me to warn you any longer," said the Fire King with the amused, proud smile still on his lips before he turned his head. "Your ambition has been heard and acknowledged, Lukas Aguilar. Despite your heritage, and your Pathforging, I dare say you have all the makings of a Fire Lord. Perhaps even a king someday. I know not what Truth that relic contains, but the Empire could do with someone like you."

And what did *that* little invitation say about him, Lukas couldn't help but wonder. Just what was it about him that made every power he came across in this world always extend offers to join them?

He didn't let the shudder within him escape. Even with everything his inner-world had right now in its arsenal, he was nowhere near prepared to face the monster before him.

It had been quite some time since he had set eyes on the Ifrit King in that borderland, and even to this day, the memory of that massive beast evoked a mix of revulsion and deep-seated fear within him.

It was so easy to forget that these kings weren't human, bremetan, or even *mortal*. Their exterior was a facade, a lie created centuries ago, a mask they had gotten so used to wearing that they themselves could forget what they truly were deep within.

But Lukas wasn't a bremetan. He was an anomaly.

Seeing the Ifrit King with his own eyes, comprehending that just the weight of its existence was enough to throw the borderland into a howling madness, a hunger to annihilate everything . . . and to think that a kami of a similar nature and power lay trapped within the soul of this being in front of him . . .

It was humbling.

"Lord Fire King," interrupted Lord Naowa. "Perhaps we could move ahead with the terms of the lease?"

"Ah, yes," said the Fire King, a little pensively. "I had almost forgotten about that bit." He regarded Lukas evenly. "Not many people know this, but before the Zwaray Keep was a svartalfar sanctuary, this entire estate was an empty terrain, with a single rupture in reality in the middle of it."

"The Well," said Lukas.

"Yes, a lava-ridge borderland, to be specific," said the Fire King. "The svartalfars were allotted this territory because, apart from getting the materials and minerals they needed for metal crafting and forging, they could maintain periodic checks on the great Arah that resides within."

"Arah—"

"A magnificent shapeshifter, the embodiment of annihilation, and perhaps the strongest spiritual entity in our world. Not even I, with all my power, can beat it. Ever since it manifested within the lava ridge, I have been studying it, courtesy of the svartalfars."

"Arah," Lukas repeated, again wishing he had a firmer grasp on this world's powers. For the life of him, the title evoked nothing more threatening than an altered variant of the dranzithl, which in itself, could have posed an incredible danger under the right conditions. Just channeling enough energy through a limited amount of aqāru had been enough to commit genocide inside the Peak. Given enough supply, the dranzithl were a significant threat to any mortal out there, spiritist or otherwise.

Soulcrafter. Meynte, on the other hand, hissed a soft warning in his head. She sounded distinctly uneasy, bordering on urgent. *I think they mean the creature that harried you back in the Desert in the first place. The one you call—*

Lukas's jaw physically dropped, and he only heard the echo on the floor as he took a reflexive step backwards, both hands coming up to his face in sheer shock.

"Wait," he began, swallowing with a dry throat. "This . . . Arah. wouldn't happen to be, oh, a couple of hundred yards long, enormous tail and wings, claws and fangs, fiery . . . A demon, would it? Loves to blow things up , hates company?"

"Oh?" The Fire King leaned forward, sudden interest in his eyes as he studied him. "If I didn't know any better, I'd say you almost sound familiar with it . . ."

"Familiar?" Lukas's voice might've been high-pitched at this point. "The damn thing tried to burn us to ash. Why for all that's good in the world would you even want to get close to that thing, let alone study it?! Hell, it had claws larger than I am tall!" He held up a hand to emphasize that he wasn't exactly a small man; the overseer snorted at the visual. "It's the size of a freaking island nation, and if it were one, its export would be violent death by incineration! And you've been using those frail little svartalfars to study it? Are you crazy or just stupid?"

"Oh?" Lord Naowa leaned forward as well, and Tanya straightened, but Lukas was too focused on the Fire King to really notice at the moment.

"So you *have* met the great Arah." The Fire King's smile grew. "And clearly, survived it as well. That makes things so much more interesting."

Lukas was still just completely flabbergasted by the sheer immensity of this idiot's death wish. "I mean all it is, is just one natural-born Ifrit . . ." He froze. ". . . King."

It came to him easily enough, surprisingly.

"I see. The Well here isn't to harvest resources. It's a prison."

"Oh" the Fire King said. "How did you come to that reasoning?"

"It's the only thing that makes sense." Lukas shrugged, lining up his reasons in his head. "Control is the hearthstone of the Empire." He ignored the sudden hiss from Tanya and the look of shock and embarrassment on the overseer's face. "And Arah is beyond anyone's control. A natural-born Ifrit King will require a Soul Capacity of over a million just for someone to bind it, which is *impossible*. And even if somehow that miracle were to occur, the binder's elemental constraint would shatter instantly. No amount of control can balance things when the Fire element is at Level 5. My personal bet is that the binder would get immolated instantly after the binding, and that's assuming they could even perform it without getting vaporized first."

"I would be careful with the phrasing, Aguilar," said Lord Naowa, almost defensively. "The Empire is blessed by gods. Not even *that* beast with all its power can face the wrath of the Pantheon."

Lukas shook his head immediately. "Gods are powerful, yes, but *too* power-ful. At least on this plane. Unfortunately, so is the Ifrit King. A god could very well successfully subdue Arah but not without sacrificing several kingdoms in the process. That creature isn't a demon; it's a walking, breathing, world-destroying catastrophe. And . . . forgive me for being blunt, I dare say that even gods would suffer from setbacks if they tried to fight the beast inside that borderland."

"Careful," said the Fire King, smiling, a tinge of rebuke mixed in his tone. "One might think you're blaspheming."

"I am not," said Lukas, unfazed. "Gods are not gods because they hold more power than kings but because the source of their power is faith. Rather than churning out power using a high-level kami or being limited by a mortal shell, a god harvests the faith of millions. Yes, on this plane, their strength is practically infinite, but inside that borderland, cut off from their faith, gods are only as strong as they can be by themselves. No, it's much better to confine the Ifrit King within that lava ridge and cut it off from affecting this plane at all, and . . . svartalfars . . ."

He straightened. His eyes narrowed, and everything clicked all at once. He met the Fire King's eyes.

"Why don't you tell me why this land was *really* granted to svartalfars as a sanctuary?"

"The plan was to use svartalfar runecraft that applies to all borderlands and maintain the stability of the lava-ridge prison," said the Fire King easily.

Lukas blinked.

"Wait," he began slowly, really trying to understand what he was hear-ing here. "Did you actually just reveal your inner agenda, just because I asked nicely?"

I suppose there are some benefits to dealing with a sane Asukan, Meynte pointed out, obviously as unprepared as he was for having the answers just given to him.

Even Lord Naowa and the overseer were gawking at the Fire King.

"*I know. Really throws you for a loop, doesn't it?*"

"The svartalfars were a balancing factor for the Empire," said Lord Naowa, noting the king's gesture. "Their runecraft speaks to the world—*every World*. It's a power that even the Asukan Pantheon cannot claim to possess. They were tasked with keeping the borderland stable, and in return, they were handed the entire estate on an infinite lease, by order of the Fire King himself. Their metalsmithing and enchantments were carefully regulated through govern-ment channels to assure them the best prices; every resource they needed was offered at subsidized rates. Even their subterranean territories were warded against the Eternal Light to grant them effective working conditions. Offi-cially, they were contracted to forge and maintain the Wells at the shrines and private properties, and in return, they enjoyed diplomatic immunity within the Empire, enforced by the Cobalt Army."

"Wait, enforced by the Cobalt Army?!" asked Tanya, sharing a quick gaze with Lukas.

"Of course," said Lord Naowa. "The svartalfars have the right to seek aid from the Cobalt Army in times of distress. Even against a Sacred Eight, if necessary. Which makes their massacre at the hands of the Shimizu even worse. Things transpired far too quickly for anyone to understand, much less react."

Lukas had debated quite extensively with Solana in the past just what role the svartalfars played in the Empire, but she had never mentioned this little tidbit. Either she didn't know, or she had played upon his ignorance and kept things from him. Even Lukas, who had probably traversed more of the Haze and its countless borderlands, had never really been prepared to consider the effect that creatures like the Ifrit King would have on the real world, or Onogoro, as they called it. He had always thought that Eternal Light stood guard against the mists of the Haze and that even the Wells were just lures to capture kami.

But what if there was more? What if there was a reason why the Empire used Wells to lure kami out when Solana had pretty much given him a quick trip through the Haze? When Meynte, and now Tanya, was able to rift through space using the Haze.

What if the Empire was using svartalfar runecraft to seal the borders of Onogoro from the Haze itself, leaving behind well-guarded and secure channels accessed through these Wells? And now, with the svartalfar massacre, the Empire's borders were in jeopardy, which explained why the Fire King himself was treating him like a welcome houseguest, now that they knew he was someone who could take up the job himself. But if he were to repair the Wells and perform runecraft then . . .

   . . . *Wait.*

Was the Fire King really handing him the job of securing the World from infiltrators? Him, who had unlimited access to and through the Haze?

This was the chance to do what he was already doing. Being the gatekeeper to this World's reality would grant him respect from the Empire while also helping the yokai travel through the Haze without suffering the Empire's wrath. It would also give him access to resources to develop his anomaly powers, as well as recognition amongst the different clans. He could truly travel through the Empire and understand the Asukan Pantheon instead of being subjected to a biased yokai version, or even worse, the ridiculous propaganda preached at the shrines.

It was tempting. Very tempting. And he was only human.

Breathing slowly and closing his eyes, Lukas calmed himself down and emptied himself of his emotions. If there was a time to forget that he was about to confront one of the most dangerous beings in this World and remember all his lessons on negotiation, now was the time.

He thought about his conversation so far and went through it in minute detail, almost as if performing Scan or Analysis. He thought about what he had come to know, the information he had received, the manner in which he was given these things, what they meant . . .

Correction. What they meant to another Asukan in his place, and then to himself. What he represented. What the Fire King represented. What he wanted. What the Fire King wanted. The means of transaction for this deal. What was on the table, what wasn't, factoring in his own nature as an anomaly and their knowledge of him being a svartalfar-bremetan hybrid.

"I can see what you want from me . . ." he began at last, weighing his words slowly, carefully. "What benefits would I get in return for my services?"

Lord Naowa was the one to respond first. "I'd believe that was clear from the very beginning. You would be granted an indefinite lease to the Zwaray Keep, as well as enjoy all the benefits the svartalfars enjoyed. Subsidies and access to quality resources, as well as a constant source of employment from the Empire." He crossed his arms over his chest, almost glaring at him. "And the greatest of them all: the patronage of the Fire King and myself would be beneficial for an aspiring Pathforger like yourself. Most people would consider that to be more than satisfactory payment."

The Fire King, on the other hand, just kept staring at him. "Why would I want to get paid for something that I'd naturally need for doing the job in the first place?" Lukas asked. Really, what was it with this World and powerful pseudo-immortal beings wanting to get him to do their bidding without proper remuneration? First Inanna, then Solana, then Everfrost. Even Meynte had offered him a similar deal.

In my defense, whispered the memory of the empress inside his mind, *you didn't quite let me explain what I wanted.*

"It's a good plate, whatever you're offering me," said Lukas, meeting the man's eyes. "But I must point out that everything you're providing me is ultimately for your own benefit. Subsidized resources and state-guaranteed fair trade could mean a lot for a fringe race that wanted nothing more than survival and following their way of life, but to me, not so much. Even before this mess, I was employed by Zuken Banksi and was perfectly happy working for him. Diplomatic immunity? You're talking to a guy who is willingly waging war against a former Sacred Eight clan, headed by a powerful warlord and sponsored directly by the Earth King. I'll admit that having the patronage of the Fire King and yourself would indeed be a great honor, and perhaps another

Asukan would give his first-born for even a fraction of what you offer, but I am not them. Positions of power. Wealth. Prestige. None of those things matter to me. While I do admit the patronage would indeed open doors and help me access research for my Path faster, I could just as easily do that by myself at a slower pace and not be bothered with all of this in the slightest. So, no, Lord Naowa, for taking up the mantle of a Gatekeeper against the Haze and all that is beyond and ensuring the security that Wells provides to the Empire . . . I don't see how this is a fair exchange."

"You do realize you're standing in front of the Fire King, boy?" said the overseer. Ah, there was that condescension again. "People have been sentenced to lifetime imprisonment for a quarter of what you've just said."

"True," said Lukas, nodding at the underlying threat. "But I'll be candid, Overseer. This isn't some clerk job you're handing over. This is a position of immense responsibility, and believe it or not, I have *some* idea of what it entails. What it means. My advice would be that an employee who willingly works for his boss is a far more credible tool than someone being forced to do the job. But you're the Overseer of Haviskali, and I'm just a vagrant, so what do I know?"

For a few moments, no one said a thing.

Until the Fire King finally spoke.

"It is a rare day when I find myself jealous of a common man. Zuken Banksi has an eye for treasure. I wonder . . ." said the Fire King. "Perhaps it is the old legends at work that have spurred your development?"

Lukas suddenly had a sinking feeling in his stomach.

"The . . . old legends?"

Lord Naowa made a loud, throaty noise.

"Ah, yes," said the Fire King, looking a bit embarrassed. "I suppose I spoke a little too soon. Forgive me, Lord Naowa." He looked at Lukas again, amusement shining in his eyes. "Do not fret about that, Lukas Aguilar. Let the Shogun know of your demands, and we will see what can be made of them. Know this, a child you may be, but without question, you hold the potential to dictate the direction the World will go, intentionally or not, the moment you take the stage. I look forward to seeing you in the future."

It was official, Lukas decided. He would never understand how these monsters thought.

"My business here is concluded," said Jimmo Asuka, a playful smile on his face. "Lord Naowa? Kindly get the Zwaray Keep ready with all the resources our young friend will need to get started on his work. Unless the beholders have read the stars wrong, the clouds of conflict are gathering and near. I should imagine fallout soon enough."

Lukas and Tanya exchanged wary glances.

"This has been a surprisingly enlightening event," said the Fire King. "I eagerly await our next meeting, Lukas Aguilar. Until next time . . ."

Neither Lukas nor Tanya spoke a single word to each other until they were done signing the relevant papers. Much as the Fire King had said, Lukas had been issued fresh new legal documents, proudly identifying him as a citizen of the Llaisy Kingdom, with the class title of PATHFORGER and official position as FORGER with the Zwaray Keep as his home and work premises. The entire land was leased to him for the period of one hundred years, or his death, whichever came later. Lukas had finally mentioned his conditions to Lord Naowa, and seeing the man's eyes twitching at their simplicity almost made him laugh. No doubt the overseer and the Shogun were wondering why he had been such a fool to stand against the Fire King only to demand such common-sense things in the end.

Only when Lukas and Tanya had walked out of the Keep did the latter stop holding back her curiosity.

"What was that? Like, WHAT WAS THAT?" she demanded. "I'm not sure if I should hug the life out of you for doing something amazing or yell at you for pulling a stunt like that! Like . . . What were you thinking? No seriously, *what were you thinking?!*"

Well, he had pretty much stood up to the top brass of the Empire and started making demands. In his defense, those demands were all things that they would probably have granted anyway if he had been more diplomatic about it but sometimes a show of power was necessary to prove one's point.

Lukas ran his fingers through his hair. "I was feeling monumentally suicidal."

"No doubt," raged Tanya. "Sometimes I just don't understand you. You're lucky they want you for Well-forging. Standing up to the Fire King, inviting his wrath like that, it could get you killed."

"We both know that Well-forging is the least of their needs, Tanya. The real job is to ensure Arah never gets out."

Tanya crooked an eyebrow, her expression one of dubious mistrust. "Arah? Arah who?"

"Arah, the Ifrit King? The one that nearly incinerated both of us?"

"What does the Ifrit King have to do with this?" asked Tanya with uncertainty, furrowing her brows at his words, clearly not getting what he was trying to say.

He tried once more: "The Ifrit King! The one we faced inside the borderland? The reason why the Fire King gave svartalfars all they had in the first place?"

She had been there with him the entire time that the Fire King had explained to him about Arah in detail. The man had been quite vocal about his agenda and what he was really pressing Lukas to do. It was why he had all but ordered Lord Naowa to accept Lukas's whimsical demands.

So why wouldn't Tanya stop looking at him like he was talking gibberish?

"Lukas," she said, utter bewilderment on her face, "are you alright? Did something go wrong when you faced the king's power?"

Lukas stared at her for several seconds. It was like they were having two completely different conversations. They just kept circling around the same point over and over again.

It hit him then.

"Tanya . . ." he said carefully. "What exactly do you remember the Fire King saying about the reason the svartalfars were given the Keep to stay in?"

"Because they would enchant weapons and build Wells for them?" *I am not sure what is more terrifying . . .*" murmured Meynte from within his mind. *That I didn't even notice this effect at the time or the very fact that none may know the secret unless deemed worthy of it.*

". . . Lukas?" Tanya asked, confused.

"Never mind," he said, suddenly feeling oddly cold. "I think I have my answer."

"You know that after this you can never pretend you're just another vagrant?"

Lukas sighed. He had noticed the way the yokai, Olfric, Elena, and Solana had looked at him. Even Tanya was probably reevaluating everything she knew about him from this latest stunt. And it was hardly surprising. No different from the way bait fish made sure they weren't in the path of a shark swimming in the vicinity. Not because the shark had a bad temper, but because it was a shark.

He was that shark now.

And that suited him, somehow. He felt raw and a little uncomfortable. Like there was something within him that needed fixing. And maybe scrubbing his skin off with moss and hot water. Maybe after he dealt with Mujin, a little distance from the yokai mob and some rest would be a good thing. At least for a while.

"Good," he said at last.

"Good?"

He nodded and scratched the back of his head. "It'll give me the privacy I need. After everything we went through and everything that's about to happen, it'll be a nice respite."

And then a thought came to him.

"Tanya . . . Exactly what does it mean to be part of the Sacred Eight? What is their role?"

Tanya opened her mouth and closed it. Then she opened it again and closed it again. She repeated the action several times, the look of puzzlement changing to confusion as she concentrated, before giving up. "I . . . I don't know. Is it important?"

The feeling of coldness intensified. "Who knows? Maybe it is."

CHAPTER 17

A chill blew through the prison chamber, the icicles beneath the floor and the ever-spinning wind within the room bringing unbearable cold to the inmate.

Said inmate was a single man, his wrists bound in lifeforce-restraining manacles, his shirtless, injured form shivering in the cold and the dark. The shadows crawled at him from every inch of the prison, and no amount of chanting the Great Goddess's praises brought Eternal Light to its deep, dank, claustrophobic darkness.

It was the worst place for Ultaf Shimizu, whose life was now complete misery. He shivered even more, feeling an odd stinging all over his body. The pain was too much. The horrible effect of the shadows and the alien ice was taking its toll on him. He couldn't even summon anger for what had been done to him.

He couldn't feel sadness as he remembered the ambush in his fortress, which should have been impenetrable. Seeing his grandfather's seat of power explode into smithereens, leaving a flat mountain top in its wake, wasn't something he'd ever have imagined in his worst nightmares.

That it was done not by an army nor by a king but by a random nobody was more than he could bear.

The sound of footsteps alerted him, and Ultaf shivered. Panic, fear, and unbridled rage assaulted him from all directions and he was barely aware of his body beginning to thrash. And then something cool and oh-so-familiar slid in front of him.

"How are you enjoying your stay, Elder Brother?" said Tanya in an almost husky tone.

Tanya slid into view, looking beautiful and provocative, her pale, pupilless, feline-slanted eyes gazing upon him almost fondly as she raised a pale hand and licked the tip of her finger. Ultaf was suddenly aware of a hoarfrost tendril crawling upon his chest that began to dig into his skin, drawing blood. He looked at the blood trickling out of his chest, then at the tendril. Then feeling the sudden drop in his vitality, he noticed Tanya licking her finger with nothing short of horror in his eyes. *That bitch!* She was sucking his lifeforce dry with just that little finger.

He had almost forgotten that she had once served as Grandfather's sword and had acted as his representative on multiple occasions before the hideous truth of her heritage had come to light.

"W—why?" he croaked out a few moments later. His body felt deliciously numb, and he wondered if he was going to die this time around.

"Oh, Elder Brother," she chided lightly and booped him on the nose with her finger. "Always so quick to demand answers. Perhaps you should start answering a few of my own."

Ultaf choked and stared at her with wide eyes.

"But you haven't asked any!" he exclaimed hysterically.

"Oh," Tanya uttered in surprise. "That's right. I haven't."

Ultaf couldn't help it; he burst into hysterical laughter. For some reason, it was the funniest thing he had heard in his life. He laughed and laughed, his body shaking against the chains as Tanya stepped back and watched him with those white alien eyes.

It really fucking hurt.

He had to remember, Ultaf decided, as he laughed. He had to remember Grandfather. Yes. Grandfather. Grandfather. The warlord. The Beast of Shimizu. Mujin. He chanted the name mentally as his laughs turned into coughs, his body shaking with weakness. Grandfather would come. He would save him. Ultaf was his heir. He wasn't aware of his lips moving but suddenly a pale hand came out of nowhere and slapped him clear across his face.

"Do not lie to yourself, Ultaf," Tanya chided. "The Peak was destroyed, remember? Along with everyone on it. Nobody knows who did it or how. For all Grandfather knows, you are dead. You see, that makes you the best kind of hostage." Her smile turned venomous. "You've played the lord card all this time, Elder Brother. You hoard secrets, secrets passed down from one lord to another. Secrets that Grandfather passed down to our father and then to you. Secrets that should have been mine. Secrets that you will reveal to me."

"I'll tell you! I'll tell you!" Ultaf blubbered. "I—I get it. I hurt if I don't tell."

"Oh yes," she said agreeably. "Grandfather was never one for Empire politics. That is why he had you take the mantle of the acting lord. So, you're going to be my little information piggy bank. I'll come in, torture you a bit, get what I want to know, and let you hang here until I need you again."

Ultaf paled.

"Or, I can set my obscurer on you. You can, of course, resist and that'll hurt like you've never imagined in your wildest nightmares. Or you can cooperate with my Obscurer and that way, there'll be less pain and you can hope to stay alive and functional at the end of it."

"Func—functional?" Ultaf accused. "You'll make me your puppet!"

"Why yes," said Tanya. "Isn't that what you've done all your life to others? Let's see how you like it for a change."

Ultaf remembered Zuken's changeling, the ljósálfar who had proven capable of Obscuration. He remembered being paralyzed by that demon, only for it to then grab him by his chin. Seeing those bright, owlish, putrid eyes and the squid-like form within them wasn't something he wanted to revisit anytime soon.

"I'll talk! I'll talk!" Ultaf cried. "Just . . . just stop this! I'll tell you everything! Everything!"

Tanya smiled. "Wonderful! So why don't you start by telling me all about Grandfather's relationship with the Earth King?"

Wonderful . . .

That was the single word that summarized the situation in Tanya's mind.

The things she had learnt from Ultaf . . . the origins of Everfrost within her, and how deep this conspiracy ran, and the people involved in this mess . . . The more she thought about it, the more she wanted to just drop it all and vanish into some borderland with Lukas. Preferably for months, and then travel to some distant part of the Empire.

The West felt like a good option. Nothing this crazy ever happened in the West.

FASTER!

She grimaced as Meynte's metallic, right fist slugged her and threw her back by a dozen feet. Even with all her power, it still felt like she had just been smashed by a cannonball. The only reason why her punishment wasn't being pressed was due to Meynte's inability to rift in her current, metallic form, which made her feel even worse.

After finding out everything she could from Ultaf about the conspiracy between Mujin and the Earth King, though the details were still beyond her, it had taken all of her strength of will not to kill Ultaf on the spot. Lukas would have been pissed off if she did that, and while she was still getting used to his strategic planning, the truth was that all of these games between the uber-powered players she was surrounded by were getting to her.

She was tired.

Mujin. Solana. The empress's shard. The entire Shimizu name and future. Lukas's deal with Lord Naowa. The Fire King. And now the Earth King's involvement. This entire debacle had exhausted her in so many fucking ways that she hadn't even imagined would have been possible. She had thought she was prepared for this, especially after the Level Ups she had gotten in the borderland. Ha! She had been an idiot. She, who had spent all these years growing up on the run, had been caught unaware and Lukas, who hadn't even *known* what lifeforce and mana were until barely a year ago, was dealing with the entire world, while keeping her safe.

She instinctively knew that Lukas was hiding things from her. Meynte's own presence was proof enough. Seeing Lukas withstand the Fire King's power had been eye-opening. Yes, he came clean with a lot, and in the grand scheme of things, it did make sense even if it was unappealing. He was in a shitty position, and while she was grateful for it, she honestly didn't know if she could handle much more.

She wanted to punch something in the face.

She wanted to scream till her throat bled.

She wanted him in her hands, talking to her in person, telling her that she didn't need to deal with this political backstabbing and this ever-escalating mess. That he was going to take her away with him.

But he wasn't here. So she had to make do with taking it out on the metallic avatar of the empress who had once drowned her in her deepest nightmares and was only instructing her because Lukas was, in a manner of speaking, her lord and master.

If only the bitch would just stop beating the crap out of her already.

Get up, exclaimed Meynte. *Cease this weakling behavior. I'm not done with you yet.*

"I'm bleeding," Tanya protested, glancing at the blood that stained her legs and her abdomen. The punch that she had just received had to have broken multiple ribs, which only intensified the pain.

You've bled before. You'll live.

Tanya gawked at her taskmaster. She had expected Meynte to be cruel and heartless in her instruction. But this was a level beyond that.

Just as Lukas had instructed, the empress had been teaching Tanya in secret, within warded boundary fields that Tanya herself had erected with her guidance. And currently, that training involved her attempting to fight using nothing but rifting and a thin blade. The empress's shard was unable to rift, but that didn't mean she couldn't detect the ebbs and flows in the fabric of space around her and react almost instantly, and often with either a metallic punch or with her double-edged broadsword. That resulted in two blades flashing in the arena, silver blurs dancing in a lethal symphony. Meynte's broadsword swept in great, disemboweling strokes that left the air whistling in its destructive wake. Tanya's blade—a thinner, smaller, one-handed version of it—wove in intricate patterns, clashing against each other to the tune of ringing steel, smiting each other in powerful, yet graceful blows, creating lasting ripples in the air around them.

As a clan heir, Tanya had been trained exclusively by experts. But this was something completely different. No resting between bouts, no breaks in between flurries of strikes. This was nonstop combat. Continuous, uninterrupted battle. There was no hesitation, and the only thing close to a pause was when Meynte said something, and even then, she'd come forward with the intent to kill while discoursing on whatever topic garnered her interest.

You've become far too dependent on your Aeromancy, said Meynte, circling her like a predator taunting an injured prey. *You've forgotten that it is but a tool like that blade in your hand.*

She spun the broadsword casually in one hand before swinging it in a slicing arc downwards, causing Tanya to roll away.

And that is what makes you inferior!

Tanya snarled and rushed at Meynte, only to be backhanded and sent tumbling away.

Tools are just tools, even if they're part of your body, said Meynte. "*You are you. The Soulcrafter knows this, hence he prevailed. That is why I bowed before the might of a Level-3 manacrafter and why he commands my allegiance and respect.*"

Like always, it came back to Lukas. It always did.

"Is that why he's vanished in some cave and left you to train me?" she growled.

Some things, said the empress, *are better kept secret. And if the Soulcrafter deems you worthy of the truth, he will tell you in his own time.*

Tanya furrowed her brow and pushed herself up again.

"Is it that bad?"

Bad? Certainly not. But you will not understand. And it will lead you to asking more questions. Questions I cannot answer.

Tanya closed her eyes as she contemplated Meynte's response. It was cryptic, and she found herself intrigued.

"What *are* you? As in . . . I could understand a memory, a consciousness taking over a similar body with similar powers, but that's just a pool of metal you're possessing right now. How do you still exist?"

Meynte chuckled. *By being forgotten.*

Tanya frowned.

"I don't understand."

I don't expect you to. By the laws of reality, I am an impossibility. As is every other creature the Soulcrafter has brought forth to do his bidding. Those of the dead must stay dead, for their souls return to the Great Mother. Even we, the wielders of Taboo, are not exempt from this law of the universe. What is born must die. And what dies, returns to the Mother to be reborn afresh.

Tanya opened her mouth to say something, only to realize she had gotten within her instructor's reach. She barely managed to defend against the strike and hastily rifted away with an almost-fractured shoulder bone. But she ignored it.

"You . . . you're influencing him, aren't you? Controlling him from inside his World?"

Influence? Yes. Control? No. Not even close. The Soulcrafter's mind is ironclad. His World holds no Rule sacred but its own. I couldn't get in even if I tried.

"I don't believe you," she challenged. "Lukas was a Level 3 when he siphoned you. You tried to end me, and somehow, he trusts you more than me about things?"

Foolish girl, the empress's shard mocked. *Weak and pathetic you already are, yet you amaze me with your shortsightedness. You bremetans never truly realize your Potential, do you? You train under pretenders. You call them "Master" and grovel before them to learn their pitiful secrets. But they are nothing in the grand scheme of things. So inconsequential that they are little more than a single droplet in a surging ocean.*

Tanya rifted and came from above. Meynte grabbed her leg, spun her in midair, drove her blade right through her shoulder girdle, and flung her back. The entire thing happened in a fraction of a second.

Forget what your wise elders have taught you, girl, said Meynte. *For they are lies twisted to become truth. Only through pain can you forge strength. Only through weakness can you forge greatness. The Soulcrafter isn't a warlord, and yet, he resisted the might of the strongest king. He is young, and yet his will is as indomitable as the universe itself. He is strong because he wills himself to be strong. That is why his will bent mine, and it will stay that way until his World itself becomes undone.*

Tanya ached all over. She bled from a dozen wounds inflicted purposefully by the empress. Her entire body felt like one big bruise.

"And how do I become like him?"

A shadow of a smile crossed Meynte's metallic features. *You are a long way from that, girl. The Soulcrafter is a monster unlike anything you have ever known. Let him be. At this moment, the only thing you should be caring about is my blade tearing through your flesh.*

"Mujin will not wait until I'm ready," said Tanya. Her heart was pounding, her throat constricting. "And I'm done letting Lukas fight my battles for me. Even with Ezzeron, I cannot match Mujin in Aeromancy. Not even with rifting. What can I do?"

Meynte looked thoughtful.

"You made me face my worst fears," said Tanya, her eyes glistening with tears. "Made me watch as you destroyed Lukas's arm. I don't ever want to ever feel that helpless again. I need to be strong. To use Everfrost like I was born to. To protect myself *and* Lukas. I . . . I need to be like you."

Meynte smiled, but Tanya thought she detected just a faint glimmer of sorrow lurking beneath.

You don't want to be like me, she said softly.

There was a hidden meaning behind those words that she couldn't discern.

All strength comes at a price. Power, even more so. None of these things come free. And sometimes, the price is something you don't ever want to give up. Sometimes, it may even cost you your bremetanity.

Tanya swallowed.

I saw you, girl. I saw your hopes, your dreams, saw the illusions you have cast upon yourself. Even with Everfrost coursing through your veins, you stubbornly stick to being a bremetan. The Soulcrafter, in his arrogance and selfishness, let open a gate through which the End shall resurface. I warned him, but he thought you could control it.

Meynte met her eyes. *You can't. You do not have it in you the strength to give your soul up little by little until you have gone so far past the deep end that you cannot even remember what you were once. You do not have within you what it costs to become Nidhogg's Vessel. To channel the power of the End.*

"Then teach me," said Tanya earnestly. "Tell me how. I will do it. No matter what it takes."

Brave words, said Meynte. *But ultimately, they're meaningless. The power of the End is a deceitful labyrinth, girl, a web that you can only tread into if you are willing to leave behind all of your foolish preconceptions about right and wrong, about power and Potential. You must be willing to accept that you do not fear to tread the boundaries of the true and the profane. You must be one with your other self, the Frost Avatar, and proceed to gain the power that calls to your very soul. If not, this is as far as you can go.*

The Empress looked at her with a mixture of pity and contempt. *If only the Soulcrafter had listened to my advice. You have Potential, girl. Potential to become a pioneer in Aeromancy or perhaps even at rifting. But to cross the boundaries and stand on the edge of the horizon, you need to be willing to submit yourself to the omnipotent power of Everfrost. A power you fear. A power that lies hidden in your core, and until you can overcome this fear, you will not be worthy.*

Tanya frowned.

Was Meynte right? Did she fear Everfrost?

The answer was an obvious "yes" for anyone who had been introduced to the power through carnage and torture. It was natural to fear things one didn't understand and, in that sense, as long as she couldn't be sure what she was getting herself into, the fear would remain. After all, it was the instinct that guided you away from danger, that made you dread the blazing flames, that stopped you from taking that enticing leap from the top of the tower.

It ensured your continued survival.

Similarly, a newborn would have every reason to fear the people around him, but eventually, trust is built upon experience, and the fear is replaced by trust. Faith.

So, could she put that faith in her other self? From her experiences? Surely not. Frost had risen within her only to kill everyone within sight. It had transformed her from a skillful fighter to a hungry beast that only loved to devour lifeforce. It was what had gotten her captured by her grandfather and had eventually killed her father. It was what had turned her into a fugitive. Even after years of fashioning a new identity for herself, her Frost-self had ended up destroying an anomaly and submerging her in Sin. How could she not fear something that was responsible for so much evil?

She stared at her fingers, flexing her hand as she watched them extend and clench, and suddenly, like a flicker of a faulty lamp, a stray thought came to her.

Did she fear her own fingers or her own hands that could accomplish so much?

Of course not. No sane person would fear her own limbs. But why? Because they were part of the body? Because they were completely under her control?

But a child can't control its limbs completely at first—for example, they can't walk from birth, but does that mean kids fear their own legs? Of course not. Something that is a part of you can't hurt you, at least not without your consent.

Then why must she fear Everfrost? The power that flowed through her veins. The power that consumed the lifeforce of others and saved her life on multiple occasions. The power that manifested in the form of an avatar that lay silent in the darkest recesses of her mind. A power that was inherently a part of her, as much as she hated acknowledging that fact.

Thus fear was meaningless.

"I'm ready," said Tanya finally.

Excellent, said Meynte, smiling wolfishly. *If it means anything to you, it took me several weeks for me to reach this mental state. The state where you feel invincible and believe you've completely accepted Everfrost. So let's make haste. For by the time you finish your first lesson, that feeling of invincibility will dissipate into thin air.*

Several miles away in the heart of the labyrinth that was once the Crypt of Fiendish Worms, Lukas Aguilar watched the events unfolding through Meynte's eyes as the shadow of the empress led Tanya toward facing her deepest fears, which included acknowledging her other half—Frost, something she hated and despised beyond reason. While this would be quite a tumultuous experience for his lover, the end result would nonetheless be what he had anticipated.

"You truly are a cruel person, Empress," he said. "You're playing upon the very fears that you put in her in the first place. You know perfectly well what lies in wait if she faces her other self, and yet you still lure her into it."

Next to him, aqāru pooled and a humanoid figure arose, forming an identical copy of the empress.

I merely informed her of what she needed to know, said Meynte, not showing the slightest sign of regret on her features. *It was her decision to partake in the perilous path to controlling Everfrost. If anything, blame yourself for putting her on this path.*

Lukas sighed. He would never understand how he could see through the first Meynte's eyes and his own simultaneously nor how his mind could process such a thing, but he had given up figuring how psionic Skills worked and instead accepted them as a fact and moved on. Anomaly or not, there were some things that were simply too convoluted for him to try make sense of.

Lukas gave her a slightly disapproving look. "Be as that may, I find it distasteful to manipulate her like this."

You knew what you were asking when you asked me to train her, Soulcrafter. Tell me you have not forgotten the promise you made to me.

I have two requests, Meynte had told him after he had captured her. *Swear never to allow the End to take root within the girl's body. And swear that you shall stand against Fimbulwinter if it ever arrives, even if it costs you her life.*

He had given her his word.

And he was going to keep it.

The longer she fears Everfrost, the deeper it shall seep into her psyche," said Meynte now. *You yourself claimed that her other self has already attempted to hold her as ransom. How long before she completely takes over? The only way to keep her from falling is to wrest control from the Frost.*

"I'd have expected more restraint from someone like yourself."

Do not worry, said Meynte. *Frost is no fool. She knows the girl is too valuable to waste just yet. It is much easier to let the girl fall under the delusion of invincibility. She will need it if she wants to survive the oncoming storm.*

Lukas leered at her as if attempting to decipher a puzzle before sighing again. "I suppose. But mark my words. I will not lose Tanya."

He looked away, canceling the vision from the other Meynte's eyes and focusing on his surroundings, at the massive aqāru pool gathered around him. As intense as Tanya's training was going to be, it wasn't what he was most troubled by at the moment.

Soulcrafter, I can stop her from going further along the path. It would be a mistake to do so, but I will, if you want.

Lukas kept quiet. He couldn't risk losing his cool now. Not when there was so much on the line. Inanna would never let him live it down when she found out.

The goddess had always stressed the importance of abandoning one's emotions while doing a job, lest they get in the way, and for the most part, Lukas agreed with the sentiment. It had been the same line of thinking that had led Inanna to self-sacrifice.

While Lukas was not as willing to throw away everything as she had, he had learned to shut himself down in certain situations. It came with hunting monsters and fighting beasts and armies and walking through corpses that he had made himself.

What would Inanna do?

It was a question he frequently asked himself whenever he was in an emotionally trying situation like this. It was a state of mind that he greatly disliked utilizing for multiple reasons, primarily because he wasn't naturally cruel or heartless. But it allowed him to come up with quick solutions to immediate problems that would get out of hand if left unaddressed.

The twisted irony given the situation was not lost on him.

"No . . ." he said at last. "As unfortunate as it is, sometimes friends must do distasteful things to one another in order to ensure their growth and survival in the future . . ."

<h1 style="text-align:center">CHAPTER 18</h1>

Deep inside the heart of what was once the Crypt of Fiendish Worms stood a vast chamber that was larger than most cathedrals on Earth. To a degree, it even resembled one. Lights played in soft colors on the walls, mostly shifting rosy hues. The floor was covered in aqāru, running in exquisitely carved furrows to produce a pattern too sophisticated and perfect to be a mere coincidence. And all of that converged to form a sink—an enormous bone-white rock pedestal—its apex morphed into a majestic throne.

And sitting on it, as if born to it, was Lukas Aguilar.

Magnificent, said Meynte, observing the entire setup with a look of appraisal. *To think that an anomaly could fashion something such as this. It reminds me of my lair.* She glanced at the massive ritual circle beneath them. *And it was to fuse two anomalies into one, you say? Two wombs of Creation, merging. A survivor beneath a cursed Desert and the remnants of a lost and forgotten World, creating a single entity that is greater than the sum of its parts. Magnificent.*

Lukas smiled. What had started in the anomaly back then had played a major role in shaping what he had become—was becoming.

Are you absolutely certain you wish to take this path, Soulcrafter? Distorting reality is something even gods and emperors are wary of.

Lukas glanced at her. "You are unusually wary, Empress. Trust me, I have tried to account for everything I could since the last time."

He had come a long way from that surprised guy with tunnel vision who hadn't thought any further than the finish line. Sometimes it was a fight, at other times a bargain with Inanna or Solana, or just developing a particular Skill. It was exactly the kind of shortsightedness that had led to him foolishly sacrificing himself which later led Inanna to do the same.

Meynte frowned. Empress or not, she knew very little about what the Soulcrafter was attempting. But that didn't mean she was completely ignorant of the nature of what might happen. Despite his impressive efforts and planning, the fact of the matter was that there was far too much that he was not aware of.

Had these unknown factors been decreased by even a small margin, the odds of his success would've been comprehensible enough to be deemed safe but . . .

"Am I absolutely certain?" asked Lukas. "No. Not at all. But this is what has the best shot of succeeding in the upcoming trials, and I can't risk attempting it without preparation."

One powder keg at a time.

But—

"I know you're preparing Tanya for the role," said Lukas, "but I can't put all of my hopes in a single basket. I've seen what could happen."

The moment he knew he had to kill Mujin, he had begun preparing multiple plans for what would follow, both in the short and long term. He knew that Mujin would show up with an army—and thus unknowingly give Lukas exactly what he needed to jump three levels to 39, where he'd be able to assimilate the entirety of Inanna's gift, instantly putting him in the same league as every warlord out there, and possibly a king or two. There was a difference between a warlord that controlled a single element and one that controlled *motion* itself.

It was a good plan. Maybe it would even work out.

But Lukas had to prepare for every eventuality.

He needed to play to his talents, which, of course, lay in his nature as a World. And in the light of the given circumstances, nothing short of king-level power, or at least within the same zip code, would be enough. And the quickest way to gain that would be to absorb king-level creatures.

Arah, the natural-born Ifrit King would be a good place to start.

Theoretically, that is. Like he had said to the Fire King, just getting within the creature's vicinity risked being vaporized and then some. And even if the binding—or Siphoning in his case—was successful, he'd be immolated instantly because of the tremendous amount of fire mana and Level-5 fire Skills taking over his body. Even Lukas Aguilar, World Incarnate, was not immune to that.

No, a better alternative was needed. A way to harness the creature's power without actually doing it himself. As the saying went, the best way to fight a war was to make someone else fight it.

Blob was arguably a useful on that front: a puppet that moved according to his will, answering to his thoughts rather than his commands. While that worked for most creatures, it wouldn't work in the case of a kami, owing to their lack of Soul Capacity. He'd need to create a synthetic prototype, a body capable of storing Soul Capacity within itself, with a physiological constitution compatible with the spirit's element.

A featherglass core and his endless Soul Capacity would take care of the former. Aqāru was more than capable of the latter. Perhaps a skeletal framework crafted using carquane, just to facilitate better conduction of the stored energy into every body part?

It would still be connected to him but only on a technical level. For all intents and purposes, it would be an independent organism.

Sapient. Conscious of its own existence.

The only real snag was his lack of a Creation skill of that level. Metaforging was great, but it was barely enough to create basic substances and elemental weapons. He could bypass some of those limitations using Level-3 Alteration to create featherglass and carquane from other substances, but aqāru was a deal-breaker. Unlike the other materials, it was spiritually potent and required a level of alchemy that was beyond his current ability, and unless he pushed his Metaforgery to Level 3 and beyond, he doubted he'd make any progress there.

As he had said, not something he could prepare for the upcoming fight.

Hence . . . *this.*

"Aqāru Boundary. Hundred feet radius. Expansion."

Unlike every other time he spoke, his words were amplified, power lining his voice as his command took effect, doing exactly as he said and creating a territory of sentient metal around him in all directions, traveling through the pre-crafted furrows, the pool of metal following his thoughts and crisscrossing each other until he sat in the center of a massive pentacle inscribed within a massive circle. The more he studied and experimented with the knowledge he had gotten from Inanna, the more he was convinced that the Asukans had only a very superficial understanding of the ritual craft they employed for the Shikigami Ritual. The pentacle was an impressively complex, intricate system that could theoretically make effective use of diversified and unpredictable variables at any time.

Unfortunately, the average mortal was incapable of harnessing its true Potential. The best the Asukans had come up with was to channel Eternal Light, maintained by their faith in the goddess Amaterasu, to employ a brute-force method to bind a spiritual creature inside. From his quick study of the broken remains of the Well at Zwaray Keep, he had determined that even the svartalfars used this ritual, only utilizing their runecraft instead of Eternal Light, to puncture through the rift and expand it, allowing people to travel into the borderland on the other side. It was crude, put it like that, but when the closest alternative were astronomical events like the Black Moon where the barriers between the real world and the Haze were at their weakest, it might as well have been considered a landmark in and of itself.

But unlike the svartalfars or the Asukans, Lukas wasn't so limited.

"Initiate Puppeteer Protocol. Five puppets on standby. Rapid-Install Prime Host prototype."

At that, five doppelgangers of himself popped out of the aqāru at the vertices of the pentacle. The liquid metal creations even had the equivalent of trousers and shirts on, adding uneven textures to their metallic bodies.

Dizziness hit him like a tidal wave. Having six of him all at once hextupled the sensory output he was receiving. Neural Suppression came to his benefit, and he quickly silenced the data influx. He just needed the doppelgangers to do one job and do it perfectly, without forwarding all the extra sensory load to him.

"Access Ley Line Network. Augment mana production. Independent assortment. Magnify output."

Power surged out of him, flooding through the aqāru into his doppelgangers.

"FIRE."

Flame Creation and Manipulation, both Level-3 Skills that belonged to the bylestyr, rose to the forefront as one of the doppelgangers erupted into flame. Within seconds, the entire chamber was alight with crimson as waves of light and heat emanated out of the doppelganger.

"WATER."

Water Creation and Manipulation, collected from the kami Shahxith that had once been Olfric's, as well as other kami he had collected from the Haze, activated in the doppelganger on the other extreme end.

Wind, Earth, and Ether followed. Within the next minute, the five doppelgangers standing at the five vertices had become anthropomorphic manifestations of the elements themselves.

Fire. Wind. Water. Earth. Ether.

Exactly in that order.

With aqāru being an effective mana conductor and dispenser, Lukas could theoretically map out a ritual pentacle on any scale. The only real problem would be to power it properly, and drawing from a ley line using Capacitance was likely to kill him first. He had used Blob to draw power at the Peak as well as the near-mindless instincts of the dranzithl, carefully shielding his own mind from being exposed to that raw power, and even *that* had sent him reeling.

Luckily, carquane provided a solution to that problem.

It was time to begin.

Unlike anything he had done before, no single Skill or even combination of Skills would get this done. He would need to perform a specific spell. Inanna had told him that, unlike Skills, spells required the caster to hold a specific mindset and attributes to cast it, and since much of it took place in the caster's mind, it was always safe to tie the spell to a name or an aria sequence. The other option was to tie the process to a particular item—say, a weapon or relic of some kind, or an ornament, like the pendant he was wearing—but Inanna had never gotten around to explaining how that bit was done.

He was attempting to manifest his inner-world within his established territory. Theoretically, it was no different than applying the Living Anomaly function within an established boundary radius, except that he was also manifesting his inner reality at the same time.

"Territory Creation Set."

Every single drop of aqāru shivered at his words, making the air hum with a chorus of metal from every direction.

Ancient hermits on Earth had a saying—*as above, so below*—referring to how the macro and the micro had structural similarities. Basically, make something happen on a small scale, then give it the energy to happen on a large scale. If he understood it right, the pentacle matrix could be used as an amplification tool for whatever he was trying to do, so long as it was within the Rules of the World, be it enacting a massive spell upon the world or affecting reality itself.

The Fire doppelganger erupted violently, the flames reaching as high as the ceiling. On the other extreme end, the Water variant had a massive form resembling a jellyfish. A fierce gale swept through the chamber, but the pentacle remained unaffected. Carquane began forming out of the Earth variant, who looked eerily similar to a svartalfar at this point—Alteration in effect, connecting it to Lukas. The carquane then segmented as it approached him, forming lines, connecting him further to the other four doppelgangers. The crystal pierced the doppelgangers, creating a core where the heart was supposed to be.

Power flowed in. Far more power than aqāru was capable of.

Soulcrafter, mana alone will not fuel what you want. You're forgetting—

The rest of her words died down as Meynte's attention was suddenly diverted by a soft clattering sound. A piece of jagged rock had fallen down to the ground. She looked and found it was still shaking. Within seconds, the intensity of the vibrations grew to the point that the fallen shard of rock shattered, and several more were beginning to fall from above. Nothing that could remotely harm either of them but definitely odd.

Lukas spoke again:

"Deny Foreign Truth."

The rattling and the sounds magnified in size and were joined by a violent rattling of wind that had little to do with the controlled gale within the ritual circle. And that sound was joined by a discordant hum that came from everywhere and nowhere and slowly increased in volume as if it were the herald of a terrible *something*.

Soulcrafter, Meynte warned, anxiety rising in her tone, *End this. End this now.*

But Lukas didn't. He had noticed, but it was as if he couldn't stop now, not even if he tried.

Power danced, forming strange and almost erratic patterns, Kinetomancy manipulating the elements, as Rules of a World that was so similar yet so very different began to slide in, substituting reality itself within the established ritual circle. A World that was the remains of a Lostbelt, one that had perished and had yet been reborn within himself.

Everything around him was disappearing, and a sea of purplish mist was enveloping the entire radius. There was no light, no life, no conflict, *nothing . . .*

Just erected crystal mounds on an endless terrain, everything within it lying in patient, eternal wait.

Forgotten.

His lips widened into a half-formed smile.

"Est—"

NO—STOP! Meynte yelled, sensing something terribly wrong was about to happen. Unfortunately, it was a little—

"—ablish Living Anomaly—"

Too late.

THRUMM!

The resounding hum shook the entire chamber. A second of quiet followed, the calm before the storm. What came next wasn't an explosion, not really. There was no light or sound or force. Rather, a mad outpouring of *something* tore through the chamber, not as a single shockwave but a thousand slow streams, flowing in every direction, targeting everything in its vicinity.

What followed wasn't a battle. That would have implied more than one potential outcome, but the moment the world around the circle lashed out in its fury, there was only one way things could end for this was an act of an almighty being.

The wrath of the World itself.

The wave of emptiness rolled forth like a tsunami, devouring the dim lighting within the chamber, and everything—including Lukas himself—was engulfed. Meynte's consciousness jumped from one drop of aqāru to another, growing increasingly desperate as the entire thing was consumed, its protocols and sentience ripped to shreds.

The Soulcrafter had plans. Defenses. Traps. Protections enhanced by Meynte's own suggestions.

They were blown away like cobwebs in a hurricane.

Meynte screamed silently in her mind—or what remained of it as the flood of erasure subsumed her, flowing down every single drop and bubble of the sentient metal, killing every single thing that contained even a trace of the Soulcrafter's inner-world from the liquid metal all around it, a defilement stabbed into the very core of the essence that was Lukas Aguilar.

And then the familiar schema popped into existence.

Error Detected
No Vital Signs found for Anomaly Body
Soul Prototypes cannot be utilized

Troubleshooting . . .
Host Prototype exists. Anomaly Body does not exist.
Incompatible
Attempting failsafe protocols using LIVING ANOMALY . . .

Meynte wanted to laugh. Of course. *Living Anomaly! What a truly lopsided function!* An utterly selfish thing that ignored everything but its own laws.

Even the complete annihilation of its body and accessories.

Was there any doubt that the Soulcrafter was what he was?

Initiating reconstruction of Anomaly Body based on Prime Host's configuration . . .

In that darkness, *something* began to reforge itself back into existence. There was not enough of Meynte left to feel it as she slipped away, her mind erased long before any lingering sensory input finally stopped and vanished into an eternal darkness. The only thing she remembered thinking was that the Soulcrafter truly was a monster unlike anything she had seen in her long life.

Several hours later, Lukas Aguilar—or an *instance* of him anyway, not that it made a difference anymore—stumbled towards his chambers, with one hand holding his throbbing head in a vice grip while another was blindly grasping the thin air for support. He should never have attempted something that crazy so quickly without considering the other factors. Meynte had warned him against the effects of bifurcating—or in this case, *hexafurcating*—his mind, but as always, he had given his curiosity and need to experiment free reign.

Reckless or not, the experiment had borne fruit. He wouldn't be exaggerating if he'd said that he had gleaned more from this one insane attempt than his entire stay in the Haze.

Obviously, said Meynte sourly. *Expect you to put manifesting your inner-world upon reality on the same level as Territory Creation.*

"I just imagined it was simply a function of power influx, area, and mental control."

NO.

Lukas winced. *"Then—"*

Why let you do it? Because you have a habit of making unreasonable demands. Do not forget, Soulcrafter, I was an empress in life. I am well used to listening to requests that could curdle milk.

He frowned. The theory was that all energy-crafting—whether it be lifeforce, mana, or anomalous—was reality-altering as it could produce matter out of nowhere, create mana in all forms, and achieve all sorts of enchantments. A skilled user could latch on to the spiritual and symbological attributes of the elements to manifest all sorts of wondrous abilities, whether it be applying the principles of Contagion to *water* and using it to connect to someone far away across geographical boundaries, to employing the symbological attributes of Earth to fortify oneself and another in all sorts of ways. Rifting could transport people through the fabric of space, and offensive spell-fire could shift landscapes themselves. A skilled terramancer could transmute objects and alter gravity and friction while a talented pyromancer could flare the emotions of every single person within their vicinity.

True, but you forgot one simple fact.

"This isn't my World."

He had been so caught up in learning and experimenting with the powers he had been given, courtesy of Inanna and the omphalos shard within him, that he had failed to take into account that this *wasn't* his home planet. As wondrous as it might appear, lifeforce, mana, or anomalous energy . . . all of it was part and parcel of this World and thus existed within the framework of its Rules.

Its Truths.

But Reality Distortion? That was man playing God.

Not small g. Capital. For even *gods* would think twice before attempting to alter reality itself. The art of Reality Distortion was too much to comprehend. It was like playing with the space-time continuum in the palms of his hands.

After all, even time was nothing but an illusion—a thread in the meshwork of reality that could be unwoven or rewoven in all sorts of ways if one just knew how.

In the face of Reality Distortion, facts were baseless, truth was meaningless, events were timeless, and reality was powerless.

In the words of Vespasian, the Roman Emperor, "Vae! Puto deus fio."

"Dear me, I think I am becoming a god."

And that was what Lukas had just attempted. The moment he tried to distort reality by bringing his inner-world—bringing the *Plains of Forget*—into existence outside his body, brute-forcing it over greater reality using raw power, he had severely underestimated the World's reaction to it.

For some reason, he had this weird feeling that this was reality just chiding him, like a parent admonishing a silly but innocent child over some wrong-doing. He didn't know why, but he sort of knew that the next time he tried to pull this off, reality would be far less accommodating.

Still, it was better he knew that now. It wasn't something to take comfort from, but fear of the expected was always better than fear of the unexpected. He knew now that his activation ritual had failed the moment he tried to bring the Plains of Forget into greater reality, so there must have been some kind of threshold he was yet to cross.

But the same could be said about Wells. Yes, one could argue that the Rift existed naturally, and all the Well did was tear it open further at the expense of energy, but that didn't undermine the fact that the Wells employed the World's energy against the World to tear the Rift open, albeit for a small amount of time.

But so had he. After all, anomalous energy was no different from the natural energy of this World, even if it came from . . .

His stomach sank.

Again, this World was so similar to his that he sometimes forgot something crucial: he was from beyond this Creation's boundaries. The rules he played under were different from the ones everyone else around him did. Even if some things seemed to have changed in a minor fashion, like the ability to use lifeforce or mana, it was ridiculously easy to just assume that Earth too had similar stuff going on before it was rendered a Lostbelt by circumstances unknown.

And then this world threw some pretty profound curveballs at him.

Like the very idea that *energy* would be different too had never occurred to him.

It took him a second to recover from that sudden realization at the fact that such a huge fundamental difference existed between Earth and this World. He had almost forgotten that the lifeforce and mana he used were actually produced *within* his body. And the only time he had drawn on energy from the outside world, it had been added to his omphalos reserves or . . .

Or directly used against the World itself.

Like in the borderland or when he had opened a rift to the Haze.

Not really, Meynte pointed out. *Remember what you did in the fortress.*

She had a point. He had used the energy from the wardstones to amplify the dranzithl's attack. Crippling as the attempt had been, he had thought he had been adversely affected because of channeling energy far greater than his body and mind could take in. But what if . . .

What if that crippling sensation had had less to do with the energy density and more with the fact that the energy itself was foreign to his body and had been poisoning him? Was that why his experiment had failed? Because he had been powering it with his own reserves—anomalous or otherwise—which was fundamentally different to this world's energy?

It was a valid theory, and the only way to prove or disprove it was through more experimentation. If it held true, then the only successful way to conduct it would be to repeat the experiment on top of a ley line with carquane wardstones digging into it. Theoretically, it had a larger chance of success, but on the battlefield, it wouldn't be very practical.

Not when you were facing an aeromancer warlord who could simply nuke the living shit out of you from above.

And carquane crystals aren't inconspicuous.

"*They're also time-consuming to make,*" Lukas mused. And time was currently against him.

But all that caution and fear meant nothing because, as of right now, Lukas was feeling as though his head might split open at any moment and his brain would leak out as squishy juice. Oh, god. That mental image itself gave him another migraine.

Staggering into his room, Lukas steadied himself to not appear as though he was mindlessly drunk, and taking a huge gulp of air, he trudged forward and froze.

Tanya was sitting in his room, her face drained of color and looking genuinely startled. The last time he had seen her like that was . . .

When he had mentioned the possibility of Tsurara being her mother.

Lukas immediately knew that something was wrong. The only other time he'd ever seen her look this afraid was her disastrous episode with Meynte.

Ignoring the empress huffing in his mind, he rushed towards her, his own headache forgotten. Tanya just stared blankly up at him, her face so devoid of feeling that it was startling. It was blank, so stripped of emotion, so . . . empty that he could scarcely recognize her. It frightened him.

What the hell was going on?

"Tan—Tanya! What's wrong?"

It wasn't until a few seconds later that some color returned to her cheeks and she began to react again.

"What's the real reason you asked the empress to train me, Lukas?"

"Tan—"

"Do not lie to me, Lukas!" she barked out harshly, her voice unusually loud in the quiet room. "I wasn't born yesterday. Neither am I blind. And let me tell you this, Lukas Aguilar, you aren't very good at hiding things from me. Or even hiding the fact that you're hiding something."

"What could I be hiding?" he asked defensively.

"Well, that proves it," she said, her voice slightly lowered. "Usually you do one of two things when confronted with hiding something, you deflect it with a question or you get defensive. You just did both."

Lukas flinched and looked away. Part of him was terrified at the notion of being so predictable. At the same time, the fact that Tanya understood him so well sent a tinge of pleasure down his spine even while ringing alarms in his head.

It didn't help that she didn't ask anything further and just looked at him patiently.

Finally, he sighed. "I just want you to—"

"Master Everfrost," Tanya finished for him. "Before it takes over."

Lukas looked at her sharply.

"Please," said Tanya. "I'm not a fool. It wasn't an entirely difficult leap of logic. You've been scarily focused on having me master Everfrost ever since all of this began. And I don't know what kind of fucked-up deal you have with Solana, but even she's been nice to me since you jumped into the Haze. I don't know what you promised her, but she's practically giddy."

Damn it.

"And if not for that, there's this look you keep giving me since you returned. Like you see me, and you feel . . . sad or guilty. So, spill."

Lukas stared at her sullenly, a little annoyed at how easily she had read him.

"I want you to control Everfrost before it takes control over you."

"But," Tanya looked at him, confused, "it shouldn't! Your goddess sealed it away. You told me—"

"That was before Meynte and everything happened. She brought forth way more than you could contain. You can't do that without weakening the spell."

"A goddess cast the spell." Tanya sputtered. "Meynte was a *memory*."

"A memory of an empress who wielded a Taboo. Not an ordinary Skill but a Taboo. The same taboo that you also wield. You are her descendant, you're both yuki-onna . . . When she possessed you and did those actions . . ."

"You're talking about spiritual resonance, aren't you?" Tanya picked up on it quickly. "You mentioned that before."

Lukas knew that even Meynte was paying close attention now.

He nodded. "Spiritual resonance between two beings so spiritually similar, sharing a deep connection with a Taboo. Plus, it doesn't help that Inanna is no more, and I've depleted nearly the entirety of her divinity within me."

"Lukas," she said, meeting his eyes. "What aren't you telling me?"

Lukas closed his eyes. "After the empress possessed you, the seal on Everfrost loosened. Frost can take over you if she really wants to, and you won't even notice it."

Tanya stilled. It was like watching a cornered animal, preparing for a last-ditch attempt at flight.

"And how do you know that?"

Lukas felt his throat go dry. He had no idea how Tanya was going to react to what he was about to tell her.

"Because she's taken over twice so far, without you knowing any better."

Tanya stayed quiet. Unmoving. Without the slightest change in reaction.

"You already knew," he realized.

"I can't control Everfrost without coming to terms with my other self," she said softly. "She told me . . . *everything.*"

Of course she did! Thought Lukas spitefully. He knew that what had transpired between himself and Frost could have debilitating effects on his relationship with Tanya. And now Frost had gone ahead and done just that.

He exhaled. "Tanya, the truth is Frost always had a far greater control over you than you realized. Yes, you were in control of your senses, but she was always there, listening to what you heard, seeing what you saw, feeling what you felt. She was there in the borderland, listening to every single thing I told you about myself, about being an anomaly, about Inanna. And ever since the empress unleashed her, she's been able to take over, whether you want it or not."

Tanya stared at him dully. "You knew all this . . . and you didn't tell me?"

Lukas flushed at her stare. What was he going to say? That he had slept with her alter ego? That he had plotted with her behind her back, even though it was all done to protect her?

"When you sat on Meynte's throne and she took over, I tried to save you. I don't know how or why, but I got pulled inside your mindscape and encountered Frost inside. She . . . she told me things. About herself. About Fimbulwinter. About Meynte. Things that helped me outsmart her."

He could feel Meynte's gaze drilling at him from inside his mind.

"You're telling me that Frost . . . my other self, *helped* you?"

"It'd hardly be the first time. You told me she helped you secure Ezzeron, did she not? Frost isn't an alternate entity. She's a form of you, a branch of your consciousness corrupted by the Taboo you wield. Every yuki-onna, starting from Meynte himself, has had their consciousness fragmented, creating a similar persona. That's what Frost is. Not nice, but not your enemy either."

"*Laying on the compliments a little too thick, Outsider,*" said Tanya's mouth, but the tone that emerged wasn't hers. Tanya's entire body froze, and her eyes widened before a wave of wintry plume exuded out of her, transforming her hair into cadaverous white and her lips into the color of fresh, purple grapes. The only clue that she was still in control was her panicked expression. And the tightening of her throat.

"You aren't supposed to come forth unless I call for you," said Lukas. It was one thing to work with her, another to discover that she could freely skirt around their bargain with such ease.

"*This seemed . . . neater, darling,*" said her mouth again. "*Seeing you trying so hard to get the weakling to accept me felt so . . . stirring.*"

"She . . ." Tanya choked out. "She's taking over! She's . . ."

"*Sshhh . . .*" spoke her mouth. "*You forget, little girl. I'm your other half. The instincts you suppress. The power you deny yourself. We are two halves of the same coin, but that coin is weighted, and one side will always turn up more than the other. Now stop fighting me and let me help you.*"

"Frost, if you—" Lukas began.

"*Oh, darling,*" spoke Tanya's mouth. "*Your care for this weakling is so endearing. Almost enough to want me to seize control. But no matter, no matter. Right now, all I wish is to facilitate your goals.*"

She's lying, Meynte warned.

"Any reason behind this magnanimity?" Lukas pressed, all but ignoring the empress's words.

"*I promised you, remember?*" said Frost beatifically. "*I will not hamper the weakling's attempts to control this power. Especially now that you are moving ahead in the Asukan world.*"

Lukas felt a shudder run down his spine. "This . . . this is about the two favors I owe you."

It wasn't a question. It was a confirmation.

"Yes," said Frost. "*Your little demonstration with the Fire King showed a lot of Potential, Outsider. Deal with your warlord first, and then, we negotiate.*"

CHAPTER 19

T he mansion was, even by the standards of the Sacred Eight, ostentatious. Mujin never really had an eye for architecture, preferring pragmatism and security over vaulted ceilings and items of ceremonial and artistic value. Given the all-around magnificence that sprawled across the estate, the owner clearly held differing notions about the topic.

For this was the Z'allar, the house of the Earth King.

A massive construct that magically faded in and out of view and constantly flowed in shape and size. It wasn't quite a "building" per se, as it was mostly built out of enchantments and Terramancy instead of stone and mortar, crafted out of a technique so complex that it was unfathomable to anyone less than a terramancer warlord.

It was the result of years of interregional research on Terramancy, the crowning achievement of the Terramancers' Guild, built in cooperation with a dozen different other guilds and homage paid by kingdoms and clans to please the one man that lived here. This majestic edifice, located in the center of Khemmel, the capital city of Luthar, was where the Earth King held court, dictating laws and orders to the Cobalt Army and the ministry. This seat of power was the place where he'd receive foreign dignitaries and more.

This wasn't the first time Mujin had been here, nor the first time he would be delivering any sort of news here. But the sheer absurdity of the situation, as well as what had transpired recently, left a bad taste in his mouth. Honestly, he had delayed coming to meet his "friend" and benefactor long enough. Any more and he'd have had to keelhaul himself for cowardice out of sheer principle.

"I already know what happened, Mujin," said Trestan Banksi. "There is no need to bother me with stale news."

"The girl isn't alone," said Mujin, in a tone that indicated how off-putting the situation was.

"I should hope not," said the Earth King softly, with just a hint of curiosity. "If she were indeed capable of shattering the wards of the Peak, I would shift my support to her in a heartbeat. I hope you didn't do anything excessive in anger."

Mujin decided to wisely keep quiet about the destroyed mountain adjacent to the Peak. "I have learned a great many things. Some are irrelevant, some surprisingly worth noting."

"Oh? That's a rarity." The Earth King sat on his throne, serving himself some wine. Despite his words, he didn't look at all curious. If anything, he was amused.

Mujin couldn't blame him. After all the posturing and Ultaf's recent actions, losing the Sacred Eight status had been the greatest shame that his grandson could have brought to his clan. And then, right after, someone had destroyed the Shimizu's greatest fortification, which had been protected by an enchantment crafted by Mujin's father—the Wind King himself.

In just a few hours.

If someone was trying to teach Mujin humility, they were succeeding.

"It is . . . curious that the Fire King is still enjoying Lord Naowa's hospitality," said Mujin. "In Haviskali of all places."

"Oh?"

"All I'm saying is that—"

The rest of his words were drowned out by Trestan Banksi's laughter. "Have you truly fallen so low as to believe in such rumors, Mujin? Perhaps you really should step down and let the girl take your place. If nothing else, she is resourceful enough to shatter a king's defenses and bind his kami successfully, which is more than anything that any of Wakamura's blood have been able to do up until this day."

Mujin bristled but kept quiet.

"But . . ." said Trestan Banksi. "You raise a vital point. It is most unusual for Jimmo Asuka to remain behind. The other clans might be baying for your blood for the svartalfar massacre, but not Jimmo Asuka."

"Why?"

The Earth King met his eyes. "If the Fire King wanted you gone, you'd be gone. You wouldn't have been standing here, talking about it. Do not mistake his affability for weakness, Mujin. That man has worn that mask for so long that he's almost forgotten what sort of creature he is behind it."

Mujin wholeheartedly agreed. His own father, the Wind King, had been just a hair short of *terrified* of Jimmo Asuka, despite being a king himself. One of the things Wakamura Shimizu did in his last days was keep ranting about the utter strangeness of the Fire King, and after Mujin had met the man face-to-face, he was willing to agree with his late father's sentiments.

It wasn't his power nor his position nor his status as a demigod.

Rather, it was the look in his eyes. At times, it was the wide gaze of a small child, full of awe and wonder. Of innocence and eager anticipation, as though about to be read an exciting story.

At other times, it was the relaxed expression of a man that was at the end of his life.

Both expressions were genuine, unhinged, and spoke of a simmering insanity. A pure, calm, peaceful, and completely unique brand of insanity.

It terrified him to his core in a way nothing else ever had before, sending chills down his spine, urging him to leave and run away from this demon as quickly as possible.

"But you're right," continued the Earth King. "Something is certainly off. It isn't in Jimmo Asuka's nature to act this heavy-handedly. Something else is afoot, and I'm more inclined to believe that the girl has something to do with the Peak's destruction. Someone out there is playing a clever game, using the Fire King's presence at Haviskali to mask his or her actions. It almost feels . . . ordained."

Mujin froze. "Ordained? You mean a Chosen?"

If the gods themselves had decided to take action, there was nothing anyone could do to stop their wrath. Of course, no one among the Pantheon would ever bother to take positions against a mortal, but it was for these situations that they had their Chosen—representatives anointed to the holy status by the Pantheon, complete with divine blessings bestowed upon them, and who often ended up burning entire towns and cities to ashes whenever one of them decided to act up.

"It can't be a Chosen," said Mujin slowly. "No Chosen would willingly side with her. Not after knowing what lies in her blood."

"Ah," said the man, his silky tone cutting through the atmosphere like a knife. "The same old fable. An ancient power, providence of a lost god from the Time Before, carried by the White Witch, who old Wakamura defeated in battle. A power capable of ending a king. A power you've promised me in return for my support for decades. A power that I now wonder is even real to begin with."

"It's real," Mujin hissed.

"Then where is it?" snarled the Earth King, and the gravity within the room multiplied twenty-fold. One moment Mujin was standing on his feet, and the next moment his knees were crushing into the floor, the inexorable pull making his body feel like it was made of dense metal. It took everything to simply hold his head up and not fall face-first to the floor.

"Do not forget, Mujin," said the Earth King. "My support is what enabled you to run those twisted experiments all this while. But for all your claims, she's successfully avoided the Great Goddess's all-seeing eye. For all we know, she could potentially survive a Chosen's inspection."

His expression grew pensive. "I'm almost wondering if I should just let this girl take over. It would likely prove to be a most interesting decade or two before I needed her to exercise my little plan."

Wonderful, thought Mujin caustically. This was the problem with dealing with the pseudo-immortal beings that were the kings. They tended to consider years and years of time like most people thought of minutes and hours. With their body also reflecting their elemental status, the kings were less bremetan and more of a force of nature in and of themselves.

Things would not end well if he criticized the Earth King. He had already lost everything—his Peak, his Sacred-Eight status, his soldiers, and his grandson. His sole remaining hope was to find the girl and extract Ezzeron from her. He knew that there was no way she would've grown that strong this quickly, which meant that someone was helping her. Someone with the resources or the skill set to break through his father's enchantments, capable of destroying the entire mountaintop in one go.

This newcomer, this stranger scared Mujin.

"I have one more piece of news," he said at last. "Lord Naowa shifted the Cobalt Army from guarding the Desert borders to the capital city."

"Irrelevant," scoffed Trestan Banksi. "It's clear that your actions lack the thought a mere man would've put into an endeavor of such significance. Did you know that nearly a year ago, an unknown energy signature emerged from the Desert, a Level 5, from what my feelers say, and I'm inclined to agree."

"But that's impossible," claimed Mujin. "Surely there's something—"

"Wrong? I think not. Especially when the feelers up there in the extreme north of the Empire also registered the same reading. Unknown element. Level 5. Exuding out of the Desert."

"But that's *impossible,*" whispered Mujin. "Even a Level-5 energy signature couldn't travel that—"

"That far?" challenged the Earth King. "Every single feeler in the entire Empire felt it. All they could garner was that someone—" He gave Mujin a pointed look. "—was casting a Level-5 spell, reaching past the horizons of the Empire, into the borderlands and the unknown."

Mujin didn't even know what to think anymore. A spell that large? Spell potency was inversely proportional to the area of effect, unless of course, the very nature of the spell was limited to esoteric parameters. But in that case, the power level of the spell would be almost impossible to detect. Clearly, that wasn't the case here. The idea that someone could cast a spell of such an impossible area of effect and yet register itself as a Level 5 from the extreme north of the Empire was both fascinating and terrifying at the same time.

No doubt the emperor himself was interested in this.

"What—what was it about?"

"To connect," said the Earth King simply.

"To connect?" Mujin repeated in confusion. "To what?"

"Nobody knows," said the Earth King, giving him a strange, inscrutable smile. "I sent my own men to investigate the matter, and do you know what they found? Traces of yokai activity inside the Desert, and the obliterated remains of adventurer camps. Since then, yokai activity all over the Southeast has risen dramatically, a rather ominous coincidence, wouldn't you say?"

Mujin scowled, not liking the insinuation in the man's words. "Yokai activity usually waxes around Black Moon Rising, Trestan. They wane down to the minimum within a month or so as the Mists recede."

"Yet this time," countered the Earth King, "we've had as many as five mist-nights since the Black Moon Rising. Another ominous sign that something is out of order. I have long since mentioned that the Chains of Unity need to be upheld at all costs, but your clan is failing spectacularly on that front. You failed to conquer Ezzeron, your son failed to conquer Ezzeron. The only person who succeeded is a fugitive, and you'd rather risk resources and reputation—yours and mine—to find her and extract a power I've only heard of than hold the Chains of Unity together. Such senility is unbecoming of you. In fact, I would much rather believe that you're doing this quite intentionally."

Mujin looked at him in confusion.

"A few months later, my wayward son Zuken barters a trade with the Zwaray Keep, and this girl, your niece, is part of the negotiations. My feelers catch more Level-5 activity from within the Haze, and the next thing we know, your grandson massacres the svartalfar populace, destroying the Well in the process. A Well, I'm told, that was one of the most significant edifices in the entire Empire, important enough for the Fire King himself to come running."

The Earth King met Mujin's eyes. "And now, more unknown activity crashes a Level-5 ward-line and destroys the defenses that have lasted for the past two centuries, handcrafted by the Wind King himself. I wouldn't be surprised if the attack was Level 5, albeit fine-tuned to a very small area."

"I do not trust words," said the Earth King. "I even ignore actions. But I never disregard patterns, Mujin. And if you examine it closely, a very interesting pattern emerges. And the pattern says that something is afoot, and your clan is heavily involved with it. One wonders, what power have you and your granddaughter unleashed that you and your clan have gone so far to hide? Why did your grandson eliminate the very population that could've explained the Level-5 activity within the Haze? Why were Shimizu battlements found in the Desert? Just what *are* you hiding, Mujin Shimizu?"

Mujin's eyes went wide as did his mouth. For a second, he was too surprised to speak.

"You are no longer part of the Sacred Eight, Mujin. You know perfectly well what that means, what fate befalls those unlucky enough to lose their Sacred Eight status. When the Sacred Eight meets in the upcoming month, there will be questions asked. Questions that will not go unanswered."

The sort of look that told him that the answers to said questions would be the ones that the Sacred Eight and the rest of the Empire would believe but wouldn't necessarily be the truth.

They were at a critical crossroads. There was no doubt that Trestan Banksi would not like the answers he would receive. And if they contained incriminating evidence, it would put a stain not only on Mujin but on Trestan as well, given how he had supported him over the decades.

The latter would be acceptable.

The issue was that, while the Earth King was no stranger to forbidden research, antiquated knowledge, and conspiracy, rarely was he the one at risk. While he had much to gain, he also had much to lose. The very idea of being forced into such a position in the first place was infuriating.

That was the reason behind this inquisition. There was far more to Tanya's powers and the recent activities that Trestan wasn't aware of. Mujin knew perfectly well that Tanya's mother was the yuki-onna Tsurara, a direct descendant of the yokai empress Meynte. Given the Yokai Kingdom was scorched and turned into this barren wasteland, it was very possible that the girl had unearthed some ancient relic to empower herself. That or her heritage was allowing her to utilize Ezzeron's true power on a limited basis. Either way, if any information of that nature came to light later on before the other Sacred Eight, the repercussions could be catastrophic.

The Earth King would willingly massacre the entire Shimizu Clan overnight rather than be subjected to such humiliation.

Especially with the Fire King involved in this mess.

"I accept your conditions, old friend. But I humbly beseech you for one last favor. I shall, of course, come clean about everything, and if you think I have wronged you, go ahead and end me. I shall not stop you. But if you feel my cause has reason, then I request military support from you to do whatever is needed to reclaim my name and prestige."

The Earth King gave him a speculative look. "Very well, say what you will, and I will judge if you're worth my support anymore."

"I was wondering when you'd finally show up," said Zuken as Lukas closed the door behind him and stepped into the room.

"What can I say?" said Lukas. "Elena's warned all of us away from disturbing you. Somehow the yokai are more afraid of her than me. Not sure if I should be flattered or insulted."

He wasn't joking either. Something about the changeling made the yokai shy away from her presence. Even Solana, with all her aged wisdom, looked uncomfortable in her presence, though she tried her best not to show it. Lukas had tried coaxing the reason out of a couple of yokai, but their best response was that there was something about her that terrified them in a way they couldn't even understand, much less explain.

The only people to feel otherwise were Tanya and Maude.

"Please, come in," said Zuken with a laugh. "I've been hearing nothing but tales of your exploits. Ever since I woke up, all Elena seems to talk about is you. If I didn't know any better, I'd have considered you competition for her affections."

Lukas coughed. *Affections?* From Elena? How?

"Trust me," Lukas said with a lopsided grin. "I already have a girl at my side. And she's the jealous type."

"I've got some experience with that. Word to the wise, those types can be quite petty."

"Oh, I'm aware of that," Lukas said airily, remembering some of Tanya's reactions about the changeling.

Zuken laughed and ended up coughing. Reaching for the glass of water placed on the table next to him, he sat a little upright, resting himself against the headboard. "Come, sit."

He crossed the distance between them and sat down on the chair next to the bed. Ever since his extradition from the Peak, Maude had been treating Zuken and constantly checking his vitals, with Elena sitting next to him and taking care of his needs. With the possibility of war imminent, the yokai were busy with preparation, leaving this section of the territory practically empty.

"How are you?"

"Still here," Zuken said with a sigh, looking at his hands. "Not sure how useful I will be without my tools, but I'll try to help you out against the Shimizu."

Lukas bit his tongue. "Sorry about what happened to your place. You didn't have to do that for Tanya. But you did, and for that, I'm grateful."

"Is that why you got me out of there?" asked the terramancer. "Out of gratitude?"

"Partly," Lukas admitted. It felt a little weird chatting with this man without it being a negotiation or needing to worry about dancing around any issues. "Tanya also wanted revenge on her brother and her grandfather. Two birds with one stone and all that."

"An interesting analogy," Zuken noted. "Two birds with one stone. I'll have to remember that. Is that a saying from your world?"

Lukas nodded.

"Interesting," Zuken said again. "Maybe when times are less exciting, you can tell me a little about it."

"Somehow, I doubt hearing about a world without Potential would interest you."

The terramancer barked out a laugh. "You weren't joking after all. Your world really didn't have Potential?"

"Potential, lifeforce, mana—none of it. At least, during my time. I mean, we had technology, not that it stopped people from turning the planet into a shithole, but it was where I had *my* shit."

"Huh . . . a world filled with people who live and grow and develop even without Potential. Sounds like the perfect place for someone like me."

Lukas raised a brow.

"I guess there's no point in hiding it, but I'm a failure at lifeforce and Terramancy," said Zuken.

"That sounds like such a lie."

"Heh! You'd think that, wouldn't you?" The terramancer laughed again, but there was no mirth in his expression or tone. "I take concoctions, specially prepared to enhance mana production. And my fractals are the best that mezals can buy—170 percent production, and they need maintenance after every three hundred days or so. That and I was inside an underground anomaly, surrounded by my element."

Lukas didn't know if it was due to Maude's treatment or the torture, but Zuken was a lot less inhibited than he remembered the man being.

"Since when did Zuken Banksi become so carefree about revealing his own weaknesses? The man I negotiated with always acted from a position of strength."

"Haha! I suppose times change," said the man, and Lukas could feel the frustration in his tone. "Back then, you were an interesting specimen, unique but within the range of my understanding. From all that I've heard, it seems like I knew next to nothing about you."

"Well, I can't blame you for that. The time between then and now has been quite educational for me as well. I know myself a lot better now, and I'm not sure if I should be amazed or terrified."

"Well, Olfric is definitely terrified. He's been claiming that you are exactly what we hypothesized back then. A demigod."

"And that takes us back to that conversation, doesn't it?" Lukas asked, chuckling. "Sorry, bud. Still not a demigod."

"Well," Zuken sighed. "It was worth a try."

No one spoke for a long moment.

"Aguilar," said Zuken, breaking the silence. "What are you, really?"

Lukas smiled. That was a loaded question like nothing else. Even he didn't truly understand what he was. Inanna had called him an anomaly. Solana called him an Outsider. Meynte addressed him as a Soulcrafter, while Frost, the incarnate of the End, had a plethora of words to describe him, and none of them were worth mentioning in polite conversation.

"The Fire King has given me an official title," said Lukas. "*Forger.* You could say I'm the new landlord of the Zwaray Keep in exchange for my services."

"The Fire King, huh? Someone's moved up in our world." Zuken laughed, though there was a tinge of hesitation in his tone. "About time, really. So, forging, is what you do?"

"I forge what I *understand.* Objects, people, spirits." Lukas very carefully steered clear of saying *souls.* "I study their properties, their Skills, their nature, and try to replicate what I understand in all kinds of ways."

Zuken gave him a flat, unblinking stare, as if judging how honest he was being. Finally, the man sighed.

"Forger, then. I suppose that's better than a demigod. The kind of Sin you've likely accumulated after destroying the entire castle and killing all those men . . ."

Lukas scowled, thinking back on that stunt he had pulled. Both when he had channeled the dranzithl's technique, and later, when he had altered the wardstones, he had been the cause of *thousands* of deaths. No wonder everyone in the territory was giving him a wide berth. No one wanted to be on the wrong side of someone who could commit genocide and walk away without a scratch.

"Speaking of forgery," Zuken began again, "there's been something I've wanted to talk to you about."

Lukas cocked his head.

"You altered those wardstones in the castle."

Oh. *That.*

"I was watching. You altered carquane crystals while they were still channeling energy from the ley line. Not even the best legion of terramancers that mezals could buy would do that, even at sword-point. And you did it in minutes. Isn't that right?"

Lukas shook his head. "Not minutes."

"Oh," said Zuken, slightly disappointed. "I imagine you made a cursory study of wardstones before attempting the ambush, then."

Lukas smiled. "You misunderstand, Banksi. It didn't take minutes. Just a moment's glance is enough."

"Just a—" Zuken paused, inhaling, and gave him an intense look. "I don't mean to insult you, but if you could prove your word. I mean, I understand you don't have to. I don't owe you anything but—"

Lukas didn't respond. He just raised his hand.

Metaforge Active

"From dead minerals to spiritual alloys, to lifeforce-wielding bremetans to body-possessing yokai, there is nothing I cannot analyze."

Condensing Anomalous Energy
Replicating Instance . . .

"And what I can analyze, I can re-create."

Altering Mana Conversion Patterns
Creating Altered Instance

In his empty palm, raw power began to coalesce in the form of a sphere, crackling with barely contained ferocity. With practiced will, Lukas guided it to the form he intended. The sphere condensed and split into two, forming a ring of dazzling white before expanding laterally into two cylindrical structures, a shape that they both were extremely familiar with. Where the light faded, shades of dark-chocolate brown began to show. Spiraling lines of silver crisscrossed the structure in familiar patterns—not one or two, but all seven of them, promising a mana-production enhancement close to 90%—the best he had seen and analyzed so far.

"That is—" Zuken trailed off.

Forging Complete

Lukas held it out to him. With trembling hands, Zuken grabbed it—a pair of fractals with seven spirals of silver. He had gotten Lukas an exact copy of this, only that one had been specifically altered to allow Lukas access to all elements. This one though . . .

"I altered the mana-conversion matrix," said Lukas. "It will only channel terramantic power. It should increase your mana production by close to 130 percent. Granted, not my best work, but in my defense, I haven't had the opportunity to experiment with fractal mechanics until recently."

"This—you—"

Lukas laughed at the way the normally composed man was grasping for words. "Does that make you feel better now?"

Zuken opened his mouth to reply, but no words came out. Instead, he silently put those fractals over his wrists and clenched his fists. Lukas felt the surge of earth mana within the man, and the next moment, Zuken thrust his right hand at the floor, and a shaft of solid rock shot out of it, hovering in midair. He twisted his hand slightly, and the slab was cut into sixteen uniform pieces. The terramancer twisted his wrist slightly, and they began to contort, each forming a screw-like end on one side. The flat end then thinned, and the next moment, eight pairs of short spears with spiral heads were floating in the air. Clenching his teeth, Zuken made a sudden thrust, and then the weapons shot at the opposite wall, piercing it.

Lukas just watched it all with a smile. Normally, he'd have gone out of his way to hide his Potential, but too many people were in the know at this moment. Too many people who he couldn't trust knew of his Skills.

Obscurity wasn't a safe option for him to hide beneath, so audacity would have to do.

Besides, Zuken was someone that had at least done something for him and for someone he cared about.

When the bremetan finally looked up from his fractals, Lukas noticed the slight glistening in the corner of his eyes. He met Lukas's eyes, and he could see the emotions swelling in them, only held back by an ironclad will. He knew exactly how Zuken felt, after all that time spent in prison, alone, helpless. To finally be able to use his power again must have felt nothing short of exhilarating.

"I understand," Lukas said, still smiling. "Trust me. I've been in your place. I understand what it's like to feel helpless."

"You, really? You?"

He laughed. "Would you believe it if I told you that when I entered this world, I had neither lifeforce nor mana?"

"No!"

"Well," Lukas said, with a half shrug, "it's true. It took me a while to even learn that there's something called lifeforce, much less learn to harness it."

"And mana?"

He smiled. "Story for another time, perhaps?"

Zuken didn't pry.

"In the interest of reciprocation, can I ask you something in return?"

The terramancer's eyes lit up. "Anything."

Yep, Lukas observed. *Definitely uninhibited.*

"What's your deal with the Earth King?" he asked. "You're his son, yet he supports Mujin Shimizu over you."

And just like that, the terramancer's face slackened slightly. "The Earth King is my father, yes, but in name only. Growing up in the Earth King's court, I always suffered his displeasure for being born with a terribly low ECR. It's why I walked away from the kingdom before my father was able to fully lose it and have me executed. All my life, I've searched for ways to increase my ECR but only managed to find hacks to boost my mana production. Like my fractals. I also found elixirs to temporarily enhance my lifeforce if needed. They are quite expensive, and overuse causes adverse effects on my health. You might not have known this, but I was in a terrible state for weeks after we took you out of that anomaly."

Lukas tilted his head slightly but said nothing.

"When we found that featherglass in the anomaly, I—I couldn't believe my eyes. I performed the tests over and over, I . . . Maybe I wanted to prove that they were fake, that such a thing couldn't possibly exist, I mean, not even the Great Goddess . . ." He trailed off. "But it was real. Featherglass of that much purity could store Skills and spiritual information. I thought if the svartalfars could reverse-engineer it, then perhaps I could find a way out for my lack of Soul Capacity. It would be a crutch, yes, but something's better than nothing."

That was the second time he had described himself like that. Was that how Banksi really saw himself? Lukas wondered just what transpired in that castle to turn the once-prideful man into a shell of his former self.

"Unfortunately . . ." Zuken sighed. ". . . that avenue is dead too. Ultaf destroyed half the Keep. And the svartalfars know that I took him there. I doubt they'd even be willing to honor our deal, assuming they even have the samples . . ."

He trailed off, as if struck by a new realization, and stared up at Lukas with narrowed eyes. "You said that you can re-create whatever you analyze. That's what you said, right? Does that mean you can create . . . featherglass as well?"

Lukas arched a single brow and said, "Yes."

"I mean, I won't be surprised if you can't. Featherglass is so rare, even the Emperor himself can't boast . . ." Zuken paused his rambling, spotting the amused expression on Lukas's face before his words finally hit him. "Wait . . . Did you say yes?"

"I did."

Lukas held his hand up and repeated the process. A moment later, a shard of featherglass, no more than half a pound in weight, rested atop his open palm.

"That—that is—" said Zuken, looking at him like he had just discovered fire.

Lukas passed it to him. With shaky hands, Zuken held it, eyes full of wondrous disbelief. He ran his fingers softly over the spiritually rich substance, careful not to exert anything but the slightest pressure. For all its wonderful properties, featherglass was a fragile thing.

The man must have been hit with another surprising thought, for he looked at the fractals he was wearing and then at the crystal. He repeated those actions again and then again before looking up at Lukas in bewilderment.

"These are not ether constructs."

"What gave it away?"

"Because—because it cannot be ether. Ether constructs start disintegrating when you channel mana through them. But these fractals are the real thing. How—how could you have possibly created it?"

"You bremetans put too much importance on ether and not enough on the world around you," said Lukas. "Fire, water, wind, earth, and ether—five elements. But have you ever considered where these elements came from? What is the source of mana? Of lifeforce?"

Zuken looked taken aback at that question. "You're talking about theology, not science."

Lukas took a moment to marvel at the fact that in this world where gods were real, a clear distinction between theology and science even existed.

"Perhaps."

The terramancer took a sip from the glass and licked his parched lips. "The priests at the shrine taught us that the Primordials created the world, into which they sowed life and Potential. The elements are the constituents of the world and are always changing from one form to another."

Lukas threw his head back and laughed, much to Zuken's dismay.

"Did I say something odd?"

"No," Lukas said, chuckling again. "Sorry. It's just that that explanation would have fit perfectly back in my world. You know, where there are no gods and goddesses but the clergy make all kinds of stories about them. About how the world came into existence because the gods wished it to be." He chuckled some more. "I mean, seriously, all that infinite space out there, with stars and nebulae and galaxies, and somehow, they're just there for the humans on Earth to stare at the night sky and adore their beauty. Like it's some kind of natural wallpaper."

His lips twisted into a sneer. "But you know what's even more hilarious? This place. You have real gods—not parables and myths but real, walking, talking gods. Hell, even your emperor was born from a goddess. And even then, your world history is nothing but a big heap of bullshit."

Had this been Olfric, he would have instantly taken offense at his words. Zuken Banksi just sighed.

"I can't disagree with that notion. Honestly, if the Primordials were really the creators of this world, then their designs must have been extremely shabby. I do not doubt that the emperor is the son of the Great Goddess, but I get skeptical when they claim that Amaterasu is the eldest spawn of the Primordials themselves."

Lukas snorted. "You don't doubt the man born of god. You doubt the god that's born of another god. Sounds legit."

Zuken scowled. "I know it sounds like lunacy when you put it that way, but I cannot fathom why anyone would create a world with so many problems, and with such diversity, and then wage a war to bring it all under the control of a single species. For an Empire blessed by divinity, it experiences a frightening number of colossal leadership errors. Most of these are just covered up, and unless you know where to look, you won't even find anything about the Time Before. You have the tale of the Nine-Tailed Fox defeating the mighty Ryujin, but none of the texts ever talks about the Norse god Odin or the entire pantheon of Asgard. Every vanir out there worships the vanir gods of old, but none of the Asukan texts ever mention them. I mean, if you are the creator, why does your own scripture contain so many errors?"

"Speaking like that would probably get you arrested on grounds of sacrilege."

Zuken grinned. "I suppose I would. Luckily, we're in yokai territory. While that terrifies the fuck out of me, I know I wouldn't find any Omnyoji around."

"I'm pretty sure I can get Olfric here if you want."

Zuken laughed. "Not necessary. But we digress. The priests at the Shrine teach us that Amaterasu defeated the Nine-Tailed Fox, and when she tried to destroy our world by crashing the Ikai Realm into it, she ascended to godhood, sharing her power of Eternal Light with the world, casting the mists away. That is why she is the Great Goddess. That is why the yokai fear the Eternal Light, because its holiness destroys all things evil."

And there was the spark he had always associated with the man. It felt good to know that the man hadn't lost it.

"But I'm still here, aren't I? Despite being in yokai territory. And not just me . . . Olfric, Elena, Tanya, you—the yokai helped you get me out. And while they fear the Eternal Light, that doesn't necessarily make them evil."

"Honestly," the terramancer rambled on, "the more I look at the Empire, the more my instincts whisper, 'Scam.'"

Lukas wondered if it was because he was simply that bored out of his mind or just so worn out by his prison time that he had lost control of his impulses, or if he was simply enjoying conversing with someone who gave zero fucks about the strict theological doctrines mandated by the Empire.

"I mean, everyone knows that the emperor does not age. That much, at least, is undeniable. You would think that with a single, immortal ruler at the helm, the society would reach its zenith. Instead, all we have are one hundred kingdoms almost constantly at war with each other."

"And you wonder if the emperor lets it happen because he doesn't care—"

"Or because he can't." Zuken finished. "I mean, in terms of power, he is supposed to be equivalent to any of the other kings. The only reason the others pay him the obeisance they do is because he is a demigod. But when you've traveled across the Empire as much as I have, you start questioning if the gods even care about their worshipers, much less the other species. Strange isn't it, given their parents, the Primordials, were the ones that created all of it?"

"The yokai have their own story of the world's genesis," Lukas informed him. "And while it has its own quirks, I personally find it likely a little closer to the truth as I understand it."

"And do you?" asked Zuken. "Understand it, I mean?"

Lukas thought back to the memory of the Origin, seeing that incomprehensible existence, seeing tiny smidgens of Potential, omphaloi arising out of the Origin and appearing in the singularities and realms in the form of new anomalies.

"Yes."

"Yes?"

"Yes," Lukas repeated and realized Zuken was waiting for a proper response. "My teacher told me that every world arises as an omphalos—an orb of pure and nigh-infinite Potential, springing from an entity that some call the Great Progenitor. An entity that existed at the very beginning of time, when the universe was nothing but formless infinity."

He paused for a moment. "She called it the Origin."

"The Origin."

"The Origin. The Provenance. The Cradle of Creation. It has as many names as there are languages. Each omphalos births an anomaly, which later evolves into a singularity and separates from the World or Realm it was born in. Finally, when the singularity gives birth to its own unique Rules, it transforms into a new Realm, completely cut off from its source."

"That's an interesting theory," said Zuken. "One I have never heard before. I think the closest thing I can compare it to is Kvasir's ramblings. I believe I gave you a copy."

Lukas smiled. "Anomalies give rise to monsters. Monsters evolve to become species. Species morph and specialize into races, like the bremetan, or the svartalfar, or the yokai. Races form civilizations—sometimes as a singular group, and at times, a cluster like you see in borderlands. In case you're wondering, borderlands are actually singularities that lie floating, attached to the infinitely vast Ikai Realm."

"And . . . gods? Where do they come from?"

"Races level up. One, two, three . . . At four, they become warlords. And at five, they gain absolute mastery of the elements. They become kings. But even at that grand stage, they are limited by the Rules of the world, by the laws that govern the universe. Until . . ." He took a dramatic pause. "Until someone breaks free of those laws and establishes his or her own law. Their Truth. Something that did not exist before, a law that alters the universe itself by its very existence."

"Like . . . Eternal Light?"

"Exactly, like Eternal Light. And through that ascension, through achieving that impossible Rule and making it possible, a mortal becomes divine. A bremetan becomes a god."

"You're claiming that even the Great Goddess and her kin were mortals once."

"Yes," said Lukas. "Honestly, from what I understand, even if the Primordials did exist, they were nothing but some old gods that preceded the current Asukan Pantheon. That would make Amaterasu and her kin demigods, just like the emperor. And the chance that all three of them—Amaterasu, Susanoo and Tsukuyomi—managed to attain their own independent divinity is so hilariously low that I'd rather bet on you defeating a king."

"You're saying some pretty outrageous things, you know," said the terramancer. "You're implying that not only did the Primordials not create the world, they might not even have existed in the first place. A myth spread across generations by the current gods to hide the true history of the world."

"Good," said Lukas. "It's about time I'm not the only one saying outrageous things. Oh, and you are ignoring another possibility."

"Which is?"

"That Amaterasu, Tsukoyomi, and Susanoo aren't godlings or siblings. Just three independent bremetan gods that came together and scammed the world populace."

The suggestion was so blasphemous that it took Zuken at least three seconds to process it entirely.

Lukas stood up. It was time to meet up with Tanya and check on her progress. Perhaps he could communicate with Frost about some ideas he had about Inanna's resurrection. Besides, he imagined Zuken would be quite busy for some time with his new fractals and the dangerous ideas Lukas had just infected him with. Turning around, he walked back to the door and was just about to open it when—

"Hey."

It was Zuken's tone that made him stop dead in his tracks, his body tensing instantly.

Zuken hadn't moved, but Lukas could feel his gaze at his back. "From what you told me, you believe that the World itself is the source of everything. The living, the non-living, the elements."

It wasn't what he believed. It simply was.

"Correct."

"Which means that the raw energy, the natural energy drawn from the heart of the World, the one that flows through ley lines and empowers wards, is the true and original source of energy. One that can create anything and everything."

Except Potential, Lukas didn't say.

"Also correct."

Zuken met his eyes, hesitation vivid in them. "And you can somehow tap into this energy . . . to forge anything and everything. And I saw you make the metal slime take the form of a muspel . . . No, not the form. It *became* a muspel. You . . . you created life."

This time, Lukas turned around.

Silence followed, with Zuken staring at the featherglass crystal still in his hands.

"If you have something to ask," said Lukas. "Feel free to ask it."

Zuken nodded cautiously. "You have an almost endless Soul Capacity. And you can use the World's natural energy and create anything—living, non-living, even rare substances like featherglass—without breaking a sweat. And you can create *life*. And Sin does not affect you."

"I still don't hear a question there."

"It's just . . . Back when you and I sat in my office, you claimed that all that Potential from your World had to go somewhere. Does that mean that your powers are derived from the World you belonged to?"

Lukas gave him a smile, somehow managing to make it look comforting and menacing at the same time.

"I was joking, remember?"

And then he opened the door—only for Maude to rush in and stumble against him.

"Maude—" he began, bending to help her stand up. Then he noticed how short of breath she was, her eyes frantically searching his face.

"Leader received word . . ." she said, breathing fast and hard. "The Shimizu . . . They know that Tanya is in yokai territory. And they're on their way to attack us."

"What?" Lukas hissed. "How did he know?"

"I—I don't know," stammered the oni. "It gets worse. Mujin isn't coming alone. He has the Earth King's army with him. Lukas, we . . . we're all going to die."

CHAPTER 20

War was coming to the Namzuuhuu Desert.

Around a millennium ago, this very place hosted a catastrophic battle between the Empress Amaterasu and Meynte. Truth and Taboo clashed here, and the result was this plain of sand that seemed to hate the living. Amaterasu's Eternal Light, or as Olfric would put it, the All-Seeing Eye, was blind within the desert's periphery, making it a perfect location for anything that went against the Empire and the Asukan Pantheon. A land of dreary sand and mist and nameless things that roamed in its darkness. A ground that served as a haven for yokai-kind, a place where those wraiths could survive without having to succumb to the Eternal Light.

A warlord could use his entire might here and not be blamed for the mass devastation he could wreak.

But it was also the perfect place to set a trap against the aforementioned warlord. Yokai could physically move around here without fear of being burned to ash. An arena where both Ezzeron and Everfrost's powers could meet the warlord's kami at full strength, without need for restraint.

"This . . . I've got a bad feeling about this," said Zuken. "The Shimizu Warlord alone is dangerous beyond imagination. But with my fath—with the Earth King supporting him . . ." He turned towards Lukas. "Do we even stand a chance?"

"Why?" asked Lukas, gently teasing him. "Are you having second thoughts about being on this side? I'm sure we can arrange a safe transport for you to Haviskali before it begins."

The terramancer scowled. "I'm no betrayer."

No. He wasn't. He was too driven and honorable for that. But Lukas could understand what he was going through. Knowing what was about to happen, weariness and despair hammering against the doors of your mind, as you waited for the inevitable as it charged straight ahead . . .

He didn't like it, but he understood.

"The Earth King is only *supporting* him. He isn't coming here himself."

"I wasn't born yesterday, Aguilar," said Zuken, clenching his hands into fists, his knuckles whitening. "I know none of you planned for this. You planned on the warlord being too prideful to seek help. That's why you attacked the Peak, to rescue me and weaken his overall strength."

"And instead, it's gotten him a more powerful force," Lukas said. "Is that what they call divine blessing?"

"Stop mocking me," said Zuken. "And the gods are actually on their side. We're depending on the demons to help us out."

"The demons," said Lukas. "Are the ones that are in true danger. I can take Tanya and you lot and escape through the Haze. Solana and maybe some of the others will do as well. The rest will be fodder for the army, especially if they're armed with Eternal-Light-imbued weapons."

"Yes," said Zuken. "Thank you for summing that up so well. Now I can comfortably say that everything has fallen apart."

Lukas snorted and looked ahead to the horizon. They were all standing on the massive embankment Solana had constructed for them, with barriers that kept them hidden from sight. Up in the sky, floated Tanya, a warring angel awaiting her nemesis' arrival. Behind him, he could sense Solana, Ryu, and Olfric standing together, while Maude and Elena were at the back, the former commanding a small taskforce of yurei, Zuken dumped with the latter's protection when the war began. The rest of the yokai army were holding positions in different locations within the territory, ready for a sudden intrusion, whenever that happened.

"Back in my world, we had a saying, 'No plan survives the enemy.' We didn't count on the Fire King humiliating Mujin like that before the Shogun Council. We didn't count on his pride shattering like that. We didn't count on him knowing about the yokai nor expect the Earth King to offer his forces, nor Mujin to accept it. Could things have turned out differently? Sure, they could. Can we do anything about it? No."

"And that doesn't scare you?"

Lukas gave him a lopsided grin. "Of course it does."

"Then how are you so . . ."

He raised an eyebrow at the terramancer. "So?"

"Confident. We're facing the might of a warlord and a king's army."

Lukas closed his eyes, took a deep breath, and walled away a small ocean of fear that was forming in his mind. As Zuken put it, a war was coming, and he'd have to face it when it did.

He opened his eyes.

"Let's just say that I have seen how infinitely large this universe is. Beyond the Empire, beyond races, beyond gods, and beyond Worlds . . . there are powers so vexing that I cannot even *try* to comprehend them. And I know that for my dream to come true, I have to challenge some of those powers. Compared to that, Mujin Shimizu is a nobody. Inconsequential."

"That inconsequential nobody can crush us all like a bug."

He laughed. "The warlord is strong, but he's just one person. He can only be in one place at one time."

"He can also destroy our entire army just standing right there."

Lukas grinned. "There's where you're wrong, Banksi. Had this been his own army, that plan would hold merit. But with the Earth King's army, he will exercise restraint. And that can be to our advantage."

Zuken exhaled audibly. "I have considered that. But even if you and Tanya can somehow handle the warlord, fighting my father's forces will come with a steep cost. If I know him, and I do, he'll be sending Level-3 terramancers along with golems to fight. Even with the yokai, I doubt we'll be able to overwhelm them."

"Golems?"

"Golems, automatons, warships . . . take your pick. The Earth King is all about control. Mujin Shimizu might not have his aeromancer army with him, but one warship can be just as destructive." He paused, his features darkening, "Trust me, I know."

"It is a risk, yes," Lukas admitted. "But a risk we have to take. We have the psychological advantage of being in the Desert. The familiarity with the terrain. The yokai's ability to possess soldiers. The lack of Eternal Light. Perhaps between Tanya and me, we can wear the warlord down. We might have a chance."

"Maybe, perhaps, might," Zuken noted. "I'm not hearing a lot of conviction from you here."

"No, but that's actually because I'm being optimistic," said Lukas, grinning. "Ideally, I'd like to win this battle before it even begins. The chances are fleeting, but we have like . . . five opportunities to get things working in our favor, I think. If even three of them work out, perhaps we'll be able to overwhelm them without losing too many lives on our side."

"You realize they're yokai, right?" asked Zuken. "They cannot truly die."

"No, but they can be trapped. I'm certain that if shit hits the fan, Solana will escape first. She's exactly that sort of creature. But even she knows that this is the best chance we have."

Not to mention . . . Lukas thought inwardly, *the desert is also a perfect place for a third thing. One that's much more important than the first two.*

But yes, things would definitely get messy. He wasn't foolish enough to think that Tanya would be able to restrain herself the moment she spotted her grandfather. And Frost held more than her fair share of resentment against this guy, especially with what happened to Tsurara, the previous avatar of Everfrost.

She might be faster, stronger, and far more ruthless than Tanya, but it wouldn't negate the fact that she was a sledgehammer down to her core.

Which wasn't a bad thing. No matter how skilled or elegant a foe might be, a sledgehammer to the head was a sledgehammer to the head.

It was up to Lukas to act as the scalpel and trap Mujin before Tanya could bash him to the ground. And he had.

He looked back at Zuken; his smile clearly had a little poison in it. "They say civilization is a thin veneer over barbarism. Let's hope the desert survives the first tearing sound."

Several hundred feet away, Olfric stared at the empty desert and sighed.

"We're going to die."

"Such pessimism is beneath you."

Olfric turned around and found a kasha standing behind him. The whiskered man looked like he had seen many years and a lot more battles, if the scars on his face and body were any clue.

"Ryu," he acknowledged. The kasha was one of the few people he got along with in the yokai camp, and the two had found an excellent sparring partner in each other. Olfric had been most surprised to find out that Ryu had been Lukas's trainer back when they had first found him loitering around in the anomaly.

"Have you not heard the news?" demanded the aquamancer. "The Earth King has supplied troops and warships to the Shimizu warlord. They know about the yokai territory. This isn't just between Tanya and the warlord. You have the freaking Empire coming down on us."

"You look like you want to run."

Olfric growled. He hated it when someone compared his being realistic to cowardice. "Accepting the circumstances is just practicality. Mujin is stronger than ever, and he probably knows everything that happened."

"Does he now?" asked Ryu, cocking his head.

"Anything that can destroy his fortress—"

"Not anything, any*one*. In this case, our queen."

"Obviously he got to know more than that. I knew it was madness to go ahead with the attack." Olfric said. "Mujin probably thinks Tanya to be a lot more powerful than she is. If he didn't, he could've just come alone and we might have had a chance. But now?" He looked around. "All these people—you, me, the rest of them—are probably going to die because of that one stupid mistake."

"You're looking at this the wrong way, my friend," said Ryu. "If anything, we yokai are actually looking forward to this war. We will see our queen fight a warlord and display her true strength."

"She isn't on his level," said Olfric automatically, only to realize how hypocritical he was being. No matter what he had done or what avenues he had tried, Tanya had always come out as his superior. To belittle her was an act of hypocrisy beyond him.

"Oh, I know that," said the kasha, smiling. "Every yokai knows that."

"Then?" asked Olfric, growing impatient. "Why are they all here? Do you people have a death wish?"

He wasn't being rhetorical by any means. Every yokai in the territory was currently standing on the dreary desert sands, ready for battle. Aguilar was ahead of them, strategizing with Zuken, while Tanya was up in the air, looking out for warships.

It was madness.

He looked down at the sand and shifted slightly. Much to his consternation, the accursed shadow beneath his feet moved with him. Just a few months ago, he would have been scared shitless at the sight of it. Even now, he maintained the belief that something might just pull him deep into that hole of blackness if he didn't stay vigilant.

At least the light inside the subterranean territory was mostly dim, even with the burning blue flames on the walls. It had been terrifying for the first few days, but he had gotten used to it. But as he stood in the morning light of the Desert, the shadows were more prominent and darker than anything he could imagine. He knew he had committed sacrilege lately, and with his continuous association with the demon kind that were the yokai, he was probably damning himself to suffer in Yomi in his afterlife. Maybe he already had.

"Several reasons," said Ryu. "Some of them are here to support the Outsider in his battle against the fearsome warlord. Those who believe in the legends believe that the Outsider will free us of Asukan tyranny and oppression. You might not know this, but the Outsider's reputation within our colony has grown fearsome. Not even the Leader's loyalists think much of her chances against him."

Olfric grimaced. He might not have known that little tidbit, but he knew enough to know what kind of monster Aguilar was. Still, Ryu should have known better than to say that out loud, especially when their skinwalker leader was standing barely steps away from them.

"And the rest?"

Ryu exhaled audibly. "For some, it is an opportunity to see the queen prove her worth."

Olfric narrowed his eyes. "I thought they already worship the ground she walks on."

Ryu chortled. "Some do, yes. But that is because she is descended from the empress and Leader Tsurara. But not all of us agree with that sentiment. Some of us actually look down on her and whisper behind her back. Some of us know what invaded the throne room and how she was possessed by the empress's spirit."

"Some like you?"

"Yes."

The kasha's bluntness took him by surprise again. After the time they had spent together, he had gotten a measure of the creature's personality. As much as he was reluctant to admit it, the kasha was someone he could relate to. His thoughts, his ideology, even his perspective on the world was similar to Olfric's own. Just as he believed strongly in the Asukan Pantheon and looked upon shadows as evil incarnate, Ryu thought of the Great Goddess as an usurper and the Eternal Light as a blight on the world.

"Maude mentioned that incident. She told me that Tanya was a perfect vessel, more than anyone else since the Great War. Not even her predecessors were better suited."

"To become a vessel, yes," said Ryu, with an annoyed undertone. "It is not synonymous with being a good ruler."

He met Olfric's eyes. "Being born with a useful quirk in your blood is not everything. I believe in power. In strength. Domination. Surely as an Asukan, those traits hold value in your eyes?"

Olfric felt like he had just been slapped. Of course he knew that. Domination was the lifeblood of the Asukan Empire. It was the wheels that drove the Empire's chariot. His own father had ousted him from his clan because Olfric had lost Shahxith and proved himself weak.

Ryu looked ahead at the two participants as they stood facing each other. "I am not saying that the queen is weak. Perhaps she was at a natural disadvantage against the empress. After all, she wields Everfrost and the empress *was* Everfrost. The only thing you cannot protect yourself from is yourself."

That made a surprising amount of sense.

"That way, this war will clear all doubts. The Outsider holds the queen's prowess in high regard, but so far, neither I nor any of the other yokai have seen that prowess in person. Yes, she trains with the Leader. Yes, she punctured the wards of the castle with unexpected skill. But diligence and tricks are not a substitute for the real deal. Yes, she is a perfect vessel, but that says nothing about her capacity to lead us. After all, if not for the Outsider, she would have been lost forever, trapped in her own mind, and Empress Meynte would have walked among us again. Is it too much to want to see if the queen is up for the job?"

Olfric winced. Yokai society was a lot more cutthroat than the Asukans'. By the Empire's policy, respect was given to those who held a superior position. You could argue against that until your voice went hoarse, but the fact was, your opinion didn't matter. And if it did, you would probably have been sitting in that position yourself.

"I suppose a lot of you despise Aguilar for that."

"Some do," Ryu agreed, "but not as many as you might think. Remember, those with the power make the rules. It is an open secret that the Outsider bested the empress's spirit and subdued the Leader at the same time, with little aid from the oni. He proved his superiority, and that is what matters."

"That sounds wrong on so many levels," defended Olfric. "You need a proper system of governance to prosper. If any random individual just walks in and attacks your Leader, your job is to protect your Leader and capture the attacker."

"Ha! What a ridiculous logic you have trapped yourselves in, Asukan. Is your society not ruled by those with the greatest power? Is that not why the warlords, the kings, and the emperor sit on their grand thrones while the commoners shuffle in the dirt? If your Leader needs to be protected, then they aren't fit to lead in the first place."

Olfric blinked. What Ryu had just said was true on multiple levels and yet—

No. That was exactly it. Asukan society was built on the foundations of power. And yet those foundations served to strengthen the strong and protect the weak. If he walked back to his clan and defeated his father in combat, the rest of the clan would welcome him with open arms and offer him the heirship again.

Only strength mattered. Your hardships, your experience, your journey— none of that meant anything.

So why exactly did the ones at the top have the greatest protection? How disgustingly hypocritical.

The irony that a yokai—an uncouth demon who survived in the desert— was showing him the inadequacies of Asukan governance was not lost on him.

"You might wonder why we yokai respect the girl as our queen. I do not. But I respect the Outsider. And even a weak vessel working in tandem with the powerful Outsider is a better option than the fallen empress. He freed her from the empress's clutches. He overthrew the Leader's power and forced her to play to his machinations." The kasha snorted. "And to think he was such a greenhorn when I first taught him the art of fighting with fire."

"You actually sound proud of him."

"I am," Ryu admitted and scowled. "It's disgusting, though. The other day we interacted, and he treated me as an equal."

Olfric narrowed his eyes. "You're disgusted that he's humble?"

"Are you not?" demanded the kasha. "He was weaker at one time, yes, and I played the role of his teacher. But the student has far surpassed the master. To even be acknowledged like that by him now paints me as someone greater than I am. It's revolting!"

"You did not share that line of thinking when we trained."

"I hadn't seen him annihilate an entire army and demolish that fortress at that point. And the Leader claimed that he defeated the empress by tricking her."

Olfric opened his mouth but then closed it.

"Don't overstress yourself," the kasha mocked. "Think of it this way. The queen's performance against the warlord will cement her position in our hearts. If she can achieve victory, not even the Leader can say anything against her."

"And if she doesn't?"

"Then she will die."

It wasn't Ryu who had spoken those words. It was Solana, the skinwalker Leader of the yokai. Her jet-black eyes stared at Olfric, as if peering into his soul. And Olfric knew that it wasn't a threat but an eventuality. Regardless of how vast the power difference and how much time it took, Solana would bring that idea to reality, no matter what Aguilar did.

"But . . . but . . ." Olfric stammered. "If she dies, then Everfrost—"

Solana smiled. It was a deadly thing, and Olfric decided that he was better off not knowing the answer.

He looked away from her dark, pupilless eyes to Tanya, who was up in the sky. Even from that far, he could see that Tanya's hair had changed to a cadaverous white. The air around her shimmered, as if her power were molding it, twisting it, making it *more*. Aguilar, on the other hand, stood on the ground, chatting with Zuken, his hands inside his pockets, looking utterly lackadaisical.

"But don't fret," said Solana, looking at Aguilar, who stood barely twenty feet away. "I am certain that the Outsider has his own share of surprises up his sleeve. That man was caught unawares by the empress and myself, and he managed to get the better of us. I am looking forward to what he can accomplish against someone he's specifically planned for."

"I doubt he prepared for the Earth King."

The skinwalker smirked and she dug out a set of vials containing a pale bluish liquid and handed them to him. "Rumor has it that you use poison in your Aquamancy techniques. The Outsider asked me to give these to you. *Backup*, I believe, he called it."

Olfric narrowed his eyes. "He—"

Solana stiffened for a moment. "They're here. Yokai, to your positions. The enemy has come to our doors. Let's not make them wait."

* * *

A figure landed on the sandy terrain. Like a falling meteor he streaked down from the sky. His impact cratered the floor, yet his feet did not touch the sand, merrily floating an inch above it, even as it was blown away from him in wide arcs as he regarded the flying woman ahead. He stood to his full height, every slight motion heavy with veiled threat. Half of his torso was bare. Pale, sickly skin stretched across a muscular chest, the color so white it was almost transparent. Hungry eyes stared out from a fiendish face, burning with the light of insanity. Four pairs of ethereal, feathery wings rose and extended from his back. They were red as blood and as cold and sharp as death.

The smile that stretched across his face was too wide, too long to resemble anything bremetan. Toothy, monstrous, it was the leer of a bloodthirsty vampire.

Around him, a hundred aeromancers descended, landing like a flock of ravenous vultures. A hundred more remained floating in the air, the wind swirling around them in the crimson sky. Double that rose up from the floor and genuflected behind him, awaiting his command.

Hiding with your kin in the Desert. I should not be surprised you returned to your wretched roots. I should have known . . . You were never fit for my bloodline. A usurper who stole my father's legacy and is foolish enough to challenge me.

His lips twisted further, as a massive warship appeared above him in the sky.

He raised his arms wide.

"Soldiers," he said, his voice loud and clear, "*that* is the enemy. The betrayer has joined hands with the profane. She thinks that the Desert and its curse will stop us from exterminating them like the pests they are. I . . . *we* will teach them better. Except for a changeling, kill every last one of them. Burn them with our sacred Eternal Light."

His voice grew louder. Deeper. "*Like the Eternal Flame of the Great Goddess, we shall scour this desert of those parasites. We will destroy their territory, kill and bind every single one of them, and take them as our slaves. I shall obliterate that wretched creature that carries my blood, regain my father's legacy, and reignite the glory of the Shimizu Clan. I am Mujin, son of the Wind King, and today, that creature and those fiends shall taste my wrath.*"

And with that declaration, the army attacked.

CHAPTER 21

What saved them wasn't the terrain but what was built under it. The Yokai Territory was a vast labyrinth of walls and doors and shadows. Thick rock walls lined by Solana's barriers were merely the first layer of protection, and beyond that lay a maze of passageways and corridors that could prove a challenge to navigate to those unfamiliar with its halls. After Lukas's stunt against her, Solana had made doubly sure to prevent Terraportation within the territory, and the barriers prevented them from actively manipulating the walls. Added together, they made Yokai Territory a natural fortress, not easily taken, provided that there were defenders willing to guard it. And those inside were very willing.

The first wave of terramancers and aeromancers poured into the corridors, crashing through the walls, shifting through rocks, relentlessly hammering against the barriers' weakest points. Demons or not, they expected them to be frightened, unprepared, scurrying away at the sight of a stronger, numerically superior foe. What they got instead was an alert army, dug into reinforced positions, well-prepared for the battle at hand.

But it wouldn't matter.

For they were the warlord's troops, answering to the Earth King himself. What were some soul-sucking parasites compared to those armed with the blessings of the all-seeing Great Goddess?

Confident in their victory, assured of their triumph, the soldiers surged into the territory and met a brick wall of resistance.

Metal-plated warriors hesitated at the junction between three hallways. The network of corridors was like a labyrinth, and they had already used a lot of Eternal Light crystals just to illuminate their way through this darkness. In the distance, the din of battle reverberated, echoing through the walls to reach them. It almost managed to mask the sound of footsteps until it was too late.

A lone man approached. Asukan, just like them. Wearing a blue set of fractals, with a metallic *something* coiling around his right wrist. Any feelings of elation died the moment they saw a demonic, metal-tailed feline standing behind him.

The soldiers pointed their Eternal-Light-imbued weapons at him. It did nothing to impede his progress in any way.

He took out a tiny vial and poured it on the metallic thing on his wrist. The substance frothed and then extended outward, forming a sharp scythe with a cylindrical hilt, connected by a long metallic chain that ended with another weighted hilt.

"That's supposed to be my backup." Olfric twirled his kusarigama expertly, showing off a bit to the soldiers. "I have no idea what it does."

He and the feline took fighting stances against them.

"Let's find out."

A little further away, a group of aeromancers chased Maude and Zuken through the hallways. Spears and orbs of pressure and wind whizzed past their heads, Zuken raising walls to intercept them before they could even reach halfway. The two of them led their pursuers through a maze of corridors before skidding to a halt. Dead end. They turned to see the aeromancers advancing on them, blades of wind ready to impale them in a hundred different ways.

Zuken and Maude looked at each other.

"NOW!"

Yurei erupted out of the walls and rushed into the aeromancers, penetrating past their defenses without care, their wind powers doing nothing to the ethereal creatures as they sank their claws into their victims' souls and twisted them inside out. The next moment, eleven aeromancers dropped their weapons, their eyes now glowing a sinister red, and genuflected.

"All of them are Level 2's," scoffed Maude, crossing her arms. "All this running and not even a single Level 3? Talk about unfair."

"Well, you have eleven 2's," said Zuken, cocking his head. "Maybe they'll get us a couple of 3's?"

Maude grinned. "I like the way you think."

Fighting terramancers sucked, and Mizo was realizing that the hard way.

Whether it be in a straight brawl or via the manipulation of the elements, terramancers always, always held an advantage. Especially when one of them was a Level 3 and the commander of the group to boot. It was why nobody in the territory ever directly challenged the Leader in a head-on battle.

There were two more with him. Aeromancers, if their fractals were any clue. The third was a beast-tamer accompanied by a bison-like creature.

If bison had eight legs, two heads, and were double the usual size.

"Juicy!" said Mizo. "Does Ryu mind if Mizo—"

"Actually," said Ryu, raising his fiery blade, "I want to fight all three by myself. Let me see what it truly means to be a spiritist in the Empire. Maybe next time we'll get something for you."

"Bully," Mizo complained.

"R'alla!" the beast tamer hollered, as his bison let out a furious cry and galloped in their direction. Ryu struck it with every bit of his strength, but his blade got trapped in the beast's flesh, seemingly immune to the flames. The monster slammed its horned heads into Ryu's stomach and held him up in the air, and two slashes of wind hacked him into three pieces, flinging them against the wall.

Ryu's head groaned and looked at Mizo, who just looked back, smug and anticipatory.

"What the hell are you doing there, smiling like a simpleton? Go take them on."

"Can Mizo have the juicy monster then?"

Ryu cursed under his breath. "Yes, now go."

One moment Mizo was standing there, the next moment, there was a blur in the air and a *creature* was clawing its way up the bison's back. It was about the size of a massive ape, except the head looked strangely canine, with equally grotesque pairs of claws in its arms and legs. Before they knew it, the bison was lacerated in five different places and was down on the floor, blood and meat spilling out of it.

And then Mizo began to hungrily feast on it.

The enemy watched, nauseated.

"Sorry," said Ryu's decapitated head. "She does that."

Ignoring the shocked looks, he pulled his body together using his arms, and the next moment, he was whole again.

Two wind slashes cut his left hand off again.

"Well, rude," said Ryu, sighing, as a flame erupted out of his now-hacked-off shoulder and fused back with the fallen appendage. "Listen, why don't you just choose who wants to fight with me, and we can let this play out like civilized people?"

Flames erupted out of his body—his arms and legs and his metallic tail. Two pairs of fiery curved blades appeared in his hands.

"Have you decided?"

A deafening sound wrenched through the air. The spiritists had fallen to their knees, clutching their heads and covering their ears and screaming their lungs out. The ceiling above them shattered, and something four-armed and massive fell through, landing before them. It had four arms, and its flesh was metallic, pierced by horn-like protrusions with flames burning around them. The eyes shone with a mad, blue, almost primordial light.

"Ugh," said Ryu, purple blood oozing out of his nose, as he stood up. "You've got to be the ugliest, noisiest bastard I've ever met. Don't tell me you want to fight one of them too."

The metallic bylestyr raised all four arms, spheres of crimson appearing on them, as it replied, ***"MEOOOW!"***

All across the territory, more than a dozen similar scenes played out—small-scale engagements that heavily favored the defenders, ambushes were sprung, traps laid out and tripped. The defenders knew the territory well and used that knowledge to their advantage. For all their power, the spiritists weren't used to fighting in the absence of Eternal Light, which heightened their paranoia to extreme levels and resulted in them over-expending their Eternal Light crystals. The yokai baited the foe into following them into darkened corners, forced them to lose themselves amid unfamiliar intersections, and tricked them into overusing their mana. At that point, those with Possession Skills higher than Level 2 jumped on them from the walls, twisting their spiritual cores and damaging their connection with their kami. Most of them lost their kami and became possessed puppets for the yokai to play with. The ones that were stronger and had survived, served as spiritists and added to the yokai regiment.

Hammer and anvil at its most rudimentary form.

Charging in blindly had been a mistake, and for the first stages of the battle, that mistake cost the Shimizu army several flanks of their forces. Half of their total count was neutralized in these savage melees that ran throughout the territory. The other half, savagely mauled, beat a hasty retreat, regrouping and trying to leave the area, only to realize that the invisible barriers wouldn't let them escape.

Never mind keeping the enemy out. No, Solana preferred to keep them in.

For a brief moment, hope glimmered, and victory for the yokai seemed a real possibility.

Then, a massive warship appeared right above the embankments, its cannons promising the total eradication of everything that lay beneath it. Orbs of pure power rained down like meteor showers, flashes of angry light creating massive craters in the sand, obliterating the embankments and striking against the barriers with a power more deadly than anything they had ever faced.

The eight-winged figure descended from the sky, floating leisurely down to the cratered remains of the dreary desert sands. Giant holes had opened in the middle of the Desert, revealing entrances into the Yokai Territory past the pulverized ward-reinforced walls. Flares of Eternal Light were being shot down into the holes, exploding outward with a luminosity that blinded everyone within its reach. And if those victims were yokai, they would instantly disintegrate, or be weakened beyond comparison.

Enough for the infantry to take them down.

Zuken, Olfric, and the rest of the survivors had gotten back to the embankment where Solana stood, using her fullest might to render them invisible while being protected by the strongest defenses she could manage. Every single one of them looked out of breath, and he knew that without a shift in the tide of battle, they wouldn't be regaining their confidence any time soon.

Lukas watched as the warlord's feet slowly touched the floor. He was clad in a suit of old, old war-plate. A suit of silver armor so dulled and darkened by age that it no longer appeared silver. Across the metallic surface were a thousand dents and cuts, testimony to a lifetime spent on the field of battle. The helm sat on top of broad shoulders equally as battered, equally as aged. An intense blue light shone from his eyes, staring out from a stylized mask shaped into the ironclad visage of an armored knight.

Even as he stood, there was an immeasurable pose. The ancient armor only added to his dignity and power. The joints didn't creak or scrape but *growled* in barely contained fury.

This was Wrath Incarnate. His body felt less human and more . . . elemental. Like a tornado condensed into humanoid form, its fury never subdued, only focused.

Power has a purpose. That was what Lukas's grandfather had taught him. Entities like Inanna, Meynte, the Fire King, and even Solana to an extent, followed that rule. Lukas had no doubts that the Fire King utterly eclipsed this warlord in terms of power, but kept it carefully confined.

The warlord in the sky? He was all power and no purpose.

In his hand was a long blade. Large and slab-like, easily eclipsing his own majestic height, it looked less like a sword and more like a massive saw to level entire buildings with.

And when he spoke, his voice was a low rumble.

"There is no use in hiding," said Mujin Shimizu, smiling. "I know you are here. Reveal yourself to me, little brat. The time for running is long gone. The cat has caught the mouse."

Yes, Lukas decided. *This is a strong contender. Exactly how I expected. No, he's surpassed all my expectations. A true Level 4, honed to the very zenith.*

Mujin Shimizu was a warlord. He was greater in power, greater in skill, and greater in Experience. In a fair battle, everything he could do against him would end up with Lukas buried six feet underground.

So, fuck fighting fair.

He glanced at Tanya, who stood beside him, absolutely stiff, and grabbed her hand. She looked at him, and he nodded at her.

After a few seconds, she nodded back. And Lukas knew what was wrong.

It wasn't just that she was afraid of his power. No, that was a given. No one, and that included Solana, would be able to best this monster in a direct battle.

If the three of them tried to work in tandem, it might work, but they'd lacked never done so before so attempting it for the first time against such a nigh insurmountable enemy seemed foolish at best.

Besides, Solana wasn't here to fight. Her role was to defend, and right now, she was trying to heal the barriers the ship had torn asunder.

He met Tanya's eyes. "You're not the little girl he captured back then."

Her eyes widened, and Lukas knew he had been spot-on. When she first saw Mujin, she had been thinking of how much more powerful he had been back then. She needed to see that things had changed, that the difference in their power levels wasn't as extreme as it used to be.

Frost might be able to fight him. But unless both sides of Tanya were in complete sync, she wouldn't be at her best. She needed to see that the man in front of them was no god, just a man with a power that anyone could acquire given time and resources.

And it was up to Lukas to show that to her.

"Solana, lower the barrier."

"*What?*" the skinwalker hissed. "If I do that, he will—"

"Just do it," Lukas said and took a step forward.

The skinwalker considered it for two seconds before relenting. The barrier dissipated, and the three of them, with Zuken, Elena and the rest of the yokai flank standing behind them, all appeared out of thin air.

Mujin's eyes instantly located Tanya, and a small, cruel smile spread across his lips at her stiffened posture.

"It's time," he said. "You have already caused me a lot of trouble, girl. Come with me, *now.*"

"And what?" asked Lukas out loud, shocking every single person around him. "You'll spare the rest of us?"

Mujin's eyes tracked Lukas as if seeing him for the first time.

Lukas rolled his eyes. Every single supervillain he had faced so far seemed to love playing into the stereotype. Until someone did something spectacular, they would keep underestimating them and treating them like yesterday's trash.

"No," said the warlord. "If she resists, then all of you will die. If she comes quietly, only *most* of you will die."

His voice was dripping with disdain. Ripe with contempt.

It deserved a similarly withering answer.

"The problem with people in big, funny armor," said Lukas "is that underneath it is a sack of hot air and a lifetime spent dwelling in inadequacy."

Ever so slowly, everyone turned to Lukas, their faces a mixture of absolute horror and disbelief. Even Solana, who had lived longer than anyone else and that included the warlord, looked like she had never been more terrified in her life.

Judging from how long it took for Mujin to reply, he was caught just as off-guard as everyone else.

"Care to repeat that, traitor? I didn't quite hear you the first time."

"Traitor?" asked Lukas. "That would imply I even served the Empire in the first place. Get your facts right before you start throwing insults around. And honestly, I'm being quite serious. All the power of a warlord and you come charging in with armor and warships just to kill a Level-3 girl? And even then, your best idea is to hold others hostage to get Tanya? Honestly, bud, you give off more of a paper-pusher vibe than a warlord."

"Did . . . did he actually say that?" squeaked Elena.

"*Lukas!*" Tanya hissed. "What the hell are you doing?"

"Ah . . . so this is how it ends," said Olfric softly, resigning himself to an assured calamity.

"I like your armor by the way," said Lukas unreservedly. "Maybe after we've taken you down, I'll keep it for myself. Tanya always tells me that I don't look like much of a warrior. Maybe putting that on would help?"

Mujin let out an extremely refined snort. "You have quite a mouth on you, jester. I'll have to make sure to take it with me after I tear you all to pieces."

"With or without the warship?" challenged Lukas. "No, believe me, it makes a ton of difference."

Surprisingly, Mujin didn't have a retort. Instead, he just cocked his head. "Do you really think you can challenge me, boy?"

"Actually, I can," said Lukas, unrepentantly honest. "It does involve a long and complex ritual, though. Should take me about fifteen minutes to prepare. Mind if I get started?"

The funny part was, he actually gave it fifty-fifty odds. The uber-powerful types like Mujin never paid much attention to time. Especially when they thought they had everything under control. And more importantly, he wasn't fibbing. It would take him a moment to actually power himself up and fuse with Blob to gain his nigh-indestructible armor, before he could even think of lasting against this monster for more than ten minutes. At the same time, it would also buy Solana some time to reinforce her barriers just in case the warships began their onslaught again.

Solana give him a surprised look, taking a sharp breath as she realized his rather-obvious ploy. Unfortunately, Mujin did too.

"Do you take me for a fool, boy?" He snorted, glaring down at him. "Even if you could amuse me for longer than I anticipate, I will not let the girl out of my grasp again."

Lukas looked around at his team, who were looking at him like he had grown a second head, and audibly sighed.

"Well, Plan A failed," he admitted sheepishly. "I guess we can try Plan B."

"I liked Plan A," said Zuken dryly.

"I thought you would," said Lukas grinning, and turned back to face Mujin. "In that case, here's Plan B."

And his eyes flashed green.

His vision altered, showing countless curves traversing the warlord's frame. Every single one of them was a possible motion trajectory followed by the wind swirling around his armored suit. Lukas grabbed them all and spun them down vertically. The man's eyes widened as he realized that his own wind and power were being used against him just as he was pulled into a vertical somersault, only to be held back by his own tremendous control over Aeromancy.

The entire exchange took less than half a second.

Fortunately, that was enough for Lukas to slam a fist straight into the air before him—

—and space distorted with its passing.

The howling wind erupted as the very air rippled, sending shock waves radially outward, tearing through the Desert like a blade through flesh, as the impossible momentum accompanying the strike hit Mujin, pushing the Shimizu warlord backwards.

Lukas turned towards Tanya, all traces of humor vanished from his face. "Prepare yourself. I need you to take over in five minutes."

And then he turned around and chanted the words that would signal the death of hundreds before the end:

"Activate Warmonger Protocol Version 2."

Loading Predetermined Skill Functions . . .
Adding Accessory Armor . . .

The liquid metal cocooned every inch of his body—a fluid suit of armor that only left enough space for him to breathe, and even *that* was only manageable with lifeforce. The Scan and Analyze functions would allow him a 360-degree awareness, and when powered up with his omphalos reserves and the extra carquane enhancements he had come up with to store extra energy, he would not be left wanting as far as raw power was concerned.

Maximizing Sympathization Ratio
Altering and repurposing structure while maintaining integrity . . .

The last time he had utilized this, he had been a Level 26. This time, he was ten levels above that. He had a greater understanding of what his aqāru armor could or could not do. The amount of raw power flooding through his body was far greater than before. Crafting a carquane skeleton beneath the aqāru armor only magnified that.

He took a step forward, just in time for the warlord to come at him with a power unlike anything he had ever faced.

Releasing All Safety Procedures
Executing and Forging Complete

Well . . . anything mortal, that is.
The man's hand came to rest in his metallic palm.

Enact

And the fight began.

CHAPTER 22

I t was faster than his eyes could follow.

The warlord came at Lukas at near-sonic speeds, his armored fist colliding with Aguilar's armored palm and sending a shockwave that Olfric could feel from even a hundred feet away. The next moment, wind blades attacked Lukas from every possible angle, leaving him no room to maneuver or escape. Aquamancy was all about trajectories and flows, and to Olfric's trained eye, there was no hesitation or imperfection in any of those attacks. A hundred different blades came at him in perfect angles, intent on slashing him up in a hundred different ways.

And then the blades vanished—

BOOOM!

—exploding fifty feet above them in the air.

Olfric hadn't even *seen* Lukas move.

"Deny foreign Truth."

Olfric felt the words reverberate through him like the ringing of a bell. He didn't know why, but they felt . . . spiritual. Like a command. Exactly what it was that was obeying his words, Olfric didn't know, but it was not unlike the feeling he got when he took part in an Omnyoji ceremony, drawing on the power of the gods above to deliver justice against the profane.

"They vanished!" yelled Elena.

Several hundred feet above in the air, both of them rematerialized, the world echoing as they met with one particularly tremendous blow. They pulled back and clashed again with the force and sound of cannons, the collision of their weapons sending shock waves through the desert. Olfric watched as the warlord slammed his blade against Lukas multiple times within a single second, only to be deflected by an invisible shield every single time. Then they would vanish and appear somewhere else to repeat the clash in less than a fraction of a second.

"Fast!" he whispered, as he tried to keep up with the sparring. "I knew aero-mancers were fast, but this is . . . beyond my expectations."

"Trust me," said Tanya, her teeth clenched. "They are only warming up."

A shiver ran down his spine. He had always known Tanya to be the fastest thing he had ever laid his eyes upon. Witnessing her massacre the Shimizu Army in the Desert during the mission, and most recently, murder her way through everything unfortunate enough to cross her path. And the warlord was definitely moving at speeds far faster than that. The real surprise was Aguilar, who was somehow keeping up with him.

Even for someone capable of using all five elements, Aguilar had what? Months, at best? That much time was simply not enough to master any ele-ment and certainly not to acquire a speed like this. He idly observed that the entire battle had paused, both sides watching as the two combatants vanished again and again, appearing in different places in a clash of metal, wind, and sound, only to disappear again. The fight was growing in frequency and aggres-sion. One strike became three. A missed kick created a small crater in the ground. A flex of power on both ends ended up with a miniature detonation.

"The Outsider has changed," said Ryu. "I cannot even recognize him anymore."

"Neither can I."

Both of them turned to Olfric's left and found Solana, the yokai Leader, standing next to him. "His body feels different. Very, very different. The shift is too pronounced, too sudden. Like he has had a breakthrough."

"Even compared to the empress?" asked Ryu.

Olfric winced, wondering if he could slowly step backwards from the two of them. He couldn't even imagine himself talking to an elder clan member like that, reminding them of their recent failure against the foreigner.

It simply wasn't done.

"Yes," said the skinwalker. "The person that fought against the empress was strong but nothing like this. Whatever breakthrough he made, it is beyond significant."

"How can you say that?" Olfric asked, trying his luck. Either Ryu's words would be proven true and the skinwalker would not take offense at his curios-ity, or Olfric would be dead and would haunt Ryu from beyond the grave. "I mean, all they've done is clash their weapons against each other. They haven't even started taking things seriously."

Much to his surprise, the skinwalker let out an extremely refined snort. "That is because, for all your observation, you do not understand it. For all his skill, the warlord is a bremetan. That is no ordinary suit of armor. It's empow-ered by Eternal Light, no doubt keeping his kami under firm restraint and letting him channel as much Aeromancy as he wishes without fear of mana poisoning. Observe the wind swirling around his armor. It's absorbing the effects of friction, sudden momentum, and the sheer force behind the attacks. But Aguilar . . ."

She trailed off right there.

Olfric didn't blame her. He could see it as clear as day.

Aguilar was meeting his strikes head-on. And no, that thin band of metal covering his body was simply not at the same level as that armor.

"I am not sure how the Outsider does what he does, but his body has mutated, or is mutating, adapting to those conditions. His physical capacity is far greater than what it was. I've seen him fight like this before."

"But this is the Desert," yelled Olfric. "Eternal Light cannot penetrate this place."

"It cannot," said Solana softly. "But it can be contained, stored, and brought in."

Olfric followed her gaze and glanced at the massive floating warship in the sky.

"Well, I'll be damned."

Solana gave him an impish smile. "You fight on the side of demons, Asu-kan. You will be damned either way."

"Look!" yelled Ryu.

BOOOM!

Aguilar was blasted away by an explosion of wind while the warlord shot forwards, several dozen blades flying at him, aiming to hack him apart . . . if not for the sudden force blast that allowed Aguilar to escape at the last minute.

"STOP FIGHTING LIKE A BRAT!" yelled the warlord. "Fight me like a warrior or die!"

The liquid metal slid down Lukas's face, allowing him to respond.

"Compared to you, I *am* a brat. Why wouldn't I fight like one?"

And then his lips curved, and he spoke in that hauntingly heavy tone from earlier.

"Alter Reality Foundation within standard Boundary Limit."

Just what was that aria? Some kind of spell he was enacting? That was the only thing that made sense.

Right then, the terrain beneath Mujin's feet exploded. The aeromancer shielded himself and shifted to the right, only for the ground to detonate again. He dodged five successive detonations before he vanished and appeared right above Lukas, aiming a punch at his head. The fist found empty air and smashed against the desert sands, creating a fifty-foot crater.

"Trickster!" yelled the Warlord. Olfric noticed that somehow they were able to hear them speak perfectly fine, despite the distance.

Lukas popped up about twenty feet away and began wiping the sand off his metallic suit.

"Short-ranged terramantic bombardment, instant concretion, and terra-portation," said Mujin with distaste. "What are you, boy? Some kind of svartalfar half-breed?"

"He's wrong," murmured Solana. "That wasn't Terramancy."

Olfric looked at her, surprised. "But he just—"

"Terraported, yes, but the others, those weren't Terramancy. The floor exploded because he made it so. He bypassed the limitations of distance and directly *inserted* the explosion beneath his feet."

"That's impossible," said Olfric. "He'd have to have been a magnitude faster."

Solana's teeth showed. "Who said he did it himself? He didn't even *move* from his place."

"But—"

BOOOM!

The warlord had shot up to the air, and was bombarding him with a dozen, two, three, five scores of pressure orbs, shooting down at him like meteor showers. Every time they hit, the sand tossed up a massive explosion. Together, it sounded like the beating of some cosmic drum, the shock waves radiating out in every direction as Aguilar dodged them. Olfric stared at him, jaw on the floor, as Aguilar survived a constant barrage of thirty-eight perfectly aimed shots, and looked at Tanya, who was staring with open shock and awe. Olfric had seen Tanya perform those shots—Wind Shear, she called them—and each one of them was capable of reducing the population of a single house to zero leaving nothing but dust and destruction in its wake. The warlord was some-how maintaining absolute control over every single one of those shots, while also keeping perfect track of Aguilar's movement.

"Watch carefully, girl," said Solana, and Olfric knew who her words were intended for. "This is how it is when titans fight. That level of parallel process-ing is impressive. And neither of them has yet given into their emotions."

"Grandfather has."

. . . what?

Olfric followed Tanya's gaze and looked at the warlord, amplifying his vision with lifeforce. A terramancer like Zuken would be able to do that much better, but even Olfric could see the glower of frustration forming on the man's face as he bombarded the terrain with aerial shots in untold numbers, striking one after another with increasing amounts of raw power. Had this happened inside a city, it would have been ruined. Really, it was taking him an absurd amount of focus to just keep track of the explosions, and there they were, tracking each other's attacks, determining their trajectories and maintaining a stalemate while operating at such speeds.

It was ridiculous. Absurd. Insane.

"Pesky little pest!" snarled the warlord. "You're quick on your feet and are using this place to duck in and out like a mole. But this ends now. You can run, but you cannot hide."

He soared into the sky, and four massive wings of crimson red erupted out of his back, each of them easily twice as long as he was tall. Around him, the winds began to twist and churn, forming—

"Fuck my life," muttered Olfric, staring at the sky with growing horror.

Wind blades.

They hung in the air, held up by invisible hands—hundreds, nay, *thousands*. Enough to strike at almost every random space within the dome. They lined up row upon row, spanning across the circumference of an invisible circle, with Mujin in the center. Olfric didn't need to be a sensor to know that each and every one of those blades had as much impact as one of those shots from earlier. They would rain down death and destruction and scorch the terrain itself, taking down their foe.

"Oh, dear . . ." said Solana, instantly doubling her barriers.

"That . . ." whispered Tanya, staggering back, her eyes open in blank shock. "That is Ezzeron's signature move. He—he duplicated it?"

"Death By A Thousand Blades," muttered Solana. "The signature move of the Wind King. Seemingly impossible to dodge. Can you replicate that, girl?"

Olfric whirled so fast that he feared he'd snap his neck.

"I . . . can," Tanya swallowed. "But I can only manage a few hundred. But . . . *that*—"

Olfric looked up at the veritable wall of wind blades, ready to crush anything and everything within its unforgiving embrace. They left no gap between the ranks, no weakness that could be exploited, and allowed nothing to slip by their guard. Lukas could keep dodging blades when they fell one after another, but not even he could survive that onslaught when they fell *everywhere* at the same time. Best case scenario, he would be forced to go deep within the ground, in which case the blades would follow him and take advantage of his slower speed underneath the sand. Trying to take advantage of the Desert's area and escaping would do him little good, either, because those blades would just follow and trap him. And if he tried to make a stand there, he'd be blindsided with overwhelming force. A man, no matter how powerful, could not hold the mountain back. Whatever Aguilar chose to do, it would lead to his doom.

It was a flawless strategy, simple in plan and execution. There was no reason to believe it would not work like it had when the Wind King had used it. But somehow, Olfric just couldn't bring himself to believe that. He didn't know why, but something within him, a deep subconscious instinct, told him that the warlord had not accounted for something. A fatal error that would cost him more than this assured victory.

Seeing Aguilar just stand there, without the slightest tensing of his body only confirmed that growing suspicion.

"Any last wishes, boy?" demanded the warlord.

"Oh please," said Aguilar, waving his hand. "It's not like you're going to vanish those blades and take me to a restaurant if I asked you to get me a fancy dinner as my death wish."

Despite himself, Olfric snorted.

The warlord's lips twisted.

"*Fire!*"

Olfric shut his eyes, not willing to see the aftermath as the untold fury of those blades came down, raining death and destruction upon—

"Establish Territory: Serenity."

The words rippled across the battlefield, their undeniable weight giving pause to everyone, even the monster flying above. Olfric saw Lukas Aguilar raise his right hand, palms open, meeting the warlord's eyes and . . .

The silence that fell upon the battle terrain was almost deafening in intensity as every eye there gazed in wonder at what they saw.

Lukas was still there, absolutely unmoving. He hadn't run. He hadn't terraported. He hadn't tried to defend himself, and neither had the Desert erupted in a thousand explosions. Solana's barriers hadn't been breached either. And the reason . . .

. . . was up there.

"I . . ." murmured Olfric, breaking the silence. "I don't know what I'm looking at."

The blades hung in midair, held back by invisible chains, a wondrous impossibility that made no sense. They hung in their majestic numbers, and even from a distance, he could see the warlord trying to pull them back, or make them move or explode, or do anything at all.

But they didn't.

They just hung there.

Floating.

As if held in place by an impossible power.

The mountain had been held back.

Regardless of mass, momentum, gravity, or Aeromancy.

"Is this . . ." he murmured, despite himself, ". . . the power of a Demigod?"

Solana's neck snapped in his direction, her eyes widening, but Olfric could not bring himself to care.

"Who are you, boy?" asked the warlord, with something like fear in his voice.

Lukas's response was to flick his wrist, and the blades—the impossibly powerful attack of the Wind Warlord—suddenly shifted direction. Instead of Lukas, they were now aiming for—"MOVE! MOVE!" Olfric could hear people yelling, as they hurried to escape their fate—the warship, dashing at a speed that would have put lightning to shame.

If left unobstructed, the power behind those blades would have sundered an entire city apart in a single second. Each of those blades had the concept of friction removed from them, allowing them to phase through nearly anything, and they would keep flying ahead infinitely into the sky. But if something did happen to be in the way . . .

Olfric watched, flabbergasted, as dozens and dozens of wards and barriers began to form around the floating warship. Layers upon layers of protective enchantments enforced by dozens of mana generators within the warship sprang into existence, turning it into no less than a floating fortress capable of withstanding extreme damage.

And it was nearly overwhelmed the moment it came in contact with the force of a full-powered Level-4 attack.

It was an unstoppable force against an immovable object. The two titanic powers erupted against one another with such might that the warship was blasted further along the trajectory, taking the entire brunt of that chaotic attack.

BOOOM!

The collision erupted violently, as though a supervolcano had just erupted in midair, blinding and deafening all there, regardless of whatever powers or constitutions they had that would normally reduce the impact. The shock wave from the blast itself was already cataclysmic and threw any bremetan without some sort of support or protection to ground them, off their feet, even from this distance. Solana cried out in agony as she was pushed down to her knees, doing her best to keep throwing up more barriers as each of the prior ones kept shattering, or else the detonation would have instantly killed every single one of them. And that was with Tanya using Aeromancy to put up her own barriers to augment Solana's.

It wouldn't have surprised Olfric if this detonation had been heard throughout Haviskali. The Cobalt Army might be coming to investigate soon. Then he remembered that Lord Naowa had shifted the army from the Desert's borders to the capital city. But when the smoke and the stars dancing in Olfric's vision died down . . .

The warship was still there, looming over all of them ominously, except for that massive hole in one side of it.

And the worst part? Lukas was down on one knee. Whatever that spell of his was, it had taken a lot out of him.

"Ha!" said the warlord. "I have to admit, boy, you have *some* power in you. I'll even admit you gave me quite the scare for a second." He chuckled. "But surely you didn't think the Earth King's warship would be destroyed so easily."

"He's fibbing," Olfric heard Zuken murmur. "For all his talk, he's nervous. And no way was that *easy*. It was a Level 4. And I know for a fact that not even a warlord can dish out Level-4 attacks one after another. He can gloat all he wants, but that attack exhausted him as well."

"But the warship's still there," said Olfric.

"The warship is functional, yes," said Tanya, "but the strain that the blast put on its resources and defenses? That's another matter entirely."

"Yes," said Olfric. "But I don't think that guy is going to let Aguilar play with another of his superpowered attacks. And I don't think Aguilar or any of us can punch another hole like that in that ship."

"No, we—"Tanya began.

Then Solana started to giggle.

He must have lost his mind, Olfric decided. Solana *giggling* like a little girl. Even her shoulders were shaking, like she had just understood the meaning of the most hilarious joke she had ever heard. It was the laughter of a woman who had been hit by an extremely surprising gift that she knew she would relish.

"That impossible man . . ." chuckled the skinwalker. "He was playing the warlord this whole time. He knew he couldn't fight him and win, so he met him at his fullest power and enraged him enough to use his most destructive attack. And use it against the warship to either destroy it or at least considerably damage it. And look, he targeted the attack, not at the total ship, but—"

"At the cannons," Olfric whispered in awe.

She turned to Tanya. "He told us, remember? 'You will face the warlord, while he will do his best to undo that man's strengths.' He's now given you an idea of how fast the man is, the nature of his attacks, and the power and concept behind his apparently most-powerful blow. And he has destroyed the cannons, so Mujin can't hold us hostage any longer. The rest is now all up to you."

Tanya smiled as her hair turned a flawless white and the color between her irises began to fade.

"There's one thing you forgot, though," she said. Solana raised her brow, and Tanya laughed. "It's been five minutes since the battle started."

With that, Solana undid the barrier, allowing Tanya to rise above the embankment to meet her nemesis, ready to enter the battle at last.

One moment, Mujin Shimizu was up in the air, trash-talking Lukas for even imagining in his wildest dreams that such a paltry attack would be able to damage the Earth King's warship. Of course, he knew that it was bullshit; the fact that a warlord even needed to bluff him made him lose whatever respect he had for the man's prowess. Suddenly, the sight of the battle-hardened warlord shifted to the image of Ultaf Shimizu, older and in possession of a far more powerful kami, and a complementary physical and elemental Skill to boot.

It was . . . disappointing.

The next moment, a lance of wind tore through the sky at him, and for a moment, Lukas hoped that his rejuvenation Skill could heal him from that wound, and then—

—Snikt!

A ribbon-like thing slashed through the lance, shattering it right when it was some feet away from striking his chest.

"Really, Grandfather," he heard Tanya say, "attacking others when they are at their weakest. I wonder if Ultaf learned that from you."

"Learned to bark, have you?" asked the warlord, swooping down on the ground.

"That and some," said Tanya. "And if you have even a bit of dignity left in you, you'll wait before I settle my matters with him. Then we can fight, and I can kill you."

The old man sneered.

Lukas pushed himself up by his elbows, heaving as he sat upright. His vision was still cloudy and with due cause. His altered territory, *Serenity*, was an alternate variation of Neutered Earth, with the concept of *Absolute Rest* applied to everything within the established territory. The real trick was to twist the direction of the blades all at once using Kinetomancy, without making them blow up, a task far more difficult than anything else he had tried so far, what with manipulating all those momentum vectors all at once while maintaining Motion Negation against a Level-4 Wind Manipulation Skill. He had made it look as theatrical as possible in an attempt to deceive the warlord while doing his best to maintain his composure as blood vessels inside his brain were popping, with the anomaly's regen factor acting on it at the same time. At least he wasn't suffering from another brain aneurysm, but it was still pretty damn close. He could barely make out Tanya's blurry form as she grabbed his hand and pulled him upright. He rested against her shoulder and gave her a lopsided grin.

"Five minutes are over?"

She chuckled. "That they are," she said. "Thank you."

"For what?"

"For giving me the chance to grow past my fears. I needed to see him fighting. Seriously, it's like every time I look away, you're there pulling my ass out of the fire."

"And what a delectable ass it is too," said Lukas, grinning.

"Idiot." She grabbed him as he lurched slightly. "Now you relax and let me take care of it."

"Can't," he said. "Need to take care of . . . that." He panted, raising a finger overhead. He didn't know if he was pointing directly at the warship, but she'd understand. "Don't . . . do you . . . think, he'd . . . give us a five-minute break?"

"No, but he is probably charging an attack right now."

"Figures," Lukas mumbled. "Like I understand he's come to capture you and kill us all, but would it hurt to be a little polite?"

Tanya snorted. "Now rest, while I finish our overdue business with him."

"Good luck."

With a smile, Tanya turned around and faced the warlord, who for once had respected her words and waited until she was done. Lukas had recovered enough to see things and understand them with clarity, maybe even dish out a couple of distractions if need be. He had all but used the whole technique to carry out his plan, rendering him exhausted beyond belief, and it was still far from done. Then again, nothing significant ever happened without equally significant effort. For once, it seemed, fate had decided to keep him out of the direct fight. Just as it had decided to hurl him directly into the previous ones.

Quickly, he checked the Screen.

Territory Creation Active
Vertical Boundary Set
Length: Indeterminate
Terraformation Active
67% of Omphalos Reserves Drained
Continue with Terraformation? (NOT RECOMMENDED)

Yes, Lukas told it. He had bet everything on this one surprise tactic. It had to work. He had gotten the idea upon realizing the might of the force they would be facing. But facing them while standing upon these sands, where everything it all started, a new plan had begun to form in his head. Options that he had not seen before were now available. He could make it work, so long as he managed to complete it just in time. The only problem was the sheer amount of power he needed to get it done, and not even the practically endless reserves of his omphalos were enough for that.

That, and he needed to stay in one place until it was over. No matter what happened.

"Grandfather," said Tanya, standing in front of him like a shield, facing the man responsible for all the wrongs in her life. Her hair was already cadaverous, though it didn't feel like Frost had taken control yet. Despite who she was up against, this was Tanya's fight, first and foremost.

Two whips of Everfrost appeared in either of her hands.

"There is something poetic about this," said the warlord, taking a step toward them. It was a psychological trick, because the closer he got to Lukas, the greater the chances of Mujin attacking and possibly killing him, which would make Tanya increasingly desperate. The warlord thrust his blade into the desert sand and laughed. "This place witnessed the end of the Glacier Queen at the hand of the Great Goddess. It is poetic for it to now witness the fall of these pathetic parasites for good as I defeat their last hope and drag you down by the hair like a pathetic slave."

"And for what purpose?" asked Tanya. There was a surprising lack of venom in her tone. "Pathetically try to steal the Glacier Queen's power so that you can call yourself worthy?"

Surprise flitted across Mujin's face.

"Don't be surprised," said Tanya. "I know all about it. The Wind King defeated my mother Tsurara in combat and imprisoned her. He was a warrior, a king, and to the winner went the spoils. I can understand that. But then you came along. A pathetic whiner, a blight on your father's name, an insult to his Potential. Even Ezzeron thought you were beyond his notice. And so you tried to steal Tsurara's power hoping it would compensate for your inferiority."

"Inferiority . . ." spat the old man. "You call me inferior? When all your life you've fled to escape my wrath? Do not think that the half-breed behind you or those parasites hiding behind those veils can save you. Make no mistake, girl. I will crush that defiance in your eyes. I will kill that half-breed and obliterate him to dust. His remains shall blow in this very desert while my soldiers crush your allies before your eyes. And then, when you lie defeated and alone and begging for death, I shall drag you back to that same prison your worthless father broke you out from. The Wind King started the process of ending these parasites. It is only fitting that I, his son and heir, be the one to complete his righteous crusade."

The words were meant to bite, but instead, they incited nothing but scornful laughter from her.

"You are no longer simply mired in your hypocrisy. You're drowning in it."

Mujin's lips curled.

"You claim that these parasites are demons, because they possess others in order to survive, and hence, your crusade against them is righteous," said Tanya. "On the other hand, you crush your own people's hopes and dreams and lives, turning them into flesh puppets that fight for you."

"I have no need to explain my actions to a half-breed," snarled the man. "A crusade requires soldiers, and while some of them may be doing so unwillingly, their protests pale in significance to the greater good." He smacked his clenched fist against his breastplate. "I am a true Asukan, and domination of all that is profane is our divine right, for we are blessed by the gods. Your spineless father lacked the fortitude to bear this truth."

"Spineless . . ." said Tanya. "Or perhaps he simply was a better man than you."

Mujin laughed. "A coward. That was all he was."

Lukas noticed the tiniest amount of tension in her body language before she regained her composure.

"Perhaps you're right. Then again, he was *your* child. The sins of the father, as they say . . ."

BOOOM!

Mujin had no witty response to that. No proclamation, no angry retort. No meeting of eyes, nod of approval, nor sign of mutual acknowledgment. One moment Tanya was mocking the man, and the next, she momentarily vanished, rematerialized, and then met his sudden onslaught head-on, her frosted whip meeting his blade without delay nor hesitation. Every time they clashed, her whips were severed to pieces by the heavy metal, but they rejoined immediately and effortlessly for the next exchange a millisecond later. Mana was gathered. Tools were repaired. Bodies reinforced. Eyes narrowed. A never-ending series of single passes that had them gambling with death every time.

Even Lukas could tell from his vantage point that the warlord was slightly weaker from channeling all that power. And the reason for that was obvious. The more mana you channeled, the more of an imbalance was created within your elemental and emotional spectrum. And there in the middle of the Desert, where Amaterasu's All-Seeing Eye was blind, where Eternal Light could not naturally penetrate, the restraints that the Shikigami Ritual applied on the kami were weakened significantly. Which meant the more you used mana, the more power you gave the kami, and if you weren't careful, the kami could severely affect your emotions and mess with your clarity and judgment.

But even so, Mujin was still a warlord. His speed was leagues above what Tanya could achieve in her current state, and his strength could crush her with even a glancing blow. Even while limiting himself, he should've been able to take Tanya down.

Weapons crashed. Bodies moved. And once more, the combatants stood still, already on the move for the next round.

Lukas had already lost count of the number of times Tanya had nearly succumbed, just as he had stopped counting the number of times Mujin should have been cursed with Everfrost.

Every time they passed, Tanya kept drawing a little more of Everfrost to augment her Aeromancy.

Every time they passed, she had to abandon her attempt to destroy his body with a single blow or stab him with Frost, lest she be crippled or worse. Her body was already sporting a wide collection of paper-thin cuts.

Every time they passed, her face turned just a little monstrous. Frost was beginning to take over her skin. Her wounds were healing faster, but her sanity also seemed to be slipping as a thirst for blood grew stronger within her.

Lukas had risen from an average human to someone capable of operating at tremendous speeds thanks to Inanna's Kinetomancy. But even then, he had to admit that the warlord had never gone all-out on him when they'd faced each other in battle. There had always been something playful in how the madman had fought him, a condescending manner that indicated he was simply amusing himself just to see what Lukas was capable of—until the very end when Lukas's little play at bombardment had annoyed him enough to take him seriously.

But now? Now there was no restraint in the man's eyes. No hint of mercy, no holding back. He was coming at Tanya like a ravenous predator after its prey. He was calling on every scrap of his power and using every bit of his knowledge and Experience in combat to bring it all down upon her.

So how was Tanya still able to keep up?

Lukas had seen her fighting against the endless hordes inside the lava ridge borderland. He had seen her obliterate the entire horde of bylestyrs with high-powered Level-3 attacks and tear through monsters like they were nothing but mindless meat before her wind blades. It had given him an idea of what her limits were. Very impressive, but that was it. That was her max. That level was far below the warlord's speed, and yet somehow, she was still matching him now. Unlike Lukas who had Inanna's blessing in the form of Level-4 Kinetomancy, Tanya shouldn't have been able to improve her performance to such a startling degree in such a short time. Why, the only creature that had been nearly as fast as she was had been . . .

Oh.

Maude had claimed that Meynte's possession on Tanya's mind had caused no *active* effects on her. That said, there were a lot of remnants of her psychic architecture—her *memories*—that had integrated with Tanya's own spiritual core and would either fade or be assimilated into her soul. Both of them were yuki-onna, both used Everfrost, and both held similar genetic and spiritual structures, which caused a resonance that allowed her to gain certain Skills and perhaps, instincts from her ancestor.

Maude was only half-right there.

Spiritual resonance wasn't just possible due to having similar spiritual architecture or their shared connection to Everfrost. The cause could have also been each of them having experienced an event that resonated powerfully with both of their souls. Meynte had faced Amaterasu's power in this very Desert, and now, her descendant and fellow Everfrost vessel was facing another Asukan who used the power of Eternal Light.

Just like with Lukas and Inanna—him facing the Ifrit King in a world of Flame, and her facing the wrath of the Vikahl Ashlands.

Mujin was right. It truly was poetic. Lukas only hoped that he appreciated the irony behind his statement.

CHAPTER 23

———

Well, this is certainly a curious development, if nothing else," said Solana idly, observing the chaos with a gleam in her eyes, her voice carrying over the wind effortlessly despite the explosions in the air. "I have to admit, I did not foresee the girl having this much talent."

"She hasn't yet rifted even once," said Maude from behind her. "The time you spent training with her has definitely borne fruit."

Solana shook her head. "You give me too much credit, oni. Much of this is novel for myself." Her agility, her control over Frost, her composure, and the way she met the warlord on an almost-equal level . . . Only one explanation made sense.

"I was right, though," she mused, out loud. "The girl truly is a spectacular vessel. It seems the Glacier Queen's remnants have genuinely merged with her, becoming one with her spiritual self. She might not be truly a Level 4, but with the Queen's control of Everfrost, she might not need that much to bridge the gap. Not even Tsurara was this talented."

Maude gave her a surprised look. "Then the training you gave her—"

"I could only help her get used to what she originally had. That plus my observations about the queen's ability within the Haze. But all of this . . . is *her*. I can only wonder what will happen if the warlord decides to up the ante and demonstrate his fullest power."

"Something tells me that the Outsider planned all this."

"As much as I'd like to claim otherwise, I can't," admitted the skinwalker. "The Outsider is the sort to pull off miracles under everyone's noses. I certainly did not expect him to pull off that last stunt, but here we are. If he had planned on Tanya being able to make a stand against the warlord, either I underestimated the girl's ability, or she was hiding her true power all this time, in which case I suppose I have to assume she has a better poker face than I imagined."

"I'm afraid you're wrong, Leader."

"Oh?"

"Lukas Aguilar . . . He has a far greater understanding of what transpired between the queen's soul and Tanya than either of us can fathom. I spent weeks analyzing Tanya's constitution, and yet he was the first to suggest a potential spiritual resonance. What's more, his words carried a strange finality, almost like . . ."

"He was speaking from experience?"

Maude pursed her lips and nodded.

Solana's lips curled. "Interesting. I suppose I shouldn't even be surprised at this point. Perhaps the legend is more than just a story passed down by our ancestors. Especially with those words he said . . ."

"You think there's more?"

Solana laughed. "I'm surprised you even have to ask this, oni. When it comes to the Outsider, there is *always* more."

Maude's lips twisted, but then a shade of concern crossed her features. Solana followed her gaze and momentarily froze at the sight before her. She had believed that the war would be on an indefinite hiatus until the warlord himself was done with Tanya.

She had been dead-wrong.

"Is that—" she began, but words failed her.

They floated above the ground but low enough that they could directly fight those below them. Mujin Shimizu was a monstrously cruel creature, but that did not make him a fool. Quite the contrary, it made him more cunning. The first wave he'd sent in had been nothing more than a scouting force. That explained why there were so few of them and why it had all felt so lackluster. Even the pack that the Outsider's friends had finished off numbered barely more than a hundred or so. And when the fighting turned against them those who hadn't been already killed by the yokai force simply retreated. And then, the warship had blown the territory apart, creating a divide.

The one that was approaching them now, however, was the true vanguard.

The second wave.

Rows of aeromancers with breastplates of Eternal-Light-blessed metal covering their lithe frames. They were followed by terramancers, clad in bulky, dark-metal mail. They looked far more menacing than their lesser-equipped brethren, and it wasn't just their armor that made them so. For amidst them were soldiers holding spears burning with Eternal Light in all its glory. Their powered exoskeletons provided them with the tenacity to endure and the power to move, the ether crystals stacked inside them granting them prodigious strength when their faith failed to do so. A miracle of Asukan engineering striding forth in battle.

"That's—the—the—" Olfric stammered, "—the Cobalt Army."

And indeed it was. Massive war hammers. Great, bludgeoning mauls. Garlands of fire and lightning dancing between their weapons. The best of Asukan technology empowered by arcane spells, blessed by the Asukan divinity, and given to their most faithful fanatics, those who would butcher in their god's name without a single question about right and wrong. In their opposite hands were strapped immense tower shields, solid barriers of blessed metal the height of a fully grown man, complete with sigils that combined the best of mana-crafting and technology to create the best siege weapons imaginable. Behind them were more support staff—Omnyoji, healers, and technicians.

This would not be an easy fight to win.

"EVERYONE," Solana bellowed, her voice carrying through the loud commotion, "the enemy is upon us. Let the queen fight the warlord. We will protect the Outsider at all costs. All of you, *CHARGE!*"

And with that, the yokai army rushed into war.

81% of Omphalos Reserves Drained
Running on Auxiliary Power

72% Activation Complete
Auto-Shutdown Commences at 94% Reserve Drain

This was getting difficult.

Lukas watched the massive Asukan army wade into the Desert, only to meet the yokai force in open combat. This second wave was far more ruthless and powerful than the former, and he didn't anticipate things going well for the yokai side. He watched as Olfric used the power of his new kami to its maximum, the biotoxin he had procured for him from the neothelid prototype being used effectively against the Cobalt Army. They might have been blessed against the yokai's possession, and their armor might have helped defend against arcane sorcery and bursts of elemental mana, but it was far more difficult to halt the flow of water, especially if it had a mind of its own and was employing the chaos all around it to its advantage.

Doubly so when it was poisoned with the deadliest toxin Lukas could think of. He was no expert, but he was sure that even a micron of it was enough to kill a man when ingested.

And Olfric wasn't the only one dealing the damage.

Lukas saw Zuken using his new fractals to defend against the attacks that were escaping past their army, while Solana's barriers were enough to halt entire rows of terramancers in their path. He saw some soldiers hesitate when Elena fell across her path, only for Maude to arrive out of nowhere and paralyze them from behind.

Not that the army had been idle in the meantime. Like a disturbed nest of hornets, they buzzed all around them, several of them trying to attack Lukas twice in a row. First from behind and then from above. He had been saved by Zuken and Ryu respectively. But the Cobalt Army weren't the foolhardy warriors Zuken and company had faced earlier. They were veterans, well-trained in their craft, and knew perfectly well how to counter the spiritual parasites while maintaining a steady assault.

Prepared hunters cornering their prey.

And the toll began to add up.

Lukas needed to do something. But what? His own plan was backfiring against him. Terraformation, by all logic, shouldn't have taken this much power. But he wasn't just terraforming. He was also expanding his created territory against the will of the World around him, and that was taking its toll on his reserves. And unlike the Shimizu fortress, there were no ley lines beneath the sandy terrain for him to reach down and draw power from. And he remembered what had happened the last time he had used Capacitance to draw power from ley lines, even if it was just enough to empower a dranzithl for less than a minute.

Damn it. They were all going to die at this rate. He needed to do something. Anything. But expending power to wipe out the army would only make things worse.

Gritting his teeth against the migraine that threatened to overwhelm him, Lukas accelerated the process.

Overclocking Skill: Terraformation
Using 200% Omphalos Power for Terraformation
Terraformation 83% Complete

No longer was it a dull, aching throb. Instead, bright, agonizing lances of pain assaulted his mind. Consciousness flickered, brief lapses of darkness that lasted for he wasn't entirely sure how long. Nonetheless, the vertical column of crystal was forming at three times the rate as before, digging deep, deep into the heart of the Desert.

A sizzling sound confirmed what he had already felt. Zuken fell limp at his side, a blade severing a tendon beneath his knee before a hit from one of those tower-shields sent Zuken into peaceful oblivion. Elena was captured, fallen on the sand, her hands tied behind her wrists. The yurei were being mercilessly wiped out by the holy enchantments imbued in those weapons. Solana was surrounded by flanks of terramancers and aeromancers, a circular wall of force closing in on her from all sides, ripping apart the sand beneath her feet. Solana had shattered the barrier and sent several of them flying, but the rest took the opportunity to fire blades of sharp wind at her, hacking into her pristine flesh mask. The skinwalker hissed, as black ichor-like tissue tried to re-form itself as she threw up more barriers only to be attacked by an even more powerful assault.

Please, thought Lukas. *Just a little more. I'm almost done. I'm almost—*

A massive blade fell.

And two pieces of Mizo, the reiki, fell on the ground, the blessed enchantment in the blade burning her form from the point of injury. Lukas saw Olfric trying to escape a group of Cobalt Army soldiers before he was jerked back and thrown into the air. Olfric slashed them with a massive tentacle of poisoned water but became vulnerable to five slashes of razor-sharp wind that seared his torso. A soldier slammed his injured body with his shield and smashed him down into the sand; lying next to the reiki, he began to choke on his own blood.

And then a soldier slammed his broadsword right into Olfric's chest.

NO, Lukas thought with growing horror. This couldn't be happening. He glanced at Tanya and found her still fighting the warlord, who was raining down showers of wind blades at her and throwing power the likes of which Tanya had never faced before. Both spiritists had taken absolutely massive forms—a winged canine for Mujin against Ezzeron's massive eight-winged avian shape—and Mujin was winning. Solana, too, was trapped and on the verge of breaking, and none of the main fighters of their crowd were winning anytime soon. This desert, where the yokai thrived for this long, would serve as graves as the Cobalt Army meticulously brought them down despite the—

Lukas blinked.

Despite the *curse.*

The Desert's Curse.

It resented all life in general, and yet it allowed an anomaly to fester inside its own heart. It allowed an entire yokai contingent to thrive in its darkness.

And it absolutely abhorred and repelled the Eternal Light.

This . . . this he could work with.

But before he could do anything, something else happened that left his jaw dropping in shock.

Olfric *gurgled.*

Lukas blinked. No, he wasn't seeing things. Lukas gurgled and coughed out blood. He was supposed to be dead, but somehow, he wasn't. Instead, he was recovering his strength. His hand went up and with a strength he shouldn't have possessed, pulled the massive broadsword out of his bleeding chest, the wound mending at a rate fast enough to make Lukas jealous. The rest of his body was also mending itself. In place of his hacked-off arm, a new limb was growing and extending; the aquamancer was now using it to push himself back up, wary and alert.

The soldiers stepped back, clearly discomfited by this impossibility. Knowing them, they were thinking he was turning into some kind of demon. And to be fair, they weren't completely wrong.

ONI
Chimeric Entity. Result of Spiritual Fusion of BREMETAN Species with REIKI Species
Presence of Symbiotic Bond with JAAN Species

Bipedal, lifeforce-producing organism. Capable of Metamancy and Aquamancy.
Mutated Soul Architecture.

Reiki. There was only one creature near him that fitted the bill. Lukas's eyes scanned for the broken shapeshifting creature that lay fallen next to Olfric, only to see that it was no longer there. Which meant—

"Did you know," said Olfric, or however the oni now identified himself. "I was an Omnyoji in training. A spellcaster. And after getting possessed by Mizo the first time, I realized that the Asukan way of channeling mana using yokai was inferior and inefficient. A perfect balance of the spectrum is required to unleash the power, but adding constraints only leads to explosion. Harmonization is the key."

"What nonsense are you babbling?" said the soldier who had driven his sword into Olfric's chest just moments earlier.

"Harmonization. Bremetan, physical being of lifeforce; yokai, spiritual being of mana. Harmonize them, you get oni—the best of both worlds. Shattering the bonds of lifeforce . . ."

The ground shook, as a sudden, immense force spiraled around him. His body became larger, thicker, his muscles expanding powerfully, promising strength that could crush nearly everything in its way.

". . . unleashing the limits of mana . . ."

Suddenly a massive cylindrical tube of water, spreading out in a serpentine fashion with a large, draconic face, appeared and coiled around Olfric. The oni took out a vial of biotoxin and poured its contents into the water elemental around him.

"Harmonization, complete."

The massive draconian serpent attacked, and Olfric followed it, the world around him exploding into a corona of water and death. His sheer power shattered shields, knocking soldiers down, blowing them off their feet, while the serpent—a manifestation of his kami, no doubt—slithered its way through the sand and the air, soldiers dropping dead at its mere touch.

A tempest of battle surrounded him, and he was at its center—calm in the eye of the storm.

Meanwhile, with the tide of the battle suddenly changed, Lukas had a new option open to him. Sending a simple thought to Blob, it slid away from him and took on a new form.

> **Creating New Instance KHORKHOI**
> **Adding Sand to Implement New Physical Configuration**
> **Found Alien Configuration: Desert's Curse**
> **Applying . . .**
> **Spiritual Configuration Complete**

A vast black, metallic shadow covered the sands with its hateful malevolence. An eerie, grating sound spread across the sands, like metal on glass. Enormous canvases of darkened metal hide, re-forged with sand crystals, that threatened to block out the sun. It twisted and turned, scales of poisonous darkness rubbing together, languidly fusing and segmenting into one another. The more they contorted, the more they morphed into a kaleidoscope of spikes and protrusions, expanding in an endless spiral. Serrated spines ran from its enormous head all the way down to its tail.

The mouth came into full focus. The stomach-churning, nightmare-inducing mass bared its thousand-fanged mouth, releasing a gale of hot, putrid breath, the stench of a decaying corpse; anything that came into contact with its aura instantly dropped to their knees, coughing up blood, their bodies paralyzed by the intrusion of an energy so corrosive that just to imbibe it meant certain death.

It brushed away all opposition. The mammoth monstrosity swam through the sands. Anyone that fell into its path was either crushed by its teeth or flung away like a rag doll, hurled aside by its immeasurable strength. Whatever was left of the army not already facing intense attack from Olfric and Solana and whatever remained of the yokai crew, had turned their firepower against this much-more-dangerous threat. Armor-piercing blades clanged and shattered against its thick hide. Every single one of their holy weapons lost their luster from a single moment of contact with its aura.

And they weren't the only ones to suffer the brunt of the curse.

Just feeling it caused Lukas pain. The hate exuding from those sands, the simmering wrath of the World against the atrocity committed by the one that called itself the Great Goddess was a power unlike anything he had ever felt. Even inside his own World, he could feel the curse take root, corrupting it with its very presence, rendering it oppressive and repulsive. Had this been a normal corruption, his organs and bodily functions would have shut down, and the omphalos regeneration would have kicked in.

Instead, it was merging with him. Adding to him. And for whatever reason that didn't quite make sense to him, he didn't have the usual feeling of being "connected" to the World's awareness as the curse took root within him. No sense of a greater existence around him. No sense of trying to exist in a maelstrom of power and Potential that was far greater than he could even comprehend. Instead, the curse acted like it was a lingering remnant of something that was once part of the World but the process of its creation had made into a completely independent manifestation.

It wasn't an anomaly, wasn't a Truth, and wasn't a Taboo.

It was a curse. A desire. Emotion given form. And Lukas, more than anyone, knew just how deep and devastating desire could be. The desire for freedom had altered a slave girl into a butcher of gods and beasts. A desire for control, for power, to have *everything* transformed her into an empress and eventually, into the Supreme Queen. Gods, demons, Truths, Taboos, even *Worlds*—nothing was beyond desire's reach to conquer and crush.

And this curse exclusively and *obsessively* rejected Eternal Light. As if Eternal Light had been keeping it from becoming something else.

But what? It made no sense. For Eternal Light could not penetrate the Desert. Not unless it had been brought in separately.

Then . . . What *was* it?

His ponderings were replaced by worry as he realized that victory was still far from reach. Olfric, as an oni, was strong. But he was but one man fighting against an entire army. Tanya was also failing to keep up against Mujin's constant onslaught. And while the Cobalt Army was temporarily weakened by the khorkhoi's aura, their weapons regained their power the moment they stepped out of its reach.

His suspicions were right. The army wasn't only empowered by those weapons and suits. There was something else as well.

Like that floating fortress in the sky.

And it was time to address that nuisance for good.

Terraformation Complete
Territory Creation Active and Set Along Established Boundary Length
Nature: Carquane Alloy
Remaining Omphalos Reserve: 8%

Lukas exhaled. Just 2% short of shutdown. Thanking whichever deity was responsible for that bit of luck, Lukas laid out his plan. Pushing himself slightly to the left, he grabbed the peak of the carquane crystal shaft, the same substance used in wardstones, a massive construction that went deep down into the very heart of the World, across thousands of feet, establishing Lukas's territory, and drawing raw, infinite energy through the substance to the very peak.

This, Lukas told himself, *is going to fucking hurt.*

> **Capacitance Active**
> **Reverse Shift Active**

Power flooded into him. *Unlimited power.* He could feel the omphalos reserves jump up in sets of twos, then threes, then sevens, and more. In less than ten seconds, he had already recovered 50% of his total reserves, and the rest came rushing in. And he knew exactly where he needed to send it.

He slowly turned himself to face the floating fortress bearing down on him. Even a kilometer away, it seemed to dwarf everything nearby. And the sheer quantity of power stored inside it was what was empowering both the warlord's suit and the soldiers fighting across the sandy plain.

Mujin requested and the Earth King sent this titanic vessel to kill the yokai using Eternal Light in a place where it was barred from entering.

They had asked for this, and they would be the ones to accept the consequences.

It was time to show them exactly what they'd won.

He gripped the length of the carquane shard that was above the ground. Terraforming substances wasn't a big deal for him, but the cost of filling it up with energy was an entirely different matter altogether. And charging it directly through his omphalos reserves wouldn't only be an incredibly slow process, but he would never be able to dish out enough energy to make a significant difference.

But if he could pull that energy directly from the World without any consequences?

> **Creating Bombardment Units with Reduced Integrity Limiters by 45%**
> **Reaching Critical Threshold for Energy Containment**

Natural energy was unstoppable and far more potent than mana. There was no chance of stopping it once it was unleashed. It was why the wards at the Peak could hold against endless Level-3 hits but were incinerated the moment the natural energy of the world rushed in through the wards.

Luckily, Lukas had no desire to trap it.

> **Set Trajectory**
> **Lock Target**

Fire.

The upper part of the carquane crystal outgrowth splintered and shot upwards, tearing through the air. One moment the carquane crystal had ripped through the barriers and buried itself deep inside the warship. The next moment, half of the flying fortress vanished in a sea of flames. Just as with the castle before, the force of the explosion was so massive that every single person on the ground and in the air was hurled away. Even Lukas had to raise a motion barrier just to keep the shock waves from outright killing him and damaging the carquane crystal outgrowth.

And he was far from finished.

Asserting and Aligning Projectiles
Setting Locked Targets
Launch

BOOM! BOOM! BOOM! went the missiles. The first pair slammed into the warship's left, which was still somewhat untouched by the two attacks. The next one hit it in the dead center, detonating the entire warship into splintered shards that flung away for miles in each direction. The very sky itself had turned into a massive white cloud of devastation.

"Well?" said Lukas, finally standing up, and feeling his own reserves recharging now back to a comfortable 90%. "Wasn't that something?"

Far away, the warlord's rage exploded with the force of a bomb as well. He kicked Tanya aside, flinging her by several hundred feet and burying her in the sand. Then Mujin conjured a massive implosion missile and sent it hurling at Lukas at sonic speed.

Even with his power, Lukas knew he couldn't shield against such an attack. Not only would the sheer momentum shatter through any shield he could conjure, the resulting collision would detonate in his face, damaging the carquane crystal, and if that happened, the entire Desert would probably incinerate, leaving nothing but dust and a giant crater spanning hundreds of miles.

Perhaps if he were able to open a rift into the Haze faster than his current ability, he could have channeled the raw power into that World of endless energy. It would be like pouring a dozen trucks' worth of water into an ocean. Regardless of its quantity, it was still insignificant.

He could always try to redirect it. Energy redirection was the very first Kinetomancy technique he had mastered. And he had already negated the motion of a Level-4 attack earlier, stopping it in its tracks, and altering its course to the warship. And unlike before, he didn't need to save his power for anything, given how just touching the carquane crystal would flood him with unlimited energy.

It would be easy too.

But truthfully, Lukas just didn't care.

His lips curved into an almost-maniacal grin. If Mujin wanted to compare the sizes of their respective manhoods so badly, who was he to say no? The warlord, despite his fearsome power, had brought in an entire tank-load of Eternal Light to constantly empower himself and those under his command. So far, that had given them the edge.

He supposed it was his chance to even the odds a bit.

Asserting and Aligning Projectiles
Setting Locked Targets

And with an indefinite number of carquane missiles at his disposal, if he didn't show off now . . .

Removing Limiters

. . . Then when?

"*Fire.*"

The topmost portion of the carquane shaft was expelled outward with immense force. Kinetomancy empowered it. Shatterpoint Intuition directed it. The immense power of the World primed it to cause rampant destruction.

BOOOM!

In an instant, the Desert was on fire. And Lukas wasn't finished.

Accessing Scan Level-3
Overclock!
Identifying Spiritual Signatures
LOCK!
Deploy!

It was time to give the warlord a taste of his own medicine.

Locked onto Mujin's spiritual signature, the next missile rushed at him, a shark after its prey. From his vantage point, Lukas watched as the warlord shot toward the sky, only for the missile to follow him. The second, third, and fourth missiles rushed after him as well, hunting him across the open skies like a pack of dogs after a fox. Their cobalt streaks danced across the sky, never failing, never clashing, never interrupting each other's path. Only when Mujin paused for a moment to raise a force-shield did one of them smash into his barrier with an intense explosion.

"Impressive!" said Tanya, appearing next to him and nodding with approval.

"I cheated," he said. "I used the ebb-and-flow properties of water to set the missiles to a predetermined target—his spiritual signature—and then powered them with Kinetomancy. Basic stuff, really."

He blinked a few times to try to get his eyes and head to stop throbbing. Scanning the bulk of the Desert to capture Mujin's spiritual signature from afar, even for a few seconds, had not been pleasant.

"Basic for you. I wouldn't know the first thing about getting that working."

"Well, you always were a bit dim."

She stuck her tongue out. "Stop being mean to me."

Lukas laughed. "I'm glad to see you're still you. I thought Frost would've taken over by now."

"I thought so too," said Tanya with a smile. "But she didn't. I don't know. Somehow, it just feels so much easier. Using Everfrost, that is. I thought it was Frost helping me, guiding me into working with Everfrost in ways I never had before, but then I realized that she *was* me. She couldn't know any new moves unless I knew them too."

Lukas gave her a knowing smile but said nothing.

"It's Meynte, isn't it?" asked Tanya, looking at him with something like reverence. "You said something about her memories causing spiritual resonance because both of us share a lot of things."

His smile widened.

"You knew this would happen, didn't you, Lukas?"

"I might have made an educated guess, yeah."

Tanya narrowed her eyes and mock-glared at him accusingly.

"There's a reason why I suggested spiritual resonance back then. I've been the recipient of it several times in the past to know what it is like, what might trigger it, and how it can be unconsciously activated. Back in the borderland, faced by the Ifrit King, I somehow triggered a stimulus eerily similar to Inanna's own, and that helped me manifest her within my body."

"And Meynte faced the Great Goddess here in this very desert," concluded Tanya. "And I was fighting a warlord, empowered by the Eternal Light."

"Two similar situations, similar settings, and similar stimuli. I had hoped it might trigger something. That was why I chose this desert as our battlefield."

That was half-true. He had chosen it because Amaterasu's All-Seeing Eye was blind within the Desert. That meant that he could get away with almost anything without fear of being spotted.

He looked up at the sky, where the once nigh-indomitable warlord was having a tough time escaping the projectiles, especially with his Eternal-Light fuel now limited if not fully depleted, thanks to Lukas annihilating his War-ship earlier.

It probably didn't help that he was constantly unleashing more of his make-shift missiles every ten seconds.

"Meynte's Skill can't help me against him," said Tanya, frowning. "Not if he does what I think he is about to."

"Oh, and what is that?"

Tanya gestured towards the sky where Mujin had halted, crafting an intense pressure orb around himself, missiles crashing against it with ruthless precision but none of them powerful enough to cause any lasting damage.

"He is about to unleash his kami. And if that happens, none of us will stand a chance."

Lukas knew that.

"That's a Level-4 kami. Unleashed, it can end the entire battle within a split second."

Lukas knew that too.

"Even if I unleash Ezzeron, he's still below Mujin's level of power. Not when he's like that."

As she spoke those words, four pairs of crimson wings were forming around Mujin, larger and brighter than ever. And around him, a misty red form was beginning to manifest, the silhouette of some great beast.

The roar that followed shook the world and yet was paradoxically silent.

The air didn't move; it was *within*, echoing and reverberating off every single thing in the vast Desert, building to a crescendo that split the skies, sending a massively powerful wave before it suddenly collapsed, crushing down into a single, crimson point. It was so sudden and moved so quickly that, between the tremendous wave of power that exploded a moment ago, and its sudden motion, almost no one had the time to notice one tiny fact until it was far too late:

It was a Level-4, warlord-class kami. Not a bremetan.

This was obvious to anyone, of course, but it did not quite get the full point across. The Beast was not bremetan, it had never been bremetan, and it would never be bremetan. Its true origins belonged to the Wind element—motion, momentum, destruction, and chaos. The commands fed into it by Mujin Shimizu, reinforced by the power of Eternal Light, and sharing the emotions of a bloodthirsty warlord while growing into higher and higher levels had created an amoral, ravening monstrosity that could never gain true comprehension of bremetan, because it could only see and act upon the worst and most destructive aspects of bremetan beliefs. Anything beautiful, anything positive, was beyond it. To the Beast, everything around it was prey. Weak. To be devoured. Would-be corpses that just didn't know that they were dead yet.

"Ah," said Lukas. "So, he lost his one ace, and already he's taking out the big guns? Like grandfather, like grandson."

"There's nothing to joke about, Lukas," scoffed Tanya, clenching her fists. "At least with his kami restrained, I had a chance. Now? Even if I unleash Ezzeron, that thing will absolutely decimate us."

"Hey," said Lukas, touching her cheek. "It's okay. I'll take care of it. Trust me."

Tanya just stared at him.

He took his hand away. "I've got to go now. Still have one surprise to pull off. But I need to trap that beast first." But Tanya wouldn't let him go. "You don't understand. With his kami unleashed like that, Mujin is no longer in control. His kami is."

"An angry opponent is a sloppy opponent."

"Not in this case, it isn't," Tanya snapped. "As he is, he has no restraint over himself. He won't think twice before annihilating the entire area for miles on end if he thinks it will destroy you. Destroy us all. It's devastation incarnate."

"It's foolish for most to chain a lion," he said, his wide eyes turning to her. "Yet chains can be forged, and lions can be caged."

He could see her running through the possibilities. Finally, she let go of him, crossed her arms and sighed. "I suppose I dug my own grave when I decided to fall in love with you."

Lukas snorted and glanced at the impossible beast. A demon as crimson as blood, leonine, with four pairs of wings spread out, long fangs and trunk-sized limbs. And floating somewhere in the center, close to its heart, protected within an orb of wind, was Mujin himself, taken over by an alien, preternatural rage.

The malevolence that arose from the beast was a physical thing. It raised its wings—each the size of a small jet, the enormous canvases of darkened crimson threatened to block out the sun—casting a shadow on the sandy terrain. Its body was lined with jagged protrusions, each of which were openings through which the great beast was launching impossibly powerful bursts of raw power that could decimate a small building within a split second. The head was a monstrous skull-like thing.

Such a creature could unleash devastation on the entire Desert within seconds.

And it was glaring at him.

Even if he managed to break the connection between Mujin and his kami, something of that size, Potential, and power was impossible to be siphoned. Not even by him. Or by Blob. Not as it was right now. Just its consciousness was enough to absolutely annihilate any form that Blob could take.

No, if he wanted to tame this beast, he needed materials of similar proportions.

Luckily, he had entire truck-loads of Blob saved up in the heart of the dead anomaly beneath the Desert, kept in reserve for this exact purpose.

And now it was time to use them.

"I take it you won't surrender then?" asked Lukas.

> **Established Connection with All Available Accessory Mediums**
> **Establishing Parity Between all Accessories**
> **Installing Selected Functions**
> **Enacting . . .**

Dozens of missiles streaked through the air towards the beast.

"THOSE MUNITIONS DESTROYED THE WARSHIP BUT AGAINST ME, THEY ARE USELESS!"

As if to emphasize its point, it sent a wave of pure power outward, hitting radially like a tsunami against a shore. The shock wave alone should've flung Lukas by several dozen feet at the very least, but despite its display of near-apocalyptic power—

—it failed to move Lukas by so much as an inch.

And then he vanished further into the Desert.

Growling, and having failed to obliterate its prey at first strike, the creature regained its form and stood on four legs, standing easily thirty-feet tall, each limb thicker than a banyan tree trunk, the outline of thick, crimson energy coating its every inch, its leonine mane and lupine muzzle indistinctly outlined by a pair of gleaming black eyes that looked like black holes devouring everything that fell within their grasp. It was a hunter, born not out of nature but of nightmares, created out of the worst aspects of Wind and of the visceral darkness of Mujin's soul.

And then with terrible smoothness, it moved.

The beast growled and loped on all fours, its size belying its terrible speed, its entire focus shifted to Lukas and Lukas alone. The yokai did not matter, the khorkhoi did not matter, and neither did Mujin nor Tanya nor the Cobalt Army. Every single leap sent shock waves through the air for miles on end as it dashed towards its prey.

And then three pairs of carquane missiles smashed into its body and the world dissolved into crimson flame.

Idly, he mused how comical it must have looked, a massive titan being smashed into the ground again and again by tiny missiles fired by an equally tiny human.

Didn't make it any less true. And in the meantime, it gave Lukas the time he needed to make adjustments to his plan.

His strategy was simple, practical, and almost distressingly fiendish. Now that he had crafted the carquane shaft and had left a small portion of Blob connected to it, he could control it and maintain suppressive fire through carquane missiles, using Shatterpoint Intuition and Kinetomancy to perfectly predict all of the Beast's movements and strike it with impossible accuracy. His own speed was a perfect way of avoiding the Beast's attacks, focusing not on killing blows but explosive attacks that cost a ton of mana to defend against. And being constantly hit by low-powered carquane crystals, their power adjusted to minor Level-4 hits in exchange for greater stability, was perfect for it. That made them harder to block and the potent World Energy far more difficult to deflect, leaving Mujin and his Beast no choice but to face it and expend more energy against them, thus exacerbating the mana-poisoning.

That had been the true bedrock of Lukas's insane plan.

Mana-poisoning was a rather simple, well-known truth that every spiritist worth their salt had to face at least once in their lifetime. No matter how skilled you were, or how many levels you had, the truth was that bremetans were bremetans—creatures of lifeforce who weren't *supposed* to use mana. Yet, through the Shikigami Ritual—a symbiosis pact between bremetan and kami—the process became twisted into Controller and Controlled: Man and Machine, through the injection of Eternal Light.

But like all things that went against the natural order, the Shikigami Ritual wasn't perfect. Far from it, in fact. If a bremetan used too much mana with the kami's mana forge, they ran the risk of unbalancing their emotional spectrum, which could physically debilitate them. Too much mana usage all at once led to spiritists slowly losing their sanity and rationality, eventually giving into the baser instincts of the kami they ruled over.

And once this process got worse, it could result in the kami being unshackled, leading to temporary or permanent possession of the host, transforming them into a berserker ruled by the kami's instincts.

The Controller became the Controlled.

The only way out of this situation was to constantly feed more and more Eternal Light into the equation, to keep the kami weakened, limited, and most importantly, completely under the control of its bremetan host. But there in the Desert, where Eternal Light could not penetrate, Mujin and his army *needed* external reservoirs of Eternal Light to keep them going on.

Reservoirs that were stored in the impossibly well-defended warship that Lukas had obliterated.

And his current plan was to keep pushing Mujin further, to use more and more power to defend against the carquane missiles, thus exacerbating his spiritual retrogression into the instincts of his kami. He, who had boasted of an entire army of mind-controlled soldiers and monsters to follow his every whim; he who had mercilessly ordered the attack on Zuken's mansion and the svartalfars; he who was responsible for all of Tanya's sufferings . . . was now turning into a berserker himself. Bereft of sanity. Bereft of control.

A tool possessed by a kami that had been his tool all his life. Mujin had lost his castle, his seat of power, his grandson, his Sacred Eight status, and now, he would lose *himself.*

It was a vicious and merciless action on Lukas's part, one that he knew for certain a certain goddess would have approved of.

Deprivation at its finest.

Maybe he was imagining things, but he thought he felt a foreign amusement emanate out of his very being at the thought.

His body tapped into the well of power that were his omphalos reserves. They were just shy of 99% capacity.

Lukas wanted to laugh. He had learned the hard way that he really was helpless against greater powers. So, it was a bad idea to try to confront such cataclysmic powers by himself.

"Activate Protocol: Dead Man's Trigger."

Thirty-three doppelgangers—crafted purely out of aqāru—erupted out of the ground. Thirty-three copies of himself, in a great circle that encompassed around a quarter-mile radius, including every single entity within the battlefield.

Thirty-three Lukas Aguilars.

He had attempted something similar back inside the tunnels of the dead anomaly beneath the Desert. Channeling all five mana forms simultaneously had hit him hard back then.

"Numbers will not help you," The beast roared. **"YOU CANNOT CATCH THE WIND!"**

Mujin was right, to an extent. He couldn't face the Beast in a direct fight. Even with the aqāru, he was too frail to take on something of that size and power, and win.

"You seem to misunderstand something. I don't want to catch the wind. I want to trap it. Seal it." His voice was emotionless, clinical. A grin spread across his lips, and his eyes shone a deep emerald green.

All of their eyes shone a deep emerald green.

The beast raised its maw to allow power to coalesce within its fangs—

"...WHA—WHAT IS THIS?"

"Oh?" Lukas rasped out with a hint of amusement at the Beast's surprise. "You finally noticed."

The Beast was completely frozen, as if the very air that encompassed its being now held it in place.

Lukas smirked and instead focused on a massive tendril of carquane that erupted from the crystal pillar, piercing through every one of his metallic doppelgangers in their perfect circle. More tendrils shot out of them, crisscrossing each other, forming a majestic pentacle across the surface of the accursed Desert. Through their shared senses, he could see the looks of apprehension and awe on everyone's faces.

"YOU . . ." Lukas had provoked Mujin's untamed rage, and he now felt a fierce attack against his motion negation. For all of Kinetomancy's flexibility, sometimes a sledgehammer to the head was a sledgehammer to the head.

"I'm a usurper, a thief that steals from this very world."

The Screen went into a frenzy.

Boundary Radius Established
Territory Creation Set
Augmenting Connective Ley-Line Network for Maximum Output . . .

The last time, he had utilized his own reserves to produce all five forms of mana together. This time, he was going for the singular.

Anomalous energy.

Drawn from the ley line beneath, conducted through the carquane, and passed through the metallic versions of himself.

Maximize Inner-world Sympathy. Alter Reality Foundation within
Boundary Limit.

Just like before, the World around him was rattling violently, like an enormous earthquake. Furious gales blew all around, but none of them even touched the interior of the massive ritual circle. And with that came a discordant hum from everywhere and nowhere, slowly increasing in volume, as if it were the herald of a terrible *something*.

The last time, it had destroyed him entirely.

Establishing Living Anomaly

This time, though . . . Power danced, forming strange and almost erratic patterns, Kinetomancy manipulating the elements, as rules of a World that was so similar yet so very different began to slide in, substituting reality itself within the established ritual circle. A world that was the remains of a Lostbelt, one that had perished and was yet reborn within himself.

Everything around him was disappearing, and a sea of purplish mist was enveloping the entire radius. There was no light, no life, no conflict, no anything . . .

Just erected crystal mounds on an endless terrain, with everything within it lying in patient, eternal wait.

Forgotten.

His lips widened into a half-formed smile, and he took a small breath.

The World around him vanished, engulfed into the endless purple mist.

CHAPTER 24

S omething tickled the end of Tanya's nose.

She crinkled her face, but the feeling didn't disappear, so she cracked her eyes open to glare at it but regretted it almost immediately, as bright light shone directly in, forcing her to shut them again, grimacing in pain.

Prepared this time, she forced her eyes open again and glared at the culprit. It was a clump of crystal—translucent yet reflecting light, making it difficult to see what was within it. She squinted her eyes and grabbed the crystal, using it as support to push herself up. It was easily twice as tall as she, studded into the rocky floor beneath and feeling as cold as ice. Frowning, she leaned closer, peering at the form inside the crystal, an outline—not very clear, but she could determine the bremetan-like shape, only significantly taller, with two bulging pairs of arms, each of them ending with vicious sets of sharp claws; meanwhile, its intense, crimson eyes were open, aware, and staring at her intently.

"Fucking hell!" she shouted, staggering back in a pure, panicked reflex. "That's a—"

Before she could even finish the rest of the sentence, Tanya froze again, her back thumping against something solid and uneven. She spun around and met another crystal outgrowth, within it a large, manta-ray-like creature with four pairs of wings, levitating. Then another, an avian with two pairs of wings, and a fourth, the largest serpent she had ever seen in her life.

She looked around and found herself surrounded by those crystals. Easily a dozen, sprouting out of the ground, as if they were trees. There were so many of them that the plethora of sharp light reflecting off them was making it truly difficult to look around without hissing in pain.

Tanya forced herself up on her feet and wobbled for a moment before regaining her balance as she finally managed to plant both feet firmly on the ground. Satisfied, she looked at the scenery around her and what she saw was . . .

. . . an endless maze of crystals.

They rose out of the ground like gravestones, standing tall, a specimen held inside each one, each creature a monster or demon of some sort—some of them tiny, others gigantic. Across the endless terrain they lay, stretching out in every direction towards the distant horizon and beyond, farther than her eyes could see.

A gentle breeze flew past her, blowing her bangs across her face. This place was like an infinite graveyard and not even the ever-reflecting radiance stopped the chill in the air around her.

The mounds almost seemed to be waiting for someone to come shatter those crystals and set the creatures free. Before she could consider the matter any further, Tanya was distracted by a discordant hum coming from above. She looked up at a starless night sky—a velvety layer of blackness that stretched infinitely in every direction. She wondered where the intense light reflecting across these crystal tombstones was coming from, and kept looking until—

"By the Great Goddess!" Tanya almost lost her balance as she leaned her head back to look at it. "Who is THAT?"

Amidst the massive, inky darkness rose a gargantuan figure, a titanic bremetan silhouette, larger than the eye could see, sitting cross-legged, hands resting against his knees, palms open and head held high. An aura of impenetrable calmness radiated from the figure as if immersed in a meditation deeper than the ocean.

Between the titanic silhouette, the endless dark sky, and the crystal mounds littering the landscape as far as the eye could see, each containing a bloodthirsty predator ready to devour her whole, she should've felt a feeling of dark foreboding.

Instead, she just felt peace.

Like she was standing inside a shrine. A sacrosanct territory, a site of worship or perhaps—

She eyed the mounds.

—of mourning.

It was as though the mounds and the monsters within them were all savoring the tranquil atmosphere as well.

It was . . . relaxing.

Her gaze slowly clouded over. Why bother with the world, the pains and suffering that everyone seemed to want to inflict upon her, when she could just forget it all? When she could—

"What the—" came Olfric's voice from her right, and Tanya almost jumped. There he was, standing alongside Elena and Zuken, but she could swear there had been no one there a moment ago. "Since when could Aguilar do THIS?"

She wanted to ask the same. Lukas had kept her in the dark. She had always assumed that his "inner-world" was a metaphor, and that the shard of his destroyed World had blessed him with strange powers that mimicked other Worlds. He was still an individual, a man, a walking, breathing man. One she fell in love with and made love to. It's not like he was going to turn into sand or rock or have literal trees growing out of him.

But this . . . this was . . .

What *was* this?

"I . . ." she said at last. "I have no idea."

"Oh? So this display is new for you as well," said Solana, who had miraculously appeared from the other side, with the kasha Ryu next to her. It was like they were all popping in randomly all around. Tanya noted that despite Solana's typically restrained response, not even she could fully hide the genuine astonishment in her voice. "Truly, that man will never stop pulling miracles out of nowhere."

Ryu laughed. "Controlling so many puppets that look like himself all at once and channeling power through them? And now an illusion this concrete? Truly the Outsider has outdone himself."

"No," said Maude, correcting the kasha, her eyes filled with wonder. "Not puppets. They were real. As real as flesh and blood. As real as this place."

"Now you're just being ridiculous," scoffed Ryu. "The real one is right . . ." He trailed off, looking around at the endless graveyard of crystals. "Uh. where is he?"

"WHAT IS THIS . . . ILLUSION?" came a loud, booming voice from afar. The response to that came in the form of a soft, yet perfectly audible voice, one that proudly identified the location as . . .

"My World."

Lukas stared at them from above, floating in the sky, taking in the sight of his manifested World with the same appreciation and giddiness as a parent seeing his child take its first step without any support. His World wasn't close to being finished—far from it—but there was definitely more to it than the last time he had been there. Whatever had caused the rapid progression eluded him, but he could return to that puzzle later.

"Your . . . World?" asked Solana softly, warily. "The World you come from?"

"No," he said, smiling. "Not that World. This is—"

He paused and frowned. Something was here that wasn't supposed to be. Whatever it was, he couldn't recognize it; at the same time, it felt like it *belonged*.

Another conundrum! He'd investigate later.

He turned towards the horizon. Right now, he had something to do. He shut his eyes and focused, searching for everyone. Despite the outer boundary being only a quarter of a mile radius, the insides of his World were practically endless, and he knew it better than anyone or anything else. He knew where everything was: every single monster prototype, all his half-baked, shelved experiments, Meynte's memory prototype, everything he had gathered about the Truth preserved within Inanna's pendant . . . He knew it all like the back of his hand.

Bringing the visitors here had accidentally scattered them across the vast plain, an error Lukas had quickly corrected, vanishing the distance between them, while making sure they were far enough from Mujin's bestial form.

He greeted them with an amused smile. "Welcome to the Plains of Forget."

He was greeted in turn by a sea of bemused faces, though he could see a flicker of comprehension dawning on Solana's. Maude's reaction caught his attention the most, however. She didn't look confused or surprised, just sad as she stared at him with . . . was that *pity?*

"Lukas . . ." He turned to see Tanya looking up at him and around, her eyes opened so wide he could practically see their whites. She wasn't the only one, either. While the majority of the yokai or the bremetans couldn't properly comprehend what was happening around them, that wasn't the case with Solana or Maude, and what was that look in Elena's eyes?

"Lukas," Tanya repeated. "Where are we? What is this place?"

"I told you, this is—"

He paused as, right then, a considerable chunk of the terrain to the right just . . . disappeared.

It wasn't an explosion per se; there was no light, no sound, no shock wave. Just an outrushing of *something* that flickered out of existence as soon as it appeared. As if a claw the size of a city bus had reached down and smoothly torn it away, leaving only a gash in the land, the edges as smooth as blue glass.

And just like that, all his excitement vanished, leaving behind a cold annoyance at the casual destruction of his World.

"LET ME OUT OF THIS ILLUSION!" screamed Mujin, and a thousand wind blades appeared all around his gigantic form. With a roar, the blades fell by the thousands, descending from the dark sky that had turned almost glassy from the reflecting light. Like meteors, they came down to obliterate everything in their path, only to converge and vanish as if drawn into and consumed by a black hole, or rather the gigantic maw of a demon that could be called a titanic ancestor to the khorkhoi. It leaped out of the terrain, swallowed the blades, and sank back again.

"Illusion?" asked a smiling Lukas Aguilar. "Trust me, Mujin, this is anything but."

Before the warlord could do anything, his animal-like paws were grabbed by hands just as massive as he was. He fought and screamed and flailed but could not escape their grip.

"You showed me your toys," said Lukas, still smiling. "Here, let me show you some of mine. Tell me, what do you think of the gigantomachia?"

Creatures of the Greek and Roman myths, the Gigantomachia were impossibly massive beings that could make even a Tyrannosaurus rex flee at the sight. Said to be born of Gaia, they were terramancers of the apex degree and capable of solidifying *anything* within their four-armed grips.

Even *air*.

Lukas had been both exhilarated and downright floored upon realizing the true significance of what it was he had been handed when Blob unlocked the monster prototypes of Lostbelt Earth during his fight with Meynte and Solana. Even discounting the Earth's later status as a planet devoid of lifeforce and mana, there had always been a history of mythologies and mythical beings that existed on the planet, at least if the scriptures and ancient engravings could be believed.

And if Earth could house a pendant within which was housed a reflection of an Akkadian goddess, then the idea that mythological races of monsters existing on the Lostbelt was hardly unbelievable.

That alone was half the reason Lukas had spent that long loitering in the Haze: cataloging, studying, and experimenting on the collection of prototypes he had gotten from his home world.

And what a collection it was!

Gigantomachia, Titanomachia, monsters of the deep seabed, legendary races that ruled the skies, centaurs that ran across the terrain, mermen and sirens of the ocean, creatures with powers so wondrous that they appeared downright magical. The problem was that manifesting them in the real world was like reverse osmosis—the data was there, borrowed from the omphalos within him, only to be filtered through his own understanding of the prototype. The more skilled he was in elemental manipulation, the more he understood a prototype, the easier the process was. The more alien the mindset was, the more strain it put upon him, when he summoned it using Puppeteer Protocol. Cutting corners made the process easier, but it could heavily degrade the final product.

And honestly, more than *half* of what he had found sitting in the collection was downright beyond him at the moment. Maybe after he became a full-fledged warlord or reached close to king-status, he could probably manifest them outside using Blob for a couple of minutes without frying his brain in the process.

But here, inside the Plains of Forget . . . now that was an entirely different ball game.

"I told you, Mujin," he said softly, "I am a tyrant. A thief. I stole your authority, your place of power, your soldiers, and your position as the Sacred Eight. And now, I am going to steal your might."

He thrust his hand out, and tendrils of aqāru—each as thick as palm tree trunks—erupted out of the ground, impaling the solidified airy form. The beast screeched and screeched and screeched, but the tendrils would not let go. The warlord threw his head back and howled in unspeakable agony as they tore his beastly kami—a Level-4 monstrosity—out of his very soul, ripping past the bindings of Eternal Light like they meant nothing. Aqāru was lethal to spiritual entities, and it devoured the kami, despite the layers and layers of psionic defenses that Mujin tried to put up with growing desperation.

Defenses. Traps. Mental pathways. Constraints put on his very soul to keep his kami from escaping.

All of that was blown away like cobwebs in a hurricane.

And then it was over, as the Screen popped in front of Lukas.

Soul Siphon Success! Absorbed Monster Prototype JAAN: BYAKKO		
Spiritual Parasite. Energy Core constitutes Mana Forge for Wind and Ether.		
APTITUDE	LEVEL	SOUL CAPACITY REQUIRED
Possession	3	5000
Wind Creation	4	50000
Wind Manipulation	4	50000
Pressure Modulation	4	50000
Translocation	4	50000
Conjuration	3	5000

Lukas grinned. He remembered the first time he had absorbed a kami, only to be surprised by the curve ball that was Aptitude. Kami were ridiculously powerful creatures, but they suffered from crippling limitations, the most significant being their inability to generate more Soul Capacity than what they were naturally born with. It was why they were parasites, possessing other beings to utilize their Soul Capacity for their own growth—a trait that Asukans took advantage of—and turned the elemental parasites into mana-forging machines, gaining the ability to manacraft in the process.

And once a kami was separated from its host, all of its elevated Skills went dormant, saved as Aptitudes, something that could only be unlocked upon getting another host boasting enough Soul Capacity.

Back when he had gained his first kami—Olfric's marid—he had lacked the Soul Capacity to convert its Aptitudes and Skills. But now, with his *infinite* Soul Capacity?

**Transferring Required Soul Capacity to Prototype JAAN: BYAKKO
Requisition of Aptitude into Skills Complete**

It was child's play.

"I am content," said Lukas, closing his eyes. When he opened them, his expression had changed. Gone was the face of the tyrant, the ruler, the absolute god of this domain. Instead, the face of a tired, relaxed man near the end of his life stared back at Mujin. A satisfied life coming to an end, and relief that the future was in safe hands.

Not happiness, merely content. He was done, and the only thing left would not happen by his hand.

The Gigantomachia dispersed into nothingness.

"Tanya," he said, slowly levitating himself and Mujin down to the ground. "I leave the rest to you."

"No, wait," cried Mujin. "Don't kill me! Do you not see what that vile wench has become? Do you not see the wrongness in her? That power—Everfrost—needs to be controlled by an iron will. That power will destroy the world if we let it. You think you're being a hero? You think you're saving her?"

Lukas said nothing.

Mujin kept yelling, frothing at his lips. "You'll fail! The pantheon has felt the stirrings, noticed the tremors. The Great Goddess herself knows that the ancient power that once sought her in combat, the power of the yokai empress is again at large. You think that killing me will solve your problem? *Fool!* I was given the task of finding out about Everfrost and its bearer. If I die, then the Earth King shall know that I was slain inside this very Desert. It took you everything just to fight me and destroy one warship. What happens when the Earth King arrives with his immense army? You, the girl, the yokai . . . none shall survive. The Earth King will crush the girl, enslave her, and drag her back kicking and screaming. He will subdue her and make her into his slave."

Lukas still said nothing.

Mujin drew a breath. Maybe he was thinking he could turn the tables in his favor.

"You see now, don't you? Yes, I'm evil. Yes, I've committed atrocities in the name of my clan. Yes, I captured Tanya and imprisoned her. You can blame me for all that. But I'm also your best chance. You've already defeated me. Taken my kami! You can easily kill me. But what good will that do? The Empire and the Earth King will come for you. If you think Tanya had a hard life up to now, she will never know a moment of peace after this. Everywhere she goes, the Cobalt Army will come for her, and they'll keep coming until she's either captured or dead."

This time Lukas did say something.

"And . . . what do you propose?"

Mujin drew himself to his tallest. "A middle ground. I know, I—I have known this for a long while—that it was a mistake. What I did to Tanya, I mean. She was a perfect success, the miracle that marked the end of two centuries of constant experiments. A Shimizu in whose veins flows the Wind King's bloodline. One who was chosen by Ezzeron to be its next wielder, and someone in whose soul hides a power that can end the world: Everfrost. She—she was my perfect successor, but I, in my hubris, imprisoned her, tortured her, tried to extract that power out of her. I—I was wrong. I was foolish. And I'm willing to make amends."

"I'm listening."

"The Empire has forsaken me," admitted Mujin. "They took away our Sacred Eight status. Obviously, you know that. But I told them back then, in front of the emperor no less, that Tanya lives. That she wields my father's kami, Ezzeron, the wrath of the Wind King himself. If Tanya rejoins my side, if she becomes the Shimizu heiress, then she can breathe fresh life into my clan's name. We can become the Sacred Eight again."

"Really?" Lukas asked, cocking his head. "You would do that for her?"

"I'll even swear by an Eztli contract never to reveal anything about you or the yokai or whatever happened here," blabbered Mujin. "Isn't that what you want? For Tanya to get another chance at a normal life?" He gazed at his granddaughter, expecting a reaction. "I'm giving you that chance. Don't you want it? Don't you want this—*YRKKH!*"

He staggered back and looked down at his own chest, his brows furrowed in confusion. Slowly, he raised one hand and looked at the sharp, jagged icicle jammed into his chest, puncturing his heart.

At first he seemed bemused by the sight, as if he didn't quite understand what he was seeing, the sight so outside the realm of possibility that his brain needed a few seconds to actually comprehend it. Then his eyes steadily began to widen as it finally dawned on him that, yes, it was Everfrost piercing his heart, and that growing numbness was his lifeforce being sucked dry by the accursed ice.

"It's a waste of time for the killer to speak with the one she's about to kill," said Tanya in a cold voice. "You taught me that, Grandfather."

And then Mujin died.

Another notification popped up, and with it, another crystal cluster.

Soul Siphon Success!
Absorbed Monster Prototype BREMETAN

And that wasn't all.

Found 61 BREMETAN prototypes
Agglomerate Prototypes to Create a Standard Bremetan Prototype?

Yes.

He looked at Tanya. She looked back at him with a satisfied smile. Beyond them, the dark, starless sky loomed, with the titanic figure overhead, and countless mounds of crystal spread far into the horizon.

Peace had returned to this place.

The war was over. They were done.

Everything was just . . . done.

CHAPTER 25

The communication crystal lit up after the fourth vibration.

"I expect you to have something worthwhile to speak about." The voice on the other side was masculine, rich, cultured, and carried an undercurrent of *power*. It was unsurprising really, given that there were few in the entire Empire that could challenge him and survive.

"Depends," said Solana from the other side of the Empire—a distance that would take even their fastest translocator several days to cover. Normally when she called, she would be received by one of his assistants. The man despised the idea of being so easily accessible to others via any means, and these calls left him just shy of irrationally irritable.

"Are you more interested in what your feelers didn't tell you, or what they don't know themselves?" She wasn't mocking him. She was asking how much he already knew.

Even if he hadn't figured anything out yet, he would never admit it. Worse, had she attempted to excuse herself for the recent absence and lack of information, it would only attract his ire.

Lady Kandra had access to the highest echelons in the Asukan regime. That didn't mean she enjoyed the same level of respect everywhere.

And it also meant playing the longest game in the world. The game of patience.

"You have gotten sloppy," he rebuked. "Lady Kandra doesn't take sides. That was the deal. And now you've played Naowa and Shimizu against each other. Had things gone haywire, your little game could've thrown the entire Southeast into a war."

Solana clenched her teeth. She knew there was a chance her activities would be discovered. She had made a public move against the Shimizu, bargained with Lord Naowa using Aguilar as an intermediary, and caused the eventual destruction of the Earth King's warship and the death of Mujin Shimizu, his long-time accomplice.

Regardless of the reasons behind her actions, as far as he was concerned, she had gone rogue.

But confusion begets confusion. The truth was what the presenter portrayed it to be. Mujin's declaration in front of the Emperor was a perfect example of that, but nothing was set in stone . . . yet. To those that were watching, this turn of events was completely unprecedented. The most powerful person in the Southeast, Mujin Shimizu, warlord and close acquaintance of the Earth King, had marched into the Desert and had gotten himself killed and the Earth King's army massacred. It would not be unimaginable to assume that something else was at work here. Something that the audience didn't know, and wouldn't know, not until the official reports came out.

So, until the final scenario was made public, the truth would still be malleable, flexible to interpretation, and if certain half-truths were added to the mix . . . Well, who could prove otherwise?

In the end, history went to the victors to do as they pleased for their own benefits.

Had Solana not contacted him, then he too would only know of what had happened on a superficial level. Just another spectator that would come to know about the destruction caused by Lady Kandra's intermediation.

It would be embarrassing. Humiliating. Unforgivable.

But she had contacted him. She had planned on informing him of the situation before the masses. She hadn't intended to do that before, but had mentally prepared for this at some point.

With this call, the veil would be lifted for him and him alone. The news reaching Lord Naowa would be limited, especially with them dealing with Lukas personally in the future. This call was for him to be ready for those that would try to attack him with the "truth" that had yet to come.

"I already know what happened. Being aware of how it happened means little at this stage," he said.

Straight to the point then, Solana decided. Still, this would require careful handling.

"Tanya Shimizu and her ally Lukas Aguilar, both close to warlord-Level, sieged the Peak, infiltrated its defenses, captured Ultaf Shimizu, and destroyed the castle. They planned on leaving behind enough cues to lure Mujin into the Desert, and ensured the Cobalt Army would be repositioned from the Desert borders to the capital city. Mujin Shimizu was killed by unknown means."

"Unknown?" he asked. There was a dangerous tone in his voice.

Solana grimaced. "My agents in Tanya Shimizu's army informed me of a massive purple mist engulfing a large section of the Desert. Mujin was later found on the sand, dead."

What she didn't say was that neither she, nor anybody else for that matter, remembered anything about what happened. All she could recall were those metallic doppelgangers surrounding Mujin in his great bestial form. She remembered that mist manifesting out of nowhere like a massive dome and engulfing everything and then . . .

Then . . .

Even Tanya—the one that supposedly killed Muijin, given how the bastard had died with a shard of Everfrost spearing through his heart—had no recollection of how he died.

Solana didn't know what was scarier. That the Outsider had the means to kill a warlord with an unleashed kami within the blink of an eye . . . Or that he could pull off a mystery capable of erasing everything he did from every single mind caught within that purple mist. Solana considered herself a master at certain elements of psionics, and yet Lukas Aguilar had played with her mind in a way she couldn't even comprehend, much less explain.

"Hmm, interesting."

Solana could've almost believed his reaction had it not been a little too nonchalant.

"Even so, you have been sloppy," he said.

"I didn't know that gaining you a new Lady Shimizu was *sloppy*, Lord Earth King."

And there was the crux of the matter. In the cutthroat world of Asukan politics, Trestan Banksi was the one figure that was fixated, almost obsessively perhaps, with a stable Sacred Eight. Solana had tried to figure out why, but everything so far had ended up with shut mouths and grave warnings.

In fact, the Shimizu's survival was the main reason behind her *services* to the Earth King. Whatever the reason might be, the Earth King wanted a Wind King really badly, and he had quickly decided that Mujin and his grandson Ultaf would never be able to make it.

It was a brilliant game played on two fronts. Mujin got a flank and a warship, and if the Warlord captured Tanya, he won. Lady Kandra on the other hand, got resources and timely intel, and if Tanya defeated her grandfather, she won.

Either way, he won.

"And what of this . . . Aguilar?" asked the Earth King. "I imagine he was instrumental in the destruction of my warship. How did he accomplish that?"

"Aguilar is capable of motion deflection on an epic scale. If I had to fathom a guess, I'd say it's close to Warlord level, if not there already. That is all I can say."

"Motion . . . deflection. An unconventional skill to elevate, but I can see the merits," mused Trestan Banksi. "One would expect you to have more information than that, Lady Kandra."

"I try not to appear overly curious in someone that has the ear of the Fire King."

And just like that, the game started.

"What is Jimmo Asuka's involvement in this?" he asked, the dangerous tone in his voice returning.

There was a reason why Solana was playing such a risky game. She did not know the details, but there had been a cold war happening between the Earth King and the Fire King for over a century now. Lady Kandra was using this enmity to play to her advantage, and much to her surprise, Lukas Aguilar had gotten the attention and patronage of the Fire King without even working for it.

Solana had laughed herself crazy on hearing about that bit.

In a way, the two kings were quite similar to each other. Both used rather grandiose, albeit practical approaches to deal with each other, playing a rather elaborate game from the shadows, using other clans as mere pieces on the board. And from her experience, she knew that both kings were playing an equally long game as her.

Both were waiting for something.

Both were biding their time.

Both were holding back.

Both were aware of the threat the other posed.

Both were playing the game in their own way.

Both believed they knew something the other didn't.

The only real difference was that while Trestan Banksi threw common courtesy away when dealing with others unless it was absolutely necessary to keep them. Jimmo Asuka *only* threw them away if needed, but could still do so without any issue.

It was an interesting inversion of otherwise identical habits.

"I assumed you already knew," said Solana in a crafty tone. "The Fire King has made Lukas Aguilar the new Forger of Zwaray Keep. And . . . if rumors are to be believed, he is the girl's lover."

". . . I see. Poor Lord Naowa."

This time she really did smile. It would have scared the shit out of anyone that saw it. "Does that mean the girl shall have your blessings when she offers her candidature in front of the Sacred Eight?"

It was the idea she had been working on ever since Aguilar had destroyed any and all chances of resurrecting the Empress in Tanya. As a Sacred Eight Lady, Tanya would open doors for the yokai to penetrate the heart of the Empire.

Through her, and Aguilar's nifty quirk of identifying loopholes and flaws in others' defenses, Solana would get closer to her goal of paralyzing the Empire from within.

Support from not one, but three Sacred Eight clans. And two of them being kings themselves. And if she played her cards right, she could even pitch the two kings against each other.

Things couldn't get better than that.

"It depends on how long it will take for her to deliver in the end," said Trestan Banksi. "I can only afford to keep an open mind for so long. Especially for a candidate that hangs around Asuka's dog. A mad dog that has the gall to destroy my warship."

"Noted," she said. her smile was gone now. "I will begin preparations immediately."

It appeared she was mistaken. She had assumed that with the Warlord's demise, the period of strife had ended and things would turn peaceful and favorable for a change.

In reality, the simple truth was that the war had only just begun.

Lord Naowa hummed as he sat down over the table, playing with his goblet of wine. If everything had gone according to plan, then Lukas Aguilar and Tanya Shimizu had just fought in the middle of the Desert. Aguilar had promised to send word about the status of the battle, an irrelevant endeavor all things considered. If Mujin won, then he'd be parading the girl with the Wind King's kami before the Earth King, and Naowa would soon find a missive for yet another Shogun's meet to reconsider the Shimizu's dormant status. If Mujin perished on the other hand . . .

his mental meanderings ceased to a halt as Tatun Kinosu, the overseer of Haviskali entered the room. Given the fact that the man only looked slightly uncomfortable and wasn't radiating irritation, Naowa could only come to a single conclusion.

"Good news, I take it?"

"The gamble was a success, Lord Shogun," said the overseer. "The girl Tanya and the Pathforger are both safe. Tanya still retains Ezzeron. Zuken Banksi is safe. Mujin Shimizu was killed, and his Level-4 kami, neutralized. We have no idea what happened to it."

"Only Mujin was killed? The Pathforger is even better than we thought," said Lord Naowa with a faint smile, internally sighing in relief. he didn't miss the annoyed look the overseer shot at him. "What's wrong? Shouldn't you be pleased as well? Aguilar has truly outperformed all expectations."

The overseer held his gaze at the table for several long moments, as if try-ing to determine how to challenge his boss's beliefs without appearing auda-cious. "A victory is only worthwhile so long as one knows how to appropriately capitalize on it. Otherwise, it is merely a more palatable defeat, sir."

Naowa's good mood died a little as he slowly digested the overseer's words.

"And here I thought your worries would be over with the good news." he groaned and shot the man an annoyed glance. "Who knew you could be so selfishly avid? Zuken Banksi is safe and can safely return to his duties. The Pathforger will take over the Zwaray Keep and continue the svartalfar legacy. And we have a potential Lady Shimizu under my wing, operating from the Eaborid Kingdom."

"I'm sorry, Lord Shogun," said Tatun, not backing down. "You are not the one that has to now deal with a new world power capable of toppling a Warlord, and withstanding the might of a king."

"We both know that he wouldn't have truly survived the wrath of the Fire King," said Naowa easily.

"True, and neither would we," said Tatun. "Or Haviskali, for that matter."

Ah. So *that's* what had his overseer worried.

"You felt it, Lord Shogun," said Tatun. "You felt it when the Pathforger resisted the Fire King's power. I have been a Level-3 pyromancer for close to six decades now, and while I might as well be a candle against the Fire King's might, I understand the nature of Flame. All of us fought against it—you, me, the girl, but not him. The Pathforger didn't just resist his power, he *ignored* it. Like the very laws of the universe that govern Fire did not apply to him for that moment."

Naowa stopped playing with his goblet.

"I have made inquiries, Lord Shogun," said Tatun Kinosu softly. "We've collected any documentation of his name. Adventurer license, dated purchases for fractals from the subsidized government stores in Maluscion, a minor listing in the local and private guilds, and even permits for a *tanning salon*. There are transfer details to Haviskali courtesy of a permanent employment contract by Zuken Banksi, and a clearance certificate from the Cobalt Army permitting entry to Haviskali."

"But?"

Tatun pursed his lips. "I called in a few favors and accessed Maluscion's citizen directory. Lukas Aguilar, if that is indeed his name, doesn't *exist*. At least not before the mess with the anomaly in the Desert. No identity with that name and face in birth records. Not registered with any Shrine. He wears fractals, but the nature of his kami is unknown. There are several mentions of him taking up jobs, but all of them are under-the-table. No known acquaintances. No friends, no enemies. Not even a bar fight. No clearance certificates from any other amy posts in Maluscion or surrounding territories."

Naowa nodded. "A hastily forged backstory then."

"The Fire King might be a benevolent Lord," said the overseer. "But he is no fool. He will make inquiries, and I'm afraid of what he will find. What *we* will find."

As a Shogun and member of the Sacred Eight, Naowa knew all about manipulating research, money, favors, evidence—false, real and circumstantial. The Empire was a cesspool of back deal games where the rules were ever-changing before the show even started. That experience told him that they were at a critical crossroads. There was no doubt that the Fire King would not like the truth of the situation, especially if it contained information that would put a stain on not only Naowa, but on himself as well.

The latter of which was especially unacceptable.

The issue was that while Naowa was no stranger to forbidden research, antiquated knowledge, and conspiracy, rarely was he the one at risk. Due to the duties they were about to put on Aguilar's soldiers, and the status his new position would grant him in the Empire, the repercussions could be potentially catastrophic.

Both stayed silent for a moment. Finally, Naowa spoke.

"Aguilar still has to come in for the swearing. I'm certain we will have questions to ask him. And questions that will not go unanswered."

"I've already prepared a list," said Tatun, holding up a stack of documents. "Especially about why he wants the Zwaray Keep free of bremetan workers."

Naowa arched an eyebrow. "And how does he plan to—"

"Golems."

"Golems," repeated Naowa. "Paranoid, much?"

"I think we are the ones that should be paranoid."

Naowa closed his mouth and grabbed the documents the overseer passed to him. The report claimed titanic explosions and massive shifts in air pressure noted somewhere in the middle of the accursed region. An entire flank of the Cobalt Army dead and gone. A massive purplish mist. Destruction of the Earth King's—

Naowa blinked, and read the page again.

"Is this . . . ?"

"We should've known something was amiss when he destroyed the Peak," said the overseer. "The wards there are King-class. We presumed that he might have infiltrated the Peak and undone the defenses. But if he could total a king's warship . . ."

Suddenly Tatun's worries seemed a lot worse. A ghost by all records, a bremetan-svartalfar hybrid, potentially Warlord-Level if not more, and a Path-forger to boot.

And he would be placed in charge of national security.

his fists tightened. It was a mistake to jump in and elevate Lukas Aguilar to the Fire King's attention. A rash decision that he had employed in his mute thrill of witnessing someone employing runecraft, and promising the continuation of Well Creation within the Empire, and saving his ass from the Fire

King's wrath. Aguilar was special, but he would be the Fire King's to command, his employee, his dog of sorts. And in doing so, Naowa had elevated Aguilar, and now, he couldn't reprimand Aguilar as easily as he could've if the deviant had stayed under Banksi's or even his own command.

However, there was a fine line between a bad dog, and a mad one.

For several long moments, Naowa stayed silent. "The Fire King has declared Aguilar to be the new forger and gatekeeper, and that shall be done. Despite our fears, Aguilar has given no reason to persecute him. If anything, we must use his infamy to our benefit. Release the knowledge about his status as a Pathforger through private channels and . . . cut off Zwaray Keep and the surrounding territories from Haviskali."

"Cut off from . . . ?" Tatun paled. "But Lord Shogun—"

"Relax," said Naowa. "It's like you said. Aguilar is a wildcard, one that neither of us can control. Thus, it is imperative that he be placed in a situation where he becomes directly answerable to the Fire King. The materials we ordered for the Zwaray Keep's reconstruction have arrived, yes?"

"Delivered at the Keep."

"Good," said Naowa. "Engrave a writ, stating that effective immediately, the Zwaray Keep and its surrounding territories are to be declared sovereign territory. Register the Llaisy Kingdom as its official trade partner and the Empire's intermediary, with rights to first refusal. I shall sign it and suspend it. As soon as Aguilar takes over, and the constructions are complete, you can activate the writ and pass it as law."

"But sir—"

"Don't worry, Kinosu. On paper, Aguilar and the Keep will be an independent nation, solely responsible for any positive or negative attention he brings upon it. Economically, he won't be able to move a finger without our say-so, and it will keep him under our thumb."

"But we will essentially be giving away the rights to a powerful Warlord-class Pathforger. As Shogun, you could command—"

"My dear Overseer," said Naowa softly. "I do not need to hold the mad dog's chain. I have Banksi for that. For all your paranoia, you have ignored one simple thing. Lukas Aguilar attacked the Peak, a Warlord's fortress protected by King-class wards, just to *rescue* Zuken Banksi. You said it yourself—power, prestige, or popularity does not interest him, and neither do favors among the upper echelons of the Empire. This is a man that just asks himself if something is right and must be done, and if it is, pursues it with everything he has, no matter who or what he might have to face in the process. This isn't a man to be restrained, but one to hold a debt over and see him go out of his way to return the debt multifold because he feels obligated to do it."

"But—"

"Kinosu," said Naowa evenly. "The Shimizu Warlord is dead. The Shimizu Clan has lost its Sacred Eight status. Surely you know what fate befalls the clans that abuse their power only to fall to the dust later on? With the girl bearing Ezzeron and wanting to revive her clan's prestige, what kind of attention do you think she will incur from the other clans? Do you truly want Haviskali to become a battleground for this covert war that is about to follow?"

That shut Tatun up.

"No," said Naowa. "We both know that Aguilar will support the girl, which means he will elevate the Keep to a fortress and center the girl and his allies inside. Unless I am wrong, he already planned for that, which is why he must have insisted on having golems instead of Asukan workers. This really should be interesting, especially in the light of . . . hmm . . ."

The overseer stayed silent, and Naowa observed him closely.

"But that's not what troubles you, is it, my dear Overseer?"

Tatun Kinosu stayed silent for a long moment. When he finally spoke, there was an edge to the man's voice that wasn't there before. "With all due respect, sir, Mujin Shimizu was *the* greatest power in the entire Southeast, not including the Earth King. The fact that Aguilar managed to kill the Shimizu Warlord is *not* something to be ignored."

"He had the girl—"

"Please do not pretend otherwise, sir," Tatun interrupted callously. "Yes, the girl is the Shimizu heiress and wields the Wind King's kami. Yes, most would assume that he used the girl to combat the Warlord directly, and I wouldn't bother to argue against it, but we know better. We know that Aguilar was the one that killed Mujin Shimizu. Stared him dead in the eyes and everything. The girl might have helped, but the deed was his."

"Are you claiming he is a threat?"

"No, I don't think so," admitted Tatun. "If anything, he is unrepentantly straightforward. If anything, he has tunnel vision about his goals, and will happily ignore everything else. *And* he is frighteningly well-informed about the Haze. You heard him state his requests in return for managing the Keep. They were not unreasonable or unrealistic. If anything, they were the most demure things you'd expect from someone of his Potential. This hasn't changed the fact though, that he has warred against a Sacred Eight clan, manipulated multiple Shoguns and political forces, and faced possibly the strongest man alive in the entire Southeast *and* a king's warship at his own personal risk just to ensure that these priorities, these goals, are upheld. And he *won*."

"What are you saying?" asked Naowa. "You claim he isn't a threat, and at the same time, you fear his presence?"

"I do!" Tatun all but snapped. Taking a deep breath, he said. "With all due respect, sir, Aguilar is currently the most powerful individual in the Southeast.

Not to mention his Pathforgery that we don't know anything about. He could very well resist the Earth King to a degree! Someone with that much power doesn't just appear out of nowhere, Lord Shogun. I fear someone very clever is playing an elaborate game with us, and I am not sure if Aguilar is a mere pawn, or something more. And the Fire King has unwittingly handed him the keys that could sabotage the Empire's security."

Naowa nodded slowly. "Fine. Summon Aguilar."

"I . . . cannot."

Naowa blinked. "I don't understand. He is supposed to take over the Keep after taking care of this little issue with the Shimizu. Surely you can send a missive through Lady Kandra again?"

"I could sir," said Tatun softly. "It's just, neither Lukas Aguilar nor Tanya Shimizu are currently in the Llaisy Kingdom. In fact, no one knows where they are."

CHAPTER 26

O h yeah, this is great."

Lukas Aguilar was on a warm beach wearing a pair of sunglasses, lounging on a deck chair. His body had completely healed itself of all wounds and looked just like any other athletic young man in his early twenties. A small smile crossed his face as he relaxed under the simmering heat of the tropical climate in this particular borderland.

Next to him, Tanya lounged in her own deck chair in a two-piece. Her hair, still snowy-white, glittered in the light and her smooth, pale skin was bronzing quite nicely—even if it was temporary. A single transformation would revert it back to her pasty pale self, but that was neither here nor there.

"Enjoyable, yes," Tanya answered, her voice warm and carefree. "However impermanent."

"Everything is impermanent," he said softly, caressing her cheek with his left hand. "Still, a bit of rest before the next bit of insanity will do us some good."

He idly watched the seagull-like creatures soaring and buzzing around above him. This borderland was particularly comfortable, unlike the dreary and absolutely scorching lava ridge where they had encountered the Ifrit King. He had found it during his time in the Haze earlier and knew that it would be the perfect place for a hideaway. Being the accomplished terramancer that he was now, it was child's play to conjure a full set of deck chairs, clothes, sunglasses, and nearly everything else one would need for a relaxing vacation, and they were set.

Just as promised.

It also gave Tanya all the time she needed to come to terms with Frost and slowly progress in her understanding of the true nature of her power.

"You don't have to lie to me, Lukas," said Tanya lightly. "We both know this is just a distraction."

Lukas flipped to his side and gazed at her. "Tanya, regardless of whatever happens, I'm not going to leave your side. Even if it means having to spend the rest of my life finding a solution that will keep you from losing yourself."

"I don't think I can be fixed, Lukas," Tanya murmured. "In the end, it's the destiny of the Taboo-bearer to channel the End in its purest form into the world, into Worlds, until nothing remains. Frost and I have talked about this at length."

"Yeah, Frost has a bit too much confidence in how knowledgeable she is," scoffed Lukas, remembering how Frost had been completely at sea upon hearing about the oddity that had affected Inanna. "Unlike Frost, I happen to believe in finding a way that doesn't seem to exist yet, instead of just giving up and accepting fate. And besides, it will be a good distraction between now and the next big thing that I—that we'll get dragged into."

"Oh? Like what?"

"Who knows?" asked Lukas lazily. "Your position as the new Lady of Shimizu? Politics, both on the Empire-level and within the yokai? Finding a way to keep your true nature hidden from the Empire?"

"You're conveniently omitting the more important things, Lukas," said Tanya with a smile. "You just want some time to come up with a convenient excuse to explain how you killed Grandfather in the end."

Lukas smiled and pulled the sunglasses off his face. Oddly enough, his eyes had gone back to the soft brown they had been before. Something had triggered within his body the moment he had gained the last three levels needed to cross the threshold that was Level 39, which had unlocked the power of the Apex-tier Level-4 Kinetomancy Skill.

A power so deadly, it defied comprehension.

A power that he could spend the next decade studying and honing and still only harness a fraction of its true capability.

A power that made him a warlord of *Motion*.

"We both know you killed him with Everfrost."

"And I'd have believed it if I *remembered* how," said Tanya seriously. "What did you do? What psionic mystery did you use?"

Lukas sighed and pretended to ignore the irritated glare she was aiming at him. "I told you, Tanya. All I did was manifest my inner-world and bring you all into it."

"And somehow, curse me with a psionic mystery so complex that not even *Frost* is immune from its effects?" she uncharacteristically snapped at him in genuine anger before regaining her composure. "You know how I feel about Psionic Manipulation, Lukas. You know of my circumstances. Better than anyone save for, perhaps, Frost. To not prepare me for what I'd experience . . ."

This time Lukas *did* flinch. She was right. He had overstepped her trust in him in that regard. He had vainly suspected that she'd accept to *that* train of thought and hoped it would prepare her for that quirk of his inner-world. However, that had been a horrifically poor and cruel overestimation on his part.

"I suppose I should've warned you," he simply replied, not striking up the nerve to look her in the eye just yet. "Honestly, there are conditions to trigger different effects inside my inner-world, Tanya. It's a unique existence and based on a bizarre, circular logic that will keep us debating here for days. Just understand that whatever happened inside my world was *forgotten* by anyone that doesn't belong to my world and leave it at that."

"What does that even mean?" she asked. Her tone had a keen edge to it.

"My world doesn't exist. At least, according to this reality."

"But you do," said Tanya stubbornly. "You're real."

Lukas laughed. "I suppose I am."

It was like seeing a character walk out from the television and into your living room. It was less about the character or his abilities and more about the fact that he wasn't *real* to begin with.

"And I think it's all because of this pendant."

He held up the azure jewel. He was still nowhere close to comprehending its Truth or even gaining a glimpse into its nature, but somehow, the pendant was able to bridge the gap between this reality and his.

"You *think?*"

Lukas let out an irritated huff. "Look, all this is fairly new to me, too. I haven't been able to comprehend a *tenth* of the mysteries of my World, and I'm the source of the damn thing. Honestly, it's scary as fuck."

"*Wonderful,*" Tanya's voice strained as Frost spoke through her. "*There are two of them now.*"

"Could you not just *warn* me before you do that?" Tanya complained, rubbing her neck. "It hurts when you tighten my vocal cords without giving me a second to brace for it."

"*Perhaps we could come to an arrangement, Outsider?*" offered Frost. "*Why not offer us another peek into this twisted inner-world of yours? If the curse affects us yet again, you have nothing to lose. If it doesn't, you will get a step closer to understanding the kind of monster you are becoming.*"

"Lukas isn't a—" Tanya began.

"*Do not lie to me,*" snapped Frost again. "*I am you, girl. I know your deepest thoughts, the lies you tell yourself. You've seen what happens when someone earns that gaze of his, when he unleashes his hidden fury. No matter what defenses they have, no matter their powers, they are guaranteed death. No matter what preparations they make. The only thing that changes is the time and manner of their execution. Tell me you cannot see the stiffness in that skinwalker's features when she looks at Aguilar. It's the same look a prey has when fending off a predator.*"

"Hmph," said Lukas. "Your concern is flattering, Frost. If I didn't know any better, I'd say you're afraid of me."

"*I am.*"

Lukas opened his mouth to speak but words failed him. He had *not* expected that.

"*I am Frost, the herald and avatar of the End. Anomalies and Worlds are my food, my prey. They are Creators, and everything that has been created, shall die. And someday, even the Creator will perish and only darkness shall remain. But you are no ordinary Creator, are you?*"

Her cadaverous gaze met his own.

"*You are an Invader. A tyrant. A World that grows, consumes, feeds upon another. If unchecked, you will become the greatest power in the universe, consuming men, beasts, spirits, parasites, kings, emperors, and the gods themselves, and then challenge the universe itself. Your very nature will not allow you to be lesser than any other. I want to stand in awe of you. I also want to crush your throat and shatter you to dust.*"

His heart skipped a beat at her words. For all her mind games, Frost hadn't lied to him. Not once. She had shown him her true form inside Tanya's mind-scape, shown him the true might of what she *would* become in time. For her to speak that way about him was . . .

Uncomfortable. Deeply so.

Frost snaked her hands around her neck and brought her lips closer to his ear. Giggling, she licked his earlobe with her tongue, and whispered in a sultry purr.

"*I cannot wait until I see that end, Outsider. You have such Potential, so much to show me. Seeing the castle erupt might scare the lowly parasites, but that display of fireworks did not faze me. I want an odyssey. A storm of legend that will last and rage and build the universe in its image. A story that will exist in rumors and lore for millennia to come. Whether it ends in salvation or damnation, I care not. Just you and me, on a hill of corpses, watching as the universe burns around us.*"

Lukas swallowed.

Frost looked him dead in the eye again. "*I wish to see this World of yours with my own eyes. As the Avatar of the End, show me your inner-world so that I might judge its worth.*"

"You . . . wish to see my World," repeated Lukas. "Do you realize what you're asking?"

Tanya agreed. It was a grave invasion of his privacy to even ask for something like that, but she was equally curious about exactly what being a World truly meant. She had seen Lukas perform some absolutely bedazzling things, some very recently. Consuming souls and storing their spiritual information, only to use it to re-create them was a power that belonged to anomalies alone. While Lukas had certainly demonstrated the former dozens of times before, his only *true* creation that could be called *alive* was Blob, and it was, in a way, *alive* from the very beginning. Lukas only injected it with different souls, transforming it to look like them and behave like them, while remaining utterly obedient to him.

Like a flesh puppet.

But unlike how Mujin enchanted the minds of his soldiers to become his loyal minions, Lukas owned them—mind, body, and soul. They weren't alive or dead, and maybe weren't even individual existences, just Skills and instincts that were freely added to a metallic slime that took on their physical shapes. Once created, they did their duty and either died in the process or were simply subsumed back into his World.

They existed for the World within him and not the other way around.

Just like any other *monster.*

He was a hyper-specialized existence that could use all forms of mana. His Soul Capacity was tremendous, but the same could be said for any king out there. His regeneration was remarkable, but again, nothing any powerfully strong magical user would have been incapable of. His ability to speak every single language they had encountered so far—Tanya didn't know what being a World had to do with that, but she assumed it was a byproduct and moved on. His growth, the swift, progressive development of his powers was fascinating to watch, and while she didn't know what exactly he was becoming, it wasn't like he'd undergone any overnight transformations to overwhelm the mightiest entities out there.

And yet, the more time she spent with him, the more she realized that for all his claims about being a World, there were certain discrepancies between what should be and what was.

Lack of alien mindset. Associating with her despite the knowledge that she was his predator. No uncontrolled or altered body parts. The desire to automatically consume new creatures (souls) that came within his (its) vicinity was completely non-existent. His control over what he did develop was so exceedingly strong that even in moments when he muted all his emotions and operated under tunnel vision, not once did he lose control of himself and let the World take over.

Instead, during those events, he became, as Frost had aptly put it, an invader. *A tyrant.* One who would use every tool within his nigh-unlimited arsenal to bring the enemy down, regardless of what happened or what kind of mysterious power they had. One only needed to look at the fates that had befallen Empress Meynte, Solana, and Mujin Shimizu to acknowledge that fact.

At the same time, she knew that something *very drastic* had happened to him, affecting his inner-world to a significant degree. What it was, Tanya didn't know, but she knew it was too great a change. Too fast. Too significant. Too outstanding compared to the state of the rest of his progression.

When it came to new Skills, Lukas was almost like a kid, enamored by whatever new toy had just attracted his attention. He would use it over and over to often tiresome degrees, going so far as to invent an entirely different fighting style with them. At first, it had been those daggers, reinforced with his astonishing accuracy and swift reflexes. Then, it shifted to his using Metamancy and those corrosive flames. Gravity was next, followed by his experiments on Blob. For someone like Tanya who believed in rigorous and continuous development of one's Skills to take them to the apex, watching how Lukas evolved felt practically insulting. He got almost to the point of mastery within a particular discipline and then switched to another, never looking back. It was as if he threw away everything he learned like yesterday's trash. By Asukan philosophy, a man like that would end up getting nowhere, stuck with a seemingly random but high number of medium-level Skills. A jack of all trades but a master of none. A self-crippling attitude like that—it was beneath contempt.

And yet, there he was, taking down one powerful opponent after another.

Lukas Aguilar . . . terrified her.

"Call it curiosity, if you will," spoke Frost through her lips. *"I am unique, the one and only in this entire universe. Maybe Tanya will be the one to reach the zenith and gain the power of the End in its entirety, or maybe she will perish in the process. I, on the other hand, will be reborn in some other form, some other existence, until I find a true avatar that will bring about the End. The World within you too, is unique. I wish to know if it is you that becomes the World or if you are just the current form it chooses to wear, only to discard it at the sight of something better."*

She wanted to know if Lukas Aguilar was the one in charge, or if he too, like Blob, was a puppet dancing to something else's whims.

"Surely something so small and trivial demands little thought."

Lukas breathed out slowly, as if gathering his thoughts. Something about her words sparked an idea inside him. After the multiple times he had been destroyed and remade, he had enough time to come to terms that he wasn't quite the human he used to be. And yet, he wasn't just a form that his inner-world chose to wear. No matter what happened, Lukas Aguilar would remain at the helm, and it wasn't *only* because of Inanna's Divinity.

But *there* was an idea.

Slowly, he put Tanya's palm in his. "What you're asking is neither small nor trivial, Frost."

"From you, it is both. No doubt you cannot manifest it without prepar—"

Snikt!

Frost trailed off mid-sentence as the World around her instantly changed. No longer was she on that tropical beach. Instead, she was in . . .

. . . an endless maze of crystals.

They ran like headstones in an infinite graveyard, standing upright in the ground, beneath a dark, starless sky, and that titanic silhouette shining from above.

And she couldn't look away.

Literally.

Next to Frost stood Tanya, equally perplexed.

"Lukas, I . . . how . . .?"

All Lukas could do was shrug. "There are no Rules that my World holds sacred save for its own, Tanya. I think of you and Frost as two different people inhabiting the same body. I'm not surprised you're here as separate entities."

"But Lukas—" She couldn't seem to finish her sentence, as Frost *exploded.*

"This is no World!" snapped Tanya's altered self. "What is it? Tell the Truth."

"I told you," said Lukas, his voice serene. "This is my World."

"This place *can't* be a World," she growled coldly. "Worlds are Creators. The Spring of Potential. Bursting with souls, with activity. With *Life.* Not this . . . *deadland.* This . . . this place is—is—"

She looked like she was seconds away from frothing at the mouth, like a rabid animal gearing up to attack. Not a good sign given what she was. Here, in his most sacred place, where the omphalos reigned supreme, he had no doubt that it would react rather extremely if Frost—no, if *Everfrost*—acted out in hostility.

"This place is unnatural! Vile! Sickening! Revolting! *Wrong!* This—this twisted abomination cannot be—it cannot *be*—"

"Frost. What's wrong?" Tanya demanded, but her other self was shaking her head in utter confusion as well. It was like she was losing her sanity with every passing second.

Lukas tilted his head, observing Frost's growing revulsion and trying to understand why she felt that way about his World. He had expected a lot of things from her—including a desire to destroy it, given the source of her existence. But the mere sight of it driving her mad?

Something didn't add up.

It was also a jarring thing to hear. It was something he would have expected of his former self when he had first found himself in the Crypt of Fiendish Worms. Half the time he had spent wandering inside those underground tunnels, he had oscillated between trying to make sense of things and being in complete denial. Denial that he wasn't on Earth. Denial that he was talking to an actual goddess. Denial that all of this was real.

To see Frost—something that was beyond human comprehension—look at him and react like that just felt . . .

Wrong.

"You're right. This place has no life. No soul. No activity. Nothing. This," he exclaimed, hands wide open, "is *Forget*."

"Forget?" repeated Tanya.

He smiled. "The infinite terrain around us represents *perpetual quiescence*—the wait that lies between the cycle of birth and death. Nothing here is born, nothing here shall suffer death, nothing here holds any individual existence. They are all *Forget*."

"Accursed thing!" Frost said with rancor. "Vile trash! Twisted blight! This place, these . . . souls. They do not *exist!*"

He blinked. Something about her words felt off. Of course, the soul prototypes in this place didn't exist, per se. And the only way they would exist would be . . .

It clicked.

He looked at the seething avatar of Everfrost and couldn't suppress a grin. "It exists here in Forget, but it hasn't been *created*. And what hasn't been created cannot be destroyed. Not by death. Not by time. Not even by the End of Potential. Isn't that why you hate it?"

"I really should've killed you when I had the chance," she whispered.

"What's—what's going on?" asked Tanya.

"That Outsider is spitting in the face of the rules of reality, of the universe. Every single soul he siphons, he isn't just taking their Skills, he is taking them *out* of Existence. Out of the cycle of life and death. They become part of *his* reality—part of *Forget*. So long as he manifests those souls using an accessory, like that blasted metal slime, he can bypass the process of Soul Creation and make them come 'alive.' Even if you kill them, the soul just returns to Forget and then can be used again and again and *again and again.* They aren't born, they aren't dead, and thus they are . . ."

"Immortal?" asked Tanya.

"*Eternal!*" Frost snarled. "This vile deadland is a nameless, eternal manufacturing factory."

"Eternal . . ." Tanya repeated, tasting the word. "That's . . . trippy, I guess."

Frost balked at her other self. "He's a thief, stealing from the Great Progenitor, hiding from the End. Everything he siphons is *removed* from reality itself."

"Forgotten," murmured Tanya, looking at him in surprise. No doubt she was remembering the words he had said to her grandfather, describing himself as a *thief.* "But how can these souls be immortal? I mean, if this is Lukas's World, then surely when he dies . . ."

She paused.

Lukas just smiled at her.

"I see," said the aeromancer. "That's why you didn't die. Lukas Aguilar the human perished, but the World was alive. It just put you back in place and rebooted you back to 'living.'"

That was partly true. It hadn't been his body that had perished but his soul. It took Inanna using her Divinity to reforge his soul, which was then pushed out of Forget into the body as the Prime Host.

"Even if you destroy his body, he still won't die," said Frost, looking at him with narrowed eyes. "For all we know, he has hundreds of those metal slimes hidden away. He'll probably be able to regenerate himself using them. Unless you can find every single thing that is connected to this abomination and destroy it in one go, the Outsider cannot be killed."

Again, partially correct. His existence could be described as a twisted mixture of a hive mind and something similar to a hydra. With interchangeable parts, no less. There was technically no core to speak of, but that didn't mean all of his resources were distributed evenly. Trying to focus on killing Lukas would be similar to aiming for a lizard's tail instead of the lizard.

Was it any surprise he had hidden away multiple fragments of Blob in several borderlands in the Haze?

Ironically, when he had done that, he had presumed that anything that could delete his body and soul in one strike would end him for good. Instead, the Plains of Forget had just created a new Instance of him.

Exposure to that memory had destroyed both his and the Crypt's souls, or whatever equivalent existed for an anomaly. And then Inanna had reforged him. By that logic, Inanna had crafted a *perfectly identical* copy of his soul using her Divinity, one that accessed the memories of Lukas Aguilar.

No, Lukas, he told himself. *You are looking at it the wrong way. You're not an individual. You are a World, an entity that was once human, constituted a single soul, and answered to the name "Lukas Aguilar." The Lands of Forget are not a separate entity.*

You are Forget, and Forget is you.

"If Forget is this confusing, what by Wind is that?"

Tanya's words brought him out of his musings. He followed her gaze and looked up at the giant figure of a human silhouette taking up almost half of the black sky. Seated in the posture of a human yogi, it looked like the outline of a meditating god.

It wasn't.

It was far, far more than that.

"That?" asked Lukas, still smiling, "I don't know. Though if I had to name it, I'd call it the Demiurge."

He wasn't being arrogant. In old Platonic philosophy, the word "demiurge" referred to an artisan-like figure responsible for fashioning and maintaining the physical universe. That being—if he could refer to it as a *being* at all—was the manifestation of the Future. Vision. Illusion. Imagination. Dream. Much like the Infinity of Forms, the Demiurge represented an ever-distant utopia where all potential Skills of all potential prototypes within Forget were realized to the fullest sense. A state when his World would be eventually deemed complete.

He wondered. Did Inanna feel like he did when she gazed upon the Origin, something that was so far beyond comprehension that you needed to become detached from reality to do it? Was that why she was so feared? Because she had ascended to a level that allowed her to comprehend the Origin itself?

"At the base of everything in Existence, whether it be the living and the inanimate, physical and ethereal, bremetans and spirits, gods and demons, there is *always* a World. From the World they rise, from the World they take form, and upon death, into the World they return. The cycles turn and turn. That being, up there, is the *Creator* of this World. It's Demiurge."

"But *you* are the World, right?"

"Then that being is me. Or, perhaps, what I *can* become. Not Lukas Aguilar the human, not the Prime Host, and not the omphalos. Whatever the Plains of Forget contain . . . *will* contain . . . will be created by the Demiurge. Alive, inanimate, monsters, creatures, perhaps even gods. If the Great Progenitor is the creator of all there is, then this Demiurge is the same for this place."

"Big words from a perpetual slacker," scoffed Frost.

He smiled. Seeing her so thrown was amusing.

"Perhaps you'd like to test it?"

"Test?" she snapped. "I want to destroy it. I . . ."

It came without warning. No tells whatsoever. So fast that not even his eyes, augmented with Kinetomancy, could catch up with it. In less time that it took to even blink, Frost conjured a dagger and hurled it at him.

Or she tried to, anyway.

The moment it left her hands, the Frost dagger *vanished.* He should have been amused at the gobsmacked expression on her face, but instead he frowned in concern.

That . . . wasn't supposed to happen. Was it? Everfrost is a Taboo, not a Truth that this World can just ignore. And I didn't even use Territory Creation. So . . . how?

She tried again, this time conjuring a blade. The third time, she used a spear. After that, pure Everfrost energy. But nothing, *nothing* she did managed to exist the moment it left her body. As soon as she hurled each out into the world, they just *vanished.*

As if this reality—his World—had erased it from Existence.

This made no sense to him.

"*What is happening?!*" Frost kept attempting to cast anything and everything, but it all had the same result. The moment she created it, it *vanished*.

Weird.

"Lukas?" Tanya asked. "Are you doing that?"

He looked at her, flummoxed, and then at his own World. Nothing about this World—no mystery, no curse, nothing he could think of—should have been able to suppress a Taboo like that. Regardless of his powers, he was a World and Everfrost was the bane of *every* World out there that was connected to the . . .

. . . the Origin.

He froze as the truth hit him like a sledgehammer.

Could it really be that frighteningly simple? Was this all he was missing all this time?

"*Get me out of this place,*" Frost demanded, seething. "*I cannot stand the sight of it any longer. Get me out!*"

"No."

The person who denied Frost wasn't the Soulcrafter but one that presided over that land with utmost authority. "You came in by your own will, but you will leave by mine."

Tanya swallowed heavily but decided to remain silent.

"*Outsider!*" Frost snarled. "*Two debts you owe me! Do not forget that! The first you may resolve by letting me passage from this blight.*"

"You do not have to hold the debt over me," Lukas bristled, pissed at himself for what he was about to do. "I'm not going to trick and trap you here. I'm not a coward."

Frost opened her mouth to retort—

"But," said Lukas, "just like those two debts, you too are obligated to help me resurrect my goddess. And *that* is why I want you to wait while I attempt that."

Whatever Frost had expected him to say, this was certainly not it. Even Tanya had gone from gaping at Frost's hostility to gaping at him.

"You're . . ."

"Yes."

"In here . . ." Tanya trailed off, conflicted. The chance of seeing something impossible happen before her very eyes was warring with her fear of the goddess he was trying to resurrect.

"Yes," Lukas repeated. "I'm going to attempt it now. It's a multi-step process, so don't interrupt me in the middle, alright? No matter what happens."

"But—"

"Tanya," he said softly. 'I have been experimenting on this for a while now, and even when things have gone horribly wrong in the past, I have gotten back on my feet. All this time, I was assuming that I had reached a point where I was failing because of the limited divinity, but I think I can safely dismiss that assumption."

The last time, things had gotten crazy the moment the Screen had rejected the divinity, calling it corrupted. He had assumed it was because "his" Inanna was a reflection of the original, and even then, her divinity had been reforged into a mortal soul—his.

But what if he was going about it the wrong way?

"Okay," said Tanya finally. Frost had just watched him like a hawk.

Outside and a World away, Blob instantly cloaked Lukas's form while extending outward and piercing the very fabric of space itself.

Searching Optimal Rift Channels Along Periphery
Opening Rift . . .

For a second, everything went completely silent, and Lukas waited for the worst to happen. Instead, every single mound on the terrain shook with anticipation, making the very air hum, a chorus of crystal vibrating from all directions.

And then *power* flowed in.

Lukas couldn't help but grin like a lunatic. The last time, he had needed a formal ritual circle, spent a significant amount of time dealing with the sudden energy influx, and focused it through specific parameters. And even then, he had been blanketed by a deluge of pure, violent pain just to achieve the nexus. Only after he had suffered through two brain aneurysms had the Screen given him the green signal for metaforging.

Now, though . . .

Nexus Achieved
Power Levels Holding Steady
Initiate Metaforge?

Just like the last time, he would require a total of five different ingredients to bring back Inanna.

First, a template to craft her identity from. A blueprint.

Second, the materials to create her form with.

Third, a forge.

Fuel was the fourth.

The final step was to anchor the spiritual entity into the world, allowing it to manifest.

Like before, the blueprint would come from Inanna's own divinity that resided within Lukas's soul. The last time, he had sacrificed his soul to serve as a creation fabric. Noble, yes, but ultimately, a stupid act.

This time, he had options.

Creating Instance of Prime Host

Instantly, a perfect doppelganger of himself, crafted out of anomalous energy and containing the soul, Skills, memories, and divinity housed within Lukas Aguilar, stood next to him. He glanced at himself, err . . . at *it*, and found his words lacking.

"This is one of those weird days, isn't it?" he asked. He? Damn it. The entire self-cloning business really made pronouns tough.

"Lukas-1," said his clone. "You're just Lukas."

"Basic, but whatever works for you."

"Yeah," said the newly named Lukas-1. "At least this is familiar. I've already perished once when Inanna cast that scrying spell."

"So have I," said Lukas.

"And when you fucked up the resurrection, and—"

"The anomaly experiment, the fight with Mujin, the last seventeen experiments we did after coming to this borderland," said Lukas drolly. "I am you, genius. All of me, us . . . are."

"Yeah," said Lukas-1. "This does make pronouns really difficult."

"So, you're Lukas," said Tanya, befuddled. "And you are . . . too?"

"Technically," said Lukas-1, "we can have as many Lukases here as we want. You should see some of our basketball games. It's really awesome trying to out-think yourself when there are twelve of you."

Tanya blinked.

Lukas sighed. "Ignore him. He's a nut. Besides . . ." He trailed off, as a twisted amusement flooded through his being. "I am him, but he is not me."

Was this why Inanna loved being cryptic? He could get used to this feeling.

"Oi," said Lukas-1. "I *am* you."

"Technically you are me from two minutes ago. Science says that the moment you and I interact and perform different activities, we are different persons that just share genetic and spiritual similarities."

"Fuck off."

"This is trippy," commented Tanya from afar.

"We basically invented trippy here," said both Lukases, who then proceeded to glare at each other.

"I have a quandary," said Frost with a conflicted look on her face. Lukas wondered if it was because she was just pissed off at him, or that there were *two* of him to get pissed off at.

"If you can just create endless copies of yourself," asked the avatar of the End. *"why not just duplicate the divinity within your soul?"*

Both Lukases looked at each other before Lukas sighed. "That's because divinity is more than just *souls,* Frost. The moment one of us gets their divinity used up, it reflects on the soul prototype called 'Lukas Aguilar.' Weird, I know, but I suppose that's what I get for experimenting with divinity."

"Alright, enough with the long face," said Lukas-1, looking far too upbeat for someone about to serve as a living sacrifice on the altar. "Let's continue with the ritual."

"Thank you," said Lukas and exhaled. He had long since accepted the fact that there was no True version of himself—just a collection of spiritual information and an always-updating set of memories that defined "Lukas Aguilar," the Prime Host, installed in the anomaly body.

Inanna had sacrificed herself to resurrect him. This was him doing the exact same thing backwards.

Sacrifice with symmetry.

Just like Inanna's pentagon.

The Screen flickered again.

Prime Host Accessing DIVINITY
Breaking Existing Conventions
Safety Off!

The last time, he had planned to use anomalous energy to fabricate Inanna's body. That would remain unchanged. As would Lukas's—or rather The Plains of Forget's—role as a forge. The energy, as always, was being drawn from the borderland outside.

And finally, the anchor. Last time, it was the pendant hanging on his neck. This time, he had something different in mind. An anchor of the greatest-possible quality.

DIVINITY ACCESSED
Maximize Sympathization Ratio
SCAN Initiated
ANALYZE Initiated

METAFORGE Initiated

Lukas-1 fell down on the floor and threw his head back, letting out a soul-wrenching scream. Quite literally, given how the ritual was ripping his soul apart. Any other person would have empathized with his pain. Even Frost had to hold Tanya back from reacting.

Not Lukas, though. He just stood through the entire thing with a smile on his lips.

Huh! Maybe he had gone far further into the abyss than he had realized. How long before he looked back and couldn't even recognize the human that he once was?

Later. For now, it was time for the next part.

Identity.

The Screen flickered.

Accessing Host Memory

Laws were broken. Rules were defied. The spiritual form became corporeal, as Lukas-1 began to disintegrate. The last time, it was him that was being disintegrated. This time, he was creating something that didn't exist before.

Four factors were already in the mix. Time for the fifth and final factor.

"Set Anchor. The Plains of Forget."

Analyzing Memory of [Lostbelt Earth]
Checking for Incompatibilities . . .
Assessing Anchorage Potential . . .

The last time, he had offered the pendant as the anchor for Inanna's form. This time, he couldn't afford to be this close-minded. The pendant was good, *great* even. After all, it was a relic that Inanna herself had worn when she was alive. She had the right to the pendant, because she had killed the god whose Truth it contained. It was her abode for all the centuries she had been on Earth before Lukas finally awakened her. But for all its qualities, it was still a relic that belonged to another.

Not Inanna.

So instead, Lukas chose a different anchor to bind her resurrected, divine form. One of perfect quality. It would break every rule in the book, but Lukas had always been a rule-breaker, much like the goddess he was attempting to bring back.

Even after she was trapped behind the Seven Gates, a part of Inanna had escaped to Earth as a reflection, one that had become lost in time, cut off from the Origin. That meant that Earth's history *registered* Inanna as a goddess. And even if her Truth had been erased from the Origin itself, Earth still retained some recollection of it.

Much like starlight after it had left a star.

It was only poetic that the same Earth, now manifesting as the Plains of Forget, would become the Real World that would host her divinity post-resurrection.

A small smile floated along the edges of his lips at the thought.

"Now," he said softly. "Give her back to me."

A massive pentacle formed in midair, and in its center, a dazzling bright light erupted, forming a human-sized silhouette around it—white, translucent and unmistakably female. The form shimmered, a blurry haze. The face was exactly how he remembered, yet there was no emotion in it. Blank, featureless, wiped clean by the neutrality that was death. Like the rest of her form, it was a transparent thing, and in the moments when the hazy energy solidified, it shone like quicksilver.

Anchorage Potential Satisfactory
Drawing on [LOSTBELT EARTH] Memory
Combining Divinity
Setting Anchorage . . .

Lukas let out a laugh.

This was happening! This was finally happening! He was resurrecting the goddess! No, he was *re-creating* her!

But—but why were her eyes still closed?

"It isn't enough."

Lukas whirled back and found Frost looking at him, something inscrutable in her eyes. *"The ritual, it's incomplete. Even for your World."*

He couldn't believe her words. Still not enough? What had he done wrong this time?

"Anchoring her to this World was a stroke of genius," said Frost. *"But she only exists in the memory of the World. You have to awaken her with something that is unmistakably her."*

"Unmistakably—" Lukas began but trailed off. Frost was right. He had assumed that the divinity alone would have provided the appropriate identity for the goddess. But if it wasn't enough, then he needed to invoke her with something that described and resonated powerfully with Inanna and Inanna alone.

He had come too far. He couldn't stop now.

And he conveniently had one such aria sitting in his mind from his dreams.

"Your selfishness knows no bounds! You'd snatch, you'd hustle, Empires would burn and pantheons would fall, yet your desire shall remain unquenched!"

The last time someone had described Inanna in similar terms, a sense of unease had run through him. Listening to that memory of that child uttering them out loud had heralded something terrible, not unlike the time when he had accessed the memories of Earth perishing. Something so anathema to his mind that his brain would choose to give him an aneurysm rather than deal with the consequences. Something alien and completely beyond his understanding.

This time, though, all he felt was cold, distant, silent peace.

As if his journey were finally coming to an end.

As if things were coming full circle.

"You are bloodshed and battle, bringing justice and misfortune in equal measure. You wander in treachery and travel with unkindness."

Power surged through him and around him. His eyes didn't register anything, but he could feel fierce hurricanes billowing across his terrain, even though they did nothing to his World. Those flames, those hurricanes—as powerful and alien as they were, they were still welcome in his World.

They were his.

"Your wrath shall break the divine thrones, your whims defile the most sacred of relics . . ."

A thousand new possibilities were forming all around him—a thousand decimated and atomized without care.

The ritual went on.

Power coalesced. Not wrathful like it was before. Calmer. At peace. It surged through him like water through a broken dam.

The body began to shake just a little.

"Existence itself is unraveled by your presence . . ."

This was the tricky part. It was an incomplete line. In the original memory, the child had mentioned the Flames of Deprivation, acknowledging them as the Essence of Inanna.

Lukas changed the wording.

"The Truth of Depredation shall be your essence!"

Two different lines. Two different powers. Two different variations. Whereas the Flames of Deprivation, picked up by Inanna in the Vikahl Ashlands, was a Taboo that simply did not belong to the current reality, the Truth of Depredation was what defined the Supreme Queen of An and Ki. Ultimately, it was simply a choice of one over the other.

Just like before, he was doing the impossible. Defying laws. The spiritual form had appeared, brought into existence through sheer will, spitting in the face of all accepted Rules.

For Potential never followed Rules. Never followed laws. Instead, it merely shaped them to its will.

Closing his eyes, Lukas exhaled and thought back to Inanna. She had used her presence to bind his shattered soul. To manifest his mind once more and awaken his consciousness after he lay dead in the anomaly. It had left her with no power, no faith, no presence, and unless Lukas managed to find a way to make it otherwise, no existence.

You were my miracle, Lukas Aguilar, she had told him. *I can only hope that you will be my miracle once more.*

Something heavy appeared in his palm. Opening his eyes, Lukas realized what he was holding and smiled.

A coffee mug that his grandfather had gifted him before his death.

The last time he had seen it, it was filled with tenemu, the wine of Sumer. Drink of the gods themselves. He had drunk it, right as Inanna had vanished before his eyes.

How suitably poetic that he was in the same position right now. Only this time, he was going to offer something in that cup.

Himself. The divinity that had reforged Lukas Aguilar, would now reforge Inanna.

It had come full circle.

Symmetry.

Harmony.

Life, Death, and Rebirth.

"*Plunderer! Trickster! Psychopomp!*"

He saw the face. Just like he remembered. Her hair was blacker than the darkest of nights, her skin as white as the finest alabaster. Her lips were the color of frozen mulberries, fitting perfectly on a smooth, lovely face that had the most beautiful green eyes he had ever seen. And yet, no matter how much he tried, no matter how perfect each one of her facial features were individually, he could not behold her perfection in its entirety.

It was something beyond the superficial beauty of a supermodel. Rather, it was the beauty of the heavens and the earth. It was majesty made manifest, the kind you saw when you beheld the depth of a valley from the top of a mountain or the rising sun emerging from the vastness of the sea.

She wasn't old. Wasn't young. Wasn't anything but stunning.

He whispered her name out loud for the final time.

"Inanna . . ."

She opened her eyes and met his gaze. Her lips moved, and her voice came out like honey and hot soup on a winter night. A voice that promised things, one that you listened to with unrelenting interest and intensity.

Just like he remembered.

She tilted her head, and spoke her first words in abject confusion.

Who are you?

T. B. Mare is the pseudonym of the authors of Stranger Than Fiction, a LitRPG adventure series originally released on Royal Road. They are a pair of dreamers who started working together in order to share with readers some of the fun of creating fantasy worlds filled with rich lore and complex characters. Both discovered their love for fantasy and magic at a young age, and the ensuing affairs have carried on well into adulthood. Hopelessly addicted to complex genre fiction—especially the darker kind—they currently work multiple jobs but are looking forward to one day writing full-time.